Salt Bones

Salt Bones

A Novel

JENNIFER GIVHAN

MULHOLLAND BOOKS

Little, Brown and Company

New York Boston London

Mulholland Books / Little, Brown and Company
Hachette Book Group
1290 Avenue of the Americas, New York, NY 10104
mulhollandbooks.com

First Edition: July 2025

Mulholland Books is an imprint of Little, Brown and Company, a division of Hachette Book Group, Inc. The Mulholland Books name and logo are trademarks of Hachette Book Group, Inc.

The publisher is not responsible for websites (or their content) that are not owned by the publisher.

The Hachette Speakers Bureau provides a wide range of authors for speaking events. To find out more, go to hachettespeakersbureau.com or email hachettespeakers@hbgusa.com.

Little, Brown and Company books may be purchased in bulk for business, educational, or promotional use. For information, please contact your local bookseller or the Hachette Book Group Special Markets Department at special.markets@hbgusa.com.

Print book interior design by Taylor Navis
Family tree by Taylor Navis

ISBN 9780316581523 (hc) / 9780316596480 (international pb)
LCCN 2024945381

Printing 1, 2025

LSC-C

Printed in the United States of America

The only legend I have ever loved is
The story of a daughter lost in hell.
And found and rescued there.

— Eavan Boland

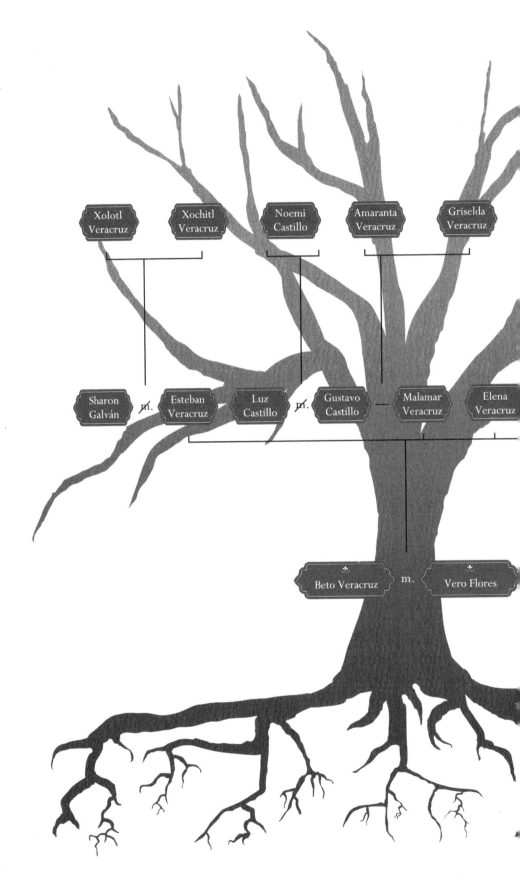

Árbol de la familia

Harlan
Callahan

Benny
Veracruz m. Salazar
Limón

Sean
Callahan m. June
Callahan

Guy Callahan m. Elva Vaughn

Salt Bones

PROLOGUE

Thick, noxious air burns her throat as she flees through the fields, mud clotting to her soles like leeches, one untied shoe after the other over the rutted vegetables.

She shouldn't run toward the water — it isn't safe. But the murk would offer cover.

She doesn't risk a glance behind her or fumble at the yellow onions bulging from the ground. At first, it's the familiar stench of sulfur bubbling from deep in the earth, mangled with the smell of rotting fish, thousands of carcasses gurgled onto the brackish marsh just ahead.

Then something intoxicatingly sweet fills her nostrils. She's not near the sugar plant on the other side of town, but those sugar beets smell like overripe dirt anyway. This is more walking into the donut shop at sunrise and ordering a maple bar and sweet tea. She shakes her head, sure her blood sugar's collapsing from starvation and dehydration and she's about to nose-dive into the fields when the sweetness sours just as suddenly as it came — and she's overtaken by the dank stench of sweat and shit.

Her heartbeat throbs in her ears, eclipsing the sound of a truck engine's roar — another predator in the night, tearing through the furrows and ruining the crops, chasing her.

Would anyone hear her if she screamed?

She can't waste the breath she needs for running.

In the distance, golden lights twinkle a mythical city arisen in the nowhere between the closest towns, neglected or desolate, and the still-living, breathing town where her people are.

But the lights aren't magical, and they're far, much too far. She'd never outrun the truck to get to the geothermal plant where someone at the gate might hear her. Let her in. But would they believe her if she told them who was after her?

A few hundred feet ahead stands a dock. Rickety and slanted, but still possible cover. She could jump into the frothy, stinking water, hold her breath, and hide beneath the battered, salt-crusted planks. Her pursuers might assume she's darted toward the wildlife preserve, climbed the chain link. Or drowned.

The fug of gasoline and exhaust commingles with the acrid sea, fertilizer, her own sweat and spit, and her blood pumping, pumping furiously. Her lungs scream. *Don't let me die out here —*

The sky lights a purple path upward — the Milky Way beckoning as if someone's holding a flashlight behind a pinpricked cosmic bedsheet. It cascades across the expansive blackness that blurs into the jagged peaks of the Chocolate Mountains beyond this stretch of desert that's claimed countless lives.

The clomping of hooves and a blaze of headlights pierce her back.

Her dark hair flaps crow's wings against her sweat-drenched hoodie as her high-tops slip against the mud.

There's nowhere to hide, no tree cover, nothing but shrubs and dirt, and the green fingers of onion bulbs wavering the hands of the dead, reaching for her, grabbing, pulling her downward.

She falls to her knees, blackening her hands with soil.

But the creature canters steadily toward her.

She scrambles up, the Salton Sea in sight, a soupy bog in the darkness.

Her feet crunch fish bones and the minuscule shells of dead crustaceans; millions of them crackle beneath her while she flies toward the pier stretching into the abandoned lake, all that "accidental" water sloshing for miles across the dusty bowl of valle, before the headlights overtake her, and the horse-headed woman cackles, her midnight-black mane scraggling down her bare back.

For a moment, she's glowing yellow, gleaming with beads of sweat. Saintly.

Then the gunshots resound.

One. Two. The deafening booms reverberate through the mountains. Aerial drills. Only this is no drill. Following the shots— metal clanks its sick *click, click. Boom, click, click. Boom.*

If anyone were out here but the night animals, the stars, they've shut their eyes. They haven't seen a thing. They haven't said a damn word to anyone.

1
VENATUS

ONE WEEK EARLIER

M al's chopping block already seeps with blood when the hinge on the door to the carnicería squeaks like a distressed house cat. Mal pays no attention from the back room where she's butchering today's cuts. Not that she'd greet whoever's entered the shop anyway. It doesn't belong to her. She just works here. Putting on a cheerful face for the customers is Renata's job.

You have to be a bitch in this business to get anywhere. By bitch, Mal means tough. Her terrible mother named her *Bad*, so that's close enough. Like bad seed. Malamar, bad sea. Mami concocted the name as a punishment for the daughter she believed kept her chained to the Salton Sea, wrecked by a series of hurricanes the year Mal was born. Still, they stayed beside the water, which sometimes

6

blossomed blood-red from the toxic algal blooms, killing all the fish and stinking to high heaven for weeks. If you ask her mother, Mal was born for this place.

She rolls back the sleeves of her hoodie, cranks up Radiohead's "Creep" on her headphones, and swings another carcass onto its hooks, dragging it toward her workstation, metal scratching as the cold, solid slab sways between her bare hands. She wears a white apron and hairnet but forgoes the restrictive plastic gloves, needing that tactile connection. Some artists work with wood or metal or glass; Mal creates masterpieces from meat.

She pops a mint-flavored Tums into her mouth, the chalky tablet mixing with the tang of blood on her palms, salving her acid reflux burns. She keeps a roll in the ass pocket of her jeans and chews half a pack a day the way Mami used to blow through cartons of cigarettes before Mal's big brother would throw them out and Mami would just run around the house screaming, "Mal! What the hell did you do with mis putos cigarrillos?" in her half-mock Hollyhood accent she'd perfected before her life went to shit.

As if Mal has the cojones to stand up to Mami. That's her older brother Esteban's wheelhouse, not Mal's. That's why he's the one campaigning for the Senate this fall, not her.

I'm a weirdo—the lyrics Mal's loved since she was a teen lull her into a flow state. She hauls the carcass to the electric saw, carving it in two, leaving half on the hook and carrying the other chunk to her block where she aims her ivory-handled breaking knife, tip curved like a lover's tongue, through the gristle, then pulls, slices, and tears the splintered muscle, ripping it from tendons and fat, until she has a manageable primal piece, born of the skill and precision of her twenty years performing this same cut.

Whole animal craft butchery is a rare art form—and Mal knows she's talented. Suppose she was working farm-to-table in an upscale Orange County or New York butcher shop? Given her experience fabricating animals of all different breeds, feeds, and finishes, she'd be able to market herself as an artisan butcher. But here? She earns just above minimum wage, like all the other cooks. Of course, they're all women. Mexican women, to boot. Lowest on the pay scale, her college-educated daughter told her when she was taking some feminist class.

Mal grabs her desert-island butcher knife and removes the tenderloins. The money cuts. She finds the natural seams between muscles and draws back with her sharp tool, gently tapping the meat. From the loin, she breaks it down into subprimals: rib loin, center cut or short loin, and sirloin—her guiding and tearing hand in disciplined choreography with her slicing hand. All that gorgeous marbling. As she cuts the thick covering of fat she belts out, "I don't belong here."

Griselda's still taking UC San Diego by storm, an environmental researcher who may one day return to salvage the ruin los ricos have made of this land. Papi's land. But Mal doesn't want her eldest daughter to come home, not really. She escaped El Valle—a feat Mal never achieved, nor her mother before her, nor hers. The only one who got away before her was Mal's sister, Elena—swallowed by the same toxic bloom that tainted their childhood. The town was quick to brand Elena a runaway, a puta who got what she deserved. But Mal has never been convinced.

She's finishing the tenderloins and moving on to the next cut, when the back door swings open with a familiar creak, and in saunters her work bestie, Yessi, carrying a tray of asada. Afro-Latina with tawny skin and wide eyes that remind Mal of walnuts, her natural coils gathered into a tight bun, Yessi's got a pinched-lip look like she's here to stir the pot.

With her usual pomp and circumstance, she leans against the

doorframe, balancing the metal tray on her arms, a smirk cutting across her lips. "Oye, yunta." Their term of endearment she says as casually as *dude* but given their history is a loaded inside joke. "Heard the latest chisme about your favorite front girl?"

Mal doesn't pause her butchering but shoots Yessi a look, one eyebrow raised. "¿Qué pasó?" She removes the earphones.

"Renata got arrested the other day for giving head down at the FFA swine barns . . ." Her smirk widens. "To some high school cha-valón, aunque she already graduated."

Mal shakes her head and slices through the meat in front of her, acid curling her throat. She pops another Tums. Why Yessi loves talking shit about her own cousin, she'll never know. When Mal's sister vanished, people said she deserved her fate. They didn't say it to Mal's face. But she heard. Everyone around her loves shaming so-called sluts. "People's business is their own," Mal says as much for Elena's memory as for Renata's defense.

"Ándale, yunta. I'm just passing along what I heard." Yessi chuckles, as though she's not offended in the slightest by Mal's rebuke. This is just how they are with each other.

Yessi sidles up to Mal, whose pulse flutters, damn butterflies throbbing her wrists at her nearness. Yunta, yes. But only because Mal's been unavailable her entire adult life.

She's the closest Mal has to a real friend, even if she only knows half-truths. The truth is, she and Yessi might've been girlfriends — they'd kissed once years ago, on their break, between the carnicería sidewall and an abandoned field, overgrown with burnt-orange cre-osote that sprouted like wildfire.

Yessi's long onyx hair had been coiled in a tight bun, her aura a blend of crushed chile and sweet lilacs. Yet something in Mal resisted, despite the soft crawl of her body toward Yessi's spunk and sass, the smeared red lipstick across both their faces. The full truth was that Mal had committed herself to a half-life with someone else twenty years earlier.

Now, in the back of the carnicería, Yessi — hands in gloves, black apron around her tank top and jeans, hairnet around her bun — reminds Mal why she hasn't let anyone know about her and Gus. *This,* right here. Everyone would say about her what they say about Renata. More to the point, they'd say it about her daughters.

Even so, Mal leans in. "How long did they hold her?" She wonders if she can still smell burnt wildflowers on Yessi. "Renata, I mean."

"Just a few hours, pero ay, qué vergüenza. Mi tía Carmen was boiling!" She's holding in a delighted chortle like she's waiting for Mal to give her permission to burst into hysterics. But as Yessi takes a hard look at Mal, she draws out a long "Girrrrrrl, what's wrong?"

Mal shrugs, and Yessi sets her metal tray on the counter, layered with pink strips of thin-flanked steak.

"Did the guy get arrested too? The high school kid?"

Mal wonders if her little brother, Benny, had anything to do with the arrest. Maybe not. He's a big-time detective at the station now, not just a beat cop. Their youngest detective.

Yessi shakes her head *no* and gives Mal a little bump with her hip. "I just served you the freshest tea, pero you look like you're about to cry." She leans her head on Mal's shoulder. "Isn't Griselda coming home for your brother's thing? You should be excited."

"You and Lisa will be at the fundraiser, right?"

"Of course, yunta. It'll be fancy, ¿qué no?"

Mal rolls her eyes. "So posh. You know Esteban. Always kissing up to the Callahans. If it were my party, I'd have barbacoa in the backyard."

"Right?" They both laugh now. "Dime, ¿qué te pasa?"

Mal stretches her neck, unknotting the constricted muscles, grasping for how to explain the malaise fomenting in her for
almost twenty-five years—and whatever darker emotion's bubbling
beneath that—but before she can reply, the back door swings open
and in steps Renata. The tension snaps like a cheap condom. "Everything okay here?" she asks, glancing between Mal and Yessi as if she
knows she's interrupting.

Yessi rolls her eyes at her younger cousin. "God, Ren, you're
such a pest. Don't make me regret getting you this job."

Renata curls her lip. She has a cheerful, round face like a toasted
tortilla and cropped, silky hair several shades lighter than Amaranta's,
which is frizzy and dark as coal. "Whatever. Stop taking breaks and
come help me. We've got a rush."

"Saturday morning. Hangover cure time," Yessi drawls, a hum
to her voice.

Menudo's the hair of the dog. The cook makes it a'yight here.
Papi's is ten times better.

As Renata huffs off, Yessi winks at Mal and whispers, "We'll
talk later, yunta," then sashays through the swinging doors after her
cousin.

A few minutes later, when the front door's whining again and
Yessi's bustling to the back room, Mal suppresses a grin. She here to
keep flirting or spreading worse rumors about her prima? Mal sets
down the boning knife and leans against the chopping block, waiting for Yessi's next theatrical burst of bochinche. Instead, she says
flatly, "Your dad and daughter are here."

They come every weekend for groceries. At home, Papi cooks—
more chicken than beef lately since he's put Mami on the diabetic
diet. They'd better pick up some pollo asado this time. Plain white
chicken breast is the worst.

Mal wipes her bloody hands on her apron—the red stains

smearing watercolor poppies on a painter's canvas—and follows Yessi to the counter, where Amaranta's staring at Renata with the focused intensity of a guard dog, which is unlike her younger daughter. Except, she *is* a newly minted teen, self-conscious about her looks in a way she never used to be, and Renata's drop-dead gorgeous. Could it be envy? Mal stays back a beat to see how this unfolds.

"What can I get you?" Renata asks Amaranta, who gives her head a dazed shake, barely noticeable, but Mal catches it. "A sample of menudo?"

Amaranta nods emphatically, the edges of her lips twitching, and Renata serves her a deep ladleful into a paper cup. But when she takes a slurp, she scrunches her face. See? Papi's is better.

"Mija," Papi calls when he notices Mal at the swinging doors, and she relaxes. Papi has that effect. His presence calms her. There was a time, after Elena disappeared, Papi's drunken stupor was almost as terrible as Mami's vitriol. But once they moved away from the sea and he took up gardening, he mostly came back to himself.

She gestures for them to join her at the end of the counter, where she hunches and plants a kiss atop Amaranta's frizzy head, careful not to lean too far, keeping her blood-spackled apron away from her daughter. She's the same size as Mal though she's only fourteen and for the moment, they wear the same clothes, some of which had belonged to Elena. The Converse Amaranta loves, for instance. Egg-yolk yellow.

Griselda's the one who inherited Elena's face; it's uncanny to walk into a room and find Mal's long-gone-likely-dead sister. Until the sunlit filter that blurred Gris into the tía she never met fades and there's the staunch and steadfast daughter Malamar raised instead.

It's different with Amaranta. Rounder, darker, with the budding of plumpness, all her childish edges going soft. She'll end up like Gus, tall and thick.

"Buenos días, Papi." Mal kisses her father's cheek. Cafecito and pan dulce with a trace of fertilizer. Back when they still lived beside the sea, in the government-provided house where Papi worked tirelessly to repopulate the waters and oversee the fish he'd introduced from the Gulf of California on the land his ancestors had toiled for millennia—back when he was jefe and felt such pride in the thriving fish and game industry—he smelled of salt and, eventually, sulfur. But he ceased working after Elena disappeared, and for too many years, he exuded a fermented odor, a loaf of sourdough left in the rain. As he's aged and made a brittle peace with his grief, he's become an avid gardener. Now he emanates the scent of soil and the tres flores oil he still slicks into his sable hair.

"What are you two doing here so early?"

"We're tired of chicken!" Amaranta moans, and they all break out laughing.

"Hallelujah," Mal says. "We're *Mexican,* Papi! Get some carne asada, for Christ's sake!"

"Ay, mija." Papi *tsks,* but he's laughing too.

"So what'll it be then, eh, Pop? Between you and me, the menudo here can't hold a candle to yours. We've got some good tripas if you want to show your nieta what's up. It's time she learns." Mal raises her eyebrow at Amaranta, who slinks a bit. She gets away with everything around the house, including leaving all the chores to her elders. Papi finds solace in his work or else Mal would put her foot down. Let him take care of them now; Mal was little more than Mami's maid during her childhood. Mal won't put her daughters through that.

"We're making birria de res," Amaranta bursts.

"I've got the perfect tender chuck roast for you." Mal retreats behind the counter to select the meat and wrap it in puckered white paper.

While she's prepping the roast, Papi chats with Renata. "I get my beef here," he says conspiratorially, "instead of the meat market closer to our house. It tastes better."

Renata nods, solemn. "It's kinda why I work here. Poorly treated beef tastes bad."

Mal hands Papi the crinkling package. She ties it with string, old-school.

"I knew I liked you," Papi tells Renata. "Not everyone can taste that difference."

He means the Callahan butcher shop, Beef Tooth, replete with factory farm cattle yard. Their families have fought Mal's whole life. It's another art, fending off the exploitation of the privileged assholes who think they own this town. Mal refuses to source her meat from Sean Callahan's and orders from a smaller, organic farm near San Diego, where the cows graze and are grass-finished.

Papi took her hunting when she was a girl and taught her to respect her kills — the lives they lead before they die. He told her the Kumeyaay word for the land is the same for the human body: Mat/'Emat. That stuck with her. Connects her to everything. Even the cows. Even the sea.

Last summer, Griselda came home for an internship and preached for weeks at the dinner table about the Callahans' unfair practices. Grisly tales of their slaughterhouse just down the road. Unexplained illnesses, water pollution, land destruction, mud-smeared cattle wedged in the packing yard, their hides glistening and sticky with confinement. The workers aren't spared from injuries, diseases, or accidents either. Not to mention the waste, that abattoir mess—shit, blood, bone, chemicals like nitrogen and phosphorus—all floating out into the Salton Sea.

Griselda's impassioned tirade sounded like a college presentation—all those gruesome details about slicing the necks of conscious cows. It made Amaranta sick. Pobrecita left the table, gagging up the sopa her abuelo spent literal *hours* stewing.

Gris's soapbox talk probably stems from Sean Callahan's only son, Harlan, her on-again, off-again boyfriend, who was back on last summer. Even though he's a yuppie who protests his own father's business while still living in his gated estate, Mal respects his efforts. The Callahans make terrible enemies, as Mal knows all too well. Harlan secretly undermining them from within their own posh home takes serious cojones. She only knows about his guerrilla tactics through Gris, and as far as Mal can tell, his dad has no idea. She'd respect Harlan even more if he moved out altogether, but dismantling an empire takes time. And resources. Mal's not one to judge someone for who their family is, and he wouldn't make the worst son-in-law, if it came down to it. Still, she doesn't want her daughter stuck with him in El Valle.

"I'm not gonna work here forever," Renata adds, as if she's been privy to Mal's thoughts. "I want to be an eco-justice lawyer."

Yessi's never mentioned her cousin's aspirations. Damn. Good for her.

"Una abogada," Papi rejoins. "Working for change como mis nietas." His voice swells as he tells her about his scientist granddaughters. "Amar es una futura científica, y mi otra nieta, Griselda, está en la universidad. ¿La conoces? She's about your age."

Mal, ever the mama bear, spies the briefest scowl shadowing Renata's face before she catches herself. At first Mal wonders if Renata doesn't speak Spanish but then realizes it was the mention of Griselda's name that struck a strange chord. Does her coworker dislike Mal's eldest? Wouldn't be the first. Everyone knows everyone in their small town. Everyone's got beef with someone. Even her own brothers, Lord help them. Splitting up the family over this damn fundraiser in two nights. Benny refuses to support Esteban since he's holding it at the *Callahan mansion,* of all places. Enemy territory. But Mal and Esteban have always been close: Chuy and Mallow Mar—like the candy bars. In high school, they were a bookish pair of Mexican nerds and scholars ¿y qué? Mal won't abandon Esteban now, not when he's so close to winning his Senate seat.

The house cat in the hinges screeches as the door swings open wide and two men in khaki and olive-green camouflage tromp into the carnicería. At first, they strike Mal as military, men who sometimes come into town from the bases dotting the outlying mountains and desert beyond El Valle. But they're missing key elements of a soldier's attire—no glinting dog tags, no combat boots or crew cuts. One guy has a Viking beard and mustache so manicured and sculpted it's comical.

Renata's demeanor changes when the hunters come in, and, in fact, she begins to resemble a house cat herself now, all coy and mischievous.

The hunters zero in on Renata, cutting off Papi midsentence. "Is Mal around? We need to discuss a job with him."

Amaranta stifles a giggle. Renata smirks too.

Mal clears her throat and steps forward, crossing her arms in front of her bloody chest.

"That's me," Mal flexes.

The hunters are taken aback—bocas tan abiertas que los peces podrían nadar en ellas, as Papi would say. He makes up his own dichos. *Their mouths gape so wide, fish could swim in them.* Mal's used to this reaction. It amuses her every time.

Hipster Beard grabs the elk teeth dangling from his keychain. "Oh, sorry, I didn't realize, but, hey, great we caught you. No disrespect. We've heard you're the best butcher in the valley. We need someone to process game for us."

The other guy chuckles. "We'd have done it ourselves, but it was a train wreck."

"Right?" Hipster Beard agrees. "We need more bang for our buck this time around." He shakes the keychain and both men laugh. Buck. A male deer.

"Yeah, I have the chops to prepare your venison," Mal puns back.

Amaranta cracks a smile and Mal winks. She's taught her daughter how venison comes from the Latin *venatus,* which means *to hunt.* Originally, the term referred to any kind of edible game, but it's used now to mean the meat from deer. It also means *hunted* or *pursued.*

Once they work out the details and price and Mal gives her cell so they can text when their kill's ready, Renata asks if they need anything else. When they decline, she leans against the counter, pulls out a compact tube of lipstick from her snug jeans pocket, and applies another greasy coat of mauve around her crescent-moon pout. The hunters remind Mal of wolves in a cartoon, grinning and nudging each other as they depart, the hissing feline of door hinges bidding them farewell.

When Papi pulls Mal aside to ask her advice about what to cook for Griselda's return and whether she thinks Benny will join them at the fundraiser even though he's not speaking to Esteban, Mal notices Amaranta suddenly light up in a spirited conversation with Renata. Mal wants to eavesdrop but also respect her daughter's privacy. Her girl's growing up. Looking for women to emulate. Far be it from Mal to deem Renata an unsuitable influence. Even if she does hook up with guys in the parking lots of swine barns.

Elena hooked up all across town and the surrounding country-side, everyone said.

A year older than Elena, Mal still had no idea who her sister was. Elena kept her secrets but Mal could've tried harder. Could've been a better role model. A better sister. She might've been a failure at the root, a bad sea as a sister and a daughter, but as a mother? At least she got that one thing right. *Right?*

2
ALL THE DOGS IN TOWN

The meat falls off the flank of the birria de res, plopping into the chile-red broth with a *plunk*. Papi said when he was a boy, they made this adobo stew from goat meat.

But Mal was right about this beef chuck. It's the perfect cut. So tender.

She tops hers with finely diced onions, cilantro, and a wedge of lime, glad to see Amaranta helped her abuelo and her chopping skills are improving. She grabs a tortilla from under the Styrofoam lid of the warmer, breaks off a piece, and scoops out a chunk of meat from the broth, staining the blanket of tortilla bright red.

Everyone but Mami's doing the same. Mami uses a spoon. Slurps loudly. The juice runs down her mouth like she's bleeding from her gums.

After dinner, Papi's washing dishes while Amaranta does her

homework at the table. A kid who does homework on a Saturday night. That's the kind of girl Mal's raised.

She has tutoring tomorrow. A boy in her class. Maybe she's crushing. But Amaranta prides herself on remaining an enigma, steeped in gender-nonconforming mystery. Mal's fine with that. Boys screw everything up anyway.

Papi's humming above the sound of the rushing faucet and the gentle *clink-clink* of dishes. His voice to the thrum of the water takes Mal back to the sea. The dock at the edge of their old yard led to Papi's little government-issued boat. When Papi was a boy growing up deeper in El Valle, his people were more than laborers in the irrigated fields—they were farmers in their own right, cultivating the land to grow and thrive.

Back then, his family, being Kumeyaay and Cahuilla, the original inhabitants of this land, were welcomed as immigrants. It's ironic, considering they'd come from this place but migrated to Mexico, moving back and forth over thousands of years until the imaginary borders drawn by los políticos restricted international travel. When the floods came again and nourished this land, they also rebirthed the sea, which for a time sustained his family—until everything decayed, and over the past two decades, Papi's borne the brunt.

Mami's nurse, Lupita, hasn't come for her shift again. Her daughter's sick with asthma. Mal remembers those days with Griselda in and out of emergency rooms—how harrowing when a daughter can't breathe. So Mal cleans Mami's pressure wounds in Lupita's place. They flush bright and toxic as algal blooms.

She lifts Mami from her wheelchair to the flowered couch, props her one remaining leg on a towel, and sets her first-aid supplies on the coffee table like her butcher's knife set. Maybe if she thinks of Mami as a carcass, the whole process will be a pinch more tolerable.

But as Mal scrapes the flesh, Mami slaps back her hand, hard.

Mal's skin turns red along her knuckles. If it'd been palm to palm, it would've been a high five. But with Mami, it's always a rebuke. "That hurts," Mami squelches. "Watch what you're doing, tonta."

Tonta—stupid girl—Mami's term of endearment for Mal, who releases a moody puff that blows the wisps of bangs from her forehead as if she were a teenager sulking. She'll be forty-two soon. Why does she still let Mami do this to her? She turns her huffs into the box-breaths her therapist taught her. *You'll choose a familiar hell over a strange heaven every time unless you reset your nervous system.* So Mal breathes in for five out for five as she digs the pus from the mealy bread crust of a scab. The hydrogen peroxide sizzles and bubbles against the little wormlets on Mami's skin.

Mal shushes her in measured tones meant for soothing and not the irritation she feels. She doesn't need another slap. Not to her hand or her face.

Still, Mami's prolonged grief seethes through her dementia. "You're the reason Elena's gone," Mami slurs, her speech slow as a borracha or niña up past her bedtime and fighting it. "You stupid, fat slut. You got pregnant when you should've been watching your sister."

Never mind that Mami got the timing backward. Mal got fat with Griselda *after* Elena disappeared, and Mal was already Baby Benny's substitute mother by then, since Mami all but abandoned him. He was born the very night Elena disappeared, Mami's wails more akin to grief than labor—like she already knew she wouldn't raise this child herself since his birth signaled the loss of her favored daughter. He would've starved if Mal hadn't stepped in.

When Griselda arrived two years later, she and Benny were more Mal's twins than her brother and daughter. Mythical cuates, born from the earth and sea, akin to the Nahuatl cóatl—twin snakes.

And never mind that Mal lost the baby weight after both her pregnancies.

Mami jabs because she can.

"It should've been *you*," Mami hisses. She's on a vitriol roll tonight. What was in that broth? Truth serum? But Mal's heard it many times before. Mami wishes her eldest daughter had disappeared instead of Elena. Her baby girl. Her favorite. Her angelita, pobrecita, muy linda, qué bonita, besito, besito. "Pero no. Dios left me with *you*. A daughter who hurts me."

Mal shushes her again, breathing in for longer, the eight counts of a curandera asking permission to enter the spirit realm for guidance, although Mal's not sure what spirit she believes in. Certainly not some white-haired man on a heavenly throne.

Mal prefers Amaranta's version; she calls it the Great Mathematician in the Sky, because, she says, we're all ones and zeros at the particle level. *Give me the strength not to dig my fingers into the black hole of Mami's misplaced rage—*

Instead, Mal takes a Q-tip and applies a thick coat of salve, Mami's wound opaquing like a cloudy window at their old beach house, filmed by a layer of salt and wet grime.

A hand grabs a clutch of hair from Mal's scalp and yanks hard, so the Q-tip snaps and flies through the living room. Black maggots drift through Mal's vision, her neck protesting the unnatural angle Mami's jerked it. Mal blinks, focusing on the dishes clinking in the background, Papi's humming above the faucet, the soft scrape of Amaranta's pencil lead against notebook paper, scratching like a rodent at the dirt. No one seems to notice or care that Mami's no longer a frail woman bound to a wheelchair by daughterloss and diabetes.

Mal doesn't dare look into the milky glaze of Mami's marble eyes.

The candles on Elena's ofrenda flicker from the small foyer to Mal's left. Dried flowers. Irises instead of marigolds since Mami clings to a foolish hope her favorite daughter will be returned. A statue of an archangel and another of La Virgen. Mal counts in for eight, her gaze locked on the picture of Elena when she was sixteen, holding a blue ribbon at the Midwinter County Fair for her art installation. Out for eight. Elena had painted a horse, a bay, braying in a field. The photo was taken a handful of months before she disappeared.

Mal doesn't make a peep as she gently takes Mami's hand, lifting each finger with the patience she'd use to clip her daughters' fingernails when they were little, or Benny's, uno, dos, y tres deditos, cuatro, cinco . . . until Mami's grasp unpries from Mal's hair, releasing her scalp with a screech of relief like untying chongos from a tight set of braids.

Instead of scolding Mami or tattle-taling to Papi, Mal's desplante takes on the cool tone of a woman growing up — or maybe just out of fucks.

"Amaranta," she says, spine straight, voice tight, "go pack your backpack, mijita, and don't forget your toothbrush. I just remembered I have to run some errands, so you're spending the night at Tía Sharon's."

Tía Sharon's house hates itself. Amaranta firmly believes this. It's as if the house looked in the mirror and cursed itself — not for being ugly. It's stately and upmarket, gaudier than most houses in El Valle. But like someone beautiful without makeup who insists on wearing every lurid shade in MAC's spring collection to overcompensate — it perceives some lack.

Still, it had a good foundation. Tía and Tío were rico lawyers. In some ways, Amaranta is proud to be the niece of a rising senator and the former mayor. There's no slapping lipstick on a pig at Tía's. Before she left her post as mayor and divorced Tío Esteban a few years ago to *become a lush,* as Abuelo says, Tía had been a powerful woman.

These days, she just seems sad, same as everyone else in their family.

Like Ma, who thinks Amaranta doesn't know why she drops her off with her two fifteen-year-old cousins, Xochitl and Xolotl, the deplorable cuates, once or twice a month, but Amaranta's not a baby. She understands just fine. Ma's too tightly wound and needs to get laid. That's how Iggy puts it anyway. Iggy lives with her sick grandma now. She and Amaranta have sick grandmas and sneaky moms in common.

Amaranta discovered the latter when she and Iggy were scrounging for weed in Ma's drawer and found actual photographic evidence of Ma's cringefest of a secret life. Ever since, Amaranta's been too freaked to think of much else. She wishes she were brave enough to just *tell* Ma she'd rather be chilling and making out with her bestie-turned-girlfriend, Iggy, than survive her nasty-ass cousins' antics.

"Can't I stay with Iggy tonight?" Amaranta had whined on the way over to Tía's, trying to produce a tear for authenticity (pinching herself on the thigh works, but she's wearing jeans).

"Another time, okay?" Ma's voice was weary and had that sharp edge to it Amaranta hates, like *end-of-convo,* when the truth was it never started.

Amaranta needs Tía to spill whatever she knows about Ma, since Tía's the only one in the family who gets drunk enough to spill the real tea, not the weak, watery stuff everyone else tries to serve. But tonight she's been too busy with her new boy toy to notice Amaranta, who watches the couple through the glass doors. They're drinking and dancing on the patio, Tía with one hand around Oscar, shamelessly pinching his nalgas, and the other clutching her cocktail.

Amaranta's observant. A scientist. It's how she learns things. Even things she's not supposed to know. The power of observation is both a blessing and a curse. Once you know, you can't unknow.

She watches until Oscar slides off his shorts, his dick swinging like a stallion's during a hot piss, stirring up a cloud of dust and steam. She's only ever seen a horse dick at the ranch beside the park that skirts her house and the New River, before now.

Tía pulls down the straps of her bathing suit, but Oscar's looking elsewhere — straight toward the sliding glass door. He winks.

Amaranta turns away, mortified. Was he winking at *her*? Gross.

Might as well see what her menacing primos are up to while she waits for her Tía to finish getting laid. Is that all grown-ups think about?

The alternative is to call Iggy to rescue her, but Amaranta still wants to talk to Tía. She needs more time. She drifts upstairs, a leaf caught in a slow current.

Xochitl's room is the first on the landing; her prima's door stands ajar, its silhouette carved out by the half-hearted glow of a table lamp. Amaranta peeks in but it's empty.

Next in the hallway is Xolotl's closed door.

Amaranta turns the doorknob, prepping to roll her eyes when she enters like she's bored of them before she's even hung out, only her nerves stingray as she nudges the door open.

The cuates sit cross-legged on a black rug. She's about to say *Sup, party people* (a phrase Iggy prefers for its gender neutrality and casual tone) when she sees what lies between them on the shaggy dark carpet. A silver blade catches the scant light.

What kind of shit are her cousins into? Amaranta curses her unquenchable scientist's curiosity and stays still. The room is so dim she has to squint.

"Your tongue shall be slit,
And all the dogs in the town
Shall have a little bit."

They extend their arms, and Amaranta would poke fun at their theatricality (is this for *her* benefit, are they putting on some kind of show?) but her insides wobble and all she can do is watch, transfixed as Xolotl picks up the blade and opens a thin red line across his sister's wrist. Then they switch, and she does the same for him. The sudden streak of spilled cherries dribbles down their arms, jarring against the room's silence. No gasps or grimaces of pain. Only their weird chant punctuated by the soft, rhythmic patter of blood drops hitting the rug. They lean in, each clamping their mouth to the other's wrist, sucking. *Ew. Ew. EW.*

Amaranta stumbles back as the cuates, in unison, perk up, predators post-kill, sensing their next fresh meal.

They swivel toward her, panic freezing her in place, and they're on her before she can react. A vise-like hand clamps down on her mouth, snuffing out her scream. *Iggy!* Shit shit shit.

They drag her back into the room.

"You're our new plaything," Xolotl teases, his breath hot vinegar against her face, his fingers tightening around the hilt of the blade. He grabs Amaranta's arm and traces the tip against her skin. She kicks and tries to scream, but Xochitl palms her face.

This is a new low. Why did Amaranta think she could handle them? She's been so stupid. Blood oozes from her fresh wound, seeping onto the carpet. Xolotl collects the blood into a small bowl.

Summoning a surge of adrenaline, Amaranta wrenches herself free, elbowing her cousin's gut. She sprints through the hallway and down the staircase to the patio where she last saw Tía Sharon. But it's empty.

Are they mating underwater? Did they move to another room? Will the cuates come down and snatch her again? Drag her back to their room? She should run out the front door and call Iggy from the sidewalk. She's about to do just that when she spots Tía in the study, crumpled on an oversized leather couch, glass in hand.

Amaranta clutches her bleeding arm and slinks into the room.

Tía Sharon offers a sloppy upturn of her mouth. "Hi, mija. Need something?"

"Your kids tried to kill me."

"What's new? They've been trying to kill me since conception." She lifts her glass like she's making a toast before breaking out into a burst of full-throated laughter.

"Look," Amaranta says, holding out her bloody wrist as proof.

Tía Sharon squints, leans closer, then blinks in disbelief. "Jesus, girl! What'd you do to yourself?" She's suddenly alert. "You need some first aid, mija. Come here, let me see."

"*I* didn't do this to myself." Amaranta's anger flares, hot and righteous. She pulls her arm away and uses the bottom of her T-shirt as a compress. "It was your sadistic children! They think they're in a horror movie."

Tía's gaze sobers. "¡Ay! Stop being a drama queen and let me find the liquid bandage."

She stands and motions for Amaranta to follow her through the pristine house, with its fancy chandeliers and dining table set like something out of a home decor magazine, to the guest bathroom where she fumbles the liquid bandage onto Amaranta's arm while clasping her drink, rambling and slurring her words. "You don't know true horror, mija." Her voice is bitter rinds.

Amaranta tries to snatch the brown vial from her aunt, its sharp antiseptic smell mingling with Tía's sickly sweet drink. But Tía bats her away.

"True horror is seeing something so bad that if you told anyone, it could get you killed." Tía slices her throat with her finger, the little paintbrush of antiseptic dripping onto the tile.

The liquid stings in Amaranta's fresh wound. Tears stab at the edges of her eyes.

"I was at a party, you know? A party. I should've been having the time of my freaking life, mija. But *nooooo* . . ." Tía slurs *no* with such a vigorous tilt of her whole body that she sloshes her drink onto the floor then erupts in a high-pitched hysterical clap of laughter that ends with a hiccup. "That was *true* horror. This is a little accident." She plops down her glass on the countertop with a clattering *ting* before retrieving a small silver compact mirror from inside her bra, its surface glinting in the soft bathroom light. "This," she slurs, waving it unsteadily, "is my . . . is like your bloody wrist." She flicks open the compact, revealing a smudge of rust. A hollow laugh bubbles. "This memento?" She waves the mirror again. "This is my life insurance."

She slumps across the toilet seat, folds her arms atop the marble counter, and hunches over. Amaranta lifts her aunt's head, but her eyes are shut and she's snoring. *Wasted,* Ma would say. This night officially sucks.

What the hell was Tía ranting about anyway? Some horror party? It's so weird every adult Amaranta knows is haunted. Do all adults have this one screwed-up night in their lives? Ma's scarred by the night of the bonfire when her sister disappeared. She talks about it all the time.

But this is the first Amaranta's heard from her tía about a similar night.

The compact glimmers up from the tile. It's got rust or something on it. How could this little thing be Tía's protection? What, is she a witch or something, and is this her totem?

Amaranta pockets it. She can't pass up a good mystery. She'll get Iggy's advice as soon as she makes it out of this freak show.

But a shadow across the bathroom door sends her chest palpating. The cuates are coming back. Shit shit shit. She turns slowly, holding her breath.

Standing in the hallway, wrapped in nothing but a towel around his waist, Oscar stares at her, eyebrows raised. Furry caterpillars squirm across his chest. His hair is slicked back and wet. There's a hot, sloshy sensation in her stomach. Her teeth cling to her gums with a sticky paste.

"Hey, mija," he says like he's already family although Amaranta's only known him a couple of months and they've never had a real conversation, only him droning on about his motorcycle and New Creations, which sounds a little cultish to Amaranta, but so does all organized religion. "She fell asleep on the pot?" He laughs. "Where are your primos?"

Amaranta squeezes the mirror. It feels cold against her warm, soggy palms.

"Upstairs."

3
NOT SO DEAD

Sulfur. The rotten egg stink of a dying sea. It sticks to her lungs. The gurgling mud pots beside the toxic water. A vomitous splashing in the sopa bowl of her stomach.

No, not sulfur. Piss. A hot stream of it against the dirt.

The awful reek of ammonia, unmucked stables, all that urine-soaked alfalfa surfacing...

It comes to Mal first as the sticky sweetness of maple syrup, cloying. But there's something of a trap already set in the sap. Dig into the silky warmth and it'll harden into viscous pools — so the stories go. Those entranced by the horse-headed woman *have* to touch her hair. And when they realize it's a mane and their schoolboy palms have clung to it like too much candy, they're already caught. How quickly syrup turns to piss. It happens every time for Mal. A whiff of something enticing before it rots.

She jerks up from sleep, a mother troubled. It's dark. She's trembling.

She checks the body beside her, the steady rise and fall of the blanket, the snore deeper and more phlegm-trebled than she expected. It's not Amaranta. She rubs her eyes and remembers where she is.

The rhythmic clop of hooves recedes to the steady drip, drip, dripping of a leaky faucet. Everything here leaks. This house, Gus's once-seaside cottage, is falling apart.

What time is it?

Her phone on the nightstand says 4:00 a.m. No missed calls. No texts. No alarm. It's Sunday. Four years since she last dreamed of the horse-headed woman who chased her the night Elena disappeared. Four years since she started therapy. Why has La Siguanaba reared her equine head now?

For a hundred years, townsfolk have claimed a horse-headed woman roams the beaches and surrounding desert as far as Mexico. La Siguanaba, they call her. Hideous one. But that doesn't tell the whole story. She's a shapeshifter. Some say she wears a high-collared lace dress, once white as wedding silk, now saturated in the rust-red innards of her victims. Some say she wears whatever a man lusts after most. Sequins. Spandex. Fishnet. Nothing at all. Legends tell of her lurking in the shadows, targeting womanizers and drunkards. Los borrachos.

No, she doesn't sneak, no se esconde. She merely approaches with deliberate nonchalance. Leaning over, she lifts her long hair above her head, as if wringing out water, and then releases it, letting it cascade into a flowing waterfall. The men catch a glimpse of her naked form and dark, ethereal hair, and they're undone.

"Reveal your face to me," the borrachos y mujeriegos implore, enticed by her beauty. They misinterpret her reluctance as coyness, inching closer and closer until their breath grazes the back of her neck. Then she turns, allowing her long, dark hair to fall away — revealing the white-boned skull of a horse.

By the time they scream, it's too late.

If she doesn't kill immediately, she leaves men lost and wandering, mad in the wilderness. Mal has long worried it's not only drunkards and womanizers La Siguanaba comes for but children. Teenagers. Girls — everyone blames women when things go wrong.

She texts Amaranta: You still up, baby? You alright?

The sick sensation that awoke her, the rumbling in her gut, burns her throat. She fumbles a hand to the nightstand again, feeling for the foil paper, grabbing two Tums and chewing while she waits to see if Amaranta's side goes from "received" to "read."

She's been tumbling Amaranta out into the night since she was a baby. Griselda and Benny before her. They're used to it. But that doesn't make the next morning any less sloshy in her gut. Mother-guilt. It burns like the peppermint on her tongue.

Why does Mal let Mami get to her?

Her therapist says self-care first, then she can care for others. So Mal crashes at Gus's place as often as she needs. Over the years, that's meant once a month. Whenever Mal's intestines twist and kink like the primal cuts in the industrial meat grinder, it's time to step away from the house. Living with a narcissist has given her irritable bowel syndrome. That's what her therapist says. For twenty-odd years, Mal's IBS has been a surprisingly accurate barometer for how much Mami she can handle before she snaps. In some ways, she's been a petulant teenager sneaking off to her boyfriend's. But teenagers often excel at self-preservation. This has been the pattern since she was seventeen and dropped out of school to get her GED and take care of Benny. While it might not be the healthiest coping mechanism, it's well-worn and rutted.

Mal used to believe Mami when she accused her of being the slut who should've disappeared instead of Elena; she'd hang on to Mami's every hateful word. But a year after Griselda left for college, she called Mal and announced, "Mom, I think you should start therapy." She gave Mal a list of numbers to call, all matter of fact. "See which one you feel comfortable with, okay? See which one sticks." Mal shoved down the embarrassment she felt at having her barely adult daughter confront her, but she called each number on the list, made an appointment with the woman who bothered her the least, and promised she'd try it for three months, long enough to form a habit. That was four years ago. So why's she dreaming about the horse-headed woman again *now*?

A paranoid thought gallops through her mind. Maybe La Siguanaba's finally coming for her. She grabbed Elena instead of Mal when they were teenagers, in the fields, by the sea. Everyone in town said Elena deserved it. Bunch of misogynist assholes. But even after four years of therapy, a tiny part of Mal is still convinced the monstrous creature could've been after her instead of her sister. Mal was the daughter Mami wanted gone, after all.

If La Siguanaba came for Mal in the past but snatched her sister instead, and she's back—who might she accidentally take if Mal's not careful?

Or maybe it's just guilt. Mal's too old to be sneaking off, living a double life; pues, it's eroding her relationship with her youngest. Mal can't bear the thought of Amaranta pulling away. She's not ready. Maybe this is just Mal's psyche working overtime, convincing her to keep her 'jita close when her therapist's challenging her to let go of the reins a bit and see what happens. *What about your closeness with your daughter is good for your daughter,* her therapist asks her, pointedly, *versus what's just good for you, Mal?* So far, Mal hasn't answered, just stared at the swirling patterns on the carpet. But the question has troubled her. *Is* she stifling her daughter with her own need? She pushes that thought *way* down — subterranean deep.

She checks her phone again. The little dots mean her daughter's typing.

Mal releases a breath she didn't realize she was holding.

Amaranta texts back: I'm fine. Was asleep til you texted. Weirdo. She adds the clown face emoji.

Mal texts back a heart. Then adds a monkey covering their face with their palms. She can't lie back down. The acid's broiling her from the inside out.

The bed groans as she gets up and pads through Gus's house, floorboards creaking. She folds her arms tightly across her chest and shivers as she passes the other bedroom, its door shut tight. It's probably locked. She never goes in. No one does.

She slides on a pair of mules, unlocks the front door, and steps outside, aware she's enacting the very motions Gus claims his daughter, Noemi, took twenty-five years before when she, too, vanished across the marsh.

The yard is littered with fish bones, scattered from the beach below, bleached white, crunching beneath her feet as she walks down to the sea. Along the way, she picks one up. It resembles a tooth.

Not the kind from Mal's nightmares, torn from her swollen gums, their roots exposed and bleeding. Nor the kind Mami knocked out of her mouth in girlhood. No, this reminds her of when she first met Gustavo Castillo, and he wanted the ones glinting at the water's edge, jutting from the salted shore.

Mal, eighteen years old, had been down at the beach with Baby Benny, studying for her GED and bird-watching.

She'd been staring at the water for hours, observing the pompous pelicans skim the surface, diving like arrows toward the blue line, then rising with slick, squirming tilapia in their beaks. The western sandpipers danced across the muddy embankments on their stilts for legs, waggling their butts and tail feathers like ladies with fancy fans, calling for the smaller fish and insects they piped into their beaks.

From the corner of her eye, she'd recognized the man with a crumpled map. He wasn't much to look at—disheveled, dejected, rejected by his wife and the remaining fragments of the town. Yet something about how he clutched that creased paper as he knelt by the salty shore intrigued Mal.

She hoisted Benny onto her hip and asked, "What's on the map?"

"Places she isn't." His voice was both gruff and earnest, as if his throat were filled with gravel or he was on the verge of tears.

"Your daughter?" Her stomach clenched like bait on a wire. Mal hadn't known Noemi except in passing. She was in the same grade as Elena. Mal wasn't too cool to hang out with younger classmates, but she didn't hang out with anyone except Esteban before he became *Stevie* consumed with Sharon—prom king and queen. The perfect couple. And Mal was alone.

Folks called Gus the Devil. El Cucuy. The monstrous beast who sneaks into the homes of disobedient children and snatches them away. In some versions, he's covered in prickly hair, akin to a chupacabra. In others, he has the slick skin of a regular man, but he's evil just the same.

Legend says El Cucuy was once a mere father annoyed with his naughty children. He concocted a punishment to teach them a lesson, locking them in the closet where they could sweat it out while he ran some errands. But when he got back, he found his house had caught fire and his children had burned to death.

Did they curse him, or did he call the curse upon himself, in his disbelief and shock and guilt? Either way, El Cucuy now stalks the bedrooms of children, checking their armarios, under their beds. But his search has grown chaotic over the years, his desire deranged. No longer does he search for children to save but to fill the void within him, the burning ache where he cannot face what he's done.

Lingering by the water, Gus didn't seem devilish, just profoundly sad.

She got on her knees and joined the search — Baby Benny cooing a gurgly, drool-gummed laugh.

At first they spoke little, but gradually their exchanges became more philosophical. Gus shared the history of El Valle, revealing that he was a community college professor before his daughter disappeared. His words often took on a Socratic, teacherly tone, like he cared about what she thought. She returned each day with Benny as they scanned the beach and surrounding desert, fields, and thermal mud pots.

Three months in, Mal pulled something shining and iridescent from the ground. A sharp incisor. Pulpy and dark at the center. Knifelike at the tip.

Gus took her back to his house, saying, "Let me show you something," in a tone that made Mal worry she shouldn't have brought Baby Benny with her.

But you didn't get as sad as Gus by *hurting* others. It comes from *being* hurt.

He retrieved a baby food jar filled with teeth of different sizes and colors, from milky beige to lurid yellow, from different mouths and various levels of oral hygiene. Some sharp enough to be animal razors, some dull as ground stone. Mal was both repulsed and intrigued.

That jar was macabre, but she held it, fascinated, examining the old, blood-crusted stumps. Tooth enamel is the toughest thing the human body makes. Tougher than bone. And yet, teeth are so easily dislodged. Uprooted. Like anything else, so easy to rot.

He pulled out that stained map and laid it on the counter beside the jar. It depicted their desert oasis adorned with Gus's chicken scratch. Thick red markings resembled tributaries, their ink seeping into the map's fabric. He'd left similar scribblings on the news clippings scattered throughout his house, dating back to the early days of El Valle and even further, delving into ancient myths and geological records.

"This where you found the teeth?" she asked.

He nodded.

"Are any your daughter's?"

"The police would have to believe me to find out with forensics. They'd have to care."

"Don't you have dental records?"

"You know how it is out here."

Mal nodded. She did know how it was out here.

The sheriff barely pretended to hide his speculations on Elena's disappearance. Fast girls run. Period. The case never closed but it'd never really opened either.

"They all girl's teeth?"

"Doubt it. Some are coyotes. Other animals."

She held one up to her own tooth and gazed at her reflection in a dusty window. It fit. She didn't have to imagine the force it would take to wriggle it out of the safebed of her gums and onto the playa floor. In that way, twisted though it might've been, she'd felt connected to Gus's daughter, and to Gus himself. A small town will make monsters everywhere. That part Mal had always understood.

Now she soaks in the duskish light dancing across the dying, drying lake. He won't leave this ghost town or move farther inland like everyone else. He's waiting for his daughter to return. No, he's waiting to die and join her. And Mal's been decaying alongside them in this purgatory. She isn't being fair to their relationship, but nothing has been fair.

A shotgun cracks, leaving a familiar pop and crackle in Mal's eardrums, snapping her out of her thoughts. She's been out here an hour at least. She tromps back through the fields toward the thunderous sound coming from the east side of Gus's property. The salted playa crackles beneath her feet the way she imagines ice would.

Mal finds Gus awake and in the yard, his shotgun aimed into the distance. His jeans fit snugly around his muscular thighs with a slight looseness at the waist that allows enough space for Mal to slip her hands between the waistband and his warm skin.

His most prominent features are those thick, dark brows Mal secretly wishes she could pluck and paste onto her own meager arches. When she was a teenager, it was all the rage for girls to pluck theirs into wispy lines; luckily, her daughters take after their father, inheriting arches of which Frida Kahlo would be proud.

A few silver foxes burrow into the dark forest of his hair, curling at his scruff—while Mal, twenty years younger, has taken to dyeing her grays a rich bronzed brown.

Birds flock into the sky. A coyote rushes past. The sun peeks from behind the mountains.

"Catch the chupacabra?" she asks, pressing her body to his.

"Damned raccoons eating my vegetables."

"You old codger," she laughs. "Viejo gruñón."

Gus harrumphs, puts the safety on the gun, points it to the ground, and opens his arms for Mal, who leans into her beloved.

His grief should've wilted him into a man much older than his sixty-one years, but his good genes have preserved him. Only a few russet sunspots scatter across his cheeks. Mal covers hers with makeup, but anyone who saw them together would assume they were the same age. Of course, no one ever saw them together. That was the point.

He smells of vanilla, bourbon, and earth, in that order. He's barefoot. Shirtless. Irredeemably handsome. She'd have had to watch out for women throwing themselves at him if they lived elsewhere. Here, Mal has him all to herself.

"I wish the girls had let me teach them to hunt," she says, wrapping her muscular arms around him. Although she's petite, Mal's full-on brawny from heaving beef carcasses above her head. Papi stopped hunting after Elena disappeared, but Mal eventually took Benny when he was old enough, passing on the age-old traditions their father wanted but refused to share with the son he didn't claim.

It's weird that Mal never took her own daughters out. She can't say why not. Griselda was staunchly vocal against it from the start. Or she was just as squeamish as Esteban. And, of course, she influenced her sweet and existential little sister who cried over a coyote one hot summer when desert creatures wandered into town searching for food and water. Amaranta wanted to treat it like any stray dog they could rescue.

"You tried, that's the main thing," Gus says.

She didn't try hard enough. As with so many things with her girls. *Their* girls.

They don't know their father at all. Over the years, there's been a murky truce. Gus stayed attentive during Mal's pregnancy without directly acknowledging the babies. He wasn't ready to be a father again.

When the girls were little, he was a shadow at the edges of parties or the park, watching his daughters play from afar. When Griselda was four, maybe five, she'd asked Mal if guardian angels could look like regular people. She'd described Gus. He'd cried when Mal told him, fat tears rolling down the puppyish slants of his eyes, down his morning-bristled, square jaw, and onto his flannel button-down.

Still, Mal hadn't wanted to bring her daughters into this — this vast, aching sadness and all the town's hatred toward him — so year after year, they'd reluctantly agreed to keep their secret.

"You were out there early," Gus muses into the gap of her silence, kissing atop her head.

She wants to admit she was torn out of a recurring nightmare she thought she'd buried when she started therapy. The truth? La Siguanaba scared the shit out of her. What if Mal disappeared and her girls never knew who their father was? She'd never meant to keep the secret this long. But if she's not careful, he'll recoil. She has to package it gently. He won't like this one bit. Not after all these years. Instead, she says, "I think you should meet the girls."

Deep ridges form in the desert sand of his face. Mal has put them there. He runs a palm along the smooth wood finish of his rifle comb but says nothing.

"You could come for dinner? The night after Esteban's fundraiser?"

"Why *now,* Mal?" He stoops down, resting his rifle across his knee, and pulls a wilted carrot from the dirt. A pale, sickly orange thing covered in soil, ringed and sprouted, the tip tentacled with roots. "Griselda's grown. Amaranta's in high school. That ship has sailed. I screwed it all up. They don't want to meet some old man."

Her therapist says if she wants her daughters to trust her, she must trust them. But that kind of trust takes guts. The mother's catch-22. Has she raised her children to accept her when she shows herself to be human? Well enough to love her, warts and all?

He brushes off the dirt. "Everything's dying."

Mal reaches for the vegetable. Snaps it in two. It crunches. The innards are bright. "Not so dead," she says, kneeling on the ground with him.

Maybe Mami and Papi could've protected Elena if they'd been on the same page, working together instead of fighting. They were distracted by the shitstorm between them. The mess they'd created. It's time for Mal and Gus to clean up their mess.

Mal's held on to her family's pain like a birthright. She's held it tight so she wouldn't pass it on to her daughters. But she needs time to let it go. "It's time."

Tears well at the corners of his eyes like broken irrigation sprinklers then fall down the black stubble at his jawline and neck, the slight protrusion of his Adam's apple. Finally, Gus sighs and gently pulls her in, kisses the top of her head again. "After the fundraiser."

A lukewarm response — but she'll take it.

4
DAUGHTERS DISAPPEAR HERE

You okay, mijita?" Mal glances at Amaranta as they drive to school Monday morning. Her sullen baby face dimples at her cheeks, and Mal's always found it amusing that Amaranta's frown resembles a smile. "Did something happen at the sleepover? Were the cuates jerks?"

"No, Ma. Jeez."

When Mal got home yesterday, Amaranta was already in the bedroom they share, lying on the bed, earbuds planted, scribbling in her notebook. She's been quiet and moody ever since. Maybe she's joining the too-cool-for-mom club. Benny and Gris are founding members. Mal hoped Amaranta would pass on the membership, she was always such a mama's girl. But she's been acting weird since Mal got home.

"Why was tutoring canceled?"

Amaranta shrugs. "He ghosted me."

Maybe that's why she's upset? Maybe she liked that boy and he ditched her? Mal hates to spring a father on her daughter if she's already going through her own teen drama. But the nightmare nags at her. *Protect your girls,* something keeps repeating inside her.

"After your tío's fundraiser, let's have una charla. A heart-to-heart. I've been gone so much lately . . . it's just this desmadre with Abuela . . ."

"Yeah, fine." Amaranta rolls her eyes and plays with the edges of her hoodie sleeve, stretching it over her hands. "Maybe you'll start telling me the truth."

"The truth about *what,* baby?" But Mal's intestines twinge with all her omissions. There's so much she hasn't told her.

"Nothing. Never mind." Amaranta jams her earbuds into her ears and retreats into silence the rest of the short ride, but after a few seconds, a silver light shimmers from her palm.

Mal squints against the unexpected brightness, annoyed by the distraction it casts on the windshield. "Mind keeping that down? The reflection is blinding."

Amaranta shifts in her seat, the light disappearing as abruptly as it appeared.

When she tumbles out of the Jeep in a flurry of backpack, mismatched cutoff overalls, polka-dot socks, and Converse — a sticky, swishing sensation barrages Mal's gut. She never acclimates to spilling her girls out into the world. How could she? Daughters disappear here.

Elena shone, a stunning mix of chola and cheerleader, with lips that shimmered like the caramel-glazed donuts she loved. And the part that terrifies Mal, as a mother? They'll never know *why* she vanished. Where she went.

Outside the classroom, Amaranta links arms with Iggy—equally vibrant in her retro punk style and short, spiky, purple hair.

"I love you," Mal calls into the chasm widening as Amaranta tromps toward homeroom in her high-tops, untied laces trailing behind her through the dirt and grass.

Motherhood means fashioning a house out of Jell-O. Wobbly, leaky, stains everything. Mal builds these walls—membrane-thin, jellyfish material, breathable. Her girls need structure but independence too. Boundaries.

She jerks her Jeep into first gear, hoping Amaranta will turn and wave before she recedes through the classroom doorway. But she doesn't. The cars behind Mal in line honk her away from the drop-off curb.

The carnicería is bustling when Mal arrives, but she strides past the counter toward the back without more than a nod to the cashier, a man around her age she hardly ever talks to. Doesn't even know his name. She slaps on her apron and lays out her set of knives neatly on the counter. Something feels off, but she slices the tension away with the flick of her wrist.

She's stripping the meat with a deboning knife down to the single barrel of muscle and tying it into a loin roast when Yessi interrupts Mal's flow.

"Oye, yunta, I'm glad you're here already. Tengo un chisme grandote."

Ugh. Another gossip fest. But Mal's not feeling it. She's too tense from her nightmare.

She must look upset. Yessi narrows her eyes. "No, wait. Something's still wrong with you. Spill."

"No sé realmente . . . no es nada. Es . . . mothering is *hard*."

Yessi guffaws, a spurt of laughter from deep in her belly. But it's not cruel. "OK pues, it doesn't help that *your* mom is legit horrible. You didn't exactly have the best example."

True enough. Mal's not usually so mopey, though. So tender. Not even when La Siguanaba was coming to her *before*. She just wants to cuddle with her girls in bed watching rom-coms and eating junk. She misses those days. Are they really almost gone? Will Amaranta graduate in a few short years and take off too? Come back only when Mal twists her arm, like Gris for her tío's fundraiser?

"I wanted us to be like the Gilmore Girls . . . Las Veracruz Chicas. I wanted to be the kind of mom my daughters trust."

"Who's keeping shit from you?"

"Amar." Mal wipes her hands on her apron, already more red than white though it's still early in her shift. "It's like she's mad at me but clams up when I ask."

A worm of guilt wriggles. Mal is the comal calling out the pot. Taking off and keeping secrets, even if it's only one night a pop, it adds up.

Yessi's been saying something, but Mal hasn't heard a word. *Dissociation* her therapist calls it. Mal would've said daydreaming. Therapists make all our traits sound so bad.

"Sorry, Yessi. Can you repeat that?"

"Ayyyy . . . you never listen to me." She's scolding, but there's a playful lilt to her voice. "No te preocupes, yunta. She's a teenager. It's her *job* to be snarky. And daughters are always mad at their moms for something. It comes with the territory."

Mal nods, the blade flashing pink with meat under the fluorescent bulbs.

Yessi narrows her eyes and leans in. "Not to freak you out more, but maybe she heard what's happening with my cousin. It's what I've been trying to tell you. It's all over town but I heard it straight from the horse's mouth . . . mi tía."

Mal finally looks up and sees the worry lines etched into Yessi's face. She missed those before.

"Wait, what? Something's going on with Renata?" It swooshes through Mal like the whistle of a kettle in another room — her coworker should be here already. What's his name wasn't scheduled for Monday's shift — *Renata was*. "She get arrested again?"

"No . . . it's worse. Well, maybe. No one knows."

"You lost me. Start at the beginning."

"Word on the street is she was supposed to run off with her boyfriend. But he flaked on her, and no one's seen her since."

"She's *missing*?" Mal's stomach clenches. The freezers hum.

Yessi nods, solemn. "Yeah, that's what I've been trying to say."

Mal sets the cleaver down. A dull ache starts at the base of her skull. "She was with her boyfriend? I didn't know she had one . . . you made it sound like . . . she's got a lot of options."

"She has a *main* boyfriend then lots of lesser ones on the side, ¿sabes? Mi tía knew something was up because Renata is, and I quote, such a good daughter who checks on her mom todo el tiempo, so when she didn't come home or call, Tía Carmen *knew* something was wrong. She went to the main boyfriend's house, aunque, and now I quote mi prima Valeria, he's a no-good cerdo sucio and she can't *believe* her daughter would date ese cochinero."

"Y qué onda at the dirty boyfriend's house? What's he say?"

"Well, that's what's loco, yunta. He claims he's *not* her boyfriend. They split up hace un rato and are only friends now cuz she was seeing someone else."

"Did your tía file a report?"

"Sí, lo hizo. But you know how it goes. They're looking into it." She makes air quotes and rolls her eyes.

Mal's whole body stiffens. The thirty-seven degrees of the processing room hits her with a frigid gust. She's sweating beneath her hoodie; her throat lodges with a thick paste. The meat hanging from its racks turns lurid as she pictures Renata — short, hazelnut, bobbed hair, unassuming features but still, Mal just saw her two days ago, applying that thick coat of lipstick.

She has a sudden, nightmarish vision: Renata stiff and cold, bluing alongside her in the meat locker, against the other slabs hanging from hooks.

Vomit — hot and acidic — rises in Mal's esophagus. She slams her hands down to catch her balance, upsetting a tray of carne asada; the thin strips of meat clatter to the floor.

"Do they suspect the ex-boyfriend? Or the new boyfriend? Where's he?"

"No one knows."

"Probably because there is no new boyfriend. He's making that up. Do I know him?"

"Raul Castañeda? He works at the meat plant and went to school with your oldest, so he's what, twenty-two, twenty-three? You've probably met him. He's friends with your older daughter's boyfriend, what's his name, the Callahan boy . . ."

"Harlan, but Gris broke up with that pobrecito when she left for college. They're . . . what do the kids call *friends with benefits* these days?"

"Fuckbuddies?"

Mal presses her palm to her stomach, but Yessi doesn't notice and keeps yammering.

"Pues nada, Renata's been gone since Saturday night. But Raul's got an alibi . . . he was bartending all night."

"I thought you said he works at the meat plant?"

"Ay, that kid's got all kinds of side gigs."

Mal can't believe Benny didn't tell her any of this. He has to be the detective on the case. Why didn't he text her?

"Where was she last seen?"

"Out by the Salton Sea."

Mal can't think beyond the throbbing in her temples. She pops a Tums then swings open the meat locker, the tundra blast a welcome relief.

"Who saw her out there?"

"Some teens fooling around behind hay bales," Yessi says above the hum of the freezer. "If anything happened to my cousin, my money's on that perv who killed his own daughter back in the 1990s. Rumor has it he's still lurking, snatching girls. What's his name? You know who I mean, yunta? That Cucuy guy?"

The cold air isn't enough. Mal peels off her apron and shoves her shoulder against the back door, emerging into the unrelenting brightness of El Valle sunshine. Sweat drips down her back and gathers in her armpits. She rips off her hoodie, revealing her tank top, damp and clinging to her stomach. She takes deep, shuddering breaths, in and out. Slowly, in for five, hold, out for five, hold.

It started with Noemi. But within a few months, Elena was gone too.

No one knows it's a horror story when it begins.

The early summer air pulsed, releasing the humidity it'd clung to through the day. The fields smelled of fertilizer and damp, vegetable-clotted dirt. Mal was walking home from the graduation bonfire alone when something rustled through the fields, weaving between the crackling crops. Mal called out, but the creature ignored her and kept skirting the edges, dragging the darkness behind her as she followed Mal, who squinted through the scrub

and underbrush, finally making out a face. The one that had terror-
ized her since, except for the reprieve before *this Saturday.* The night
Renata disappeared. Holy shit.

Those glowing red orbs in the deep-set eye sockets and, where
a nose should've sat, a long, spongy muzzle with thick black slits
at the nostrils. A plaintive neighing split the night. Mal might've
believed she'd seen a wild horse, but as the creature emerged from
behind a hay bale, she revealed the curvy body of a woman, fetlocks
for arms, splattered in blood.

Yessi's been standing beside her the whole time Mal's been trying to catch her breath. "Yunta," she whispers. "I shouldn't have
opened my big mouth. You know how I am with true crime and
chisme. I get obsessed, but I should've realized it was too close for
comfort. I'm sorry." She puts a hand on Mal, who recoils. Yessi steps
back. "I don't *really* think something happened to my prima. She's
probably just had it with this podunk backward-ass town and took
off for Los Angeles. I bet she'll call us from there." Even as she's saying it, Mal can tell she doesn't actually believe it.

This can't be happening again.

Iggy rolls the joint behind the portables at the other end of the PE
field. It's lunchtime but no one ever comes back here. The proximity
to the garbage bins makes it unbearable. That also makes it a haven.
From regular losers and homophobes, yeah. And from Amaranta's
stupid cousins. She slips her hand beneath her sleeve, the splotchy scab
reminding her of what liars her family are. Even Ma. Especially Ma.
Sneaking off at night and leaving Amaranta to get mutilated by the
cuates. She's such a hypocrite.

El Valle's not the worst, probably. But it's a tiny town. And people are jerks everywhere. At least, that's what Iggy says. They've

never been anywhere besides San Diego to visit Amaranta's big sister and the beach. The real one. Not the crusty, fish-gut travesty they have here. They have plans, though. Amaranta's grades are good enough for Ivy Leagues if she wants. Iggy would follow her, she says, to the ends of the earth. Or Boston.

Iggy lights the tip, and the tissue paper crinkles black and gray. She takes a drag, then offers a hit to Amaranta. These are technically Amaranta's since they stole them from her ma's drawer where they found those cursed pics (or dick pics, as Iggy screeched when she saw them—they weren't really dicks, but they may as well have been). Anyway, Iggy keeps the weed at her house and in her backpack since, if she gets caught, her grandma's too sick to care.

Amaranta takes a puff, holding the smoke in her lungs before releasing. It makes her tongue feel thick and her thoughts less stabby—they curl and waver like the gray wisps she releases from her mouth to the air above the trash cans.

"What'd your mom say about you taking off from your aunt's house?" Iggy asks, taking the joint back.

"Nothing." Amaranta puts her backpack on the blacktop and plops onto it, cross-legged. "She didn't even know."

Iggy nods. "Parents don't know shit."

She means grandmas too.

Amaranta reaches into the kangaroo pouch of her hoodie and fingers the silver compact, tracing the indentations. Tía said this mirror had something to do with a party gone wrong. *True horror,* she said. Like the nasty-ass pics in Ma's drawer. Those images would horrify Amaranta forever whether they featured a monster or not. But this mirror. Tía said it was her protection. From something she witnessed? At a party? Like the one Ma's always talking about? The one Tía Elena disappeared from?

"Could your aunt be lying about the whole thing?" Iggy breaks into Amaranta's labyrinthine speculations. "Some weird game she plays like her kids?"

"I don't think so. Adults usually tell the truth when they're drunk."

Iggy takes another puff and makes a show of expanding her lungs like she's a peacock puffing out her chest, then blows hard. She licks her fingers and clamps them over the black-rimmed mouth eating the paper. Amaranta hates when she does that. She'll burn herself. But Iggy's always trying to impress her with how macho she is. It'd be cute if it weren't stupid.

"Besides," Amaranta adds, "it's too much of a coincidence, isn't it?" She doesn't say aloud the part that's been bothering her most. Iggy already knows.

"Should we drive to the police station after school, then? Show the evidence to your uncle Benny?"

A swishy sensation passes through Amaranta. Partly the nausea from the weed. Mostly the fear that Ma's been lying to Amaranta her whole life.

"I'll text my uncle, okay? We're not even sure what it's evidence of."

"It seems pretty clear to me."

"It's not." Amaranta tries to say this the way Ma does, like *end-of-convo,* but then she feels bad for snapping at Iggy and adds, softly, "Don't do anything . . . you know . . ."

"Impetuous?" Iggy moans, scaling a garbage bin then jumping off it, grabbing her sneakers in midair like she's on a skateboard doing an aerial trick.

Amaranta rolls her eyes but half-smiles, despite herself.

Iggy kneels in front of her, bare knees to the blacktop. She nuzzles her nose against Amaranta's neck so the hairs on her skin prickle. A few weeks ago, this would've been heaven. Now, Amaranta's all twisted inside. If only it were Renata breathing on her neck. But that makes her feel like crap since it would crush Iggy. She kinda wishes she could put the whole girlfriends thing back in the bag. It was so much simpler before.

"Oh, hey, how was tutoring yesterday?" Iggy pulls back and looks Amaranta in the eyes.

Amaranta stares at the grass in the field beyond. "Fine." She stands, makes a big deal of putting her backpack straps on. "Boring."

She won't tell Iggy that the junior in their physics class, Mateo, canceled on her and that she's kinda heartbroken about it.

At the carnicería, Renata wore jeans and a T-shirt, bangles halfway up her wrist, long beaded earrings that dangled practically to her shoulders, and a quarter-sleeve jean jacket. By all accounts, gorgeous. Renata's too old for her, sure, and Amaranta doesn't trust her gaydar. There's something loveable in every girl, gay or straight.

Smiles are free, though, and Renata flashed her a sweet one.

She really hoped she'd see her this weekend at Mateo's.

She hates lying to Iggy about where she's been spending her Sundays, even if she's not doing anything wrong. Lately, the only one who truly sees her is Iggy. It's ironic that you can't tell the closest person to you that you like someone else. Is this what it means to grow up? The closer you get to someone, the more you have to keep from them?

Luckily, the bell rings, saving her from her melodramatic thoughts.

Iggy links her arm through Amaranta's and walks her to class.

5
GHOSTING THE PRESENT

Griselda reaches one of three stoplights in their dead-ass town (and nobody from outside better call it that because it's *her* dead-ass town!). *Huele a pedos,* Abuela says of the air, thick with dust and pollution. It smells like farts. El Valle — in its sunken basin two hundred feet below sea level — traps not just air but people like Mom who wish they could get out but stay and stay.

That won't be Griselda.

She hasn't been back since Benny's wedding in June but Mom convinced her to come for Tío's fundraiser (Benny had some shit to talk about that). It's just, so what, the Callahans are backing Tío's campaign? Benny's such a purist. At the end of the day, she loves and supports them all, especially since Tío's doing such good for their community. *Sí, se puede* and whatnot. She wishes Benny would let it go. All that matters is the cause. Harlan's taught her that.

¡Ay! There she goes, thinking of Harlan . . . she *could* turn left onto Cattle Call Drive toward his grandiose house like she used to throughout high school and last summer. If he were anything like his family, she wouldn't be so drawn to him. Rich kid, set to inherit the valle his family stole from Griselda's family's people — they could be a movie. But he's sweet and goofy and lovable. She's a damn insect, and his place glows in the night.

Instead, she forces herself to suppress the impulse as if snapping a rubber band on her wrist — *flick*. She smothers it with thoughts of Nana Dora's puffy quesadillas two blocks down, golden, flaky tortillas fried and filled with too-thick jack cheese so the grease oozes down her chin with each bite.

If she went to Harlan's, two things were inevitable: First, she'd sleep with him. They're magnets that can't keep apart. She's got no cool when it comes to Harlan.

In fact, her inability to let go is keeping her from throwing herself a hundred percent into San Diego. She's got no crew or dating or sex life to speak of. It's pathetic how attached she is to El Valle and Harlan. Sometimes she wonders, doesn't she *want* to detach?

Second, they'd end up at the protest Harlan's coordinating tonight — stealing calves away from his dad's facility — which would invariably circle back to the first thing.

Her phone's been buzzing like an incessant beehive, every text a plea for her to join him at the cattle yard. He's been woke about animal rights since before woke was a thing, but his dad doesn't know he secretly undermines him at every turn. In some ways, she agrees with the Sun Tzu he touts: sometimes you *must* utilize the enemy's maneuvers to enact change. A devotee of *The Art of War,* he says, "The greatest victory is that which requires no battle" and practices this philosophy by using his parents' and grandparents' money to destroy them from within. In an act of subterfuge he relishes, he organizes underground protests and sit-ins — tonight he and a small group of friends will snatch animals, nurse them back to health, then send them to shelters and sanctuaries. But the little kid inside her is just plain scared of getting caught. Jail time would *not* be a good look for her résumé.

But Griselda also worries that the colonizer's tricks will never undo the colonizer's damage. She can do more as a scientist than an agitator, can't she? More as *herself* than Harlan's girlfriend? She can't keep letting Harlan or her well-meaning familia suck her back into their drama. Into El Valle. She's *only* here for the long weekend. And she'll science while she's here. If it weren't so dark, she would head straight to the sea for soil and water samples.

Nope. She'll just take Amaranta out for dinner. Her hermanita always gets her mind off her own shit. She's the best justification for beelining straight home instead of Harlan's house or the sea or venturing out alone.

Griselda parks in the driveway then bursts into the house, a flash against the drab interior. "I've gotta pee," she shouts as she swooshes past the oppressive air of the dining room where her abuelos sag like waxen figures at the dinner table. Abuelo, newspaper spread, lingers over the crossword puzzle while Abuela, his wife of almost fifty years, stares blankly toward the living room television screen set to a novela, the sound so low she couldn't possibly hear it, even with her hearing aids. She seems harmless, but that's not how Mom tells the stories.

"Wait, what about my kiss, Elena?" Abuela's voice crackles with age.

Although Griselda grew up with Abuela, the elder woman often doesn't know her granddaughter. In Abuela's fading memory, Griselda becomes her lost daughter.

"I'll be right there! Long drive," she calls after blowing a kiss to the ofrenda, a shrine to her missing tía halfway down the hallway with the dingy wallpaper lined with family photos.

"Just two hours from San Diego," Abuelo Beto chimes in, his laughter following her. "You down a Big Gulp?"

"Slushee!" Griselda hollers back before slamming the bathroom door. Once she's finished, she heads to her little sister's bedroom. "Hey, kid," she calls from the doorway.

Amaranta's engrossed in her headphones as she absently rubs her wrist. When she notices Griselda in the doorway, she stiffens and yanks down her sleeve. Griselda settles beside her hermanita on the bed, pulls one of the buds from Amaranta's ear, and slips it into her own, their heads butting in a tender collision as their dark hair intertwines.

"Smashing Pumpkins, huh? That's what's up. Kickin' it old school."

The edges of Amaranta's mouth creep into a sly smile; she gives a noncommittal shrug.

When the song ends, Griselda reaches for her sister's phone. The playlist's called Anarchy. She arches an eyebrow.

"You approve or what?" Amaranta asks.

"Better not bait and switch me with some boy band shit," Griselda teases, scrolling through the rest of the playlist, her finger hesitating over each song title.

"You wound me." Amaranta mimics a stabbing motion at her heart.

Griselda ruffles her sister's hair, the color and texture of damp coffee grounds. "R.E.M., Velvet Underground, the Wallflowers, Natalie Merchant, the Cure. When did you get cool?"

Amaranta leans back on her hands. "Ma listens to this type of thing."

"Good point. I guess it's not *that* cool." Griselda wrinkles her nose playfully.

They both laugh, Griselda letting her laughter turn into a sigh. She nudges Amaranta with her elbow. "You have to admit, though, Mom's *kinda* cool."

Amaranta rolls her eyes but gives an exaggerated groan of agreement. Mom's a waif of a woman who wears classic 1990s grunge — the last person you'd assume would be a badass butcher.

Griselda glances around the room she, her sister, and Mom shared until her bruncle Benny moved out after graduating from the police academy five years ago. After that, Mom offered Griselda Benny's room, claiming a teenager should have her own sanctuary. While she embraced the offer, Griselda suspects it was more about Mom's loneliness than anything, her need for an everlasting slumber party with at least one daughter.

It was forever before Griselda realized that's not how most kids grow up. When she was younger, she thought having a mom who was more of a sister was the coolest thing in the world. Now? She's pretty damn sure it's dysfunction at its finest. Mom has no idea what boundaries are. Granted, she raised Benny since she was seventeen and had Griselda when she was nineteen. She might not know *how* to be alone.

"Hey, where's Mom anyway?"

"Abuela was screaming at her again. It's the new norm. But Ma couldn't handle it."

"She say when she'll be back?"

"In the morning, to take me to school."

"I'm supposed to go out to the Salton Sea with Abuelo then, but if Mom's not back in time, I could take you."

"Nice, thanks." Amaranta squeezes Griselda's hand. "In Ma's

defense, Abuela was saying some truly shitty things. Everything was her fault. The hurricane. Tía Elena's disappearance. Shit like that."

"Damn. Is Abuela's nurse here? Lupita?"

"Nah, she's been at the hospital."

"Her daughter sick again?"

Amaranta nods. "Iggy's grandma's breathing is getting worse too."

"Pobrecitas."

When Griselda was little, air hadn't fit through her asthmatic lungs. She mostly outgrew it, but kids in El Valle die of asthma more than anywhere else in the United States—they're mostly Mexicali kids, so no one does squat. And it's getting worse as the Salton Sea dries up, exposing the poison-laced playa, wind-swept into the noses and mouths of everyone still breathing out here. That's why Gris is getting her master's degree in ecosystems, studying the effects of the pesticides on living things—that virulent cocktail of lead, ammonia, and arsenic encrusting the lake bed from decades of field irrigation runoff and wastewater that ends up in the sea (since everything in the sea ends up in the fleshy pads of El Valle's rib cages).

Griselda's phone buzzes again. It's Harlan's umpteenth text: Got a trailer for 30 calves. Ur great with animals. Don't let our shit stop you from being great 🐮

Amaranta reads over her sister's shoulder, then pesters, "Come on, Gris. Let's go."

Mom would *kill* Griselda if she took her hermanita. But if Amaranta's there, Griselda won't go home with Harlan, right? It would *just* be about saving the calves. No sexy business.

"Will Renata be there?" Amaranta asks.

"How do you know *her*? She's a lot older than you."

"She works with Ma." Amaranta's face turns suspiciously red, giving her an unnatural rose-blushed look (since she forgoes makeup and all that other "girly shit").

Damn. Someone's got a crush. Griselda smiles but won't embarrass her little sister by saying more. "It's too dangerous. Mom would have my head if you got hurt."

"It's never too dangerous to do the right thing."

Her sister's wide-eyed earnestness gnaws at something inside Griselda. She wavers.

Amaranta snatches the phone and texts back: Drop the deets.

"You'd better not make me regret this," she says, letting out a sardonic laugh.

Amaranta pokes her in the ribs, then reaches between the mattresses and pulls out a black ski mask. "We could take your Batman mask."

"Hey, how'd you know about that?"

Griselda reaches for it, but Amaranta hides it behind her back.

"I've known you sneak off to these protests for years. You're not that slick, sis."

"Listen, you little smart aleck. I'm serious about the calf rescue being dangerous. It's one thing to talk the talk but another to walk the walk. You *sure* you can handle it?"

Amaranta rolls her eyes. "You're not the *only* one who can plant a thousand trees to save El Valle, you know."

Griselda snatches the mask. "Almost *two* thousand."

As a test project with tribal leaders and the California Conservation Corps, Griselda and Harlan worked their asses off last summer planting native mesquite and palo verde, digging through the dense clay of the playa with measuring tapes, skid steers, and donut-shaped biodegradable water reservoirs called cocoons. They dug two thousand holes in the salinated soil and filled them with trees.

"Exactly," Amaranta says, squeezing Griselda in a side hug as the text from Harlan comes through with the address.

"Why're you wearing that big ole hoodie anyway? It's not even cold yet." Nights in the desert in October can get cold, but this year's been sweltering.

Amaranta shrugs and plays with a piece of loose thread on her sleeve.

Griselda rubs her back, recalling how hard it was to be a young teen with body image issues. Hoodies are the teen equivalent of armor. She stands. "Want Nana Dora's on the way?"

"Duh." Amaranta springs off the bed.

Before they race out the front door, Griselda wraps Abuela in a warm hug, still not correcting her when she whispers gleefully, "*Elena!*" Let Abuela believe her eldest granddaughter is her disappeared, likely long-dead daughter. What's the harm?

"Bring me cheese fries," Abuela says, a conspiratorial gleam to her eyes, her raspy voice pitching higher and making her sound young again, despite the half-gloomy, half-regal wheelchair and the grays peeking from beneath the box-dyed caramel Mom hasn't retouched yet.

Griselda tries to imagine her as a glamorous starlet. Mom says Abuela wanted some rich Hollywood producer to discover her. Back in the day, when Abuela was a young woman, El Salton Sea was this Hollywood-glam hot spot. People from all over would flock there for fun in the sun. Even Desi Arnaz came to fish and boat after golfing in Palm Springs. But all that disappeared the year of the hurricanes. The year Mom was born. Griselda thinks that's why Abuela's so cruel to Mom. She was a bad omen, signaling the end of her dream.

"Cheese fries?" Abuelo laments. "Esa onda no es buena para tu diabetes, Vero." He says her condition with a Spanish inflection— dee-ah-BEH-tehs.

With a dramatic gesture toward her pansa (as she calls the little paunch in her midsection) and a roll of her shoulders, Abuela declares, "Mira, I should be watching my waistline in case a movie star notices me, but just this once."

"I would, Abuela, but we're gonna catch a movie in El Centro so the fries would get cold," she fibs. Why's she lying to her abuelitos? If Mom's gone, she's gone for the whole night, and her abuelos won't remember where Griselda said she was taking her hermanita anyway. But deep down, she knows she shouldn't be taking her to the calf rescue.

"Dame un besito, Elenita. ¿Dónde estabas? You had me worried."

See? Cheese fries are already forgotten.

"Lo siento, Abuela. I'm here now."

She plants a taut kiss on Abuela's cheek, which smells of peppermint lotion and overboiled chicken. Griselda's affection for the elder woman seeps through her annoyance and concern that Abuela might be making Mom's life a living hell, thus harming Amaranta.

What's it like, slipping into the past, ghosting the present?

The mirror above the dining room table shows her Elena's face. When Griselda was a child, she had no idea growing up would mean becoming a dead almost-woman. Yet, here she is, twenty-three when Elena only made it to sixteen.

And still, she wears her long-gone tía's ghost face.

Mal turns the key in Gus's door but before she can open it, he's already standing in the doorway, pulling it ajar. "Did you hear?" she asks, her voice husked with fear.

"Yeah." His face is disheveled.

She's a wreck, on the verge of tears. She came right after her shift ended. Well, after she made sure Amaranta was home. Griselda's on her way from San Diego. But Mal can't sit around doing nothing. She has all this terrifying nervous energy. *The clomping. The stink of piss. The visions.* Dammit. Maybe La Siguanaba *has* returned. "It's happening again."

"It's not." He says this gently, but there's something in his voice that assures her he's just as scared. He feels it too. The déjà vu. The aura that it's all happening again. She wants to ask if he smells the maple that festers to ammonia. Hears the stomping.

He opens the door wider and sure enough there's the corkboard they've been working on for nearly twenty-five years, tracing leads, compiling notes. It makes them look demented. Maybe they are. Noemi. Elena. And now Renata.

"Have you been to the beach?"

He nods.

She presses the flashlight button on her phone, lighting up the front porch.

"Let's search it again."

6
STAMPEDE

Amaranta tugs her sweatshirt over her arm so Griselda doesn't see the slash mark purpling across her skin and turns up the music from Gris's dashboard. They belt out "Zombie" by the Cranberries as they drive past shadows that tower across the dark back roads.

The fields are dotted with the occasional light from a farmhouse or ranch. In the distance, the geothermal plant glimmers. When Amaranta was little, she thought it was a city gleaming and sparkling. Now she knows it's an energy company injecting water into the bubbling, volcanic mud pots beside the Salton Sea. In her scientist opinion, this process is infinitely cooler than some made-up mythical city. The mud boils and pops.

"I'm glad you finally deem me mature enough for your grown-up adventures," she says with a mock-haughty lift of her chin.

Gris leans over and ruffles the top of her head. "You dork." But she's laughing.

This is the happiest Amaranta's felt since before the sleepover with her stupid cousins. Since before Iggy spent the night at her house and showed her . . . how screwed up her Ma is.

"You know, kid, you cannot tell Mom about this ever. Pinky swear." Gris holds up her right pinky to interlace with her sister's, steering the car with her left hand. "And if I tell you to do something, don't hesitate, just do what I say. This stuff can be dangerous, and it's not technically legal — "

"What's right and what's legal often aren't the same." But she connects her pinky.

"Look at you, wiser than your years." Gris gives her pinky an extra-long squeeze.

Except, she doesn't *feel* wiser. She feels knotted and confused. Should she tell her sister about Ma . . . and the compact Tía said was her life insurance . . . or would that endanger her somehow? Could Tía have been right? Is Ma mixed up in some twisted shit? Amaranta doesn't believe in curses or monsters. If someone's after Tía or Ma, he's flesh and blood. He has a name. But would Gris even believe Amaranta or dismiss it all as a childish overreaction?

Mostly, she's worried about shattering Gris's illusion of their mother. It slayed Amaranta. She doesn't want to do that to her sister. She clenches her fists and nods with what she hopes is a stoic warrior expression as they turn down a washboard road rippled like waves in a brown ocean. Gris lowers her headlights, the dust and silhouettes of hay bales, farm equipment, and alfalfa stalks blanketing the dark. Like they're driving into nothingness.

She maneuvers onto a ridiculously narrow path and comes to a stop, cutting the ignition and turning to Amaranta as though she's Ma about to give some big *keep-you-safe* speech.

"Pull your hood up and wear this over your face," Gris says, handing her a slate-gray pañuelo from the glove compartment. It smells like chamomile lotion and french fries. Not unpleasant. "Don't get in the way, okay? I can't watch you every second, so keep up with me."

Amaranta nods, stifling a laugh at how different from Ma her sister sounds. She squashes her curls into her hoodie.

Other cars are already parked nearby; a hulking Ford F-350 is parked down the road, hitched to a horse trailer large enough to hold seven to eight horses.

"Wait here a sec."

Griselda gets out, closing the door, and heads over to Harlan, whose face erupts into a dumb grin like she's a much-anticipated present on Christmas morning. She points to the car, but when they both turn toward Amaranta, his happy-go-lucky expression sours. Whatever. She's here and there's nothing he can do about it.

Griselda's saying something, probably *be nice to her* because his face does the whole *calm down* routine as they stroll over. Amaranta raises an eyebrow, debating whether to roll her eyes. Griselda's word is law in Amaranta's book. And apparently, in Harlan's too.

She gestures for her to get out of the car. "You have to be careful tonight, Amar. Don't pull any stunts. We'll look out for you, but we have serious business to handle."

Amaranta rolls her eyes now, taking a deep breath, "Yes, Madam Serious. Got it." She turns toward Harlan, who's twining his fingers through Griselda's hair like a lovesick puppy. "Will Renata be here?"

"Re — ?" His face shrivels like he's bitten into the saladito in the pulpy center of an orange, all that rocky salt at once. "I mean, I don't know."

"You two are buds, right?" Griselda asks, her forehead crinkled, her face smooshed against Harlan's chest. "She comes to these protests?"

Harlan leans in and kisses the top of Griselda's head in a weirdly paternal way. Hetero-normies. Amaranta does *not* get them.

"I mean, I guess we're buds. You could say that. My buddy Raul's been seeing her. He's over there." He points out a guy in a gray hoodie standing beside a bale of hay, smoking a cigarette. He doesn't exactly exude approachability. "You could ask him."

But Raul never gives her a chance. He's all business.

As they meet the others masked in hooded glory, Amaranta's lovesickness dissolves into pure nerves. The whispered chatter around her sounds more like distant white noise over the thumping of her own heartbeat.

People group off after they get their orders, Griselda pulling Amaranta toward the big truck bed. When the engine starts, they snail through the dirt, lights dimmed, like a hayride through a haunted corn maze. Except Amaranta doesn't believe in ghosts.

Though when the beef plant comes into focus, it's definitely a horror scene.

Amaranta forces herself not to gag, front-row to everything her sister warned her about this cattle yard. "It's like a zombie cow movie . . ."

"Focus," Gris hisses.

Along the road, flashlights direct them to a side gate — a massive chain link with barbed wire. A tall, lanky guy with a mask and hood jumps down from the cab, sprints to the gate, and cuts the lock with massive bolt cutters. He rushes to open it, gesturing for the truck to hurry, then sprints toward the sea of stalls.

Holding pens, hundreds of them, all crammed with cows, most standing but some lying on the ground. There's no way they can rescue them all. Amaranta's chest squishes. How will they decide which to save and which to leave behind?

"Are the ones on the ground dead?"

"Some, yeah, but some are too sick to stand and have to be dragged out by forklifts and hauled to the meat plant. Pobrecitos."

These cows are not the bright-eyed farm animals she imagined but grotesque creatures, their bodies emaciated and covered in sores, their eyes hollow and empty. They let out low moans that echo through the yard, sounding almost human.

Harlan passes her a nylon rope tied like a noose with a ring at the end, and Amaranta's hands shake as she takes it.

A guy in tight Wranglers and dirty boots barks, "Only take the calves."

"Adult cows don't deserve saving too?"

The ground is slick with mud and excrement, and the cows press in on her from all sides. Their hot breath on her face makes her shudder. She reaches for a calf, but it won't budge. Small and frail, its eyes wide with fear, it won't leave its mother.

"Come on," she whispers, tugging on the rope. "We have to save you." She hates that they're leaving the mother behind, but the calf won't budge. Its wobbly legs are surprisingly strong. "Come on, stupid," she groans, wrenching as hard as she can, terrified she'll choke it.

Gris must see her struggling because she comes up and smacks the calf on the butt, and it stumbles forward. Amaranta leads it to the trailer where she passes it to the Wrangler guy, then repeats the process, each time more sickened by the scene around her. The cows extend in all directions, their moans growing louder and more frantic as the group works.

Her senses overload — the stench, the pitiful mooing, the shitty muck she's sloshing through — when chaos erupts. Sirens are blaring around them, bright lights cutting through the darkness. Amaranta freezes. She looks up from the calf she's pulling—a group of protesters has flung open the stalls, letting loose all the cows, who crash into each other, trying to escape. Gunshots split the night. Amaranta's chest contracts and her vision blurs. The cattle yard spins. She lets go of the rope to cover her ears as several more shots fire, and the calf she was holding clambers off with the grown-up cows.

"No, wait!" she calls, but it's no use. She can't see it in the dark sea of bodies.

She's trying to decide whether she should run after it or climb a fence to avoid the stampede when a large, hairy hand clamps her arm. She screams.

A heavyset man with a goatee, a gun holstered on his waist, snarls something, yanking on her, but Amaranta can't make out his words. His ropy hands burn her skin as she twists to jerk free like those poor, stupid calves.

His lips move, but all Amaranta hears is the stomping of the cows, hundreds of them hurling themselves toward the open gates, their grim, monotonous lowing incongruous against the high-pitched wail of sirens. "Gris! Help!"

The hairy guy reaches for his gun, and Amaranta kicks him as hard as she can in the balls. He keels over and releases her with a roar of pain that breaks through the din.

Amaranta stumbles backward as the guy recovers and points his gun at her, snarling, "You little bitch."

He's going to shoot her.

But out of the ruckus, Gris rushes behind him with a shovel. Its sharp metal edges are covered in cow shit. In one swift motion, she brings it down on the man's head with a *thwack,* and the man crumples to the ground. Blood pools around his dark hair, slick against the shit-encrusted yard.

The ground beneath Amaranta's feet liquefies, the mud and excrement blending into a treacherous sludge. She sways, her stomach contracting. She might fall . . . except Harlan grips her arm and rips both her and Gris away from the rushing stampede, which quickly blocks the man from view.

"Run!" Harlan shouts, and Amaranta focuses on nothing but her sister beside her, steering her through the black-and-white chaos. As she runs, her lungs trill like swallows fluttering in her ribs, her breath hot and sticky against her mask. They scramble into Harlan's truck, the engine growling to life, and Amaranta tears the mask off, gasping.

His hands on the wheel are covered in something wet and glossy.

As they drive away, Amaranta looks back, a thick clump of dread rising within her. She can't see the man through the mud-slaked coats of the cows, but she imagines his blood-crusted face pressed beneath their hooves.

"I think the cows trampled that man," she whispers to Gris, still trying to stop the world from spinning around her.

But her sister is frozen, her face stiff and rigid. Did a bullet hit her?

Amaranta's checking for blood, shaking her sister, but she doesn't seem to have a wound or anything.

"Gris?" she whispers.

Her sister shakes her head slowly.

Harlan's watching from the rearview mirror and softly says, "He'll be fine, Gris. You did what you had to. You were protecting your little sister."

Amaranta squeezes Gris's hand and realizes she's now whispering, more to herself than Amaranta or Harlan, "He's fine. He's fine."

"Are you hurt, Amar?" Harlan asks.

Amaranta shakes her head *no* and squelches back the tears threatening to fall. She musters a fake grin to cheer Gris up. "Beef Tooth Cattle Yard: One-star experience. Would definitely NOT recommend." But her sister says nothing. Doesn't even crack a smile.

Amaranta holds the slash across her wrist. It burns and burns.

7
UNA LIMPIA, UN EXORCISMO

B y 7:00 a.m., Mal's back at the house Esteban picked out after returning from Stanford with his swanky law school degree. He bought Mami and Papi this place on the modest side of Main Street and himself a fancy one al otro lado; then, when he and Sharon divorced, he gave her that house and bought otra, as if he were a lizard and his house were his tail, so hassle-free to regenerate. Probably because he's the Callahan lawyer, one of the few Mexicans on the rich side of town. But Mal's grateful. It's kept a roof over their heads.

"Lupita here for Mami?" she asks Papi, who's in a robe in the kitchen with a cup of café, humming an oldies tune.

"Ay," he says, rolling his eyes. "She didn't show otra vez. I hate to do it, but I may have to fire her and find someone more reliable. And your mother's in a *mood*. Cuídate, mija."

"She yelling at you too? La Gritona . . ."

"She doesn't mean it, though, mijita."

He still only sees what he wants to see in his wife. Mal changes the subject. "You ready for Esteban's fiesta? You need me to iron your shirt? Your suit's clean, ¿verdad? You told me not to take it to the dry cleaners, but I could stop by—"

"Sí, sí, ya está limpio. And I can iron my own shirts, muchísimas gracias."

"Well, con permiso, señor," she laughs. "Where are the girls?"

"I haven't seen them yet this morning. Mija, Griselda asked me to take her out to the lake today." He starts humming his song again, searching through the cupboards and finally pulling out a box of bran he scowls at like it's a rodent.

"Oh yeah? Well, don't be late tonight, okay? Esteban *needs his familia there.*" (She mimics her brother's oratorial voice at that last part.)

Papi groans. "Why does he have to throw una fiesta junto con esos ricos, eh? Esos cabrones. ¿Por qué no aquí, en nuestra casa, o en su propio rancho?"

Mal's laughing because Papi's saying everything she's been thinking and finds it hilarious that he calls Esteban's manicured estate a rancho. But she promised her brother. "Aguas, Papi. You sound like Benny. Don't you start también."

"¡Ay, qué la fregada!" Papi grumbles under his breath, which is the closest he ever comes to cursing. Mami's the one with the wild tongue. Papi's has always been milder and in Spanish. Even when he was practically a drunkard, un borracho, from the time Benny was born the night Elena disappeared until Esteban moved them to this new casita when he took up gardening and that tactile connection with the land, the soil, growing things over time started returning him to the papi she loved. While Griselda haunts Mami like a ghost, she seemed to heal something in Papi—a second chance at raising a daughter not to disappear. "Estaré allí," Papi assures Mal, kissing her on the cheek. "We all will. Tal vez con Esteban como jefe, al fin se hará algo en El Valle, ¿eh?"

Mal can only hope her brother will turn it all around. Back in its heyday, in the 1950s and '60s, jovial announcers on TV and radio programs trying to drive wealthy suburbanites out of the sprawling Los Angeles metropolis and onto Mal's family's ancestral land had declared, "The Salton Sea truly is a miracle in the desert. Here is where you can find the good life in the sun."

Now the sea's known only for being deserted. Toxic. Apocalyptic, even. A dire warning to the rest of the world about the coming ecological crisis, although no one is listening. Except for Esteban, who's trying to convince los políticos El Valle is worth saving.

People see it as a wasteland, when really much of El Valle is still lush with irrigation water and brings in over a billion dollars to California every damn year. That land should go back to the people. Not stay hoarded by the Callahans and their land baron ilk.

And if anyone can turn hobnobbing with los ricos into political revolution, it's her brother. Esteban can change like a magician pulling a rabbit out of his hat, only he pulls out *Stevie!* His whitewashed alter ego who can kick it with anyone. He's versatile así. Earned an honorary degree in code-switching. Unlike plain old Mal, born and raised in El Valle. Never been anywhere Mal.

"Bueno," she says, opening the pink box she's been holding behind her back. "*Now* you can have one."

Papi's face lights up. "What did I do to deserve una hija who feeds me donuts instead of bran flakes?" He takes the jelly.

* * *

"¿Qué pasa?" Mal asks upon walking into the girls' room and seeing her daughters on the ground. Griselda looks wrecked — either from partying hard, which she never does, or pulling an all-nighter, which makes no sense because she's here for the long weekend. Amaranta looks queasy, too, but more frightened or guilty. "Did something happen?"

"Drank too much last night, that's all," Griselda mumbles.

"You let your little sister *drink*?"

"No, Mom! *I drank too much,*" Griselda groans, rolling her eyes like she can't believe her mother has accused her of something so ridiculous.

Mal inspects her two daughters. Griselda's face is splotched and pasty. Her sister is still in pajamas, which is out of character for her usual studious self. Amaranta's motto is *If you're not early, you're late.* Normally, it bugs Mal, who's as laissez-faire as they come. At the carnicería, they've created a special "Mal's schedule" where Mexican time flexes even stretchier, allowing her to juggle her job and motherhood.

But it worries Mal that her daughters are sitting on the floor, not even pretending to get ready. What aren't they telling her? Before Mal can grill Amaranta, her youngest bounces up, grabbing her clothes and leaving the room in a huff.

Griselda slumps into a seashell, resting her cheek against the carpet.

Mal's sigh comes from a badgering twinge deep within her. "She's been acting like this since the weekend. Maybe longer. She won't talk to me. Did she mention anything to you?"

"No," Griselda whispers in a way that scares Mal.

"Why'd you drink so much, mijita? Everything okay in San Diego?" Mal sweeps a hair from Griselda's face, but she pulls away.

"I'm fine, Mom. It's just, this Valley. It's a lot."

"Tell me about it." Mal takes a deep breath. "Did you hear about Renata?"

"Amar was *just* asking about her . . . that girl who works with you? Why, what happened?"

Mal shrugs. "I don't know exactly and was hoping you could fill in some blanks. Yessi says she's missing."

Griselda sits up slightly. "Have you talked to Benny?"

"He's not answering."

"Me neither. Jerk. I'll stop by his place after Abuelo and I go to the sea."

Mal nods. "Don't be late to Tío's thing. He'll throw a stink. And while you're at it, see if you can convince Benny to come. He listens to you."

"He doesn't listen to anyone."

It's true. Ay, Benito. She loves him. But he's as mulish as they come. As if they need more drama. Mal rubs her temples, pushing back the aura of a migraine. *Not today, El Diablo.*

Amaranta returns, fully dressed but mismatched, hair in tangles.

"You could've changed in here, tontita," Griselda teases. "Since when are you shy?"

"I'm tired of phonies," Amaranta says, straight-faced.

"Who are you calling cuentos chinos?" Mal asks wearily. "Me and Gris?"

"Whoever the shoe fits." She's serious.

Mal stifles a laugh. "Fine," she says, standing and marching across the room. "Dame los zapatos."

"What?" Amaranta screeches, bewildered. "Ma, it's a *met-a-phor.*"

"No, no. ¡Dámelos!" Mal stomps over to el armario and pulls out the hand-me-down Converse, scuffed, yellow, and covered in ink. Mal kicks off her chanclas, grabs a pair of polka-dot socks from their shared sock drawer, pulls them on dramatically, then puts on her daughter's shoes. "Perfect fit." She lies back and holds her feet up in the air like a cockroach.

"You're such a weirdo." Amaranta's trying to suppress her laughter but can't.

"We're a family of weirdos and I love us!" Mal heaves herself off the bed and positions herself squarely in front of her youngest, resting her hands on Amaranta's shoulders. "Mi amorcita, I'm not *lying* to you about anything, okay? I'm just . . . trying to keep you safe."

"Too late."

"Why, what's going on?"

Mal looks from one daughter to the other, but they both shrug.

"Look, girls. I don't know what you two are up to, but just be careful, okay? Promise me. You know that cashier from my work, Renata?"

Amaranta's cheeks get all rosacea-stained and she looks at the ground.

"What? You know something about her?"

Amaranta shakes her head, and Mal looks to Griselda who makes a show of shrugging her shoulders emphatically and widening her eyes.

"*Anyway,*" Mal sighs, trying to figure out what the two of them are up to. A sister joke? Or do they know something? Come on, Las Veracruz Chicas. Open up! "She's . . . well . . . Yessi thinks she might be . . . missing?"

"You don't think she's . . ." Amaranta makes a squeaky noise, and Mal pulls her into a hug.

"No, no, just . . . be careful. After all this fundraiser bronca ends, we need una charla . . . *all* of us. I'm making dinner tomorrow night."

Gris groans and sets her forehead against her knees. "We need una limpia." Her voice comes out muffled, but she's right. They do need a cleansing.

"More like an exorcism," Amaranta mumbles.

"Yessi can do one for us." Mal sweeps back Amaranta's thick fringe of coal-black bangs punctuating the middle of her acne-constellated forehead. "A *limpia*, not un exorcismo."

Amaranta rolls her eyes but then, unexpectedly, rests her head against Mal's chest. Mal takes the opportunity to hug her daughter tightly, inhaling her apple-scented shampoo. "Group hug," she shouts, crouching down and gathering Griselda into their outstretched arms like *London Bridge Is Falling Down*.

"I'm so hungover," Griselda laugh-groans. "What if I need to puke?"

"You'll have to puke on us," Mal deadpans, and her daughters yell out, "Gross!" in unison. But Mal can't let go yet. She clasps her girls closer and whispers, "We're stuck."

Amaranta has explained entangled particles. No matter how far apart they are in space-time — across the universe, light-years away — they still know what each other are up to and follow suit. Einstein didn't believe in spooky action at a distance. Einstein wasn't a mother.

Mal should've squeezed tighter. She shouldn't have let her girls go.

Griselda saunters toward the kitchen, a towel wrapped atop her head, as Tío Esteban bustles in, arms full of Walmart bags. The only Walmart used to be two towns over in El Centro, past a shit-load of farmland. But a few years back, they put one in at the town entrance, and not just any old one, a *supercenter*, qué fancy. It's their mall. There's even a car wash. And, get this, a Starbucks. The kids will never know the struggle.

Although the family should be helping Tío with his fundraiser tonight, he's still taking care of the abuelos. Typical Tío, but Griselda finds it endearing. Some people would dramatize the fact that they do everything for you, martyr-style, holding it over your head. But not Tío. He's a reverse Grinch, born with a heart several sizes too big.

Sweat shimmers across Tío's bronze forehead, highlighting his receding salt-and-pepper hairline as it trickles down his face. His square glasses slant down the bridge of his wide nose, but with his arms filled with grocery bags, he can't push them back into place.

Tío's objectively handsome if not as gracefully aged as Mom. He looks like the much-older brother, not just by a year. And compared to Benny? Tío Esteban could be his dad.

Griselda rifles through the bags, refrigerating items as needed. She heaves a sigh when she reaches the bottom of the bags with nothing to show but fruits, vegetables, lean protein, and Abuela's Ensures and adult diapers. Where's the good stuff?

Abuelo comes in and points to the pink box above the microwave. Donuts! Score! Griselda grabs two maple bars. Maybe sugar can cover the stress of what happened last night since alcohol didn't work.

"Hey, Pops. Don't be late for the party tonight," Tío calls to Abuelo. "I'll come get you and Mami. Is your suit clean?"

"Why does everyone keep asking me that?"

"We just want you to look guapo."

In old photos, Abuelo was a lean, ropey fisherman, his russet skin weathered from years steering boats and leaning into the sea. These days, his teeth jut diagonally, slats of a crooked fence, and his nose hairs have turned into fluffy white stalactites.

Tío continues, "I hear you're exploring the sea this morning with La Científica, hey, Pops? Don't overdo it. It's rough out there."

"I'm the parent, hijo. I still know my ass my from elbow."

"No, I know, Pops. I'm just helping."

"Del dicho al hecho hay gran trecho, mijo," Abuelo replies, his eyes kind but stern. They love volleying dichos. *Actions speak louder than words.*

Tío's face crumples but he composes himself. "I'm stressed, Pops. Elections are just around the corner."

"You're a shoo-in, mijo."

"I wish it were that simple."

Abuela wheels into the living room, cutting him off. She holds up a crocheted blanket, her eyes bright. "Stevie, I can't believe you're graduating high school already!"

The dementia could be alcohol-induced. She doesn't drink anymore; no one lets her. But Griselda found a bottle stashed away in Abuela's bathroom. She's a magpie with little nests of trinkets and stashes of stolen family belongings hidden away.

Before anyone can correct her, Abuela's telling him, "Tell Elena to come eat breakfast before school."

"No, I'm here, Abuela. I'll eat before school," Griselda answers, unsure when she got stuck in this role, playing a dead girl.

As Abuelo and Griselda journey up Highway 111 toward Interstate 10, they pass the beef plant. She almost retches remembering last night. What has she done? Harlan texted her again this morning that the guy's fine, according to Raul. But she still feels like shit.

"Qué desmadre," Abuelo mutters. But he's not talking about the cattle ranch.

He hasn't been back to the sea in a while, and it gets worse each passing year. They stop the car at the salty crust of the beach and get out. His wide nostrils flare at the dust swirling in the wind. Griselda takes out two masks and hands him one.

"It's a damn shame," he mutters, looking out at the water. "A white man, railroad money in his pockets, came here in the late 1800s and declared the soil the most fertile he'd ever seen. If only there were water." He lets out a half-laugh, half-sigh. "Be careful what you wish for. My people called Lake Cahuilla home long before the Anglo settlers and railroaders came to this desert. This lake was no accident till they got here."

They walk along the shore, crunching on the salt-laden ground.

"Entonces, ¿qué pasó?" She loves his stories. Even the sad ones. This one is helping take her mind off her own drama.

"In 1901, they dug trenches to bring water from the Colorado River."

Abuelo bends down, picks up a smooth stone, and tosses it into the water. It skips twice before sinking, a skim of muck frothing where it fell. It reminds Griselda of soup.

They reach a sitting area, wooden benches worn from exposure to the elements but turned a sick shade of green.

"For a while, it was a dream, mijita. Gente from all over this country and Mexico wagoned into this desert to cultivate their little plots, building beside the irrigated fields. It was the California rush not recorded in the history books."

He pulls in a breath as if gulping underwater, his mask sticking to his lips.

"Are you okay, Abuelo? Should we go?"

She pulls a cantina of water from her bag and offers it to him. He lowers his mask, takes a few sips, and wipes his eyes.

"No, no. I haven't finished the telling. Where was I?"

"The floods come next, don't they?"

"Yes. Spring of 1905. Torrential rains. The Colorado River

swelled, and the Alamo Canal broke. Farmland, homes, all lost to the ancient, reemerged, renamed *Salton Sea.*" He says this like it's bitter on his tongue, then removes his hat and runs a hand through his gray hair. "The white folks were shocked. They hadn't bothered to understand the history of the place. If they'd asked the ancestors, they would've known how the basin has filled in an ebb and flow for millennia."

Griselda nods and turns toward the corroded railroad tracks leading into the water. "I remember you telling me about the enchanted railroad tracks."

Abuelo laughs. "I was born in 1948 after several more rounds of floods. My father told me those submerged tracks, where the railroad had carted our gold to the East Coast Anglos, led to another world under the water."

He leans back on the paint-chipped bench, scabbed with barnacles.

"You know, mija, I didn't mean to get so caught up with this sea. I wrote a report on native and invasive species for Fish and Game, and they liked it so much they put me in charge, esos güeyes. It was my brainchild to bring saltwater species from the Sea of Cortez." He shakes his head sadly. "Look at them now. *I've worked all my life and all I have is my broken body.*"

"You're quoting Dorothea Lange's photo of an old Mexican laborer."

Abuelo touches the tip of his nose and winks. "You always were attentive, mijita. Cesar Chavez and I went to the same school, have I told you that? We were at Hidalgo Middle together in the forties right here in El Valle. Most Mexicans and Indians couldn't go to school back then, but we did." He points his thumbs to himself as if he's holding up invisible suspenders.

Although he's recounted this many times, she nods. Normally

she would bring up Dolores Huerta and her importance in the
United Farm Workers movement as Cesar's partner in organizing.
But today, she steers the conversation in a different tangent.

"Can I ask something off topic?" Griselda hates to interrupt his
storytelling, but he's in a mood to share some truth, something
she's desperately needed lately. Especially after last night. And
now . . . what Mom said about that girl, Renata. It's all too weird.

"Ask away, mijita."

"Would it bring you any peace . . ." She clears her throat, hesi-
tant. "To know whatever happened to Elena? Even if it's something
terrible?"

When Abuelo looks at her, his eyes go milky. She swallows hard,
thinking she's crossed a line and he'll scold her for asking, but then
he answers, "You look just like her."

Griselda has asked her mother about Elena over the years with
the morbid curiosity of a budding scientist, then as a cautionary tale:
How could a person disappear without a trace? It violated the laws
of physics. Matter is neither created nor destroyed. Elena must've
gone *somewhere*. She hadn't *disappeared,* although this is what her family claimed.

To Griselda, several possibilities came to mind. Tía could've
been dead for twenty-five years—either by natural causes, an accident, an overdose, or murder. Alternatively, the land itself might've
swallowed her, a coyote den or the swampy sea her final resting
place. Or perhaps she'd been kidnapped, her body dumped, buried,
or chopped up and discarded.

Still, although it flies in the face of statistics, Griselda wants
to believe she's living her best life somewhere. The movie starlet
Abuela Vero never became, Tía could be sipping iced tea in Portugal
or Spain, a caftan the color of pottery draped around her perfectly
sculpted bronze shoulders, her shining, sun-glazed legs dangled

between a lover's, poolside; her angular face and wasp-stung lips, her dimpled nose and high-arched eyebrows, her hazel eyes—the face Griselda shares—shaded by an oversized sun hat. Tía, who made it out of El Valle for good and never looked back. Not even for the family gutted by her absence.

Griselda wouldn't begrudge Tía if any of the latter were true.

She rises from the bench, dons a pair of gloves, and walks toward the water, bending and gathering a scoopful into her test tube, capping it before collecting another. The shells scattered around her on the shore resemble teeth. Fish corpses litter these toothy remnants like the discarded meal of some monster who's spit out the bones.

A glinting in the shoal catches her attention. The debris down here is called *hash*, like breakfast hash, a mixture of millions of minuscule broken shells. But in the sunlight, the jagged edges of something more fibrous than nacre become discernible.

Abuelo spots it too. "Is it an elk or deer bone?"

"In the water?" Griselda picks it up with a gloved hand and turns it gingerly, inspecting. Abuelo comes close to examine, rubbing his bare hands against the bone. "Don't touch it, 'buelo."

He scoffs. "Ay. You may be the scientist now, but I've been doing this since before you were born."

Griselda chuckles and refrains from rolling her eyes, which would be disrespectful, although she suspects he wouldn't mind one iota.

"It's more of a fossil than a recent remain," she muses aloud, turning it over. "It looks kinda like a cactus pod without spines. Look at those empty sockets."

"A jawbone," he murmurs, wincing.

She too shudders at the thought of the force required to break it into pieces.

She rubs it with her thumb. "It's weird how *stonelike* it is. Warmer saline waters of the Salton Sea can strip flesh from bone, leaving a stark whiteness behind. But mineralization — where bone turns into something akin to stone — typically occurs —"

"In *fresh water,*" Abuelo finishes her sentence for her.

"Exactly."

Griselda read an article about a couple of retired scientists who volunteer to locate the bodies of drowning victims. Could the experts have helped locate her tía, if her family had reached out? Assuming she was in the water, of course, and that was a wild assumption. The amateur sleuths with their sonar equipment could detect bodies in lakes much deeper than the Salton Sea, which is only sixteen meters deep and drying rapidly, having lost a third of its water over the last twenty-five years. Why do they do it, the couple was asked? *People need to see a body to grieve well and let go. They need to see the bones.*

Griselda's family has never let go of Elena. Not her abuelitos, not her mom, none of them. "Humans hate being in the dark, don't we?" Griselda says. "We're such curious animals."

"Indeed, we are, mija." He sounds underwater, lost in his own sad thoughts.

"We should show this to Benny so he can test it in forensics. Just in case."

"No, mijita. This can't be human," he says, his voice somber. "Probably elk or deer. Human jawbones are distinct . . . they taper more at the joints." He gestures to the bone. "I've been handling game since I was young, and these traits are unmistakable."

She's fairly certain he's mistaken, but she won't press it. "I'm sorry, Abuelo. I didn't mean to open wounds."

"Gotta open wounds to let them air out properly," he declares, ever the sage, but his voice sounds weary. It's time to go. She's asked a lot of Abuelo, coming out here.

They return to the car in silence and tuck the test tubes into a large ziplock marked BIOHAZARD with her other specimens to take back to San Diego for her dissertation research. The effects of El Valle's toxicity on every living thing. And dead.

She sets the specimens in the trunk along with the broken bone and slams the lid.

8
BAD SEA

The hours blur past, as stressful hours do, until Mal can fetch
her and Gris's used prom dresses and Amaranta's borrowed
suit from the dry cleaners. She texts Benny again about Renata
but he ignores her. Her message stays "received" instead of "read."
She needs her little brother at that damn fundraiser; he'd have more
than gossip about Renata's case. Goddamnit, Benito.

Next door to the dry cleaners, she picks up three sweet teas
from the donut shop. She needs sugar to pull through. She resists a
donut because Griselda's homecoming dress fits her, but only just.
She doesn't want to split the seams during Esteban's fiesta. Qué
mitote.

Mal climbs into her truck and blasts the air-conditioning; there
are myriad ways to describe El Valle from May to October, including
but not limited to the sweltering broil of a barbacoa in hell, or her

favorite, the devil's crotch. Some days, humidity from the irrigated fields turns the air into a sauna. Still, despite the heat, most kids in this small town walk home. Buses are reserved for those coming from surrounding towns or the countryside. The Veracruz house is just a mile away, but Mal chooses to baby her daughter because she can. Or maybe she's just terrified, deep down, to let her walk alone. Especially today.

Renata has dug into the wormy place inside of Mal, the place where Mami still calls her, shouting, *Malamar*—malísimo, very bad. What was Renata doing down by the Salton Sea? The very night Mal was out there sleeping with Gus.

She can't stop the buzzing in her head since Yessi told her about Renata. The thread across time and space that seems to connect her with the girls who went missing so many years before. Like Elena.

That night, too, was a party. Esteban was headed for Stanford in the fall. Local teens were congregating in the countryside between town and the sea. Elena went with a group of her friends. A keg, a bonfire, and a field draped with drunken teenagers. Sometime around midnight, she disappeared. Mal left the party early, and when she got home, the only one there was Mami—full-on crowning with Benito, whose timing has always been terrible. Papi spent the night drinking at the local watering hole. Everyone there vouched for his whereabouts. Including Gus. Ironic, both fathers should be drowning their sorrows. What was Papi so upset about? He didn't even know Elena was gone until the next morning.

Mal washes down the acrid taste in the back of her throat with the teeth-numbingly sweet tea. It coats the painful swishing. She pulls up to Amaranta's school with time to spare and parallel parks beside the iron gates surrounding the school like a prison yard; these weren't here in the 1990s. She'd walk to Johnny's for fries with cheese or taquitos smothered in avocado. This gate might make parents think that their kids are safe, but it hides the insidious truth, doesn't it? We're never safe.

Her phone vibrates with a text message: Parents! Come support our future leaders at the career fair tomorrow. She gulps down the rest of her tea before she notices him — leaning against the bars, his hat dipped down low over his face, as if that would hide him from anyone. She blinks, making sure it's really him and she's not hallucinating. What's he thinking?

Anger prickles Mal's skin as she marches toward Gus. She pushes through the tension in her diaphragm, forcing herself to drink in air for the requisite five seconds, hold it, release, repeat, before she shakes her shoulders. She's shaken. Or as the girls would say, she's shooketh. If girls are going missing again, he shouldn't be hanging around a high school.

Yes, women and girls disappeared disproportionately to men and boys. And in this country, Brown and Black girls and women, like Renata and Elena and Noemi, aren't found — not even as remains, not even as bones. The media doesn't care. The police forget or have other cases. Yet you know who didn't stop searching? Who didn't forget? Gus. That's how Mal knows he *couldn't* have killed Noemi, no way, nohow. And he had nothing to do with Elena's death. Mal knows that. But the rest of the town doesn't. And they all have eyes.

She stops close enough to have a conversation without drawing attention to themselves as a pair. She doesn't want parents gossiping about Amaranta's mom and El Cucuy.

"What are you doing here?" She hisses through clamped teeth.

He shifts, flushing a deep shade of crimson — wine soaked into dark wood. "I was worried about her."

Mal lets this settle in. "Because of Renata?"

"It's . . ." His face crumbles.

"I know." She sighs, wishing he would've called her instead.

He scratches his stubbled jawline, frowning at Mal. He reaches out as if he'll gently touch her hair then remembers himself. "You have a little chunk of — what is that, beef? Pork? The other white meat?"

They're not looking directly at each other but glancing over their shoulders, Mal focusing on the passing cars beside the stop sign and the liquor store across the street where she'd always get the kids Mexican candy and paletas when they were little. She's painfully aware how much attention they've probably drawn to themselves. El Valle doesn't have a Real Housewives vibe, but people love to talk shit. If they got caught, would it be a relief? Freedom at last?

"We said dinner tomorrow. Why'd you change the plan?"

The dark pools of Gus's downward-sloping eyes whirl and eddy. "It's like I woke up and realized I've lost three children. Even though two of them are alive. They've been alive this whole time, and my dumb ass just missed everything."

"You haven't lost Gris and Amar," she whispers, wanting desperately to embrace him. "You'll see. Tomorrow . . . at three?"

He nods, his eyes drizzled with tears, his thick brows folding. "I'm sorry I intruded. I'll see you tomorrow."

"You're never an intrusion. I'll text you later."

As the release bell rings and he walks away, Mal, still shaking with adrenaline, scans the sea of teenagers for her own. She spots Amaranta laughing with Iggy, huddled together as if they're the only two people in the world.

Mal raises a hand to signal her presence, and Amaranta's expression changes, like she's acknowledging the existence of the parallel universe where her mother lives.

Mal shares this quality with Amaranta — the mental compart-mentalizing. Seeing Gus here at Amaranta's school was an utter shock. Could they really ever combine their worlds?

Her daughter's voice rises above the din of chattering teens. "My ma's here. I'll call you later. After my uncle's stupid party."

The girls share the meaningful smirk of an inside joke Mal desperately wants to be in on.

Amaranta tries to zone out with her abuelitos at the kitchen table; their ridiculously vibrant fruit cups brimming with melon, pineapple, mango, and jícama speared and sprinkled with Tajín seem to laugh at the black hole inside her that's sucking everything into its singularity.

The scratch beneath her hoodie stings. It better not be infected. Stupid cuates. She takes a bite of the chile fruit, which stings too. She's been chewing her cheek.

The door catches her eye as Tío Esteban strides into the kitchen. Not the tío she needs. Tío Benny's usually awesome but lately his superpower's been ghosting her. She's not sure she could explain it over the phone, and, anyway, she's scared to get Ma in trouble whether Amaranta's right or wrong about her hunch. And even though he's the police, he would listen to Amaranta and give her the kind of advice she desperately needs, wouldn't he? If he would just answer his dang phone.

"Hey, Pops, how was the sea? You didn't get too tired, I hope. Or sunburned."

"Estoy bien, mijo. El sol es bueno para mi salud."

"Okay pues, Pops. Whatever you say. Oye, is Lupita coming to help Mami get ready? This is a big night for me," Esteban says, emphasizing *big night*. "For us all."

"Sí, sí," Abuelo swats him away like a pesky mosca buzzing around the fruit. "We'll be ready for your big mitote."

"Pops, don't call it that. You'll jinx it."

Amaranta stifles a grin. Ma's been calling it that for weeks behind Tío's back.

"Lupita's not coming, though," Abuelo says like he hasn't heard Tío. "So the honor of helping la bella Vero is mine."

Abuelo groans with effort as he gets up and shuffles to the cabinet, retrieving a small bottle from the top shelf. He pulls out a pill and saunters over to Abuela with a glass of water. "Mi amor, I have your vitamin. Take it, and we shall dance the evening away."

Abuela makes a puckering face but complies, taking the pill and sipping the water. Abuelo unlocks the brakes on her wheelchair, takes his wife's hands, and sways as he serenades her. "*Que será, será. Whatever will be, will be. The future's not ours to see . . .*"

Amaranta focuses on the bottle label: *Ativan 4 mg — take as needed for agitation or anxiety.* Would they notice if she pocketed a few pills?

Her sister's homecoming made everything worse. Amaranta can't get the squish of the cattle ranch out of her head. That gun aimed at her. Gris with a shovel. That guy's face, smashed.

"Where's Mallow Mar?" Tío asks, his voice overly bright.

Amaranta shrugs.

"You okay, mija?"

"Yeah, sorry, just tired."

"Get some rest before the party, eh?" He smiles as he pats Abuela's shoulders then passes through the door to the living room.

Here's her chance. She could snatch a few; her abuelitos wouldn't notice. Lord knows she needs them. She has enough agitation and anxiety to fill the Salton Trough.

But before she can open the bottle and dump a few of the little white pills into her palm, Abuelo turns to her and calls out, "Mijita, come dance with us."

Guilt stops her. She places the bottle back on the counter and heads toward the center of the tile floor, taking Abuela's soft, wrinkled hands and swaying slowly, staring into Abuela's distant expression. A bit of spittle crawls down Abuela's lips onto her chin and chest. Amaranta can't afford to peace out. Not when Ma has let a murderer into their midst.

Benny lives in the apartments catty-corner to Cattle Call, home of the national rodeo. The houses that overlook the park are million-dollar mansions—would be, if anyone else but the current occupiers could afford them. No one else comes to this town besides the residents. Everyone else is trying to get out.

Griselda parks in the small lot outside Benny's apartment, climbs the metal stairs, and pounds on his door. "Let me in, loser."

Below, a school bus yawns and releases a steady stream of back-packed children running in all directions.

A shuffling inside tells her someone's home. She sits cross-legged on the doormat (it does not say WELCOME), her back to the door. "I'm not leaving, so you might as well talk to me."

The door opens a crack, and she falls back slightly. She looks up. The latch is still attached, and an eye appears. Brown. Not Benny's.

"Hey, Gris." His tone is as casual as if she came over daily.

Salazar Limón's thicker than Benny, with striking, jet-black hair he tries to lay flat with gel, but that flares up like a duckling's down.

"Sal, hey, where's your new hubby?" Their summer wedding was the cutest, but she feels bad she hasn't talked to Sal since. She gets to her feet while he unlocks the rest of the door and pulls it wide, allowing her in. The place is a mess. "He's been ignoring the whole family."

"Yeah, you guys have turned him into a bigger pain in the ass than usual lately."

"Why, what's going on?"

"Nah, just the stress of the job and Mal's nonstop guilt trips."

Sal's been playing video games on the couch, surrounded by take-out detritus. He's not wearing a bathrobe but might as well be.

"You guys need a housekeeper."

"I am the housekeeper." He pulls her in for a side hug and noogie, knuckling her scalp.

"You're fired," she laughs, wrestling away. But then she looks at Sal's face, crestfallen.

He's been out of work a couple of months now. Layoffs at the hospital fell mere weeks after the guys' wedding — twelve department heads decapitated at once, including Sal's position in Marketing and Public Relations. While Benny's career has been steadily inclining, Sal's has taken a nosedive. CEOs blamed Medi-Cal patients (yet their own salaries skyrocketed).

Same as it ever was.

He brushes off her comment without getting all sentis. "Want a beer or something?"

"Nah, I've got Esteban's thing. You guys should come."

"So Mal roped you in, huh? That why you're here? A last-ditch effort to drag us over?" He grins and plops onto the couch, grabbing the Xbox controller. "Benny's a step ahead of you."

"Where's my cuate anyway?" Mom's been calling Benny and Gris that since they were little and it stuck. She glances toward the bedroom, door open, bed unmade but empty. There aren't many places to hide in this tiny apartment.

Sal's already engrossed in his game, playing as that sheriff from *Stranger Things* but dressed as Indiana Jones, creeping through a Southern gothic mansion, chasing a little girl in a white hat through piano rubble. Gris is half-tempted to sit beside him and play. "Went for a run."

"Rain check on that beer, okay?"

"Where are you going?"

"To grab my running shoes from the trunk."

"You think you can catch him?"

She winks. "Oh yeah. See ya!" She's been running after Benny since they were babies. He's two years older and always several paces ahead, but that's never stopped her.

When they lived at the Salton Sea house, she'd toddle after him on the beach or Salvation Mountain in the Slabs (where artist enclave meets hobo encampment). Built from the debris of a crashed hot-air balloon and nearly condemned as a safety hazard for its lead paint, the Jesus-themed mountain was preserved as a national treasure. Benny calls it an eyesore, but Griselda loves it.

Through high school and when Benny was training for the police academy, they'd run together around the blacktop road encircling Cattle Call Arena, then up the twenty-foot hill out of the basin, back through the rich neighborhoods, stopping at the Donut Shop a few blocks from their house, where they'd pick up a donut, sweet tea, and walk the rest of the way home. She laughed at the counter-productivity of it every time, but he'd say they weren't trying to lose weight, just boost their endurance, and sugar was a great motivator.

Now she cuts through the horse pens and show ring and finds him climbing the bleachers, knees to chest as he runs.

"Hey, pendejo," she calls out, laughing as he turns, loses his balance, and almost stumbles down.

She joins him on the bleachers, her muscles bitching at the knee raises. Or the hangover. She's been running on the beach in San Diego but hasn't done stairs in a while. And it took a bunch of drinks last night with Harlan (once they'd made sure Amar was reasonably

untraumatized and could fall asleep) to cover the literal and prover-
bial shitshow.

She glances at her bruncle, step in step beside her. Normally he's
as handsome as they come. Dark, wavy hair that lies smooth across
his head and falls devil-may-care into his face. A shock of bright blue
eyes. Taller than Abuelo and Tío Esteban. Today, he looks like shit.
Purple bags swollen under his eyes. She nudges his sweaty bicep.
"Why are you ignoring everyone?"

"Mal's relentless. She's got Amar texting me now too." His
words are punctuated by shallow breaths. He's pushing himself
hard. "I told you all. I'm not going."

"You working on Renata's case?"

"Yeah, you know her?"

"A little, from school," Gris puffs. "She was dating one of Harlan's friends."

"Raul, yeah, I questioned that guy. I might've passed him off as
a lowlife were it not for how hard he works. He's got a job at Sean's
meat plant *and* moonlights at the hunter's lodge. Spent most of the
night there bartending an extra shift. It turns out he and Renata
are both involved in those protests with your . . . what's your status
these days? Booty call?" He gives her a little jab with his elbow. "But
I can't find any connection there to her disappearance."

He's always teasing her about Harlan. She'd call their relationship
friends with benefits. But after last night, Benny's innocuous comment prickles. They reach the top where an American flag waves in
the breeze, then turn around and head back down. Sweat pearls at
her forehead and drips into her eyes, salt stinging. It's infinitely more
humid here than San Diego.

"So what do you think happened to her? Same as Elena? And
Noemi?"

"You mean, disappeared without a trace?" Benny's voice takes on an almost manic tone, an impotent rage that boils within him. He's never hurt a fly, but all her life she's seen that anger simmering beneath his surface, searching for a crack from which to explode. "You should see her poor mom, Gris. It's awful. I . . ."

"You'll find her, Benito." Her belly flops as she says this, though. The truth is Renata could be anywhere. Lying in a ditch on the other side of the border by now.

"I've been having these nightmares."

"About what?"

He stops, bends over to catch his breath, hands to knees, then looks up at her like she'll think he's crazy but what's new. "The Devil?"

"El Cucuy. Again?" She ruffles his sweaty hair then wipes her hand on her shorts. "It's all Mom's stories. She terrified us as kids. It's nothing."

"Renata's mom and a few nutcases around town are convinced it's that guy who still lives out by the sea . . . Gus." He takes off running again, out of the arena and back toward the blacktop.

Damn. No wonder he's having nightmares of El Cucuy. Griselda had seen him around . . . a psycho waiting to snatch kids. The weirdest thing? Griselda has these . . . not quite memories . . . more like ink splotches or wispy spiderweb impressions of him in the darkest recesses of her subconsciousness. They come out when she's faded or high, which is seldom. But it's unnerving.

She gathers a thick, humid clot of air into her protesting lungs before she pushes her sore muscles to chase after Benny. "Why's her mom convinced you should look into *that* guy?"

"Renata was meeting some dude out by the sea. But who? And what for?"

"I bet you'd find out if you came to the fundraiser tonight. All those chismosos, someone's bound to know something. They'll all be getting drunk enough to slip."

"You think the rich folk know what's up? Renata's as poor as they come."

"So she wasn't kidnapped for a ransom." Gris refills her lungs to get up the hill, but halfway through she's gasping and stops for a puff of her inhaler. Benny stops, too, waiting.

"You be my eyes and ears at the party, yeah? I've got other leads to follow."

"Hey, speaking of leads, let me show you what I found at the sea earlier."

At her trunk, she takes out the jawbone. "Abuelo says it's from an animal, but it looks human to me."

He examines the fragment, jagged where it snapped. "Damn." He takes the plastic bag. "A small human. A girl, maybe."

Her stomach cramps. It couldn't be Renata. This bone's far too bleached. But any of the other missing girls?

"I'll have forensics take a look."

She nods, almost opening her mouth to mention the calf rescue and the guy she whacked on the back of the head. How she'd left him there to get—what? Stomped to death? Mired in cow hooves and shit? She's at the top of a toxic heap now, alright. And Benny's not just her bruncle. He's a police officer. She opens her inhaler lid instead and takes another puff.

97

9
TO KILL A COYOTE

The lights of the Callahan house twinkle into view like sudden stars in the night sky as Mal drives down the block overlooking Cattle Call Arena. This is Rodeo Drive, not pronounced the fancy way they do in Beverly Hills but how a cowboy would— Road-ee-o Drive! Yeehaw! Mal squints into the dusky basin, almost mistaking a herd of horses for the ghostly apparition stalking her again. She dismisses the syrupy piss and wet alfalfa stench as a false alarm.

As she pulls closer to the ostentatious mansion, she fights the urge to make a quick U-turn and drive her and the girls through a taco shack before heading home and snuggling in their pj's. It'll be harder to get through the night when she's so upset about Renata's disappearance. But here she is, parking her Jeep, stepping out in Gris's old homecoming gown, slit thigh-high.

The Callahans' horseshoe driveway, long and spacious enough for ten cars, will fit far more tonight. Callahan hired some young guys from the country club to valet. Mal smirks. This oughta be good. They're gonna destroy this rico's yard.

She reluctantly hands over her keys to a teenager, whose eyes linger on Griselda before he peels his attention off her eldest, long enough to notice Mal's breastbone. Some folks would call Mal's plunging dress inappropriate for a woman her age, but she couldn't give a flying fuck. The only dance she went to back in the day was a triple date with her siblings and Sean Callahan, qué payaso. She deserves a do-over. She'll get through this night with her daughters by her side.

She ferries them up the ornate driveway, arm in arm, an unbreakable line.

In the dining room, Mami and Papi, dwarfed by the wealth around them, perch at a far table looking more dapper than Mal's seen them in years. Mami's wearing pearls Papi probably strung around her neck, and Papi's hair is plastered to his head with Tres Flores, slick and shiny.

All around is dark, polished wood. So clean it's like these ricos don't use their stuff. Mal wants to relax but can't, not wanting to disturb or agitate anything. Look at the monogrammed pristine hand towels in the bathroom, so white they can't have cleaned a child's jelly-stained mouth! And everything's initialed. Maybe they're worried someone will steal their shit so they've written their names on it for safekeeping — a phone number stitched onto the tag of one of their stupid, pearlescent hand towels: IF LOST, PLEASE RETURN TO 555-0123.

The tats on every artifact could've been Old Man Callahan's wife's doing — Elva Vaughn, celebrated equestrian and daughter of one of the area's largest landowners, whose marriage to Guy doubled the size of the Callahans' land like feudal lords expanding their kingdoms. Elva descends from El Valle's pioneers who arrived by train right when only white folks could homestead and scoop up not only the land but the stubborn water rights that even the Supreme Courts have upheld, so she clings to her maiden name. Old money christened this place the Imperial Valley, engraving their European names on the signs and conveniently overlooking the Cahuilla and Kumeyaay peoples, including Papi's ancestors, to whom the land actually belonged. But at least la gente took back the name — everyone calls it El Valle.

Now they're barreling toward the largest ecological disaster the country's ever seen but the only thing anyone cares about are these ricos' farms. And only for what they produce.

Should farming here collapse, the nation would have to settle for canned vegetables instead of fresh. Imagine soggy, salty, canned green beans for little Jimmy and Jane in Minnesota or Maine? A travesty of epic proportions. The sodium content alone. Might as well serve them canned soup. All that MSG.

Still, if farming goes belly-up, the Callahans have fallbacks. Old Man Callahan bought several geothermal plants surrounding the sea and is investing in lithium for cell phone batteries, and Sean owns the beef plant Harlan routinely sabotages. At least one Callahan son is trying to undo the generations of damage. Mal has some hope for this family. Maybe it's Griselda's influence on the little prince. He's had a crush on her since elementary school. And she can be quite convincing. La Abogada. If she weren't a scientist, she could've been a lawyer.

Whatever the reason, Harlan might actually have the guts to fight his dad. And win.

Elva hovers at the edges of the gathering, eyeing it with a mixture of polite regard and slight distaste, conversing with her daughter-in-law, June, and son, Sean.

Until Mal's junior year, Sean was merely a clown who played pranks and ditched classes. Set to inherit everything, he felt no need to lift a finger — so he didn't. After their triple date, Mal saw what makes the Callahans so dangerous. They think they can have whatever they want.

And to a certain extent, they can.

Sean's wife, June, was the Cattle Call Queen when she was a senior in high school (and Mal's life had fallen apart). El Valle royalty. She may not have been born into it, but horseback riding and barrel racing in tight, rhinestoned jeans in this rural place gave her more than a leg up.

Elva's older than Mami but has that money-can-buy-youth look, whereas Mami's crinkled into herself. Elva's lowlights mask any grays, coiffed and sprayed into place. She wears a sequined faux-gown pantsuit with a trainlike peacock feather cascading down her skirt. Mami, sunken into her wheelchair beside Papi, almost makes Mal feel sorry for her. *I was made for the movies,* Mami claimed throughout Mal's childhood. She could've rivaled Dolores del Río or María Félix for beauty, with her classic features prized in that era: slim nose, wide-set eyes, dark hair, and olive skin. She praised these same features in Elena. But the reality was no studio would hire her.

Deeper into the corridors, the house grows less imposing but still a far cry from the comforts of the well-worn Veracruz household. A majestic mahogany and marble wet bar with cowhide stools and a bartender, both plush. Vintage liquor bottles. Everything bathed in hues of forest green and adorned with striped patterns. Oil portraits of hunting scenes.

Amaranta hovers near an elk head jutting from the wall. Her face says it all. Who hangs dead animals? Bunch of sadists. Mal's not one to talk, but she respects the animals she butchers enough not to decorate with their carcasses.

She reaches for an appetizer, some weird little piece of toast with crema and tiny black pearls. She should be used to the briny taste, being a fisherman's daughter, but her familia's never been fancy enough for caviar.

Esteban seems to have acquired the taste for it just fine; at the epicenter of this bash in his honor, he stands out in his expensive suit and Windsor knot, navy blue, crisp white. He reminds Mal of a conductor, waving his arms with charisma, directing servers and campaign volunteers, shaking the hands of his guests and contributors, laughing in his deep baritone.

He *would* have his fundraiser here. But even if Mal's an outsider, for tonight, she's holding her own in a house built on stolen land. And that's something.

At some point, she realizes her daughters have whisked away without her.

She stuffs another tangy, briny caviar crema toast into her mouth and scans the room, trying to quell the dizziness she feels at her girls' absence. A burst of unexpected joy pulses through her as she spots Yessi with her girlfriend, Lisa, in matching plum dresses, taking selfies and holding up champagne glasses. But as she starts toward them and catches a snippet of conversation from another group, her joy melts into a nagging fear. "That poor girl's still missing. But you know, you get what you give."

"I heard it's El Cucuy up to his old schemes. No girl's safe is what I think."

Two hens, pecking. But they hit the nail on the head. No girl *is* safe. Not here.

Mal sticks the rest of the toast in her mouth and makes a puckering face, burning a hole into the backs of these cabronas' heads, about to give them a piece of her mind when Esteban appears before her, smiling in a genuine way Mal could never achieve in this social setting.

"Hey, sis. You managed to have some fun yet?"

"Still working on it." She forces a smile, then realizes she's got little fish eggs stuck between her teeth and clamps her lips tight, tonguing them away.

"Mami and Papi are asking about Benny. Couldn't you convince him to show support?"

"You knew he wouldn't come."

Esteban sighs, dropping his shoulders. "Maybe after the election."

"Maybe," Mal echoes.

"Where are the girls?"

"Around here somewhere." She tries to sound casual, but something quivers inside Mal.

"I'll bet they found the dance floor. There's a banda in the backyard taking requests." He puts one hand akimbo and the other to his hips, swaying with an easy grin. "Put me on your dance card for a cumbia, okay, sis?"

Mal glances toward the kitchen and French doors leading to the backyard. "Make our parents go afuera también. They look so stuffy and sad cooped up in here with strangers."

"These aren't strangers, Mallow Mar. We've known them our whole lives."

Mal doesn't recognize anyone. They all blur together.

He's about to walk away when she grabs his arm and blurts out, "Chuy, it's happening again. I've been trying to shake it off but can't."

It takes him a moment to register before Esteban's eyes widen. He clears his throat and lifts his shoulders in a minuscule move

103

Mal recognizes as trying to ward off an uncomfortable emotion. "Renata?"

Mal nods, the twang of her earlier headache pinching her eyebrows. "It's . . . like before . . . with Noemi then Elena."

Esteban sighs, shaking his shoulders rigorously. "I'm sure it's *not, sis.*" He kisses her cheek, and she unclutches her hand from his arm, realizing she's left little half-moon indents in his skin. "Help me mingle and put in a good word for me, okay? Eat some hors d'oeuvres. And try to have some fun. It's a party."

As he strides off, straightening his posture and taking another deep, forceful breath before replastering a smile and greeting more partygoers, a flurry of noise erupts from the entryway.

Flanked by the cuates, Sharon struts through the front entrance in a little black dress, emphasis on *little,* commanding the spotlight as if the gala were hers. Any space Sharon bumbles into becomes infinitely less breathable; she sucks out all the air for herself. It's not love lost in Esteban's expression when he fastens his gaze on his ex; there's something more complex beneath the surface, an enigmatic mix of emotions Mal struggles to decipher. His veneer of stateliness escapes him for a moment and he's a schoolboy again.

Sharon's entourage includes her New Creations vato, bedecked in his fanciest cholo wear: starched and hood-pressed khaki Dickies, plaid button-up opened to reveal a white undershirt, and blue Puma tennis shoes. Beside him, the cuates look bored. In the past few years, they've gone from cute children to striking teenagers, possessing an undeniable attractiveness. Still, there's something *off* about them, an indiscernible coldness.

Since Sharon came home from Stanford flaunting the diamond Esteban gave her, she acts like she was born with that rock on her finger (pues, Mal still doesn't understand how he *paid* for it since his scholarship should've covered only rent and tuition). So her cuates honestly believe the world's been gift-wrapped just for their entitled little hands. They smack too much of Mami — who beat the shit out of Mal whenever the world disappointed her. Who will the cuates take their frustrations out on if the world doesn't cough up? Fortunately, Chuy works his ass off to keep the money flowing so Sharon can keep up her facade. She'd served one ineffectual term as mayor and didn't run for reelection. She does nothing with the law degree she earned alongside Esteban but lives as fancy as ever.

Entitlement in El Valle is as common as love triangles in telenovelas.

When Tía Sharon and the cuates appear in the doorway, a sick, squirmy sensation rankles Amaranta. She wishes she could talk to Ma about it. *Mathematician in the Sky, why is life so complicated?* Why can't she go back to the way it was *before*?

Rather than face any of them, Amaranta heads to the backyard, where the lights sparkle against the swimming pool's surface. Gris took off once she saw Harlan. Of course, she'll only confide in him. Never mind that Amaranta's the one who almost got *killed* last night.

She scans the mannequins tottering their plates of slimy fish eggs and paste. One bland face after another — they're all pretentious, Tío Esteban's crowd. She's about to retreat inside and call Iggy when a hand clasps her shoulder, spinning her around. She recoils, an instant replay of that guy last night, clutching her, and for a second, she's sure he's found her.

But it's just Tía Sharon, gorgeous and made-up as ever but all nervous and twitchy, a complete 180 from her usual buzzy socialite vibe.

"Amar," she whisper-shouts. A vein in the middle of her forehead throbs. Spittle lands on Amaranta's nose. Gross. She tries to back away but Tía grips her tight. "My silver compact. The one I showed you the other night. Did you take it?"

Amaranta shoves her hand into her suit pocket and clutches the compact, cool against her sweaty palm. "No, Tía. I haven't seen it . . . maybe your brats took it."

Tía sighs but her grip on Amaranta doesn't relent. "They claim they haven't seen it either."

"They're liars, Tía. You know that."

Tía stares into Amaranta's face, her breath close enough that Amaranta can smell, for once, Tía hasn't been drinking. Normally there's a sweet-sour tinge to her. Right now, she's stone-cold sober and smells of peppermint, which is startling as hell.

Amaranta does her best innocent face until Tía finally releases her, eyes hemmed with pink like an Urban Decay eyeliner. "It's important, Amar. Did *you* see it? Did Oscar?"

"I have no idea. When you passed out, I took off to my friend's house. End of story."

Tía nods. "Sorry I scared you, mija. It's just . . . that damn mirror. I need to find it."

"*Why, Tía?*"

"I can't——" Tía glances around, ensuring their conversation remains private. "Just please, if you find it, let me know *immediately.*"

She's tempted to reach into her pocket and hand the damn thing to her aunt—end her distress. But she has Ma to think about. She can't just give up the one thing that might . . . *protect* her ma? She's not sure that's right. Implicate her, maybe. Or rescue her.

"I really do think the cuates might've taken it. You should check their rooms."

Tía Sharon considers this for a moment, her expression softening into something like despair. "Maybe," she murmurs before slipping away into the crowd.

If she can't find Tío Benny at this stupid party and he won't answer her texts or calls, she has no choice but to find more evidence on her own. Something that'll connect all the dots and nail the sicko Ma's seeing... (all Nancy Drew and shit, but this is real life and real scary).

She makes her way inside again when the live band stops playing and the music screeches to a halt.

"El Chupacabra!" someone screams, crossing themselves. A fury of screams and shrieks. She cranes her neck to find the source of the tumult, a party trick or —

An animal whose dark skin and fur are warped with gashes, bunched and scabbed over, its neck and legs longer than usual, its ribs jutting, making the whole creature appear skeletal. It's a coyote suffering mange, surely, not the hotly contested vampiric creatures who puncture the necks of goats to suck their blood. Gris would back her up on that if she were out here.

"It's diseased," she hears among the chatter.

The coyote stands at the edge of the yard as if surveying the guests.

"Coyotes are getting bolder," another partygoer comments with an air of authority. Amaranta wonders if all adults turn into know-it-alls at parties. Maybe it's the wine.

A man starts yelling toward the coyote, "Go on, scram."

It bares its teeth, hunching low on its haunches.

One partygoer lobs a glass toward the coyote, another, a bottle of champagne.

By the time Tío Esteban and Old Man Callahan come out, the pool is cluttered with floating shards of broken glass and the remnants of spilled alcohol, a fresh glass of wine diffusing like a watercolor.

"What the hell is going on?" Old Man Callahan yells, and Amaranta discerns the slightest wince from Tío Esteban.

"It's the damn coyote," a man in a cowboy hat calls, nodding across the yard. "Possessed or something, won't move for nothing."

As if to prove his point, a man pulls out a pistol and aims it toward the animal.

"Don't you dare," Amaranta yelps, her blood roiling with indignation, her cheeks burning. It's not that she's altogether against hunting. Her ma and abuelo are excellent hunters. But this hardly seems fair to the coyote. Besides, they wouldn't be shooting it for food. Just out of fear and a sense of ownership.

"El Chupacabra," the same woman repeats, crossing herself again as if for good measure.

"Pobrecito, está tan enfermo," a woman calls, and Amaranta turns. It's Ma's friend, Yessi. Finally, a voice of reason.

"Bet it has rabies."

"Mange."

The crowd murmurs assent. Tío Esteban's got beads of sweat gathering at his temples and above his lip as he stares at the coyote.

"Shoot it," someone calls.

"Isn't it against the law to shoot game, even on your own property?"

"Coyotes ain't game. They're pests. You can shoot as many as you want, your property or not. If they're threatening your livestock or pets or getting too close, you can shoot 'em. Just have to chuck 'em in a landfill after."

Fat, salty tears are welling in Amaranta's eyes by the time Ma comes outside and wraps her arms around her. Amaranta can't help it. She nuzzles her face against Ma's arm, the sparkly fake rhinestones on the recycled gown scratching her cheeks and forehead. For once, she's glad Ma's a helicopter. "Don't let them kill it," she whispers. "Not like that."

"Might be the kindest thing, mijita," Ma whispers back, although

Amaranta can tell that she's on the verge of tears herself. "Come on, let's go inside." She turns to her brother. "Chuy, *do* something."

"Yah," he calls, the way a cowboy might in a Western, signaling a horse to giddyap. "Get out of here." He claps his hands and walks across the bridge of the pool, hands out, palms flat in surrender.

Amaranta pulls Ma through the French doors. "He'll get bitten."

Ma nods like she's agreeing but says, "He knows how to handle wild animals, don't worry, mija. We grew up in the boonies."

"But that animal's sick."

"They often are."

Tío's still skulking forward as the coyote inches backward then turns and leaps over the fence. Amaranta watches as far as the cliffs, where it blends into the shadows of the mesquites.

The crowd cheers Tío Esteban, whose shoulders slouch. Amaranta catches an almost imperceptible motion before he turns. When he does, a bright, wide smile splashes across his face. His straight ivory teeth gleam against the lights that encircle the fence and patio beams. Those same lights cast a glimmering reflection in the pool.

The man with the pistol reholsters, hidden now by his suit jacket.

Amaranta exhales as Tío calls, "I've got you, mi gente."

The crowd cheers louder, calling out, "Steve for Senate."

"Go find your sister, okay?" Ma says, squeezing Amaranta's hand.

Does she think Griselda's hiding in the punch bowl or what? Sigh. Mothers.

"Are we leaving? I haven't found Tío Benny yet."

"He's not coming."

Amaranta's stomach falls. "I need to talk to him."

"Yeah, me too." Ma's voice is clipped, her lips drawn tight.

Amaranta treks down the gaudy mansion halls lined with closed doors—closed but not locked. She opens each one, searching for her sister. Maybe she *can* talk to her about what's going on. If she can pry her away from Harlan long enough. Maybe she'll know what to do.

Griselda's naked ass presses against Old Man Callahan's ornate, mahogany desk, where she and Harlan are going at it.

The stereotype that scientists are dowdy could not be further from the truth. Understanding the body's needs and being existential bitches, scientists know how to carpe diem, perhaps better than most. If this is all there is, live it up.

Papers scatter as Harlan thrusts into her. She grips the back of his shirt so hard buttons fly off. Normally, she'd be laughing. Right now, she's working off some serious guilt.

"Marry me," he whispers into her ear. Clearly, he's working off his own shit.

She covers his mouth with her finger, shushing him. His eyes plead an urgency that only Griselda's body is willing to answer. Whatever else he wants or needs from her will have to wait.

Minutes before, they were screaming about the calf rescue. Griselda *almost* considered turning herself in. She assaulted a man. She needs *proof* he's okay. But now here they are. And all she wants in this moment is oblivion.

Of course, that's too much to ask because her little sister barges into the office, yelps like a wolf cub, then darts out, slamming the door behind her.

"Shit, Amaranta, wait!" Griselda calls out, piling *more* shame onto her steaming heap.

"What?" Harlan's back was to the door, so he didn't notice the interruption.

Griselda presses her palms to his chest. "My sister saw us."

"Oh shit, Gris. I'm sorry, I thought I locked the door. Want me to stop?"

She rolls her eyes as he goes limp inside her. She tries not to focus on how handsome he is or she'll get worked up again — and she needs to stop getting so carried away whenever they're together. Not if she ever hopes to escape this valley for good. She risks a glance at his neck, noting the slight protrusion of his Adam's apple amid the ropy veins. How one person gets to be so rich, kind, and sexy still seems unfair. You'd think he'd be a douche like so many of the spoiled kids of landowners set to inherit, but he's not.

"I'd better make sure she's okay," Griselda says. "Especially after last night."

He stuffs himself back into his boxers and zips. "Yeah, that was a clusterfuck. You know I'm sorry . . . I didn't know it would spiral out of control like that . . . but she'll be fine. Kids have seen worse by her age."

"Worse than her sister maybe murdering someone? Doubtful." Griselda pulls her dress down, smoothing it against her ass, hips, and thighs. She slides her feet into her high heels. "Stay here. We need to finish . . ."

His eyes shine, but she slaps him softly on the arm. "We keep getting ourselves into trouble." She steadies her breath so it emerges in even streams instead of shallow puffs. Now that the high of sex is wearing off, she just feels awful again.

Right outside the door, Amaranta's wilted against the wall, her knees to her vested chest. Her suit and bow tie crumple against her knees. Her curly mass of hair sloops over her scalp, covering her face so she appears faceless. Griselda worries about her hermanita in this town where anyone who stands out bears a mark. She yanks her hand, pulls her to standing, then ducks her back into the office she and Harlan just defiled.

Amaranta blushes when Harlan pushes his sand-colored hair out of his face and gives her an equally embarrassed but charming smile. "Don't be upset you walked in on us, Amar. We should've locked the dang door. That was my bad, okay?"

Griselda wraps her sister in her arms and kisses her on the cheek. "Forgive us?"

"There was a coyote in the backyard" is all Amaranta answers. "Tío Esteban got it to run back into the wild."

"Weird," Griselda murmurs, but her pulse speeds back up to what it was a moment ago.

"I'm surprised no one shot it," Harlan says, acerbic.

"They tried to shoot it," Amaranta answers. "It was scary."

"I'll bet." Griselda ruffles her sister's hair. A stitch of guilt stabs her side. "So listen, kid, about last night . . . Raul said that guy was fine. He checked into the hospital with only minor scratches. I was thinking about telling Benny, but . . ."

"What good would that do?" Harlan finishes her sentence, not exactly the way she would've phrased it. "We were there for a just cause. He was defending my dad's unethical practices. And anyway, Griselda, you were literally *saving* her," he nods toward Amaranta, "from getting *shot*." He lets out a deep breath. "We were in the right."

Amaranta doesn't look at them. She picks at her fingernails. "Yeah, I guess."

"Go check out the theater down the hall, last door on the left," Harlan says. "There's a popcorn machine in there. And a cappuccino maker last time I checked."

"Like, a *theater* theater?" Amaranta bites a hangnail.

"With theater seats and everything."

"Your family is too much," Griselda says, rolling her eyes.

"You want to come watch something with me, Gris?"

"We'll be there in a few minutes, okay? Put something on and make popcorn."

"You're not gonna . . ."

"No!" Gris's face flames. This is so awkward. "We just need to *talk*."

"You should use a bedroom and *lock* it. What if I'd been Ma? Or Tío? Or one of those old rich people? Oh, Ma told me to come find you, by the way."

As Amaranta pivots to leave, she pauses in front of the wall beside the door, cocking her head as if she's about to say something but doesn't. She scrunches her face.

"You're not gonna tell Mom, are you?" Griselda calls after her, and Amaranta whips around, her expression unsettled.

"About what?"

"Any of it, I guess." Griselda's Harlan-induced irresponsible behavior the past twenty-four hours.

Amaranta gets a look on her face like she wants to say more, just not in front of Harlan, but she turns the lock on the handle instead, whips around, and shuts the door behind her.

Later, when Griselda and Harlan check on Amaranta in the movie theater, she isn't there. The screen is dark, but there's a cold batch of popcorn in the glass case.

After the bizarre coyote incident and Esteban's big speech (introduced by the sheriff with all the Callahan butt-kissing that entailed), folks inundate Mal's brother with questions. He's thriving on this shit. He shines brightest under attack. Not that people *attack* him. More like, offer him opportunities to prove them wrong and himself right. His savior complex has never bothered Mal because beneath his macho veneer he cares about the people and the community.

Martín Sanz with the Comité Cívico del Valle stands to pose a question.

"With a billion dollars in agriculture coming through El Valle, why do we never see none?" Martín asks. This isn't the kind of crowd who would cheer for such a remark, but Mal nods. *Preach,* she wants to call out, but won't irk her brother. Before Esteban has a chance to answer, Martín presses, "How would the lithium plant be any different? You say it'll bring much-needed funds, but the rich won't stop getting richer off our backs just because we hope they will."

Mal bets Esteban wishes he hadn't invited Martín, the agitator. But she feels the same way. Their whole family does.

"We all want to see El Valle flourish," Esteban answers diplomatically, but sweat pearls at his temples, belying his confidence. "It's when we work together and set aside our differences that real change happens. That's why we're here tonight. We want the same thing."

Martín counters, "I went up to Sacramento and overheard los políticos patting each other on the back, assuring each other not to worry about us because, and I quote, *Only a handful of people live down there anyway, so they don't matter.*"

"That's why I need your vote, hermano," Esteban says, but his voice is softer than before.

Mal steps out the front door to call her daughters, neither of whom returned. If she were a smoker, she'd light up. She can't handle hearing any more of Esteban's campaign prattle.

The music from the banda in the backyard wafts to the front porch where Mal leans against the railing, massaging her temples. The valet boys lounge on the grass near the curb, smoking. She's tempted to bum one just this once when a figure clacks up the arched driveway, his cigarette flickering orange. For a moment, it's Gus making his way toward her in his navy suit, wingtips, hair slicked back with gel, face shaved smooth against his square jaw.

As the figure draws closer, the illusion of Gus dissipates, replaced by the unmistakable silhouette of Sean Callahan, his reddish-blond hair streaked from hours in the sun. True, the Callahans don't just sit in their trucks and tractors but actually get out in the fields. That's one thing they love to tout—how they get their hands in the dirt and pick alongside their workers. Even if it's mostly for photo ops.

He tosses his cigarette aside, the ember briefly illuminating his face before it's crushed under the heel of his polished shoe. This party is dead. Mal needs to find her girls and get out of there.

"¿Qué onda, Mal?"

Ugh. She hates when Sean chameleons his father, putting on that friendly El Jefe demeanor. "Quit with that schoolboy Spanish. It's blood and sweat you're parroting."

Sean's gaze is too knowing, too familiar, and Mal wishes she hadn't borrowed Griselda's low-cut, thigh-high dress.

"Just trying to keep the embers burning."

"Ashes don't burn, asshole."

He puts his hands up in surrender. "No need for hostilities. Heard you've been making a name for yourself. The guys at the club were singing your praises. Said you're gonna dress their kill." Sean's voice is casual, but his eyes are keen, watching her closely for a reaction. "It's not every day you hear about a butcher with such *artisanal skills*."

Mal stiffens. The club is a so-called exclusive gathering of El Valle's elite sportsmen. Snooty, self-congratulatory men who believe their ability to track and kill makes them kings. Mami waitressed there when the club on the Salton Sea went patas arriba after the hurricanes destroyed everything on the shore, before

Baby Benny was born, but Mal's never been. She had no idea the hunters in the carnicería the other day were members. It's creepy, come to think of it. Those hunters were hitting on Renata. Maybe Sean knows something about her through them.

"How's business at Beef Tooth?" she bandies.

"Can't complain. Business is thriving."

"Thriving's one way to put it," she replies. "Exploiting is another."

Sean guffaws, his eyes crinkled with what seems genuine appreciation for her caustic wit. It's infuriating. "You've always had a knack for carving things up. Remember prom?"

"I could show you what else I've learned to carve." She stares at his cojones, daring him to say more.

"Ah, right. Well, how about a dance, instead? For old times' sake? I'm not the same guy who stepped on your toes."

"I'm not a girl who lets herself get stepped on," Mal retorts. He acts like the Del Río Country Club dance was a fond memory instead of a nightmare.

It was Esteban's machinations that landed her on that triple date in the first place. He convinced her Sean was harmless, his jokes hiding a sensitive guy underneath. Yeah right.

Thinking back, Esteban probably wanted Sean to rent the limo. His dad was the only one who could afford it. Esteban was always trying to impress Sharon, even then. Social climber. She's not being fair to her brother, but that was the one night he got everything disastrously wrong. She's never really forgiven him, even though Mal agreed to go. She had hoped it would be more about the three siblings having fun. She was naive.

Elena was too young but wanted to go to prom too. She got herself invited by a senior whose name escaped everyone. He was a placeholder. But Mal never knew whose place he was holding.

Who actually held Elena's heart? She had so many secrets. At any rate, her prom date wasn't there by the graduation party and Elena's disappearance—or he'd have been a suspect. She can't even recall his face, let alone his involvement in her sister's paltry investigation.

At the country club, Sean had offered his arm to Mal. With his easy laugh and smoother talk, he'd dominated the dinner conversation—the clinking of silverware punctuating discussions about futures as planned as the landscaped golf course. Mal stayed quiet. She had no plans, only vague notions of adventuring—exploring. But she kept those to herself.

Elena was going to be a Laker Girl cheerleader, she said. As soon as she turned eighteen. Tryouts were held in El Segundo, close to the beach. She was good enough. Everyone agreed, if anyone could do it, Elena could. She'd rock those yellow and purple midriff and booty shorts.

As the night wore on, Sean pulled Mal to the dance floor, the heat of his breath, the press of his body, invasions she endured because she, what—wanted to fit in? Pretend to be as natural at this as her siblings?

Elena looked happy, jumping on the dance floor with no-face-no-name, Chumbawamba's "Tubthumping" playing, *I get knocked down, but I get up again.* Esteban and Sharon were grinding against each other, their legs intertwined like railroad tracks at a crossing.

Cumbia. Strobe lights. Girls crying. Nasty punch. Sweat crust. Humid as a frog biome. Amphibeal. Slick. Sweat and sex. Nasty everything. *Tin roof, rusted.* The taste on her tongue.

Did someone spike the punch? Or was she just this socially anxious? She hadn't yet learned to box breathe through the *oonce-oonce-oonce* of house electronica. The eclectic deejay.

Girls with mascara-streaked faces clung to each other, their laughter piercing the dense air, as boys in ill-fitting suits prowled the edges, coyotes, all of them.

All of them except Gus. But he came later. And he wasn't a boy.

The after-party meant piling back into the limo that ferried them to Sean's. That was the last time Mal stepped foot in the Callahan house, before tonight. What he'd tried to do. Pushing her to the chaise lounge in his downstairs guest room when she came out of the bathroom, dizzy and exhausted.

Papi must've woken at 3:00 a.m. to start making breakfast burritos he drove over to the Callahans' at 6:00 a.m. where they devoured them then fell asleep like puppies on the floor. All except for Mal. She waited in Papi's troque, chorizo and eggs going cold in her tortilla. Her corsage crushed and wilted. The tasteless nothing of breakfast burritos and salsa.

"Mal?" Sean asks again, all *Earth to Mal*. "Dance?"

The suggestion hangs like dirty laundry on the line between them. Yet in a twisted effort to find out what Sean might know about Renata, she extends her hand and accepts his invitation, moving slow to the melody so different than the cumbia or *oonce-oonce* of house beats. What would his former Cattle Call Queen of a wife say if she spied them dancing alone? The inappropriateness of it swells like a sausage in the sun of her stomach. His breath, thick with something rotting beneath, chokes her. Tobacco and pickled ginger?

"I'm curious why you keep tabs on the sucesos in my shop. It's a little . . . stalkery."

"Oh, you know how it is, word gets around. I make it my business to know who's doing what in our field. And speaking of who's doing what, Harlan and Gris have a pretty remarkable connection, huh? Star-crossed lovers, can't keep apart."

Mal cringes at her daughter's name on Sean's lips. "Are you seriously comparing our kids with those suicidal fools from Shakespeare?"

Sean chuckles. "Come on, Mal. Give me a break. I can understand why Harlan would be smitten, though. You Veracruz women are hard to resist. And what's so wrong with building something that lasts on familiar ground?"

"Gris is only here for her uncle's fundraiser, Sean. She's heading straight back to grad school after this weekend."

He hums like a little kid with a secret. "I heard she was thinking about sticking around the Valley for good."

"You heard wrong." A surge of protectiveness gurgles through Mal. Griselda's gonna be the one who gets away. "Griselda's too good for this Valley." When the words are out of her mouth, she knows she means them.

"Right, well, Harlan and Griselda seem to be doing better than we ever did."

"There's no *we*. Never was. Nor is my daughter looking to be someone's trophy."

"Just like her mother, then. Always fighting."

"Women shouldn't have to fight all the damn time."

"You make it sound like we're all monsters when you know the stories go the other way around. It's La Siguanaba who ensnares men, Mal."

"Why would you bring *her* up?" A sticky sensation flows through Mal. It starts at her neck, a prickling strangulation, then trickles like hot, warm blood gargling down her skin.

He's laughing, almost guffawing. "It's a *ghost story,* Mal. Lighten up. Jesus."

"Sean, what do you know about Renata?"

That wipes his smug smile away. He looks startled. Good. Let him squirm.

"Renata? Why would you think I know anything about her?"

"You seem to know a lot about what goes on. You knew about the hunters and our kids. It's not a big leap."

Sean looks away, his gaze drifting over the remnants of the party before settling back on Mal. "Renata's disappearance is a tragedy, but I, unfortunately, know nothing about it. Let's not start all this again."

Mal's skin crawls. Yeah right. She sees Sean for what he is—a predator.

"Shouldn't you ask your little brother the cop?" His tone has turned acidic, his smile and charming demeanor vanished. He pulls away as the song ends, and Mal feels the pressure release. He gives a curt nod then turns to his father's house. She's left hollow, drained, but intact.

Slumped against the wall by Old Man Callahan's stuffy office, Amaranta brings her knees to her chest again in what she'd like to think is an artistic, tragic-heroine kind of way. Barging in on Griselda's . . . uh, personal *moment*? They could've spared her the trauma with a simple turn of a lock. But noooo. Now she's replaying their sexcapade in her head.

At least it's better than that guy's scruffy face squashed under hooves.

The clacking of footsteps makes her raise her head to listen. Probably some poor partygoer lost in this maze, desperately looking for the toilet. A snarky part of her wants to shout, *Wrong way, genius!* If they only knew they're about to encounter her guarding the Hall of Embarrassment. No one else needs to see that cringefest.

Except those aren't the haphazard footsteps of a bathroom

seeker. There are two pairs, for one thing. Heels tapping on the wooden floor, like the slow clap of an unimpressed audience. And they're too . . . deliberate.

Amaranta peeks up, recognizing those designer shoes anywhere. Who would spend hundreds of dollars on plain black shoes? Oh, right. Her cousins.

Posh, prissy, and positively the *worst*.

They're both wearing clothes so ridiculously trendy they're more like costumes.

In a juvenile, unoriginal move, they start murmuring that creepy rhyme. Reject lullaby.

"Your tongue shall be slit,
And all the dogs in the town
Shall have a little bit."

"Leave me alone." Amaranta dips her head between her folded knees, covering her ears with her kneecaps, muffling their singsong taunts.

"Your tongue shall be slit,
And all the dogs in the town
Shall have a little bit."

She peeks through her shield at their wicked grins. "Villain starter pack, much?"

In a total invasion of her personal space, they kneel beside her, flanking her like prison guards, one on each side, and continue hissing it into her ear, emphasizing each word, drawing the rhyme out, enjoying it. She stifles the urge to jam her elbows into their faces. She hates them.

She could start the fight, but they'd finish it, and they all know it.

"Snitches get stitches."

"Oh, how original! Took you all night to think of that?" But she's trembling.

They rise in unison, as though they've planned this flash dance, and saunter away.

She watches as they leave, and they must realize it, because, in sync, they turn one last time and slice their fingers across their throats in the same motion their mom made the night she showed Amaranta that compact.

10
WATCHING YOUR SISTER

Although Mal woke with the bitter remnants of last night on her mind, today promises sweetness. She's baking a tres leches cake and introducing her daughters to their father. And Gus to her parents. Ay. They can start to be a family. Tres leches just happens to be a favorite both Amaranta and Gus share.

She steps onto the front porch, a blast of humid morning air slapping her in the face as she reaches down for the newspaper. Papi's religious about reading it in print and not on a screen. She gazes out beyond the neighborhood toward the open lot lined with palm trees and the sun sliding over the New River. From this distance, the water doesn't seem toxic. Amaranta has described Saturn's moon Titan in a similar light: rivers, lakes, and seas abound, yet all of them consist of ethane and methane due to subzero temperatures. A beautiful poison paradox.

Mal's gaze drifts downward, toward the driveway. Gris's little Honda isn't there. Did she make it back last night? Mal's stomach clenches. She whips out her phone. Why didn't you come home? We're having a guest for dinner. Get home by three please with prayer hands for emphasis. Her daughters know she hardly ever uses emojis. She calls through the house, "Amaranta! Are you ready for school? Breakfast!"

Back in the kitchen, Mal removes the chilled cake from the fridge, its surface glistening with a skin of moisture. The sponge, delicate and airy, sits poised beneath a crumb moistened by the three milks, its golden interior speckled with vanilla seeds. She'll cover it with plastic wrap and leave it to set in the fridge while Amaranta's at school.

"You sleep funny last night, mijita?" she asks, side-eying the mess of tangles Amar is sporting as she trudges into the kitchen.

"Nightmares."

"Me too. But I made you eggs with applesauce. It's on the stove."

Mal made this concoction for Amaranta when she got her tonsils out in kindergarten because all she'd eat, besides popsicles, were scrambled eggs and apple sauce. Separately at first, but when they accidentally mixed on her plate, she loved it. That icicle mealiness of the mushed apples coating the bland egg sponge. She still eats it though it sounds repulsive, perhaps because it got her through the bodily trauma with a bit of sweetness.

"Are you trying to butter me up?" Amaranta asks, regarding her mother skeptically.

"It's an apology for dragging you to such a boring party last night."

"Boring is an understatement, but nice try with the eggs."

She kisses Mal on the cheek and takes her plate to the kitchen counter where she hops onto a barstool and begins to eat, nothing like Mal's other two: Griselda and Benny would shove food into their mouths as if racing against time, but Amaranta savors each bite. She possesses a Zen quality Mal envies.

"I'll drive you to school as soon as you finish," Mal says.

"I could walk."

"No, La Siguanaba's roaming," Mal responds, then clasps her hand over her mouth. She promised herself she'd stop torturing her girls with ghost stories. What made her bring up the horse-headed woman today? She's been trying to keep the nightmare far from her mind.

"Maaaaaa," Amaranta groans. "La Siguanaba's not real."

Mal ruffles her hair. "Hey, let me braid this mess real quick." She sections her daughter's hair in two, then plaits down her back, nothing fancy.

"Hey, speaking of La Siguanaba, have you heard anything new about Renata?"

A kick to Mal's rib cage, that ghost bird in her corazón. One of the braids unravels in her fingers. She reweaves it quickly and ties it in a knot.

"No," Mal says. "Have you?"

Amaranta stiffens, her eyes narrowing as if she's about to divulge something that would shatter the fragile peace of the morning. Instead, she rises from her chair, leaves her unfinished breakfast, and says, "Never mind, it's just a rumor. Let's go, I don't want to be late for school."

Mal sighs. She won't press or pick a fight today. "Don't forget I'm picking you up from Johnny's at one o'clock sharp. I need your help with dinner. We're gonna have that plática, okay?"

"Fine," Amaranta says as she shoves her earbuds in.

On the way out, Mal stops at the ofrenda for her sister, its velas perpetually burning. *Keep my girls safe,* she whispers to Elena as if she were an angel who could do anything but stare back from the photograph of her and that imaginary prize-winning horse.

At lunchtime, Mal drives thru Johnny's for a half order of fries with cheese and avocado plus sweet tea, then munches her snack from her Jeep in the barbershop parking lot across the street, windows rolled down. She'll give Amaranta a few more minutes inside with Iggy.

Teens amped for the home game swarm the parking lot and neighboring streets, filled with the buzzing energy of an early release. Ah, to be young enough that a Friday football game is the peak of existence.

¿En serio? Those nights playing at the games with the band were some of the best of Mal's life. Their halftime performances on the field. The crispness of her uniform and squelch of her leather shoes. The sturdy brass neckbone of her flute against her lips. She'd play up and down its spinal cord, a few hours of pure release. Esteban on the saxophone. Somehow he made being in the band cool, and girls in the stands watched him, *Stevie,* as much as the football players, all starry-eyed and shit. Elena in her cheer uniform, her long, wavy ponytail secured with a blue-and-gold-ribboned bow at her crown, the pleats of her short skirt flapping against her thighs as she sprang and jumped, spread-eagle, legs high in the air. So free. They all were. There's something to be said for unknowing. There's so much Mal wants to unknow — wants her daughters never to learn.

It might be too late for Griselda, but not Amaranta.

They say grown-ups are wiser than children, that our years yield us perspective and experience and the understanding to match. Mal's not so sure.

She was a smart girl, Papi liked to tease—"Eres bastante inteligente *para una chica.*" You're smart enough *for a girl.* He didn't mean it as sexist as it sounds. In his pretty Spanish, it was the compliment he intended. "Eres más duro que un chico," he'd also point out—how much stronger than a boy she was, since she enjoyed the hunting trips with Papi more than Esteban did. She was a better shot. Could field dress better. *Field dress.* Like a gossamer summer garment to wear in a field of wildflowers. When it meant skinning and gutting a dead animal. But she didn't mind. She was tough. Smart enough and tough. And that was alright by her.

Papi's teasing toughened her up, casting her a lifeline she needed to survive Mami's temper and delusions of grandeur. Mal didn't know they were delusions then. When she grew up and needed a therapist to deal with all her Mami basura, that's when she learned it. And box breathing. And boundaries. If only she could've gone back and given little Mal all those tools.

But she had the Papi-infused toughness. Shooting. Field dressing.

And anyway, that's what daughters were for. Mal couldn't go back and protect her little inner child. But she could keep her daughters from harm.

One would think Mal hates her mother for making her the kind of woman she is. Distrustful. Self-reliant. Resilient. Dura. Unbreakable. After all, if she'd been lavished with unconditional love, she could've afforded to be soft.

Mal is *not* a soft woman. But her brother loved her well. Her father. And Elena, in her way, the trickster. One time Mami brought yellow fabric. When Mal got home and went into the room she shared with Elena, the tube of stretchy yellow material was folded on the end of her bed, and her sister said, "Look what Mami brought! A dress for you!"

Mami? Brought *Mal* a yellow dress? What kind of nonsense was this?

Mal unfolded it — a five-foot tube of a dress.

Elena said, "Here, let me help you put it on!"

So there was Mal, wearing a yellow tube from neck to floor, and Elena drawled, straight-faced, "Oh, it looks beautiful on you!"

Mal was trying to understand if she and her sister were seeing the same thing when Elena burst into a fit of giggles, rolling around on her bed, clutching her sides.

"You look like a chiquita banana!"

Mal was so mad at her sister, but looking back, maybe Elena's love language was practical jokes. Maybe Mal could've learned to laugh at herself and take life less seriously. Maybe she wouldn't be so anxious now if she could've laughed at the world like her sister did.

The honking of a car snaps Mal back to the red-and-white pole of the barbershop parking lot. Her cheese fries have disappeared and the sweet tea's nothing but crushed ice. The effervescent horde of teenagers has dispersed to a few stragglers jaywalking the three-way intersection. Mal checks her phone for the time. One thirty. An hour? What's Amar doing in there, rolling the tortillas herself? She knows Mal's picking her up. What's the holdup?

Mal opens her phone and clicks on Amaranta's thread to check for a missed text.

The last message was a few days ago, a meme of a dog smiling with oversized teeth.

Mal types, Hey, baby. I'm here. Are you ready?

She waits for the confirmation that Amaranta's read it, but it stays "delivered" not "read."

Mal waits a few more minutes then calls.

"If I don't know you, I doubt I want to. If I do, I'm probly already with you."

Mal doesn't bother to leave a message. Kids these days never check voicemails.

She removes her keys from the ignition, grabs her wallet, and crosses the street to the tiny corner lot of the restaurant. Mal scans the parking spaces and surrounding curbs for Iggy's *slug bug,* as her daughters would've screeched, punching each other. It's not in this lot.

She flings open the door of the small building—a neighborhood market in the seating area with a counter for ordering from the kitchen. In another part of the country, Johnny's might be called a deli or taquería or bodega, but here it's just Johnny's.

A quick skim of the faux-wooden booths, soda and iced-tea machines, one-person bathroom, and ordering counter—all one room—reveals neither girl.

Mal's been waiting in the damn parking lot for nothing. How rude of her daughter not to apprise her mother she'd gone somewhere else for lunch. Gris never put her through this shit.

One of the servers behind the counter, Estrella, lives down the street and is an acquaintance of Griselda's; the girls used to carpool for Science Club. Mal shakes off her frustration and the fear simmering below it long enough to flash what she hopes is a friendly smile.

"Hey, Estrella. How's your mom?"

"Oh, hey there, Ms. Veracruz. She's good, thanks. What can I get you?"

"No, nothing. I ate already."

"I *thought* I saw you in the drive-thru. Was something wrong with your food?"

Mal releases a stiff breath. "No, it was fine. I just . . . weird question.

Have you seen my younger daughter Amaranta here today? With her friend Iggy?"

Estrella's dark brows knit below her thick fringe of bleached bangs. "There were a lot of kids cuz of the early release. I didn't serve 'em all, so I might've missed her. Sorry."

"No, that's okay. I guess she went somewhere else. Maybe it got too crowded in here."

"I'll keep an eye out for her."

"Yeah, thanks."

"Say hi to Gris for me."

Mal squelches the disquiet wriggling from the subterranean of her psyche — where Elena resides. And Noemi. And now Renata. But her daughter was out with a swarm of other teenagers in broad daylight. She's *fine*. Mal slams this last word down in her brain as she dials Iggy's number, trying to ignore the shaking of her hand holding the cell phone.

Iggy answers on the second ring. "Hello?" she asks tentatively, her voice sleepy.

"Hey, Iggy. I'm at Johnny's, but you girls aren't here. Did you head somewhere else?"

The line goes silent a moment, and Mal checks to make sure it hasn't disconnected. "Hello, Iggy? You there?"

"Yeah, sorry," she mumbles, stifling a yawn. "I . . . um . . . I'm confused, sorry Ms. V. Amar's not with me . . ."

A seasickness washes over Mal, throbbing her eardrums. "Wait, what? She *said* you'd be at Johnny's together when I dropped her off. Where is she then?"

"I didn't go to school today cuz I'm not feeling well. I texted her this morning. Have you tried her cell?"

"She's not answering."

"I could try her . . ."

"Yeah, do that." Is Amaranta mad at Mal? Did she say something wrong this morning? She pauses, trying to think rationally. "She's just walking home, right? Her phone died? She forgot to charge it . . ."

"I'm sure she just forgot." Iggy sounds fully awake now, but there's a brightness to her voice that sets Mal on edge. They both know Amaranta's not forgetful. She's a walking encyclopedia. She keeps everyone else on a tight schedule. She's obsessive, even. She wouldn't *forget* to call Mal.

Iggy's saying something else but Mal can't hear her through the wind tunnel the pressure in her head has created. She lets out another deep breath and focuses.

"Do you have the Find My Phone app?"

"I do!" Mal is such an old fogy, she forgets the tech available at her fingertips. "I'll check it, hang on." Mal squints down at her phone, types into the search icon "find my phone" and the app pops up. She clicks on a picture of Amaranta and waits for it to home in on her girl.

The little bubbles blink and blink.

Finally, a wide circular berth surrounds her daughter's picture. It reads, "Approximate location" and a time stamp from "one hour ago." The circle entails the high school and a two-block radius surrounding it, which includes Johnny's.

"Shit, this isn't helpful. She was either here or at the school or somewhere surrounding the neighborhood an hour ago. What does that mean? Where is she *now*?"

"The location isn't always exact, depending on the nearest cell phone tower. I guess . . . she turned her phone off?"

"Why would she do that?"

"Maybe it died . . ." But Iggy's tone sounds uncertain.

"Call me if you hear anything. I'll see if she's still walking."

Mal hangs up, ordering herself to stay calm as she climbs back into her Jeep and makes a slow lap around the perimeter of the high school for any lingering students or staff who can say whether they've seen Amaranta.

The student parking lot is empty, the school itself deserted of teenagers, although a few community members and parents are disassembling booths in the quad. Mal spots a familiar face carrying a banner that reads NEW CREATIONS toward the curb. Sharon's new vato, Oscar.

She rolls down her window and calls out, "Hey there, Oscar, right?"

He squints like he's looking into the sun before a warm smile spreads across his face, brown and smooth except where his shaved-bald hairline meets his forehead and wrinkles like a bulldog. "Oh, hey there, Malamar! Sharon's sister!"

Ex-sister-in-law.

"Hey, have you seen Amaranta?"

"Yeah, she came by the New Creations booth earlier. Qué cariño. You raised her right, mama."

A cringy sensation spiders across Mal's skin, but she keeps a tight smile plastered to her face. She hates asking this man they barely know about her own daughter. "Did she mention where she was going after school?"

His face crinkles even more. "Nah, sorry."

"If you see her, tell her to call her mom."

"Híjole, your 'jita's giving you the runaround, huh?" He chuckles. "It's probly nada. Teenage rebellion. The good Lord knows I did my own share of mess when I was her age. And more when I was grown!" He laughs again, a sound that grates on Mal's nerves.

"Well, thanks——"

"Actually, that's what your 'jita and I were discussing, come to think of it," he cuts her off. "New Creations."

"Amaranta wanted to know about New Creations?" Mal can't hide her incredulity. Her daughter's *not* religious.

"Yeah, for sure. Your 'jita's a good egg, mama."

Mal cringes again.

He keeps rambling, oblivious. "I wish Sharon's 'jitos would listen. Those cuates give your sister a headache with their drama. Oh, hey. Want me to call Sharon and see if she's heard from your 'jita? She's home now with the cuates..."

"Sure, thanks. Tell her to call me," she responds. It's too weird, getting parenting advice from this stranger. "I'll check the office before heading home." She tries for a laugh, but it comes out as a weird, pained groan. "I'm overreacting. She'll be annoyed with me for doing the uptight-mom thing..."

Mal waves as she drives away and parallel parks in front of the gate where she confronted Gus yesterday afternoon. The school is eerily quiet. Every other parent has picked up their kid or they've all walked home. Mal gets out and makes her way toward the office, whispering under her breath, *This is not like before. This is NOT like Elena.* She considers making the sign of the cross again. Is that the smell of maple sugar that'll ferment to piss-soaked hay? *No. NO.* She had a tea. It's her own sweet breath.

Either Amaranta's at home or staying after to talk with a teacher. Or she got detention. Okay, that's far-fetched. Her girl's much too fastidious and respectful. Mal might've believed she'd stayed to hang out with Iggy in detention, but Iggy stayed home from school.

Mal turns the knob of the office door and peers into the room, hoping to spot Amaranta perched on one of the hard plastic chairs, twiddling her thumbs and looking up at Mal with a guilty expression to which Mal would just raise her eyebrows and smile in a way that meant *rules are made to be broken* and *let's go have some tres leches.* Milk cake covers a multitude.

But the room is devoid of teenage girls.

Mal's palms slicken against the doorknob she's gripping for balance.

"Can I help you?" the desk clerk asks like Mal's just one more inconvenience before she can kick back for the weekend.

"Um," Mal sucks at the sick paste in the back of her throat. "Have you or anyone in the office seen my daughter? She's a ninth grader, Amaranta Veracruz. She should've been at Johnny's with her friend Iggy, but neither was there. Amaranta's not answering her phone."

"No, I haven't seen her, but I'll check with detention and her last-period teacher if they haven't left campus yet." Does she sound condescending?

Mal nods, and while the clerk makes the calls, Mal focuses on the bland, beige decor and inspirational posters so she doesn't spiral out. The clock on the wall says 1:45 p.m.

A minute later, the clerk says, "I'm sorry. Her teacher, Mr. Baker, has left for the day. And the detention monitor hasn't seen her."

Mal's a skydiver without a parachute.

She thanks the clerk and gives her cell phone number in case Amaranta shows up, then returns to her Jeep and pulls out of the abandoned school lot, heading back down Imperial onto A Street, scanning the liquor store as she turns left, the trailer park beside the apartments, the baseball diamond, skate park, public swimming pool, and football field. Groups of kids huddle, most of them locked into their phones but a few skate or ride bikes. None of them are Amaranta. It's been an hour since school let out. She must be at home. Mal's being ridiculous.

She should've called Papi, she realizes, mentally slapping herself on the forehead, but she's so close to the house now, she'll talk to them when she gets there. Just another quick turn onto the jack-knife that breaks A into West A where they live.

Griselda's Honda is still absent from the driveway. Mal dials her again, but it goes straight to voicemail, same as Amaranta.

She curses under her breath, unsure whether she's disconcerted or relieved.

She settles on tentative relief. The girls are probably together. Amaranta probably called Griselda to pick her up for lunch once she realized Iggy was home sick, then she forgot to tell her mom. But Mal hits that snag again: Amaranta is not forgetful.

"Amaranta?" She calls out as soon as she flings open the front door, her keys still jangling from the lock.

No answer.

She calls out again, louder, half chastisement, half question. "Amaranta?!"

Like most teens, Amaranta's ears are usually plugged with those annoying buds, music cranked up so loud she can't hear her mother calling her for dinner or chores.

This is no different, Mal tells herself as she strides through the house, calling out to Papi now as well as Amaranta. There's no use in calling Mami, who won't answer or be of any help even if she does.

The living room and kitchen are abandoned but tidy. The house unnervingly muted. Mal strides through the hall trying to keep her mind blank as she scans the bedroom she shares with her girl. It's in the same state of disarray it was when Mal left Amaranta asleep to start the tres leches and breakfast. Amaranta's backpack isn't tossed on the bed or the floor. It's clear: she hasn't been home.

Mal envisions the smell of ginger to suppress the oncoming nausea, but it reminds her of Sean, which makes her stomachache worse. She reaches into her back pocket for a Tums but pulls out an empty wrapper. Shit. She chalked Amaranta's sulky behavior to hormones. A necessary rebellion. But what if it was more? *You should've been watching your sister!* Mami bellows through the caverns of her mind. Has Mal not been watching her daughter?

Every moment as a mother has felt like tending a fickle garden. Too little water, and they wilt from neglect — just as Mal did under Mami's inattention. But just as overwatering a succulent can drown it, too much affection can be a burden. Mami doted on Elena as she choked out Mal, and neither girl turned out okay. Mal doesn't blame Mami for Elena's disappearance on a conscious level, but something screeches in her intestines. It never stops screaming.

She stops her inward spiral by gently pressing her hands to her sternum and pulling out the imaginary box she can breathe into.

She's letting past trauma inform the present story. She's juxtaposing two moments that might not be related. What does the evidence in front of her factually support?

Her daughters aren't answering their phones. They're probably together. They're probably safe. She dials Griselda again. Still no answer. She leaves a voicemail and a text, both echoing the same urgent message: Is Amar with you? Call me ASAP.

Mal steadies her trembling hands as she makes her way toward her parents' bedroom. Why is everything so quiet? Normally Lupita would be chattering away to Mami.

In the kitchen, tres leches ingredients fill the sink. She meant to wash the dishes before she went to pick up Amaranta, but time got away from her. She's about to call Gus when a voice drifts in from the backyard.

A flutter beneath her ribs signals her to calm down. They're in the backyard! She got all worked up for nothing! Oh...a silly, relieved grin plasters across her face and fills her whole body as she slides open the glass door and tromps outside onto the back patio.

Her parents are positioned halfway across the sizable stretch of quarter-acre backyard, the upside to a small house on a large plot. Papi is bent-kneed on a rolled-up towel to keep his joints from locking while he kneels before the garden as if in prayer, his work pants and white T-shirt spotless although his gardening gloves are coated in a thick coagulant of coffee-dark mud.

A few feet away in her wheelchair, Mami, in an oversize sun hat to keep her olive skin from blooming more brown spots, rests beneath a hundred-year-old willow whose leaves hang on it like a fur around a stately woman's shoulders.

Except for Papi squinting against the sun, making him look like he's frowning deeply, her parents look content, their chatter pleasant, and any other day Mal might lean against a rafter beneath the awning to watch them, a little girl again, enchanted by their defiant love for each other. But this is all she sees.

She scans the rest of the yard quickly to be sure, then calls out, a thistle-like sharpness prodding her throat, "She's not here? Where the hell is she?"

"¿Qué pasa, 'jita?" Papi sticks his trowel into the dirt and removes his dirty gloves. He grunts as he supports his weight with his hand on his thigh and lifts himself to standing.

"I can't find her," Mal answers, airway constricting, tears welling despite her best efforts. "She wasn't at Johnny's with Iggy. Did she check in with you?"

Papi's face scrunches deeper. He wipes sweat from his brow. "Oye, she did come home, didn't she, mi amor?" As if Mami's memory would be more reliable than his. "Por poco tiempo, before she gusted off again como una hoja en una tormenta. Always in a rush, estas jóvenes."

"She came home? Bueno. Está bien, está bien." Mal's been holding her breath, she realizes. She lets it out now.

"Sí, she spent the night with her novio but had to go to work . . ."

"Wait, what?" Dammit. He means *Griselda* came home, not Amaranta. "Papi. I meant Amar. Have you seen *Amaranta*?"

"Oye, no, mija. Lo siento. Not since . . . the fundraiser, wasn't it? Last night."

"When Gris came home, did she mention picking up Amar from school?"

"She didn't say, pero I think she went to the Salton Sea a trabajar."

Mami doesn't appear to be paying them any mind. She's reaching for a pepper from the garden, plucking it, and sucking on it like a candy.

Mal whips out her cell phone and dials Gris again, but she still doesn't answer.

"We were out there ayer, mija. Hardly any reception," Papi says. "That's why she's not answering." He pauses a long stretch, wiping his hands. "Pero por si acaso, have your brothers ask around town while you head out there. We were near the old house. Start there. I'd go contigo, pero tengo que quedarme con tu mami. Lupita todavía no llega para relevarme. Anda, mjita. Voy a llamar a la familia y los neighbors."

Mal nods numbly as she dials Gus instead of her brothers, the sulfuric match of her guts scraping the wet box against her organs. He answers on the fourth ring.

Without any preface, Mal blurts, "Can you go look for our girls?"

Mami's been humming to herself quietly, stripping the fire-orange skin of her pilfered pepper, but at Mal's words, as if a trip wire has been pulled and Mal's holding the fuse, Mami shrieks loudly, pointing at Mal, screwing her once-placid face into a portrait of rage and anguish. "You!" she spits. "You lost your sister! You lost my Elena! Get out of my sight!" Mami turns to Papi, her voice a mixture of a child's whine and a banshee's wail, pleading, "Beto, get her out of my sight!"

Without a word, Mal turns away, sprints into the house, and slams the door behind her, breathing hard, her back against the wood.

The muffled subaquatic panic she's been fighting to keep at bay for the past hour has morphed into the sharp sting of motherfear.

If in the unlikely event her daughters aren't together, Amaranta will *need* Mal to keep it together. She refuses to fall apart. The first forty-eight hours are critical, Benny's told her when working on any case, but especially a missing person. After the first forty-eight hours, your chances of finding the person decrease by half.

"Mal? Mal are you there?"

Gus's voice seems to come from under a thick blanket. Mal stares at the cell phone in her hand. He's still on the line. She quickly presses it back to her ear and fills him in, the ligaments of her rib cage compressing. She rubs her chest in circular motions as she talks.

"I'll meet you out here," Gus responds, but his voice is thick. She hears his anxiety.

When they hang up, Mal dials Sharon and as soon as her ex-sister-in-law answers, Mal bursts out, "Is Amaranta with you or the cuates?"

"Ay, Mal. Oscar told me what was happening," Sharon drawls — whether from concern or a hint of early afternoon alcohol, it's hard to tell. "The cuates and I haven't seen her, but we'll jump in the car now. Have you talked to your brothers?"

"I'm about to call them."

"I'll call Stevie for you."

After they hang up, Mal leaves one more message for Griselda — Mami's words serrating through her, *You were supposed to be watching your sister!*

Then she texts Esteban: Emergency. Amaranta's missing. Meet me at the beach by the old house, grabs her keys, rushes out the front door, and dials Benny at the station.

11
THE FIRST MISSING GIRL

I n the dilapidated house beside the Salton Sea, Mal and Esteban are camped out in her room where he's snuck in contraband. They are seventeen and sixteen, in high school, and Esteban has gotten cool, but he doesn't care. He's still the best brother in the world when he feels like it. He'd be a better brother if he helped Mal more with chores and dinner.

"Hey, Mallow Mar! Look what I've got." Esteban grins, the peach fuzz on his seventeen-year-old upper lip coarse. They didn't have many nights left before he'd turn into a man and go in search of whatever it is men search for. Soon their late-night junk food sessions will be obsolete. He'll go off to college, and she'll—she has no idea what she'll do. Where would she get the money for college? Esteban will go on a scholarship.

He pulls out a bright yellow package of Hostess Ding Dongs and a colorful box of Razzles. In a mock-deep voice, he says, "First, it's a candy."

Pause.

They both say through their laughter, "Then, it's a gum!"

They watch too much Nick at Nite — all those old-fashioned commercials, cheesy but they love them. No one understands Mal like Chuy. Everyone else thinks she's a dork. A weirdo. They're both nerds, but Chuy can pretend otherwise.

She peels back the tinfoil around the chocolate, stuffs the soft little cake into her mouth.

He gapes at his sister's puff-adder cheeks, wide-eyed.

It takes a while to chew her way through it, but eventually, she swallows the sponginess and gifts him a chocolate-covered grin. The cream squishes between her teeth. "Beat that!" she whisper-shouts. Slam, bam, takedown.

He accepts the challenge with forced stoicism. His dark eyes focus. He sucks in an epic breath and opens one tinfoil wrapper then another and another. He holds all three cakes in his palm, darts Mal a pointed look, then shoves the Eiffel Tower of Ding Dongs into his open maw.

Mal stifles a guffaw so she doesn't wake Elena across the room and have to share this junk food extravaganza with their snooty sister.

Or worse, wake Mami. Wait. She's not here anyway. She's out again, wherever she goes.

And Elena sleeps like the dead.

Esteban's cheeks puff like a chipmunk as he struggles the sweets down.

"Don't choke!" she whispers, ready to swat his back if he does start choking.

Finally, he takes a last thick swallow, his Adam's apple jutting with the effort, and pumps his fists into the air, triumphant. Then he reaches into the backpack he brought into her room and pulls up two bottles of Coke, pops the caps on the windowsill, and hands Mal one.

"You've got the corner shop back there?" she laughs, swigging hers down. It fizzles inside her. "Where'd you get all this?"

He grins over the rim of his own bottle, drinks the Coke half-way down, then pins Mal with a more serious expression that reverberates the bubbles. "It's the least I can do, sis."

It's the first time she can recall he's acknowledged in any way — besides slapping Mami's hand so it can't reach Mal's face — that the scales in their home are skewed. If they're dipping in your favor, why speak up? But Mal knows that's not what keeps him quiet. Mami's their *mami*. Papi treats her like a queen — and so, she is.

A boom shakes the night. Military drills from the Chocolate Mountains regularly reverberate through the desert and send ripples through the sea.

"Did you hear that girl Noemi went missing?"

Mal nods and Esteban looks away.

"Papi says it's a chupacabra. Or La Siguanaba."

"What?" Mal's pulse unspools, threads wild at her wrists and neck.

He is sheepfaced, embarrassed, as if he can't believe he's spouted such nonsense.

"Never mind, forget it."

"Chupacabras eats animals, right? Not people."

"Yeah. No, I'm being stupid. I ate too much sugar."

He slugs Mal playfully on the shoulder. "Finish your Coke."

The fizzy coolness slushes down her throat, expanding her rib cage with the carbonation. Mal pictures the chupacabra's fangs as it slogs into her sugar-filled stomach, into that pit.

"And anyway, it's weird. Which is it? An animal-eating beast? Or a horse-headed woman? Like, the MOs are different, right?"

Before he can answer, Elena's sitting up, her hair a mess, her face all scrunched. "Would you two *shut up*? I'll tell Mami . . ."

"Oh, give it a rest, cabrona," Chuy says. "She's not here."

"Fine, I'll tell Papi."

"What, that we're *eating candy*? What's your problem?"

"No, that you're not letting me *sleep*. I have cheer practice early in the morning."

She throws a pillow at him, but it falls to the floor, missing by several feet.

"You sneak out all the time late at night so don't act like you're all innocent," Chuy prods. "Besides, Papi's not here either."

The soda and sugar fizzle in Mal's gut. "Where'd he go?"

Chuy shrugs, then scratches his face, which he always does when he's nervous or upset. "Out looking for Mami. You know . . . to drag her home."

He's been doing that a lot lately. He's been drinking a lot more too.

"At least give me some candy, then," Elena says, and Chuy throws her a bag, but she doesn't eat it. Just tucks it under her pillow and turns back over.

Later, once Chuy's gone to bed, Mami staggers through the front door, drunk and obnoxious. She stops in the girls' room, spies the candy wrappers, and starts slapping Mal, no questions asked. Mami's breath reeks of something at once sweet and acidic. Candy gone bad. Elena's deep breathing stops. She's awake again. But she does nothing.

Mal's trying to pull herself into a ball to avoid the hardest slaps. "I didn't do anything."

"¡Babosa! ¡Cochina! Stuffing yourself with junk and soda! You fat pig!"

Tears are leaking down Mal's face, the skin where Mami's hand meets her own, smarting and tender. "Just leave me alone."

A hand grabs Mami from behind. At first Mal thinks it's Papi, taller than Mami and strong enough to pull her away.

But it's not. It's Chuy.

His face is fire, Mal can see how angry he is even in the scant hallway light fizzling into her bedroom. She wipes the snot from her face, watching as Mami turns in horror to see her son, still tightly grabbing her wrist, admonishing her, warning her.

"You need to *leave her alone,*" he says like he's the man of the house because the real man of the house has changed and none of them knows why.

And Mami does leave Mal alone. For that night. But she's wary afterward, never as quick to lay a finger on Mal again—at least while Chuy's around. Mami's accountable to someone in the family. Not everyone's under her spell. Someone's watching out for Mal.

12
BUT BLOOD, HER OWN

T he stench of alfalfa soaked in ammonia. Masked by that cloying sweetness. It's unmistakable as Mal speeds through the
back roads, dodging tractors and slow-moving vehicles. A crop
duster flies low over the vegetation and unclenches its metallic jaw,
gasping loose its poisons upon the land and anyone crouched picking
below. Drowning out the plane noise? Clomping hooves. Rustling in
the fields. In the weeds.

She grips the steering wheel so tight her hands ache. Tears pelt
her cheeks. She's catastrophizing but can't help it. She *won't* let this
happen again. Not to her girls. She should've been at the career fair.
That damn text invited parents. If she'd been there, she would've
known where Amaranta went after school. Or she'd have taken her
out to lunch herself. Whatever choice a mother makes is the wrong
one. Whatever choice Mal makes.

This sea steals girls. It's not safe. Renata disappeared out here days ago. Mal *knows* La Siguanaba haunts the water. Any body of water. Why didn't Mal *do more* to keep her daughters safe? She *knew* La Siguanaba had returned.

She dials Griselda again and almost swerves off the road in the process. When the phone goes to voicemail, Mal curses under her breath and hangs up without leaving a message. She can't help picturing Amaranta trudging through the stalks of alfalfa, slipping into the New River.

"Siri, dial Iggy," she calls out to distract herself from spiraling, and when Amaranta's bestie answers, Mal snaps, "Have you heard from her at all?"

Iggy sounds wide awake now — and scared. "Not yet."

"Do you have any idea where she could be?"

"I'll check all our haunts." Iggy's voice sounds small and unsure.

"What haunts? Text me all the places she could be. Were you planning on going to the game tonight? Was Amar?"

"No, cuz I'm sick."

"Call me if you hear anything," Mal snaps and the line disconnects. She doesn't care how rude she sounds; she blames Iggy in the nonlogical way of fear. There's safety in numbers. Two girls are harder to grab, pull into a van, drive away with. Does the same hold true for the supernatural? An animal — clumped and matted — curls in the road. Mal swerves before she realizes it's already dead. Judging by the tawny, blood-soaked fur, the peaked ears, and narrow-pointed muzzle, it was a coyote . . . like the one in the Callahan backyard last night. Except the organs and intestines of this hapless creature splay across the packed dirt.

She replays the night she found out about Noemi's disappearance. Back then, Esteban actually believed it could've been a chupacrabra or La Siguanaba. Papi too. Since then, they've stopped believing. But Mal's not so sure. What if the police haven't found nada because the police *can't* find evidence of the supernatural?

She speeds past Gus's house — then the shuttered bar where Papi and Gus were both drinking the night Elena disappeared. The red eyes Mal saw that night... she searches for them in the fields now. Is La Siguanaba out here somewhere? If so, she'd better leave Mal's girls alone.

Her intestines churn so badly she debates pulling over to the side of the road but instead presses harder on the gas, kicking up dirt and thrashing over the ruts and dips.

At the moldering beachfront property, with its decades-old for-sale sign bearing a spray-painted X over the realtor's face, Mal stumbles from the car and climbs the porch, holding her swollen stomach. The house is even more decrepit than she remembers, paint flayed like scorched skin, shutters broken-necked at the hinges. Sea air mixes with rotting wood.

"Girls?" Mal calls loudly from the porch, scanning the shore.

Griselda's Honda isn't parked on the beach, but that doesn't mean she hasn't parked farther downshore. Mal would start trekking across the beach now — but if she doesn't get to a toilet, she'll shit herself. Damn her IBS.

She pulls open the front door. Inside, the house has the quality of a pneumonic lung — wheezing with damp and mold. Furniture's chopped into kindling, probably by squatters on freezing desert nights. Burn marks char the carpets where winter fires leaped and licked. Black-splotched wallpaper peels back to reveal a constellation of holes in the plaster beneath. The floor — littered with broken beer bottles and discarded condoms like shriveled jellyfish — smells of sewage and the sharp tang of urine. Have people no shame? Condoms are bad enough, but piss on the floor? The toilet still flushes!

Esteban insisted on keeping the water running, arguing for the dignity even squatters deserve.

The bathroom door is flung open, revealing more graffiti than porcelain. She ignores the mildew infestation on the toilet and rushes in. The windows are barred. The tub is ringed with a hypnotic mix of mold and street art.

She follows the graffitied ring around the tub, tracing it in circles until she spaces out—and an image of herself a few weeks after Elena disappeared wavers into view.

Knees to chest, she shivered in lukewarm tub water with a fever so high her brain could've broiled like cabbage in the sunstroked fields, teeming with white flies.

Mami was there, for once, trying to cool her daughter down, but in Mal's fevered state, as the waves of Mami's dark hair cascaded across Mal's body, Mami morphed into La Siguanaba.

She opened her mouth, her teeth the size of boulders, her eyes two ruby stones glowing fire. And clamped down.

Mal juddered, dripping wet, Papi hovering above, his dark eyes brimming.

It was the beginning of the nightmares. Her family was mostly dead inside the house overflowing with garbage and rotting fish. And she, dead Mal, joined them in their afterlife. Her waterlogged eyes blinked away the bathwater. Mami. La Siguanaba. Mami. La Siguanaba.

"Beto," Mami called out to Papi. "Get some ice. She's too hot."

Mami soaked the cloth and wrung it above Mal's head until the balloon in her brain began deflating. The water against Mal's face turned warm and sticky. Horse-headed Mami was eating her whole as her body steamed in the bathwater. And then she was out in the sea. Only, it wasn't filled with salt. But blood. Her own.

It had to be a dream. *Wake up, Mal.* But sometimes, she couldn't wake.

Mal flushes, washes her hands as best she can without soap, then gives a last glance through the decay of the living room. Her daughters aren't here, and why would they be? Except for the nightmares calling her back.

She's rushing toward the front door to search the beach when a jarring, high-pitched screech cuts through her. She whips around to find a long orange beak, the sagging pocket of a throat, and the black eye mask of a pelican. One of the last. It gawps at Mal through the grimy window then raises its long, jagged wings, all that furtive pomp as it tucks its baggy neck and beak groundward the way Mal holds a long knife to her butcher's block.

The loud pounding of boots against the floorboards tears her attention from the bird.

Someone bursts through the front door, and Mal's poised to donkey kick them in the stomach when she realizes it's Esteban, worry lines carving his cherrywood features.

"Mal, what are we doing here?"

"I can't find the girls. Papi said Gris came out here, so . . ."

"I don't think they'd come in *here,* though, do you? It's disgusting." His face is anguished as he looks around at their childhood home.

"No, I . . . just needed the baño," she admits. "Pues, Amar hates this place."

She's not sure that's true or why she said it; Amaranta's never shown affinity or animosity for the house. She hardly knows it beyond the fact that her family used to live here. She hasn't been here in years.

He checks his watch. "It's almost two thirty. Might as well give it a quick scan since we're here. But be careful, the floor could be unstable." He grabs her hand and gives it a squeeze.

A smattering of rodent droppings dusts the kitchen and oven like black poppy seeds; the sink is piled high with moldy dishes. Weeping from the walls, spray-painted initials and haunting phrases seep like blood: *Everything must end. Live free or die. Dead birds only. Hopeless zone.*

In the dim hallway between the bedrooms, empty spaces on the wall mark where the Veracruz family portraits once hung. One such void stands out like the afterimage that lingers when you stare at the bright bulb of the sun too long then close your eyes. It was Elena. Before she hung above the ofrenda in the new house, illuminated by candles, she'd haunted this wall, holding her prize-winning painting of a horse. Did she ever even ride a horse? Mal can't remember.

Esteban places a hand on her back, guiding her forward. She climbs the stairs.

"Over here," he says, pointing toward Mal's childhood bedroom door. It's closed tight. She shared this room with Elena until she didn't.

Mal tries to ward off the rising panic that she might find her daughters, hurt or worse, before pushing open the door. The room is filled with old furniture, covered in dust and cobwebs. In the corner, a scrap of fabric, bright pink and patterned with flowers.

"That looks like one of our shirts," Mal says, her voice barely a whisper, her heartbeat wonky. "The girls' and mine."

Esteban moves closer to examine the fabric. "Could've left it here when we moved."

Mal shakes her head as if rattling a broken appliance. It's the toxins making her dizzy.

A mouselike squeak emerges from her throat. She swallows it down along with a thick, bulbous clump of indigestion, like hair clogged in a drainpipe. "Look!" It's a takeout box from the carnicería. "Do you think Renata was here?" Mal whispers.

"That missing girl?"

She nods toward the cardboard container.

"Could be a coincidence. Every teen across El Valle comes out here for sex or drugs or God knows what. And folks on their way to the Slabs..." He prods the box with his shoe. "But you can tell Benny about it."

The thought of adding her daughters to Benny's list of missing girls hits her so hard she can't breathe. She rushes to the blackened window and pries it open, gasping mouthfuls of hot, stinking sea air. Amaranta once told her we spend six years of our lives dreaming, so the chances of any moment being a dream are startlingly high when you consider that. And of those, how many nightmares? Please let this be a nightmare.

Across the sea, a figure wades through the water. Another stands on the shore.

"Girls?" she calls as loud as she can, but they can't hear her. They're so far away she can't tell who they are.

The Salton Sea is a still expanse broken only by the black cormorants that dive like suicide bombers and disappear beneath the surface. Griselda's hip-deep in the water, her waders slick with scum as she gathers samples, when an internal alarm bell rings. There's a presence on the shore. Squinting against the bright, hot sky, she turns and catches the silhouette of a lone man. His gaze is intense, like he's studying her.

She shouldn't have come out here alone. It's remote and isolated, and she left her cell phone in the car so she wouldn't drop it in the water.

She considers her options as she stomps through the muddy water, gelatinous and toxic, reminding herself she's an eco-warrior. She can't let some creep scare her away. Besides, the guy might be a fellow scientist or a tourist trying to catch a glimpse of the apocalypse.

She sidesteps toward a distant point down the shoreline, hoping to maintain a buffer between her and the stranger. A crane lands on a leafless snag, searching the skin of the water like the steadfast angler it is, not realizing the fish are gone.

She's up to her waist now, mindful not to splash near her face or mouth. The lake spits putrid and sulfuric. Another black bird plunges in. Abuelo's told her how Fish and Game ordered him to burn the birds in incinerators, smoke filling the sky above the fields of alfalfa, cebolla, broccoli, lechuga — and all the migrant workers picking, picking. El Valle residents are all unwitting participants in a vast, ongoing science experiment.

Griselda vowed she would only help as a scientist from now on . . . then got involved in Harlan's activism and look where that got her. She tamps down the awful images taunting her since the botched calf rescue. That swinging shovel, the squish of metal —

Amaranta's terrified yelp as she hid her face in Griselda's chest.

She looks up.

Along the embankment, the man has followed her.

Much older than she, slender but toned, he has salt-and-pepper hair and a quizzical expression on his face. He raises his hands in an *I'm not here to harm you* manner that sends a chill down her spine. What does he want? With a slight wave, he backs up, inviting her to come ashore. What should she do? Swim for it?

Her throat goes dry and scratchy as she scans the shoreline for debris to fight him off if necessary. The beach is confettied with the detritus of its former glory and the funky art installments of the avant-garde who still claim to find beauty in what's become of this lake.

A few feet to her left, a moldering dining room chair with a sign nailed on that reads: END OF THE LINE. She'd have to pry the wooden legs apart to use it as a weapon, but the feet have sunk into the playa. Farther away, mailboxes to nowhere, rusted metal, rooted too deep in the sludged earth to pull out quickly enough. Same with the dilapidated and rusted playground, half-swallowed by the water. There's a smattering of broken beer bottles she makes her way toward.

"I didn't mean to startle you," the man calls across the bone-littered marsh.

The seashells crunch beneath her waders. She tightens her grip on the vials, her breath catching as he edges closer. Holy shit. El Cucuy. This is the guy Benny needs to bring in for questioning in Renata's disappearance. She doesn't hesitate. Her waders squelch as she runs feverishly away from this perv, checking behind her to make sure he's not following.

She's out of breath by the time she reaches her car. She grabs her bag for her inhaler, but her phone catches her attention before she can take a puff.

Eight missed calls and six texts, all from Mom. She presses the last missed call to dial her back. As the phone rings, she turns and watches El Cucuy trudging away through the sand, his shoulders hunched. What the shit was that about? Her heart's still cantering as Mom answers.

"Gris, tell me you have your sister." Her voice is frantic.

"No, why?"

As Mom recounts the details, bile fills Griselda's mouth.

"Where are you now?" Mom asks.

"About a mile from the beach house."

"I'm at the beach house now. Get over here."

Griselda strips off her waders and boots down to a pair of shorts and a T-shirt and stuffs the stanky gear into the trunk, then slaps on a pair of chanclas and slams the trunk. She floors it through the dirt toward Mom's old house, guilt and fear gnawing at her like a wild animal caught in a trap, chewing its own fur and skin and bone to get away. What if this has something to do with the calf rescue? Shit shit shit. What if someone saw them there? Followed them home? What if this was payback for what Griselda did? What if someone's after her too?

She stops the car a few hundred feet from the old house, swallowing back the acidic tang in her mouth. Why'd she take Amaranta to that damn protest? She knew it was wrong.

Mom's kneeling beside Tío Esteban in the waste of a yard near the rundown for-sale sign. Griselda stumbles out of the car, legs wobbly, bracing for a slap as Mom, who must have figured out where she took Amaranta, stands and rushes at her. Instead, she's enveloped in a tight hug, Mom's tears saturating her shoulder and dark hair before she pulls back just enough to clasp Griselda's face between her hands.

"I already called Benny. He's sending officers to the school and surrounding neighborhood. We'll find her, okay, mija?" The words seem like burrs pricking Mom's throat.

Tío Esteban joins them, putting his hand on their shoulders. "We've checked the house. Let's make a plan so we're all on the same page and can cover the rest of the town quickly." Like a conductor, he waves his arms in the directions they should take. "I'll canvass Main Street with the picture of Amar on my phone. Mal, you're heading home to meet Benny, right? Do you need Gris to go with you?"

Mal hiccups another sob but shakes her head vigorously no. "We should split up to cover the most ground, like you said, Chuy."

"Okay, so Gris, you can head over —"

She has no idea where he tells her to search. She already knows where she's heading.

13
MILK TEETH

The Veracruz house cramps with people, a thick soup of humidity and the sweat of too many bodies in this tight space. Papi's been making phone calls to the whole town. Through the din, Mal's family buzzes. A hive — or flies atop a dung heap. It's not them, exactly. It's their worry. Their fear. Palpable and sickening. And so damn loud. They've been through this before, this gnawing that leaves them helpless and desperate. *Bzzzzz.* A frayed wire spilling frenzied energy around the living room. It hovers above the candlelit ofrenda for Elena.

Benny showed up with a team, a barrage of officers rifling through their house for clues to her daughter's whereabouts, scouring the place like ants marauding, perhaps to demonstrate they're taking this seriously. Benny's her brother, after all, and a good detective.

The months following Elena's disappearance, Baby Benny had

gnawed on Mal's finger. He preferred the salt of her finger over the waxy rubber of the pacifier. Mal couldn't keep offering bottles; overfed, he just spit up the milky bile. Papi was no help. And Esteban? Pacifying his grief with Sharon, abandoning Mal to Mami and Papi's grief—and the son they refused to raise. So Mal carried him around noche y día, affixed to her hip, his mouth seamed to her pinky like a starfish to the pier of her skin. His bright blue eyes burned as she sang to him.

She can't hum the lullaby she sang to him and all her kids without devolving into sobs (*Arrorró, mi corazón . . . Hush-a-bye, my heart*) but it runs through her head as she grabs a wad of dark hair from Amaranta's hairbrush to give Benny for a DNA sample, before she realizes they all use the same brush. "Will it work if her hair's all mixed up with mine and Gris's?"

"No," Benny says. His eyes are still bright blue, but the years have softened their edges. "We need something definitively hers."

Only Amaranta's. They share everything.

"I've got a lock from her first haircut . . . and some milk teeth," Mal offers, her breath hitching. She never thought she'd need them for this. "I saved what she left the tooth fairy."

"Perfect," Benny concedes. "Those'll work."

Mal scrambles to the closet and retrieves the artifacts then returns to the pressure cooker of a living room. As she hands Benny the teeth—bulbed with dried blood—Yessi busts through the front door, clutching a clipboard and a stack of flyers with Amaranta's face, a photo so recent it seizes Mal's chest. "Oye, yunta," Yessi says, her voice threaded with sadness. "Lo siento."

Mal tries to respond, but her mouth fills with a thick paste. It glues her lips together. She's the chisme now, isn't she? Her daughter has followed the other missing girls. Tears are rolling down her cheeks when she realizes Yessi's been saying something.

"I'll hit the streets and post these all over town. We're organizing the search party."

It's strange how Yessi's treating this so much worse than her own prima missing. She didn't make posters for Renata.

Benny gives Yessi a brief nod. "Appreciate it, Yessi. Set up command outside, though. We need to keep the inside clear of foot traffic."

Yessi offers Mal a supportive hug but her touch stings. She does her best to stay stone-still and not shrug her friend away.

"We'll find her, yunta."

Mal nods. It's unreal.

When Yessi retreats, Benny introduces his lieutenant, but Mal can't hear her name through the beat of her own pulse pounding like too much bass in her head.

The lieutenant's badge reads Hernandez Pierce. She has a stern, no-nonsense look, hair slicked into a bun, gaze unflinching. "When did school let out?" the lieutenant asks.

"About two and a half hours ago . . . No, I guess three."

Those three hours are devastating. The thing about El Valle is Amaranta could be en route to Mexicali by now. In the back of a truck to Arizona, Los Angeles, or San Diego — through the desert in any direction. Three hours away from El Valle is a long way.

"Why'd you check out the Salton Sea when your daughter was last seen at school walking toward Johnny's?"

"I thought she might be with her sister, Gris."

Hernandez Pierce stares at her a moment longer than seems warranted before jotting something in her notepad. Mal looks to Benny, who avoids her gaze.

"Does your daughter party out there? At the sea? Or have friends who do?"

"I mean, no, but . . . my dad told me to check where Gris was researching since her sister's often in tow." Mal can't tell this staunch and stuffy uniformed woman that she also followed the stench of urine and the whisper of a horse-headed woman.

"Ms. Veracruz?"

Mal blinks.

"Are you okay? Do you need something to drink?"

Mal shakes her head, sits on the armrest of the floral-printed couch, several decades out of style.

"Gris is your eldest?"

Mal nods.

"She home?"

Mal scrolls back through Chuy's plan: he headed to Main Street and Mal came home. Where did Griselda go? Mal can't remember. "No, she's out looking" is all she can manage.

"And Amaranta's father?"

Mal hesitates, glancing to Benny at the lieutenant's implication. She knows why they're asking: Could this be a custody dispute? But how can she begin to put the complexity of their relationship into words? Benny raises his eyebrows but says nothing.

"One-night stand," Mal says, holding her head high, daring the lieutenant—or anyone else—to judge her.

The lieutenant pauses, her expression unreadable before she nods. "Understood," she says, her voice neutral. Her gaze flickers briefly toward Benny, who keeps his face blank, then returns to her notes, pen poised. "We'll explore all angles, including those outside of school. It's crucial we check with everyone close to her."

Mal's pretty damn sure Benny remembers Gus. They've never talked about it, but she dragged him all over the Salton Sea with Gus. And when Gris was born two years later, she carried them both around. There were no babysitters. Mal was the childcare, period.

If Mal shows any indication she's lying, the lieutenant doesn't seem to notice and Benny's silence corroborates. The script of questions continues. "When did your daughter leave school?"

"I'm not sure." If she *knew* that, they wouldn't be in this situation.

"We'll check with the staff. See if anyone saw her leaving campus."

"I checked with the office clerk first thing. She hadn't seen her. I got to Johnny's an hour after school let out, enough time for Amaranta to have grabbed lunch with Iggy. But Iggy was home sick." Her voice trails off, lost in the what-ifs whirling through her mind.

She's about to correct herself—first she spoke with Griselda's friend at Johnny's, then Sharon's vato, Oscar, but, as if from a nightmare, Mami wheels out of her room, her eyes occluded like a monsoon is rolling through her brain.

"What's happening? Why are all these people here?"

Benny ignores Mami's question, glancing around the living room as though the nurse might pop out. "Where's Lupita? Why isn't she watching Vero?"

"With her sick kid again," Mal says flatly.

"You need a new nurse."

Mami turns on Mal. "This is all your fault! *You* lost your sister!"

A wildfire ignites within Mal, but she forces herself to inhala, exhala. Her temples throb as she releases the hot and sticky tar of anger. She mouths to Papi, *I can't deal with this.*

Papi nods, his face creased with sadness as he starts wheeling Mami away, but she screeches, "You couldn't take care of your own goddamn daughter. And now she's gone!"

Mal opens her mouth que los peces but nothing comes out. For once, she understands what Mami is saying. The accusations she's flung for years on end—they've never been meant for Mal, have they? Mami's blaming *herself*. The loathing, the fear, the guilt—it's distinctly mothered. Festered over two decades into a monstrous mother.

They retreat down the hall, Papi humming "Que será, será" quietly into her ear.

Their family must be cursed. Who would steal two daughters from the same family? One lost daughter shatters a world. When there's nothing left to shatter, what else can break? What else but *everything*?

Hernandez Pierce punctures the awkward silence. "Which route did you take, and did you notice anything unusual?"

"East across A toward the school, right onto Imperial, past the high school, left on D, then into the parking lot across the street from Johnny's."

"The barbershop lot? You remained in your vehicle while you waited?"

Mal nods, a hot sheepish shame rushing her. She should've gotten out of the Jeep first thing and checked on Amar. She sat there while her baby girl could've been fighting off an attacker. Mal just fucking *sat* there.

"What time was that?"

"They got out at twelve thirty. I told her I'd pick her up at one thirty. It must've been one."

She was focused on introducing the girls to Gus and how dinner would go over. She'd wanted everything to be perfect. She'd made a cake.

The lieutenant is jotting down notes and asks without looking up, "Did your daughter make new friends or acquaintances recently? She start hanging out with anyone new?"

"No," Mal says automatically. "Amar's a passionate introvert. When she cares deeply about something, she can break out of her comfort zone, but she prefers to stay behind the scenes. She's had a handful of friends her whole life, and now she only hangs out with Iggy. She does stay over at her cousins' house sometimes, the cuates, but otherwise . . . no."

"She has a cell phone?"

Mal nods.

"Does she have a laptop or use a family computer? We'll need to check her email accounts and social media."

"She has a laptop, but I don't . . . she doesn't even have social media."

"TikTok, Snapchat, that kind of thing?"

Mal's one of those dashboard swivel heads. *No, no, no.* "She says she's not a seal flapping and honking for fish and won't pander to strangers for virtual rewards." Mal's laughing as she says this, but her eyes are leaking. Amaranta is so damn funny. She prays to the Mathematician in the Sky. *Please let my daughter be safe. Please.*

Mal can't breathe. Her eyes flutter back. No one else seems to notice.

"Just the same, we'd better check. And we'll get the phone records from the phone company. You use . . ."

"T-Mobile." She's boarded the wrong train; they're not asking the right questions. They're wasting time. "What's going on in Renata's case?" Mal interjects, directing her question to her brother.

He shakes his head as if saying, *This isn't the time.*

"There could be a connection, couldn't there? They've both disappeared, what . . . less than a week apart? That can't be a coincidence."

"Can we send out an Amber Alert?" Papi asks from the hallway.

"Only if we knew what car she got into. *If* she got into a car," Hernandez Pierce says. "Or someone saw her with an abductor. We need evidence she's in imminent danger —"

"Send out the damn Amber Alert," Mal cuts her off, turning to Benny. "Of course she's in danger! Or she'd have come *home!*"

Benny doesn't look Mal in the eyes but focuses on her nose, like a child averting their gaze when they've done something wrong.

"Look at me, goddamnit." She doesn't recognize the frantic pitch of her own voice. Mascara, tears, mucus, and salted mud globbed across her face, contorted with rage. No one says what they're all probably thinking — Mal's acting like Mami.

The tale goes when a daughter's lost in hell, her mama's lost with her. Or her mama's soul flies to her — and stays in hell. Mal already feels her soul leaving her body.

"We have protocols for Amber Alerts, Mal," Benny says. "We might not meet the criteria, but Yessi's got the search party going. We'll find her. Now's not the time to lose it."

"I'm not *losing it*," Mal snaps. "I'm trying to find my daughter."

Benny hesitates, "Could she have . . . run away?"

"Like Elena?" Mal's voice is ice. He must know how angry this conversation makes her. Too often, they don't believe a brown girl is worth searching for. Because Elena was sixteen, they assumed she ran. Benny should know better. "Elena didn't run away. Neither did Amar."

The lieutenant steps in. "We've alerted Border Patrol and will put out a BOLO." Mal must be making a face because the lieutenant clarifies, "*Be on the lookout.* We'll start our search around the high school, expanding from there. We'll also ask around at tonight's football game."

Suddenly, Mami appears again, still distressed, "Why are all these goddamn pigs here?"

Why does she keep escaping? Why won't Papi lock her in her damn room?

Mal thwarts the impulse to snap something cruel or inappropriate, but instead pulls a thick clump of air into her throat and counts to five *twice* before she says, "It's okay, Mami. These officers are just trying to help us find Amaranta. They won't hurt you."

Mami snorts, her eyes glinting with suspicion. "I don't trust 'em. They took my nieta."

"Vero, we're all trying to find Amar," Benny says. "We need your help."

She scrunches her face. "What do you want me to do? I can't even walk no more. My damn leg's gone."

"Mi amor, we need you to tell us if you remember anything peculiar before I came back from el mercado and took you out to el jardín conmigo." Papi's soothing tone irritates Mal. "You were aquí en la casa solita por una hora. Did Amaranta come home, ¿sí o no?"

Mami's occluded eyes grope around the room. "No me acuerdo de nada."

Mal leans in, the peppermint mouthwash of her mother's breath masking the rotted smell beneath. "Try to think. Did anyone come to the house? Did you hear anything outside? Did Amaranta come home at all? Did you talk to her?"

Mami's cat eyes narrow slightly, and Mal holds her breath. "Stevie brought me a mazapán rosa, but the girls didn't come home from banda practice."

Mal nods, fighting the urge to roll her eyes or cry at her mother's retreat into the past. She loves those little peanut marzipan candies. "Okay, thank you. That's helpful."

Benny shakes his head at Hernandez Pierce, who's been jotting in her notebook. She catches his gaze, and he mouths, *Strike that.* The lieutenant crosses out her last notes.

Papi pats Mami's hand gently. "It's four thirty, mi amor. Time to take your vitamins."

"Her Ativan," Benny whispers to his lieutenant.

Hernandez Pierce turns to Papi. "Was her nurse here today, did she see anything?"

"No, Lupita's got a sick kid. I was here all day, except for the hour I went to the store."

"I see." She jots more in her notebook. "When was the last time the nurse, Lupita?" She looks up from her notes, and Papi nods. "When was the last time Lupita was in the home?"

Papi considers. "La semana pasada."

"Can we have Lupita's contact info anyway? We should check in on her. See why she hasn't been here in a week."

Just then, Esteban comes inside, and a surge of hope flows through Mal.

"What happened? Has anyone on Main Street seen her?"

Esteban gives a disheartened shake. "I even stopped at the ice cream parlor June Callahan runs. Lots of kids there, but no one saw Amar."

"No one saw her at all today?"

"I'm sorry, Mallow Mar. It's just one street. There are plenty more to scour."

It's the main artery of the town. It runs from boca to culo. Mal was sure someone would've seen her.

"Could this be about Esteban?" Papi interjects. "Is there someone who means him harm? Something about the campaign?" He turns to his son. "Have you made any enemies, mijo? Anyone who'd want to hurt our familia?"

"It's politics, Pops," Esteban says. "It's the nature of the beast to get ugly. But I can't imagine anyone would stoop so low as to kidnap a child. I mean . . . God." The early-onset wrinkles in Esteban's face deepen.

"We'll need names if there've been threats," Benny says, his tone measured but edged with something sharp.

Esteban whips his phone out. "Let me get on the horn with my campaign manager, Lucinda, see what she can tell us. She's the brains of the operation. Then I'll call around."

Benny rolls his eyes and mutters under his breath, "I'm the actual *police* but sure, call your friends."

Esteban pauses and gives his shoulders a hard shake but says nothing as he steps into the backyard, disappearing into Papi's garden.

Mal perches on the edge of the sofa and runs a finger over her daughter's milk teeth on the coffee table, the trauma replaying through her — stained yellow with the stench of hay bales in the summer sun, yellow as the map Gus gave Mal where she'd marked red X's across her side of the Salton Sea and Chocolate Mountains, scouring for teeth and clues through the creosote and mesquite, one canteen of water strapped around her waist along with a knapsack to carry whatever evidence she found. Razor-sharp incisors, yes. But maybe other clues. Bones.

Baby Benny strapped around her in a baby carrier, a bottle tucked beside him, sweat pearled at her forehead. Something sharp crunched beneath her Converse, leaping from the ground, striking her ankle. She screamed, putting her hand to the pain. Benny shot out a gurgled cry of surprise at her sudden movement. But it wasn't a snake. Just the barbed end of a barrel cactus. A few drops of blood seeped down her ankle, pinkening her sock and shoe. She dabbed some spit on her thumb and held it to the prickling wound.

When she'd spotted the first tooth against the browning sand, she'd been surprised: it wasn't white but meat-colored, blackening at the root, already rotten. She'd crouched, balancing on her haunches, and turned the bulbous, pulpy tooth over carefully. Sharp at the biting end but swollen at the stringy root, like it was bleeding from within, at the gums.

She'd pinched the tooth between her finger and thumb for a closer inspection.

Could La Siguanaba leave behind teeth from the victims she takes? Scattering them on the shoreline and waiting? Another lure for her deadly games?

The tooth's bulbous root throbbed. It quivered.

No, *she* was shivering. In eighty-degree weather without any cover of shade, the sun boiling down. She was wet, sweating. Cold sweat.

She chucked the tooth to the ground where, before her eyes, it crumbled.

She shook her head like a wet dog wringing itself out. Looked again.

The bloody tooth was still there.

Baby Benny cooed. She felt his forehead. Not hot.

Dizziness swished through her. Maybe she was getting sunstroke. She should've worn a hat. She lifted her shirt atop Benny's head, took out her canteen and chugged back several gulps.

A pain at her mouth where the water touched. She winced as the coolness struck the nerve. The pain seared across her gum and up the left side of her face. She dropped to her knees in the sand, keeled over as nausea fishhooked her belly. Baby Benny wailed out to have been dropped on his nalgas, but she ignored him; her hand to her mouth, there it was—in stringy globules, the blood she'd searched for in the desert sand. It was coming from her own mouth.

She tugged. A crackling, then spongy as the bulb of a cactus flower being pulled from its spine—there, in her palm, a sharp incisor. Pulpy and dark at the center. Knifelike at the tip.

Her scream echoed like laughter. At the edges of her vision, the horse-headed woman glimmered like a mirage, stomping her hooves. She brayed as Mal pulled herself up and ran Benny all the way home. She tried telling Papi when she woke the next morning, showing him the empty space in her mouth, making a wide grimace. "Look, Papi. It's *gone*. An adult tooth."

The slur at the edges of his speech with morning beers was just beginning. "I told you to stop eating so much sugar. Don't think I didn't find all those soda pop and candy wrappers," handing her the basket of laundry to fold. "Pues nada, it was a baby tooth, un diente de leche. Mira." He pressed his thumb against her sore gum. "You can feel the grown-up tooth pushing in."

"It's weird it took so long," Mal stammered. "Besides, I could've sworn the baby one already fell out, and the grown-up one already came in a long time ago."

"Well, I feel it. Are you calling your father a liar?"

"No, of course not, Papi."

He patted her atop the head. "Está bien, mija." His breath was sour. Like musty bread left out too long. Molding at the edges. She missed Elena. She missed Esteban. But most of all, she missed Papi. The way he was before. He was drunk the rest of the day. The rest of the year. Un borracho until they moved away from that beach.

She's back in their living room in town, sunk deep into the floral couch cushion, breathing hard and clutching Amaranta's baby teeth. Through the glass of the French doors, she hears Chuy saying, "Luci." He's still talking to his campaign manager. She looks around the living room but no one seems to notice she's been gripped by a daymare. What does it mean?

Is La Siguanaba taunting her? She took her sister then, and she's taken her daughter now?

When Esteban returns from the patio, he sinks back in Papi's leather recliner. His face is drained. "No direct threats, but we've ruffled some feathers with farmers and activists... I just can't believe anyone in El Valle would fight that dirty."

Benny's frown deepens. "It's not just about the farmers and activists, Steve. What about stockholders, campaign contributors, they all have a stake in this Callahan lithium plant you're pushing. I wouldn't put it past them to dirty their hands to protect their investments." It's like he's forgotten he's here to be a detective, just arguing politics with his brother around the family table. "The people funding you have a lot of power. And they're not above using that power to get what they want."

The pelitos on Mal's neck stand on end. "Amar's a teen girl, not a politician or activist."

"You might be onto something there," Benny replies. "Gris *is* an activist. Or, at least, her boyfriend is. Has she taken Amar to any protests?"

"No." Mal shakes her head, slamming this shut. "She would never do that."

"Protests?" the lieutenant asks. "What protests?"

"I'll fill you in later," Benny says. "We should talk to Gris about Harlan's activities. The lithium plant could bring jobs, money, attention . . . but it could also mean corporate profits screwing the people over like always. And water for the plant might be diverted from El Valle's already dwindling supply. I wouldn't be surprised if folks took drastic measures to prevent it."

"As far as I know," Mal says, "Harlan protests his dad's beef plant, not his grandpa's proposed lithium plant."

"No one would kidnap a *child* over *politics,*" Esteban insists. "Isn't it usually someone the kid knows?"

"I *saw* someone at the school who might've seen Amar," Mal bursts, "but it has nothing to do with Gris's activism or Chuy's campaign. Just your ex-wife."

"What did Sharon do this time?" Esteban asks, heaving a deep sigh.

"No, it's her new vato."

"That guy Oscar?" Benny asks. "I'll have him looked into."

Esteban stands. "And I'll offer a reward for any intel that leads to her safe return." He heads toward the back door, phone in hand.

Benny rolls his eyes and lets out a snorting sound.

Mal stands too, a wire ready to snap, "Benny, I'm going with you to question Oscar."

He ignores Mal and turns to Esteban, stopping him before he heads into the backyard. "Steve, a reward could just call the crazies out, not to mention send us spiraling through a maze of false leads. It's a bad idea."

Mal grabs Benny and turns him to face her. "Benito, *I'm coming with you*. I've watched enough detective shows to know how this works. We need to check with her BFF, Iggy. She was supposed to go to Johnny's but stayed home *sick*." She says this last part with incredulity.

Benny's expression hardens. "Mal, you're not coming with me. This isn't a TV show. Stay at the house in case she calls or comes home."

Mal turns to Papi, "You can stay, right?"

"Of course, 'jita. Your mami and I will be here and help with the search party."

Mal turns back to Benny. "See? I'm coming."

"I've sent patrol cars to look for her out by the school. Stay put at the house." Benny locks his hands on Mal's shoulders. "Amar's case will get attention. All eyes are on Steve. The community will rally behind his niece too."

He starts out the door, but Mal follows, close on his heels. When he realizes she's right behind him, marching toward his unmarked sedan, he turns, sighs loudly, and rolls his eyes. "Come on, Mal. I can't take the victim's mother out on an interrogation —"

"Don't you dare call my daughter *the victim*," Mal cuts in sharply. "She's *not* a victim. She's coming home safe."

"That's not what I meant. But see? You proved my point. I need to keep my family and work separate. It's our best chance. You let me do what I do, and I'll find her. I promise."

"Don't promise me nada, Benito. Your family *is* your work. I'm coming. End of story."

"You want me to break every rule in the book? With the sheriff breathing down my neck? Besides, it's counterproductive. Who'd admit anything with the vic —?" He stops himself, his jaw popping. "With the kid's *mom* right there? Trust me. This is what I need to do."

"Oh, please. It'll be a chat with friends and family." Tears are forming in her eyes, and she decides to cut the crap and level with him. "I can't just *sit here*." Like she sat in the Jeep, windows down, music on the radio while her daughter was being abducted—or worse.

Mal cups his face between her palms. This tall, sculpted brother-son of hers. She stares with every fiber of mothering persuasion she can summon as he squirms beneath her gaze.

"Benito, stop arguing. I trust you to do your job, but it's *my* job to protect my children, okay? I'm *coming* with you."

She lets go, and he clenches his jaw. He looks like he hasn't had a good sleep in a week. He takes his cases seriously. First Renata. Now his own niece.

He groans the way adult men do when they know their mama is right. Even if it means they'll hear about it from their spouse or friends or boss. He checks his watch. "I can't believe I'm doing this. We have until seven before the game."

Mal squeezes his hands.

"At least clean your face," Benny says, kissing her atop the head then reaching into his pocket for a handkerchief. She raised the kind of man who carries one. "You're a mess."

Through the doorway, Papi calls, "We'll find her, mijita."

Did he tell himself this when his daughter disappeared? Does he still tell himself this—twenty-five years later?

14
YOU OKAY IN THERE?

Griselda tries to squash the dread building within her as she heads toward the more affluent side of town, scanning the storefront windows of the shops and restaurants as she crosses Main Street. How can Amaranta be lost in this tiny town full of busybodies and chismosas? Someone's bound to have seen her. Unless she doesn't *want* to be found.

No, her hermanita's not cruel. She wouldn't intentionally put her family through this.

Could she have been kidnapped?

Except that circles Griselda right back to her initial question. Wouldn't the window-watchers of the town have seen something while peering through their drapes? Surely, someone would've noticed a kid being snatched against her will. Especially a kid as vibrant as her hermanita. Amaranta wouldn't have gone quietly—she's tougher than she looks.

She's probably tucked away in a quiet corner of the library, engrossed in one of her sci-fi novels, oblivious to the world around her. Tío Esteban's canvassing Main Street, so he'll cover the library. He'll find Amaranta reading, unaware she's flustered everyone.

What nags Griselda, however, is if she *were* at the library, she'd answer her phone.

What if something terrible has happened? What if it's Griselda's fault for taking her to that stupid calf rescue? For hitting that awful guy with the shovel? Someone saw? Someone's paying Griselda back? An eye for an eye?

A stately wrought-iron gate marks the Callahan property, beyond which a winding driveway stretches toward a red-bricked, white-trimmed mansion that practically puffs out its chest, lording itself over the rest of the neighborhood.

She pulls in but leaves the engine running, dropping her head to the steering wheel, spiraling. What will she say to Harlan? *Did we get my sister hurt or worse? Could it have anything to do with Renata? Have you heard from her? Oh, by the by, you asked me to marry you last night but you've just been a placeholder until I work up the nerve to admit to myself and everyone I love that I don't belong in this town.*

What she saw as a hookup, he saw as a marriage proposal. If he'd only asked during sex, that would be one thing. But he said it again that night, when they were cuddled in his bed. She pretended to be asleep.

If she hadn't known him since elementary school—what an utter goofball he was, so heart-on-sleeve—it would be creepy. But he's put her on a pedestal their whole lives. He's a hopeless romantic and cries at all the rom-coms he's made her watch over the years. *The Notebook* and *Crazy, Stupid, Love* are his faves (he has a serious guy crush on Ryan Gosling). In middle school, he'd make her practice the move from *Dirty Dancing* where he holds Baby over his head, except Griselda insisted they do it in his pool since he used to drop her before his growth spurt in high school when he got buff enough to do it on dry land. He held her in the air a full ten seconds when they tried it, a little tipsy, at their graduation party. Then she went off to college while he stayed in El Valle to take over the farms as the Callahans do. Sometimes she wishes they'd gone off together, like Tío Esteban and Sharon went to Stanford. Still, look at them now — divorced. Griselda guesses all relationships are doomed in their own way.

A knuckle raps against the driver's-side window, dredging her up from her spiral.

"Gris? You okay in there?"

Harlan's dad glances in, all fatherly concern. He's got on a bomber jacket and muddy boots, and his cheeks are flushed like he's been exercising. All the men in this family are pretty damn good-looking. Even Old Man Callahan's kinda hot for an old guy. Word is, he used to be a heartthrob. He had rizz. Makes sense, given what a stud Harlan turned into. In the nerdiest way.

"Hey, Mr. Callahan," she says, rolling down the window. "Things have been better. My little sister didn't come home from school. I came to recruit Harlan to join the search."

His expression goes from fatherly concern to neighborhood watchman. "That's . . . alarming. How long has she been missing?"

"Just a few hours, but she knows better than to put our mom through this, so . . ."

He nods. "Well, sure. With what your family's been through." He leans against the car, resting a hand on the open window. "Tell you what, June and I will join the search too."

"That'd be great, thanks," Griselda manages.

"I'm sure Harlan's loafing around somewhere."

She nods, shuts off the ignition, and grabs her things. Sean steps back and holds his hand out to help her alight from the car like he's a chauffeur.

"I'll join you kids in a few. June's out in her garden. Let me clean off." He gestures to his dirt-stained designer jeans and mud-caked work boots. "There's a party forming?"

The way he says *party* makes it sound festive. Gris shrugs. "I'm sure my mom's friend Yessi's organizing something. Or Tío Esteban."

"Good ole Steve. He'll have this well in hand, I'm sure."

He walks with her to the edge of the lush, green grass that mocks the droughts and water wars since the floods destroyed Mom's seaside town and Old Man Callahan ignited a decades-long legal battle by accusing neighboring farmers of profligate irrigation.

While the oldest water rights stayed with a handful of the wealthiest farmers like the Callahans, water barons who control a whopping *seventh* of the Colorado River's flow, the rest of El Valle's water got siphoned away to Los Angeles. The unintended side effect? The new laws that enforced stricter irrigation practices so farmers' hoses stopped dripping their leaky noses into the Salton Sea dried the playa, setting the toxins free. Old Man Callahan kept his water but launched an environmental cataclysm in the process.

Gris almost jabs at Sean's watered lawn but decides against stirring the pot. She's too worried about Amaranta to start a mess with Harlan's dad.

Sean gives her shoulder a warm squeeze and says, "Just go right in," then tromps toward the back gate, leaving mud clots across the grass that landscapers will no doubt scoop up when they come in their trucks.

She stands on the porch. It's weird not to ring the bell like usual.

Screw it, she has permission. She swings the door open to a grand foyer with marble floors and a crystal chandelier. A pair of matching armchairs upholstered in white sits below a large oil painting of Harlan's great-grandparents. The family loves to remind everyone how long they've been in El Valle. Over a century, they've staked their lives and livelihoods to this land.

"Harlan?" she calls as she heads toward his bedroom, an attached mother-in-law suite off the family room toward the back of the house, which in a truce between his parents' mismatched styles, drips a Western theme that clashes with the posh front decor. Mounted antlers, a tree stump coffee table with a leather sofa, hunting rifles on the wall beside a flat-screen TV alongside stiff animal heads and family photos. One shows Sean and Harlan holding a dead elk. Another is a framed USDA certification for Beef Tooth.

That sharp metal shovel flashes through her mind. It strikes her sister's head. Of course that's not how it happened. But she knew the protest was stupid and dangerous. She just had no idea it would spiral so badly. Lead her to assault someone . . . Lead her sister to . . . disappear.

"Gris! What are you doing here?"

Griselda jumps at Harlan's voice. He's sporting a towel that barely clings to his V-shaped hips and sex lines, hair wet and slick, face ruddy and dripping.

He must realize he sounds like a douche. "I mean, hey, Gris! Come here, babe!" He saunters toward her and pulls her in for a kiss, but she stays rigid, not in the mood for their banter that inevitably leads to sex. Especially when there's nothing but a towel between —

He looks into her face. "What's wrong?"

"Amaranta didn't come home," Griselda breathes out, chest constricted.

"From the fundraiser last night?"

"No, from school. She should've been at Johnny's with a friend, but when my mom went to pick her up, she wasn't there." She pulls out her inhaler and takes a puff.

"You sure she's not just running around the neighborhood?"

"She wouldn't do that to us."

"Sorry, I'm an ass." He's got the kind of open and expressive face where whatever he's thinking shows up there, so earnest it would be endearing any other time. "Should we start driving around looking for her? You called the police?"

"Yeah, all of that, but . . ." A split sack of feed scatters in her stomach. "I'm scared this has something to do with what I did . . . Amar shouldn't have been there. What if someone's *after her because of me?* What if they saw . . ."

He pulls back, running a hand through his wet hair. "Nah, don't think like that. Your sister has nothing to do with any of it. She just tagged along."

"Any of what?" She clutches her inhaler tighter, the plastic creaking under her grip as she tries to steady her breath. "*Is* there something going on? Did Raul say something?"

"No, I told you. Raul said we're in the clear."

"We're obviously *not*," Griselda insists. "And I don't know if I want to be in the clear anyway. Maybe I should just confess so the police can look into everyone who was at the cattle yard that night. Have you heard from Renata?"

He sighs deeply and pulls at a thread on the towel. "No. But, I mean . . . she's a big girl. She can take care of herself. And anyway, no one's after any of the protestors, I promise you."

"How can you be sure? What if your dad's sick of us fucking with his business. What if he hired . . . I don't know . . . some thugs to get rid of us."

Harlan's not usually a gaslighter, but his condescending expression could win mansplainer of the year. "Come on, Gris. *My* dad? He's a chump. He's not a *thug.*"

"He's a bully at the very least. *He absolutely could do something like that*. We're costing him a fortune in missing cattle. He's a *business-man*. I think it's time to fess up."

"Gris, cut it out. My dad's *not* behind this——"

"Then why hasn't that guy's injury been in the newspaper? If he was just a regular old security guard hospitalized after an attack, wouldn't *someone* have reported it? Why's it all hushed up if your dad's not doing something shady?"

"Because nothing happened, I told you. There's nothing to report. That guy's *fine*. Will you drop this already?"

"How do you *know*?" She says this slowly, like she's speaking to a kindergartener.

"Raul told me." He answers her the same way. "He erased the security footage. We're clear, Gris. I'm sure this has nothing to do with your sister."

"What if he . . ." she whispers into the crook in his chest where his breastbone meets the indentations of his abs. "Kidnapped Amaranta? As payback——"

"He didn't."

"Stop being so cavalier." She's shaking so hard she has to clamp her hands around her chest to steady herself. "This isn't like you."

"I'm sorry . . . I just don't want you getting all worked up over this. You cried for *hours* last night. You got shitfaced the night before. I'm worried about you."

She's not listening. "I mean, maybe you're right, it's not the security guy . . . but it's still not *nothing*. My baby sister is *missing*. Literally a *week* after that Renata chick went missing. What if it's a serial killer? First Renata, now Amaranta?" She's been keeping these kinds of terrifying speculations at bay, but they won't stop churning inside her. "What if it's El Cucuy?"

"Well, which is it? Did she get kidnapped for payback or taken by a monster?"

She's crying now. He wraps her in a tight hug. His muscular chest, still damp, smells like citrus and cedar.

"Gris, you don't believe in monsters."

"I know. But people can be monsters."

"Let me get dressed, and we'll sort this all out." The way he says *we* like they're already a married couple balls a fist in her gut.

Just then, Sean and June appear in the family room doorway, hand in hand. June's slacks and pearls contradict her husband's ruggedness, like their varying styles in the house.

"Honey, I just heard about your sister. I'm so sorry, but I'm sure she's fine. Harlan used to scare me senseless. He gave us so many sleepless nights, darting off without telling me." June's voice is TV-Land-mom kind, but Griselda clenches her teeth as now the third member of this household suggests Amaranta simply ran off. "But we always found him . . . up to some mischief or another. We'll find Amaranta. Even so, I know what your family has been through, and this must feel just awful . . ." June smooths down her pearls. Her expression is genuine, but with all due respect, how can June know what Griselda's family has been through?

Griselda only nods.

"Harlan, honey, don't stand there dripping water all over the floor." June says it like she's just noticed him. "We're joining the search party."

She's so resolute and upbeat, it's like the whole family believes themselves — like their good fortune will rub off on the rest of the town's lowly subjects.

It'll be like a hunting party with hound dogs and a fox and an elegant banquet afterward, a chance to show off the latest fashion and gossip. Of course, they'll find Amaranta. If the Callahans are looking for her.

15
WHAT'S A LITTLE HORROR

From the driver's seat, Benny lets out a deep, pensive sigh and turns to Mal as she's buckling her seat belt. He puts a comforting hand on her shoulder. "Lieutenant Hernandez Pierce will file the missing person report at the station and then check with all the hospitals as well as review the footage from the two traffic cams on Main. We're also exploring whether anything was captured by the high school cameras, Johnny's, or any security systems from the neighbors. You went out to the Salton Sea . . . should we extend our search out there?"

"No. It was a gut thing. Esteban and I already checked the old house. Nothing but rats."

"Okay, so we'll talk to Oscar first. He's the last person to see Amaranta." He types something into his phone. "I'm asking Hernandez Pierce to run a background check on him."

"Sharon will love that."

"Where's Sharon searching, by the way? With the cuates?"

"No idea."

"Okay, I'll have my lieutenant call her too. You have her number?"

"You mean you don't?" She nudges his ribs. Benny's never liked Sharon, whether Mal's opinions rubbed off over the years or he just has better taste than Esteban. Sal Limón, Benny's new husband, doesn't come over much since Benny doesn't come over much. But he's a keeper.

"The game starts at seven. Half the town will be there. You'll go center field and make a plea for information. My guys are already canvassing around the school in case anyone in the neighborhood saw anything. Plus, the field's on her way home."

They drive in silence, the only sound the quiet hum of the engine and the soft whir of the air-conditioning, before Mal muses, "Sometimes I truly believe we're cursed."

"Yeah, I know what you mean." The way he drums his thumbs on the steering wheel reminds Mal of the stimming he'd do as a child, sitting in Papi's recliner and knocking the back of his head against its soft cushion, sometimes vocalizing in a low moan almost chantlike, sometimes silent, until he fell asleep.

"Renata's disappearance can't be a coincidence, Benny. You know more than you're telling me. Whatever it is, I can handle it. It could lead us to Amaranta."

The thrumming on the steering wheel goes chaotic, as if his thumbs are spasming. After a few moments of what sounds like a frantic heartbeat, he clears his throat with a loud hum, another one of his tics since childhood. It sounds like he's blowing his nose inward, imploding.

Finally, as Mal knew he would, he relents. "She was last seen alongside the sea."

"Yessi told me as much. Give me what the chisme chain doesn't already know."

"She was out by the highway waiting for a guy."

Mal's insides twinge. "What guy?"

"Well," he sucks his teeth and lets out a breath. "Her mom and ex-boyfriend have a lot to convey on that subject."

"Who's her mom? Do I know her?"

"Carmen Ruiz. Her family were campesinos, picking up and down the state. She settled in El Valle a few years after having Renata. She lives in the Section 8 out by Malan."

"Who does she suspect?" As if Mal needs to ask.

Another gust of congested nose-blowing. "Gustavo Castillo."

Mal lets out a slow exhalation. It never hurts less. "But did anyone *see* him out there?"

"Nope." He says this like he's blowing out a smoke ring. A fat puff in the shape of a zero.

"Who saw Renata out by the highway, then? Are they a credible witness?"

"Her ex, Raul Castañeda. He's the one who dropped her off."

"You verify his alibi? Yessi mentioned he was bartending, except he works at the meat plant."

"Yep." As they turn onto Sharon's street, Benny's thumbs go quiet on the steering wheel. "Raul dropped her off and then went to his bartending gig, seen by plenty. Including the Callahans."

"Where's he bartend?"

"The hunter's lodge."

"Figures." That same club Sean was talking about the other night.

"He claims he wanted to wait out there with Renata, but she told him to take off. Said it would be weird for her ex to be hanging around when her current man showed up."

"And why are Raul and Carmen so convinced her current man was Gus?"

"I don't think they were. In their minds, her man *didn't* show. Gus did."

Mal mulls this over. She could just tell Benny she was with Gus all Saturday night. He probably already knows. "Isn't there some kind of record of who she was talking to? On her phone?"

He makes a noise somewhere between a frustrated grunt and an amused chuckle. "You'd think savvier tech would make my job easier. Digital footprint and whatnot. But people have gotten smarter too. She used a secret messaging app. Encrypted, burn mode, untraceable."

"Dang. What was she hiding?"

"That's the thing. Maybe nothing. Kids all use these things now. It's like they're practicing to become spies or cheaters. These apps are ubiquitous, designed to look like games or, get this, calculators. Fools will do anything to avoid getting caught. Hide My Text, WhatsApp, Signal. At any rate, she did most of her messaging through the encrypted app as far as we can tell."

In the 1990s, when Elena disappeared, people just swallowed the notes they passed in the hallways. Or set them on fire with Bic lighters, watching them burn like joint paper sizzling on the blacktop.

There was a pay phone by the band room. That was as close to anonymous or encrypted as anyone got in El Valle back in the day. Before caller ID, people could press *69 to call back a number, but if the call came from the pay phone, they were shit outta luck. There's a picture of Elena in her cheer uniform posing in front of the pay phone. Mal never knew who her sister was calling — some guys don't want people to know they're dating the town slut. Maybe Renata's secret boyfriend was the same.

"What about that chavalón she was seeing? The high school kid? Yessi told me she got arrested at the swine barns. Has anyone talked to him?"

"Yeah, a friend of her little brother's." He shakes his head and offers a little mirthless chuckle. "He was at a youth group function for his church, go figure. A sleepover thing in the church gym."

"Church *gym*?"

"That big church out on the highway."

She sighs. "You don't think Amaranta went to those protests, do you?" The thought's been wriggling around inside her like a worm in the tequila bottle since Papi brought up the possible implications of Esteban's politics.

"Have you asked Gris?"

"Not yet," Mal admits, fending off a bout of nausea at the strong stench of piss. Not again. She rolls down the window, a gust of autumn heat blasting her in the face, making her eyes sting. The horse-headed woman creeps behind stop signs and fence posts and mesquite trees, following Benny's car. Mud and soil wedge beneath her fingernails. She's digging frantically. She looks up, her muzzle slick with black loam. Her face is Mami's face . . . is Mal's face. Mud gives way to wet earth, then a pool. A well. No. Blood. A thick, sticky pool of birthing blood and afterbirth. She dives in face-first, squirming and wriggling through the earth, searching, pulling hard at the squish of umbilicus until it snaps taut, and Mal gasps, realizing what it's snagged on. Curling like snakes, the fleshy rope tightens around her younger daughter's neck. *"Amaranta!"*

Mal thrusts her fingers through the bulbous noose that threatens to choke her daughter, whose lips are purple and swollen, her eyes bulging.

But as Mal pulls her up from the ground like a root vegetable, gnarled and dirt-encrusted, it's clear she's bound to something else, dragging behind her by the cord around her neck. Stringing from Amaranta like pearls on a necklace come three other girls, each as blanched and death-slick as the previous. Renata. Elena. Noemi.

"Mal?"

"Huh?"

"We're here." Benny parks his unmarked sedan against the curb.

They're in front of Sharon's house. Mal blinks a few times, reorienting herself to the waking world. Benny's staring at her.

"You sure you're alright to do this? I'm going out on a limb here letting you come."

"I can go to my brother's house anytime I want." She flings open the passenger door, huffy and indignant although she's still shaking from whatever the hell she just saw.

"It's not his house anymore," Benny reminds her.

"It sure isn't. She's letting it go to pot." Mal looks it up and down, this house Sharon won in the divorce, along with the cuates except for the weekends, although Mal's pretty sure Esteban gave Sharon todo eso sin lucha. He always placated her. Pues, the cuates *are* little shits.

A VOTE VERACRUZ FOR SENATE sign adorns the front lawn like a pink flamingo. Sharon's stayed loyal to his campaign, probably just to mooch off his political glow-up.

As Benny and Mal approach the walkway, she scrolls back to last weekend's sleepover. Before today, she hasn't thought about Oscar one way or the other, but it troubles her now—this new guy living here. He's supposedly a church man. That doesn't mean squat though.

She follows Benny to the front door, combatting her shallow breaths with as deep an inhalation as she can manage, her chest resisting as she counts to five. She's clenching her fists. Her short nails dig into her skin, leaving crescent-shaped imprints like well-worn ruts. If that vato touched a single hair on Amaranta's head . . .

Sharon answers in high-waisted jeans and a bustier, drink in hand. Mal rolls her eyes. Of course she's home drinking instead of out searching for her niece. Typical Sharon. It's bad enough she's vying for *Real Housewives of the Borderlands*. But she couldn't put her drink down long enough to *pretend* she cares about Amaranta?

"Mal! I was about to take the cuates out searching. I just needed a quick pick-me-up." She says this without a trace of embarrassment or shame, mascara smudged across her temples.

"It's been three hours, Sharon."

"Hey, Shar. Good to see you." Benny is tactful as ever. "Oscar here? We have a few questions."

"Oscar? Why? He's been here with me all day."

"Except when he was at the high school?"

Sharon looks into her drink, clinks the ice back and forth, takes a swig. "Yes, of course. Except for that."

Mal has the sudden urge to grab her ex-sister-in-law by the shoulders and shake her.

Sharon opens the door wider like she'll deign to grant them entry. Mal looks around.

Sometimes when kids run away, they go to family's houses. Amaranta spends time here; it's not impossible she might be here now. Sharon's always billed herself as the fun aunt. The cool aunt. A sharp pang nudges Mal's rib cage as she trudges toward the staircase, calling out, loudly, "Amaranta?"

Benny and Sharon exchange a glance.

"She's not here, Mal," Sharon says flatly, like she's wounded Mal would think she's hiding her daughter. "I told you that when you called earlier."

"You *also* told me you'd go out searching for her."

"I will! I am . . . I just needed a drink."

The pouty act might work on Esteban but Mal's inured. It's one of Mami's favorite manipulative tools. "You don't mind if I look around then?"

The cuates saunter to the balcony atop the stairs like they've stepped out of some gothic, overpriced fashion catalog. Seriously, it's like the Olsen twins went emo. They're fraternal, but their whole vibe's a double vision.

"Hey, Wednesday and Pugsley," Mal says, "have you seen your cousin?"

They shake their heads, perfectly synchronized, then turn away in an obvious snub. These assholes *can't* be her brother's kids. Seriously. Why doesn't anyone in this house care that Amaranta's *missing*? It's not normal for family to act this way.

"I'm going upstairs," Mal says, already lunging after the cuates, who've disappeared into one of their rooms.

"It's a mess up there," Sharon protests, but when Mal whips her head back to glare at her ex-sister-in-law, Sharon shrugs.

She starts with Xochitl's bedroom. It's not bedecked in magazine clippings the way hers and Elena's was, nor spackled with science posters like Amaranta's and Griselda's side.

It's blisteringly pale and sterile like she's walked into an air-sealed research lab. Everything's white, pristine, tidy. White walls, furniture, bedspread. The floor, hardwood, is the only thing with any color but equally bare and cleaner than their kitchen table at home. She checks under the bed. Nothing but hardwood, the diametrical opposite of hers and the girls' beds, where the underside acts as a brimming storage space.

A quick scan of the closet shows no Amaranta hiding—and why would she be hiding here? But Mal *feels* something, same as at the house at the Salton Sea, like she *needs* to examine Sharon's house closer. All the clothes are variations of black and white. A colorless wardrobe for a colorless niece. What does Amaranta do while hanging out here? What could she possibly have in common with her cousin? She regrets sending her here so often. She'll remedy that as soon as she finds her daughter. They'll have their heart-to-heart.

Xolotl's room appears much more normal, gradients of color, posters of bands on the wall, bric-a-brac and clutter without the compulsive tidiness of his sister. And yet, the starkness in the center of the room is the twins themselves, just standing there, staring at Mal like she's another species.

"Just checking," Mal finally says. "You understand."

They make no indication they've heard her, just keep staring like creepy children of the corn. She needs to have a serious talk with her brother when this is all over and Amaranta's safe. WTF is wrong with his kids? She'd pegged them as spoiled posers. But they are acting, what? High?

She sighs while they watch her get on her knees and check beneath Xolot's bed. Not as bare as Xochitl's. She won't mention the porn mag that reassures her.

It's the closet that startles her. She yelps when she opens it, turns quickly toward her niece and nephew, whose faces grow smug, the slightest expressions of amusement prickling the corners of their mouths. They're enjoying her discomfort. El Clóset, she'd call this, haunted. No hanging or folded clothes, no laundry basket, no boxes of memorabilia, shoes, games, nor anything else one might usually store in a closet.

"Do your parents know about this?" she asks.

Xochitl lets out a high-pitched shrill of laughter. Just one. A chihuahua-like yelp.

"They don't care what we do as long as our grades stay high enough for Ivy Leagues," Xolotl peacocks, puffing his chest in a way Mal recognizes as defensive.

"This is twisted, kids. I mean...I...did Amaranta see this?" She's half-stammering, half-simmering. "Did you include her in this?"

This life-size cut-out goes beyond *Twilight*. This is some vampire porn. Not sexual, but pornographic nevertheless. She's not being a prude either. This is some twisted shit. Two vampires, a young man and a young woman, taking a victim from behind, their fangs sunk into a bare neck, blood curdling down the throat, splattering their chest, like an IV has sprung a leak. The nonconsensual look on the victim's face feels so *wrong*.

Mal peers past the disturbing scene at something infinitely worse.

Her intestines pinch.

The built-in shelves are lined with dozens of little glass jars, each sealed with a screw-top lid. Each has its own label with a person's name. Maribel Sanchez. José Rodriguez. Emma Elliott. Dayton Joseph. Classmates? People in town? Neighbors? Made-up characters? Please let these be fake people.

Because inside each jar — pooling at the bottom, congealing at the sides, crusting at the golden or silver lids, brick-brown or bright red, unmistakable — blood.

"Please tell me that's paint," Mal whispers, her throat ragged. The cuates are full-on smirking now but stay silent. The vibrations of their barely contained mirth clash with her unabashed horror. "What are you doing with all this *blood*?"

A little refrigerator hums from the side of the closet. Mal lurches forward, flinging it open, terrified she'll find a jar with Amaranta's name on it.

These jars remind her of the jar of teeth at Gus's place.

The sharp incisors of the bloodsuckers in the cardboard cutout leer like the canines on a chupacabra. Goat-sucker.

A hard shiver clamps the nape of her neck and shakes her whole body.

"Benny!" She pivots hard on her heels, glaring at the twins, yelling past them. "You'd better come up here!" Her voice echoes through the little closet, and she steps into the bedroom to yell again, "Benny, I found something weird."

Xolotl sighs and Xochitl giggles, a hollow sound. Xolotl whispers something imperceptible in his sister's ear, and she nods.

"This is truly *not* okay, you two. I hope you know that. Where did you get this blood? Did you *take* it from people? And *how*? Blood can't just *sit* in jars like this. It's growing bacteria. Please tell me you don't do what I think you do with this blood."

Benny's heavy footsteps up the staircase reverberate through the hallway, Sharon's high heels clacking on the hardwood behind him.

His somber expression turns into deep concern when she ushers him into the vampiric shrine.

"There's a phlebotomy kit here." He points the tip of his pen to a first-aid box of hypodermic and butterfly needles with lock syringes and blood sample tubes with screw-on lids.

Sharon stands behind them and mutters, "These fucking twins, I swear to God, they'll be the death of me," then gulps down the rest of her drink.

"We need to find out if this has anything to do with Amaranta, right?" Mal asks Benny, her voice quavering. She wobbles. "The cuates won't tell me anything. None of these jars have Amaranta's name, but still. You need to question them and test this stuff for her DNA, right?"

"We could—but it'll take weeks to get results on this many

specimens. A week if I call in a favor. But we need to find Amar *now*, Mal. You know that." He looks around the room with distaste, perhaps even repugnance, or is that Mal projecting?—but what's missing in his expression is suspicion or concern. Like he's saying *This shit can wait*. "I'll talk to them, my gut says let's go find Oscar."

Why are both Sharon and Benny downplaying this? Mal's seen *20/20* exposés about kids who kidnap and kill. It's chilling. "What *happened* at that sleepover, Sharon?" Mal demands.

Sharon scoffs, all sentis, even as the evidence of some weird-ass shit from her son's closet stares them in the face. Mal wants to slap the fakeness off her. The thought startles her. She's never reached for violence.

"Nothing happened. Amaranta can't take a little joke, got upset, and I calmed her down while she waited for you to pick her up. You know the rest. You came and got her. That's it."

"A joke? So that's not blood? Not human blood?"

Sharon shrugs.

"And what do you mean *I came and got her*? She didn't spend the night?"

"No . . . she left. I thought . . . you picked her up?"

Mal's shaking her head. So Amaranta *has* been lying to her.

If she left Sharon's last weekend . . . and Mal was at Gus's all night, where did she *go*? Saturday night. When Renata disappeared.

"Do you know what time she left?"

"Lord, I have no idea. After dark, I guess."

"Shit," Mal says. She turns to the cuates, who've both plastered such fake innocent expressions across their faces Mal can't stand it. "This is more than kids being kids," Mal whispers to Benny, clamping a hand to his shoulder. "Mira, Benito, they might be family, but they creep me out. And Amar was here on Saturday, okay? Pues, she's been acting weird. Something was *off*."

His face is inscrutable before he takes a deep inhalation. "Okay, I'll call a team over here to see what we can find."

Sharon has joined them in the huddle.

"You're being ridiculous," she says, her voice a bit slurry. "You won't find anything. We'd never let anything happen to my niece. I love that girl. We all do. So my kids are a little screwy. After that divorce, who could blame them. That doesn't make them monsters."

"Kids make mistakes," Mal says flatly.

Sharon swishes the dregs of her glass. "This isn't a lead and he knows it, but he'll do anything Mommy Mal says."

"That's enough, Sharon," Benny warns.

"*That's enough, Sharon,*" she singsongs back, and it's hard for Mal to imagine this woman was ever mayor, she's so infuriatingly immature, one of the countless reasons Esteban called it quits, no doubt. What will he say about his twins' bloodthirst? The thought sours her stomach. She's not squeamish. She's a butcher, for fuck's sake. But the idea that her niece and nephew have been bloodletting other *children,* maybe her own *daughter* who's now *missing* . . . Does Chuy know his kids are this messed up?

Within the hour, Benny's uniformed officers are scouring the rest of the house for any trace of Amaranta. Meanwhile, Mal and Benny are out back where Oscar's tinkering with his motorcycle near the garage in a white tank top and long Dickies shorts that meet his white knee-high socks and white leather Adidas like it's a regular Friday evening.

His earbuds remind Mal of two swollen black ticks lodged in his ears. No wonder he's heard nothing. Either he's a dumbass — or he's a full-fledged sociopath who's done something horrible to her daughter.

"Oh, hey," he calls warmly when he notices them, yanking out the earbuds and stuffing them into his khaki pocket. "Have you found our girl yet?"

The way he says *our girl* makes Mal sick.

"That's why we're here," Benny says with a level of diplomacy that grates on Mal's already frayed nerves. She wants to cut through Benny's niceties, jab her knee into Oscar's spine, pin his hands, and bellow into his ear: *What did you do with my daughter, you piece of shit?* She's jumpy and combustible. Is this just what it feels like? For the world to split open and swallow her child? Oscar saw Amaranta last; he admitted as much when Mal drove from Johnny's to the school where he was still "cleaning up" after the career fair. What if he was stashing Amaranta in his trunk? *He was the last to speak to her.* The reality of that simple fact and her feelings about it — their force and vehemence — dunk Mal's head in a cold bucket.

This is *exactly* what the town thought of Gus. Why his ex-wife left him. Did Luz prod her knee into Gus and demand he relinquish *their* daughter? He was the last to see her — the last to know she was safe until she wasn't. Didn't that make him somehow guilty?

Mal's never seen the situation through the eyes of Gus's ex. It jars her.

"Sure, how can I help?" Oscar wipes his hands on a rag and stands, shaking Benny's hand. He goes in for a hug with Mal, which would be weird under normal circumstances. She tenses hard until he takes a hint, nods awkwardly, steps back, and clears his throat.

"Great setup you've got here." Benny gestures toward the repair stuff in the garage like Oscar owns this damn house. "But tell me, why work on the bike now? Planning a trip?"

Oscar wads the rag in his hands. His self-deprecating smile folds all his bulldog wrinkles. "I figured I'd make more headway in the search with my bike than Sharon's car. It'll handle rough terrain and tight spaces, so we can double down our efforts. It just needed a quick adjustment. But we were heading out, I swear it, Mal."

He pats the motorcycle like it'll confirm the veracity of his statement.

She swallows back a clod of bile.

Sharon plops onto a sunken patio chair as if nothing happened upstairs with her children. Mal didn't even notice Sharon refilling her drink, but it's somehow magically full again. The bright blue facade of the pool sparkles beside them, lurid and fake like her.

Except, the raccoon circles around her eyes are darker now. She's been crying.

Maybe she's not as good an actress as Mal thought.

Slowly, as Mal stares, the coal black smudges like ink over the milky white of Sharon's scleras so her eyes become oil wells, gushing. The slick ebony jets down her cheeks until she's covered in it like black baby oil—until from her long, wide jaw emits a plaintive neighing, her raven mane scraggling down her body, and the entire pool fades from turquoise to bleached piss-yellow.

The tale goes that La Siguanaba was a washerwoman scrubbing clothes in the public water tank or river. Mal's ancestors were always cursing women beside the water. And the women would always strike back.

The pool's fountain gurgles into rivulets and small whirlpools—the ghost of Amaranta's laughter filtering through the putrid air. Mal winces. She can almost see her daughter splashing and bobbing from the deep end where she'd play with her cousins while Mal, Benny and Sal, Griselda when she was home from school, and sometimes even Mami and Papi would all sit under the wide umbrella on patio chairs while Esteban barbecued and Sharon rubbed bronzer on her bikinied body, crisping like bacon in the broiling sun. Back before the divorce dissolved all this and Esteban moved to a nice but not nearly as lavish place by himself, sans pool.

Mal blinks back to her brother.

Benny takes out his notepad. "You've been living here, what? A month?"

Mal needs something to write with, something to *do*. She sets her hands on her hips.

Oscar scrunches his face and turns toward Sharon, who raises her eyebrows and nods. She's back to her bronzed and highlighted Real Housewife self. "Two months, more or less," he says. "I was in between places before this. Now I'm home."

Yuck.

"And in that time, how often have you interacted with Amaranta?"

The way Benny says *interacted* makes Mal want to get in all their faces and scream— *What the hell is wrong with you?* But this rage threatening to bust her is *exactly* why Benny was loath to bring her in the first place. She has to chill out. At least on the surface.

"She's a cool kid. We talked a little."

Benny nods then asks, "So why were you at the school today?"

Finally.

"The career fair," Oscar replies, a slight shakiness underpinning his otherwise deep, confident spit shine. "I was spreading the good word, telling the kids about New Creations and the outreach we do there."

At the fundraiser last night, Oscar waxed poetic about New Creations, a Main Street storefront church mostly for reformed gangsta types, reciting their Bible verse motto: *Therefore, if anyone is in Christ, he is a New Creation. The old has gone; the new has come!* He probably has it tramp-stamped.

"And what did you talk with Amaranta about? Specifically?"

"Specific?" He shakes his head. "We were just shooting the shit, you know . . . Hey, what's this about? You think I . . ." His face screws at the corners, giving the whole thing a pinched look. When he thought they came here for his help, he was eager to play the hero. But now that it's finally dawned on the dumbass they suspect him, he's searching for the nearest exit.

Benny stays neutral. "We're not accusing anyone of anything."

Yes we are.

Unlike her neighbors, Mal's never been one to jump onto any half-cocked bandwagons — especially not one intent on vigilante justice. She's uncomfortable with how quickly she suspected Oscar. Yet she can't nudge the suspicion away, which tells her it might be less *mob mentality* and more *mother's instinct*. The twins and their jars of blood. The sleepover. Oscar talking to her daughter right before she disappeared. It all connects. Mal just can't see *how*.

When Elena disappeared, there was no one to blame. No leads.

No body, no crime, no nada. She vanished into the night of the keg party and bonfire smoke. She was a ghost. One minute, drinking with friends. The next, gone.

Here, with Amaranta, they have one solid lead, and they can't blow it.

Sharon releases a sound that lands somewhere between a snort and a horse's whinny. "You're accusing my kids of something."

"Sharon, cut the shit," Benny interjects, finally showing some cojones. Except, *mwop-mwop-mwop*, his demeanor resumes its casual, friendly air as he turns back to Oscar. "Walk us through everything you remember about your interaction with Amaranta. Any little clue could be helpful in finding her. Anything you might not think is important could turn out to be a key to her whereabouts. No detail is too small, okay?"

Oscar takes a deep breath and pulls at a frayed thread on that dirty-ass rag. "Yeah, okay. She was with another girl. Real close. You know what I'm saying? Hey, I don't judge."

"What did the other girl look like?" Benny asks.

"Small frame, big personality. Purple hair—"

"That's Iggy!" Mal cuts in, stomach dropping. "She said she didn't *go* to school. Are you *sure* you saw Amaranta talking to her *today*? Not even five feet on her tippy-toes, fair skin, short, spiky purple hair, electric violet?"

"That's her. And they weren't just talking . . ."

"What's that mean?"

For a thick, muscular, tatted vato like Oscar to look embarrassed must take a lot, but he does as he glances from Mal over to Benny, his expression like, *Dude, should we tell her?* But as Benny's expression softens and he glances at Mal, she understands.

"Why didn't she just tell me? She knows I'm cool. We practically threw you a coming-out party, mijo. And your wedding with Sal . . . I mean. Why would she hide that from me?"

"It's probably not even about the queer thing, Mal," Benny says, his voice soft and reassuring. "Kids need time to figure themselves out. Most kids don't open up about their love lives to their parents. Amar and Iggy have been friends forever, right? This might just be new territory for her, something she wanted to navigate on her own before letting anyone else in."

"They were comfortable with PDA at school," Mal says, then realizes she sounds like a sulky teenager herself. Benny's right; she's centering her own reaction like a narcissist. This is about finding Amaranta. *"Why did Iggy lie, though?* Why didn't she go to Johnny's? Or *did* she?"

"What time did you get there again, Mal? And what time did school get out?"

It should be getting clearer with every retelling, but instead it's growing blurrier.

Sharon calls out from the lounge chair, "The dismissal bell rang at twelve thirty-six. Oscar called me at one thirty, give or take, asking if I'd seen Amar because you, Mal, had talked to him at the high school and appeared agitated, his words. I told him no, I hadn't seen her, but that we would go searching. And we will. If you two stop accusing us of doing something awful to my beautiful niece. Anyway, if Oscar were a suspect, would he have hung around? *No.* The cuates pulled into the driveway around twelve forty-five, so obvi they didn't have time to do anything else. Would you quit being morons? I have a headache."

Who's to say how Sharon would react if the cuates came home with their cousin tied and gagged — or an hour late and told their mom they'd done something horrifying? Some people can justify anything when it comes to their own kids' behavior.

"You have any home security cameras, Sharon? So we can verify the times they came home? My team's already checking the cams around the school."

"Of course, I'll send you the footage."

"Okay, Oscar. When Amaranta went up to your booth, was Iggy with her?"

"Nah, she went off on her own. I didn't see where."

So Iggy might've gone home when she said she did. No. She said she *never* went to school in the first place. She's lying either way. But she might not have been lying about Amaranta going to Johnny's on her own.

"What did you talk about? Did Amaranta indicate where she was going after school?"

"Let me think. She's a funny kid, ¿sabes? Made me laugh."

The way this vato talks about her daughter has a serious ick factor.

Benny's poised to take notes but his phone rings. "Excuse me a moment."

He listens intently to what the person on the other end is saying. Mal catches snippets of the conversation but can't make out the details.

"What is it?" Mal asks when he ends the call.

"We need to take Oscar in for more formal questioning."

"Why, what happened? Who was that?"

"My lieutenant. Looks like Oscar here's been holding out on us."

Mal's heart thwacks. What did this perv *do*?

"The fact that I'm a *New Creation* speaks for itself, brother. I never purported to have a clean record. Only a clean heart. Cleansed by the blood of the lamb." He picks up the cross around his neck and gestures toward the heavens.

"You're a registered sex offender, prohibited from entering school premises. And I'm betting you didn't get permission from the school or a judge to attend this career fair. So I'll ask again, and I want the truth this time. What *were* you doing on school grounds?"

Oscar eyes his motorcycle like he's debating whether to make a break for it. Old habits die hard. Benny must see it too, because he grabs the bike. But that fleeting war on Oscar's face settles into something determined, almost serene. "I was doing God's work, man. I told you, the old has gone. Christ's blood covers a multitude of sins. I was behind a booth, spreading the gospel. I'm not sorry for telling youngins how God's son can wash us clean as snow."

"That may be, but unfortunately Christ's blood does not wash away the law." Benny takes out a pair of handcuffs and grabs Oscar's thick tattooed arms. "Oscar Molina, you are under arrest for unlawful entry into a school building or on school grounds by a registered sex offender. You have the right to remain silent . . ."

Mal stops listening. Her breath is ragged as Benny calls another officer outside.

"Goddamnit, Benny. Goddamnit, Oscar." Sharon drags herself from her lounge chair and marches with purpose toward the patio, where she stops in front of the wet bar and pours herself another drink. "I did not need this today."

The cuates gloat down at them from the window above. When they see Mal looking, they retreat behind the curtains.

"Benny, you should take all of them in," Mal says. "They're all lying their asses off."

16
EVIDENCE, NOT LEGENDS

The sun sinks precariously low as they step out of Benny's car in front of Iggy's house. Imagine if Amaranta was here the whole time? Sprawled on Iggy's bed, headphones in, lost in indie punk beats with raw lyrics that speak to two queer teens? What if she's annoyed with Mal, and Iggy's been covering for her, so she lied on the phone? Mal has no idea what she could've done to tick off her daughter, but she'd take teen angst and camping out at her girl-friend's in a heartbeat over Amaranta being lost or worse.

Benny slams his car door and makes his way around the sedan toward Mal on the curb. Weeds nudge through the chain link around Iggy's yard, patched yellow and clumped with dirt. They hurry up the plank-wood porch, paint-chipped and peeling. The tract houses resemble apartments, this one so squat, even eight hundred square feet would be generous. They won't need a team to search this place thoroughly. That both relieves and unsettles Mal.

Iggy opens the door before they knock. Must've been watching from the window. Her purple hair contrasts her pale skin, lending her an ethereal glow. Compared to Amaranta, Iggy seems fragile, a waif next to her warrior counterpart.

"I was sorta waiting for you to come," Iggy says, stepping back to let them in.

Waiting for us to figure out you lied, Mal wants to shoot back, but better to let Benny do his good-cop thing first.

The house is small and choked with accouterments of illness. Green oxygen tanks. A snakelike tube coiled at an elder woman's feet. Must be Nelly, Iggy's grandmother and sole caretaker. She's hooked to a breathing machine that whirs like a vacuum cleaner.

While they move through pleasantries, Nelly nods curtly and mumbles something indecipherable — the ventilator masking half her face.

"Is it okay if I keep making dinner for Grandma while we talk?" Iggy asks.

Benny agrees, and Mal keeps her mouth shut so she doesn't scare Iggy into not sharing something that might be important. Mal's been so preoccupied lately that she hadn't given much thought to what was happening with her daughter's *bestie* — a term Mal realizes Amaranta and Iggy must've used as a private joke or code word for girlfriend.

Iggy heads into the cubicle of a kitchen and cuts open a plastic tube of ground beef, squeezing it like toothpaste into an ample plastic bowl. The pink meat reminds Mal of worms.

"Can we help you with anything?" Benny asks, his polite charm astounding Mal. But when Iggy shakes her head *no,* Benny surprises

Mal again by digging right in. "Why'd you tell Amaranta's mom you stayed home sick today?"

Iggy shifts uncomfortably. "Someone needs to take care of Grandma," she replies, as if this answers anything. "The dust triggers her COPD, so it's hard for her. She needs me."

She shapes the pink lump of ground beef in the bowl, digging into the soft, squishy meat like a child sculpting Play-Doh. With a hand coated in meat chunks, she grabs the ketchup bottle, which belches and hiccups as she squirts in a thick glob of lurid red sauce and then kneads the bloody mixture together.

"That still doesn't explain it," Mal snaps. Iggy reminds Mal of herself when she was younger. They look nothing alike; otherwise, the resemblance is uncanny: two parentified girls. The house sparkles, which must be a credit to how hard Iggy works.

"We spoke with someone at the career fair who saw you girls together," Benny presses, his voice kind and unrushed.

Iggy's entire face and neck flush bright as the tomato-clad meat. Still, she says nothing of substance. "I'm sorry" comes out just above a whisper.

"Did you do something to be sorry about?" Benny coaxes.

Mal's blood pumps in her ears. "Is Amaranta here, Iggy?"

Again, Iggy bobs her head in denial.

"Was she here at all today?"

"No." It comes out defensive. But that could be because she's a teenager and programmed to sound that way. Mal's bullshit meter wheezes as Grandma Nelly's breathing machine growls like a hurt animal from the other side of the room.

"Do you mind if we look around to be sure?" Benny asks.

"Yeah, fine. Won't take long." Iggy points out what Mal was thinking earlier.

Benny searches the house while Mal stays in the kitchen.

"What can I say to make you talk to me? To trust me?"

Iggy pours dry oats into the mixture without measuring, a sign she's either clueless or seasoned enough to measure by heart. Mal suspects the latter as Iggy squishes the oaty mixture between her fingers, creating more wormlets. "Why wouldn't I trust you?"

"You tell me." She senses an unspoken block that needs releasing. Yessi would suggest they perform a limpia, cracking an egg into a cup of water to identify the problem. The way the egg behaves—floating to the top, bubbled and stringy like octopus tentacles, or drooping limply to the bottom of the cup—reveals what's unsaid.

Mal grabs an egg from the counter. With one hand, she cracks it on the edge of the plastic bowl. The yolk oozes out, mixing with the clear and goopy whites that sit atop the raw meatloaf.

"Just one?" Mal asks, and Iggy nods, digging back in and resuming her messy mixing.

Benny returns. "No sign of her."

"She could've run out the back," Mal tries, glancing out the kitchen window toward the small plot of yard. Nothing but a concrete slab with a folding chair and a few potted plants. The waist-high chain-link fence is the only barrier, but Amaranta could've easily jumped it and fled from the neighbor's catty-corner yard. Except, why would Amaranta do such a thing? "Has Amaranta mentioned anyone messing with her?" Mal presses. "Like her cousins?"

But before Iggy can answer, Nelly's beleaguered breaths drown out any other sound. She removes her ventilator mask, revealing a face marred by deep red indentations. She gasps like a creature cornered. A mixture of antiseptic and a raw, organic smell fills the air, burbling Mal's stomach. When the woman's face tints blue, Mal screeches, "Can she breathe?"

Iggy wipes her hands on a dishcloth and leans in to help, but Nelly waves her off.

"The desert is more than sand and bullet shells," the elder woman croaks. "It's home to old legends . . . gods and monsters . . ." Her voice cracks as she struggles for breath. "La Siguanaba and her lover, El Cucuy, entwined in fate . . . in vengeance . . ."

Iggy, looking mortified, cuts in, "She's always rattling on about old myths, Ms. V. She's kinda obsessed."

No, this isn't any old myth. This is some seriously weird shit. Mal's been *seeing* La Siguanaba . . . since the night Elena disappeared . . . and now, *again*. Mal had pushed the visions away—she needed to be present as a mom and refused to become as crazy as Mami. She'd dismissed them as nightmares, superstitions, a wild imagination mixed with grief and exhaustion. She'd kept them at bay with talk therapy.

But what if these visions are showing her some dark and horrible possibility? Whatever happened to her sister . . . and the other girls . . . Amaranta? Mal's been smelling horse piss and hay. She's been tormented by the horse-headed woman. Nelly can't possibly know that—or that Mal's in love with a man the town calls El Cucuy.

Mal leans in as Nelly's voice fills with thick phlegm. She gasps out her words, interspersed with coughs. "La Siguanaba takes . . . the lost girls . . ." A phlegm-soaked spurt of coughing stops her.

"Takes them *where*?" Mal presses, heart pounding, skin crawling with escalofríos.

But before the elder woman can say more, Benny cuts in, "Thank you, Grandma Nelly, but I rely on evidence, not legends."

A lump lodges in Mal's throat. "Benny, we should listen to her . . ."

"She says crap like this all the time," Iggy says, a bright red rash spreading across her cheeks and neck. "Her bronchioles are inflamed with sludge. Not enough oxygen reaches her brain." She turns to the elder woman. "Grandma, stop scaring Amaranta's family."

Mal wants to ask Nelly more, but the elder woman is already

snoring, her head lolling against her recliner. Dammit. That *couldn't* have been a coincidence, could it?

She turns back toward her daughter's girlfriend. "Listen, Iggy . . . I know you and Amar are *together*. It's okay. You can tell me whatever's going on between you two . . . what are you sorry for? Did something happen? Did you girls have a fight? I won't be mad. Just tell me what's going on so we can find her."

Iggy's whole body sinks, like whatever she's been keeping in has been buttressing her, and now, she's been given permission to release it. "Yeah, I guess we did have a fight. It was stupid. She knows I take care of my grandma. That's nonnegotiable. You see how Grandma is."

She's abandoned the meatloaf and stands motionless, leaning against the kitchen counter, her hands coated in slimy pink tufts of beef.

"And Amaranta didn't *want* you to take care of your grandma?" Benny asks. "Why not?"

"Not exactly . . . she just . . . I guess she thought she needed me more than Grandma did today, and I couldn't be there for her."

"When? Why did she need you to be there for her?" Mal asks.

"It's a lot of stuff. It's kinda been snowballing. Honestly, I don't even know everything. She won't tell me the whole thing. But it's gotten bad lately."

"What has?" Mal's pulse unthreads, prickling at her neck and throat.

"Start at the beginning, Iggy. Has she been talking to someone new? Is she in danger?"

"I mean . . . maybe?" She picks at the meat on her hands, peeling off clumps of the mixture and flicking them back into the bowl. "I guess it started about two weeks ago when I was staying over at your house, Ms. V."

"Okay, good. What happened when you were staying over?" Mal tries to neutralize her stance and expression, tucking away her instinctual armor.

"You weren't there. You've been gone . . . kind of a lot lately?"

Mal's muscles tighten against her rib cage. She tries to nod encouragingly to keep Iggy talking, not showing any outward sign of judgment or reproach. Calm, neutral expression.

"Amar's been complaining about it a lot. How you're always running off when shit gets real." She looks intently at the stove, not daring a glance at Mal, whose breath becomes shallow and ragged. "I mean, Grandma Nelly's a pain and says weird crap all the time, so I get it. She's not *cruel* to me the way Abuela can be to you, but still. It kinda sucks you ditch Amar."

"Let's stay on track here, Iggy. Keep telling us what happened when you stayed over at Amaranta's house and how that might have affected where she is now." Benny's calm demeanor steadies Mal, although she's screaming inside, her intestines spasming.

"She was *pissed* at you, Ms. V, for taking off all the time, especially since we found something, and . . . let's just say it looks bad. Makes you look . . . totally sus."

"What did you find, Iggy? Tell us that."

How does Benny stay so calm?

"Promise not to get mad about this or get me in trouble?"

"We'll do our best," Benny says noncommittally, and Mal's afraid Iggy won't buy it. He could try harder.

"Like, I mean, I don't want to get arrested or anything, you promise?"

"I can't promise that but . . ."

Mal shoots her brother a warning glance.

"Alright, sure, I promise. You won't get arrested. Just tell us what happened."

"We were digging through your drawers, Ms. V. I mean. Not underwear. But like, looking for a . . ." She glances away, then says in a small voice, "A joint?"

Mal sighs. She smokes weed every now and then to relax. She got it medical grade at first but now it's legal—and cheap. But if the girls were rifling through her personal things . . .

"That's not even an issue right now, Iggy, okay? Just tell us what upset you girls," Benny echoes Mal's thoughts, but she's bracing herself.

"Some pictures?"

Mal's an idiot. She shouldn't have left *anything* for them to find. Not weed. That's whatever. They'll deal with that later. But she'd jokingly taken a risqué Polaroid of her and Gus and meant to leave it with him, only she'd tucked it away in her things. The girls never went through her shit. A few things were off-limits. Wait. So. The truth slams into Mal's chest like she's face-planted onto concrete. "She knows?"

Iggy nods, and she too looks scared.

"She said you've been sleeping with . . . a murderer?" It's like Iggy's choking on the words. "And that if you knew . . . maybe you . . ."

"Slow down here, you two. Amaranta knew *what*? What picture are we talking about?"

"A Polaroid, Benito . . ." Embarrassment, shame, and something stickier are pooling inside of Mal. "I took one of Gus and me . . ." She doesn't have to say *nude*.

"And you left it lying around for your girls to find?"

Boundaries. She needs stronger boundaries. A room of her own. A life of her own.

She was going to tell Amaranta about her father tonight with context and story, laughter and explanation at a beautiful family dinner with tres leches cake. This is a disaster.

"Wait," Mal breathes out. "She thinks *I* . . . what?"

"I mean . . . we've been kinda scared of you, Ms. V. Like, obviously, I don't believe you're a . . . like, a killer or anything."

"Can I use your bathroom?"

"It's a mess but——"

Mal gets there just in time to burst.

The nightmares she's been having. The latest showed *Mal* as La Siguanaba. A monstrous mother. Because her daughter thinks she's a *murderer*? Or an accessory to murder? What the actual hell? So she, what? Ran away? *To get away from Mal?*

She splashes water on her face and stares at herself in the mirror.

Before now, Mal believed the hardest part of raising daughters was behind her. Of course, there were challenges: Griselda's childhood asthma, teenage parties. But she'd always maintained one rule: *Call me, day or night, if you're in trouble. No questions asked.* Mal prioritized their safety over moral judgments. She armored them with self-respect——*Be smart, be firm. No means no. Everyone errs, but persistent disrespect? Intolerable.* She never wanted them to go through what she did. She wanted to be their unfaltering support system.

How has she failed so unforgivably?

When she returns a few minutes later, Iggy's telling Benny, "Ever since she stayed at her cousins' house, it's been worse. She's been fidgety and won't tell me what's going on except she got confirmation her mom's boyfriend is a sicko. She said she had *proof* he's El Cucuy and *murdered* her aunt Elena, but she wouldn't tell me . . . she said it would put me in danger."

Proof?

"Did she describe the danger at all?" Benny asks. "Was it a person? Did she give you any hint about what or who was dangerous?"

"I mean, kinda? In a cryptic way. Last night at her uncle's fundraiser thingy, she called me saying we had to go to El Cucuy's house, but then she texted me a few minutes later and called it off but wouldn't say why. Her crazy cousins were up to something again and she had new evidence but couldn't tell me about it. Which kinda pissed me off. Then she stormed off."

"Anything else you can think of, Iggy? You're doing great. You said she asked you to go to El Cucuy's house. Does that mean Gustavo Castillo's house? Out by the Salton Sea?"

Iggy nods.

"And did you go with her?"

"No," Iggy cries. Tears are welling in her eyes. "But I'm scared she went without me and something bad happened to her!"

"Could someone else have given her a ride?"

Iggy shakes her head, letting out a wobbly breath like she's needed permission to release it. "I guess she went somewhere with her big sister the first night she was in town. Something bad happened, but Amaranta wouldn't say what. But like, it might've been terrible."

Benny whispers to Mal, "Gris didn't say anything?"

Mal whispers back, "Apparently my daughters don't tell me jack shit."

She can't blame them. They think she's a liar. Why should they confide in her?

"Did she give you any details about the night? Any clue as to what might've happened? Do you think it was connected to her plan to go to Gustavo's house?"

"She was mad that no one in her life would listen to her. I asked her to hang out here while I watched Grandma, and we could talk, but...I guess my house and Grandma kinda weird her out or whatever. I'm sorry I lied. I was ashamed we had a stupid fight and I didn't stay with her. Like, what if she got hurt and I could've stopped it? I guess I didn't—"

"Want to get in trouble," Benny finishes for her. "It's alright, we understand. You're not in trouble. But if she contacts you, you've gotta let us know immediately, okay?"

Iggy nods, then sticks the meatloaf in a glass pan and shoves it in the oven.

Nelly's gone quiet, breathing in and out, in and out. She's no longer tinged blue. As if whatever was blocking the pathway to her airway has dislodged.

Mal's trembling as she ducks into Benny's sedan and slams the door shut, the evening humidity swallowing her like the dank mouth of a cave inside the vehicle before Benny gets in and cranks up the air-conditioning.

He refuses to look at Mal as he gets on his radio and over the static makes the call.

Lieutenant Hernandez Pierce agrees. She'll head over to Gustavo Castillo's place now and bring him in for questioning.

Mal stays silent. What can she say? They're wasting time? Benny's on the wrong track? Grandma Nelly might've had it right? Benny should arrest a monstrous horse-headed creature who slinks along the bone-scattered shoreline? Mal's shaking so hard, she can't think straight. She needs to pull herself together. She can't fall apart.

She tried so hard to protect her daughters—only, keeping parts of her life secret from them, she endangered them. She enacted the very thing she was trying to stop. Not because Gus was dangerous. Of course he's not. But because her girls *think* he is. Amaranta might've gotten into a car with a stranger or a creep trying to prove her dad was a monster. This is all Mal's fault.

She wanted to tell her with a fancy tres leches cake when she should've just spit it out!

Intergenerational trauma is like a train leaving the station against our will — it keeps barreling relentlessly down the tracks.

Over and out.

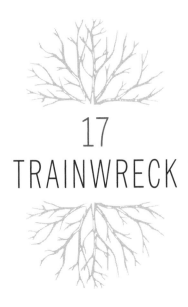

17
TRAINWRECK

Cars sardine West A and wrap around the block like someone's throwing a quinceañera. The neighborhood seems to have shifted its pregame tailgate festivities from Warne Field three blocks away to Mal's house. Neighbors and strangers huddle in the cool breeze that cuts through the air now that the sun has vanished. Canopy tents and folding tables have materialized on the Bermuda grass and sidewalk like a pop-up food cart outside a pulsating discoteca, ignited by vibrant floodlights. People have brought trays of food for the searchers, creating a macabre barbacoa that reminds Mal of a funereal after-party.

Benny releases a subdued exhale. "They went all out," he mutters.

She says nothing as Benny pulls up behind the cars crammed in the driveway. Her gut churns, a punch bowl filled with something sticky and swishing. Tears are dripping down her cheeks. Her baby girl has vanished. Iggy says Mal's the monster. The reason her daughter's gone. And now, she's given Benny a reason to go looking for Gus.

The front doors flare open, propped with a brick, reminding Mal of a dicho Mami says: *En bocas cerradas no entran moscas.* A closed mouth catches no flies. The flies must be swarming into Mal's home now.

She's near hyperventilating as Benny puts a steadying hand on her shoulder. She swallows back the acrid tang of bile mixed with blood from biting the fleshy pads of her cheeks.

"I'll be back as soon as my lieutenant and I talk to Gus," Benny says, clearing his throat with an inward implosion. "Until then, don't do anything foolish."

"Are you gonna arrest him?"

He sighs, a deep, solemn sound. "Mal... that all depends on him."

"He didn't do this, Benito. Not to any of the girls. He wouldn't."

"He's Amar's dad, isn't he?"

She nods, the tears flowing freely now.

"That's reason just to talk to him, okay?" He fiddles with the cuff of his shirt and makes another loud throat-clearing noise. "They'll take me off the case if they think I'm hiding evidence. The sheriff's already making shit harder for me since I won't give the Callahans the special treatment he thinks they deserve. I don't need him getting wind of this. I've gotta do things by the book here. We're just bringing him in to rule him out."

She grabs his hand and squeezes hard.

"Look, Steve's here. You two go to the football game. Spread the word."

Mal nods, glancing toward Esteban and Yessi who are busy checking people in at the command post tent.

Beneath the screwbean mesquite at the yard's center, in a surreal reversal of the fundraiser held in their posh backyard, the elder

Callahans staff a table scattered with maps, clipboards, and flyers featuring Amaranta's face. For a flickering moment, Mal's daughter seems to stare back at her, eyes hollow and accusing.

The horse-headed woman emerges from the hedges as Mal spills out of Benny's car, bracing herself. *Where's my girl?* Mal hisses in her mind, as if La Siguanaba can read it. As if they're connected some-how — and aren't they? This horrible creature has been plaguing her with nightmares that've seeped into the daylight, darkening every-thing, stealing away her child.

Before she slams the door shut, Benny says, "I'm not gonna rail-road your guy, Mal."

La Siguanaba throws back her disproportionately wide head, her wild bray echoing through the front yard. No one else seems to notice. As she screams, her lips flap like torn sails, revealing a row of gnarled, yellow teeth dripping with saliva.

"Mal, over here," Yessi calls, waving her over.

Mal threads through the crowd, losing La Siguanaba. But that sickeningly sweet smell stays. It settles onto the bodies of everyone she passes as she crosses the lawn.

Before she reaches her friend, Papi's standing in front of her, holding on to her arm. "Mjita, who were you talking to?"

"Huh?"

"Just now. You were looking at the bushes and talking, pero no hay nadie."

Shit. She's going as crazy as Mami. Talking to bushes.

She tries to brighten her voice. "No one, Papi. How're you hold-ing up?"

"Mijita, I hate to bring this up now when you have so much on your mind ya. Pero have you seen your mami's pills? I've been trying to calm her down but I can't find them."

"Her Ativan?" Mal asks.

"Sí. I know I had that bottle in the kitchen. But there's been so many damn people everywhere, maybe someone stole it."

"I'll let Benny know," Mal promises. "Give Mami a Benadryl. That'll knock her out."

"Bueno," he says, kissing her cheek before lumbering into the house through the crowd. Of course he's considering Mami first in all of this.

Mal's standing in front of her brother and best friend, trying to focus as Yessi explains the canvassing procedure. This crowd must be their joint effort—the two of them are practically the PTA committee of the whole damn town.

"Thanks, Yess," she replies when Yessi pauses, although she has no idea what her friend has been saying. "Chuy," she says, leaning against him for support. "Benny says we should head to the game and make an announcement at halftime."

"Most of the town's already here." He wraps her in a hug. "It's a wonder they didn't call off the game."

"So you don't think it's necessary?" Her tears are flowing freely again.

"No, it's a good idea."

"No one's heard anything?" she asks, her salty mocos streaming down her big brother's shirt, but he doesn't seem to mind.

"We're just getting started." Esteban squeezes her shoulders. "I've called in a favor from San Diego. They're sending a team of bloodhounds—"

"*Blood*hounds . . ." Mal repeats in a whisper. An inky image blots her vision before she can push it away: her daughter's blood coating the dogs, their snouts deep in mounds of her sticky, viscous liquid. It triggers a vertigo that sends her reeling.

"The sooner we do it, the better our chances of finding her . . . Sis, you okay?"

Her whole body's smattered with piel de gallina and she's wobbling like a flimsy screen door during a thunderstorm. By the time her knees give out, both Esteban and Yessi are surrounding her in a bear hug, squeezing her so tightly the shaking subsides some.

But the horse-headed woman is back. In the shadows beyond the fanfare on the grass, behind the mesquite, she widens her maw, letting out another silent scream. All that flapping, all that dripping. Her long ink-black mane tangles into the branches behind her as the tree splits open, gushing thick black tar. The yard tilt-a-whirls. Floodlights. The horse-headed woman. Bloodhounds. Black, sticky tar covering everything.

"Whoa, Mal, hang on." Esteban's carrying her inside, setting her on the couch. "Gris, can you help me get your mom some water, por favor, mija?"

Gris is here, good. Mal watches her daughter head toward the kitchen, Harlan at her heels like a puppy. *Pull yourself together, Mal. Do not fall apart. Snap out of it. Get up and look for Amar.* But before she can make her body obey, Gris is handing Mal a glass, and behind her stands not Harlan but Sean, balancing an aluminum food tray.

"What's *he* doing here?" Mal's wide awake now, pulling herself to an incline. She thrusts the glass back toward her daughter.

"Mal, come on, give the guy a break," Esteban says. "Everyone's helping us —"

"No, he — you." She glares at Sean, her voice filled with twenty-five years of vitriol.

"Good to see you again so soon, Mal. Not under these circumstances, of course." Something behind the faux concern in his bright blue eyes terrifies her. He's *enjoying* this.

"You probably orchestrated these circumstances," she spits, the pieces fitting together in terrifying unity. What he did to Mal at prom . . . and when she rebuffed him, her sister disappeared. Last night, he tried again to, what did he call it?—*strike up an old flame,* dancing with her outside his dad's house—and now her *daughter's* gone.

Esteban steps in front of Mal, but she pushes herself off the floral cushions, her head spinning, and manuevers around her brother, her eyes trained on Sean, who says, "If I'm not welcome here, I'll leave—"

"Damn straight you're not *welcome here,* you asshole."

The tray in Sean's hands wobbles as someone comes to see what the fuss is all about and bumps into him. That's when Mal realizes Sean's holding the tres leches cake she baked.

She lurches toward him to grab the cake from his faltering hands, but he flinches as if she's about to sucker-punch him, and when he deflects, the tray tumbles from his grasp.

Mal's cry fills the room as the tres leches slips and crashes onto the living room floor.

Sean takes a step back. He opens his mouth, closes it. The cake is ruined.

Mal grabs him. His breath is rancid ginger, blowing in her face.

Esteban stares between the two of them, horrified, like this was another campaign opportunity and Mal's blundering it.

"Mom!" Griselda snaps. Harlan's standing beside her, his cheeks flaming like hot Cheetos. They both look mortified. Mal should be ashamed of herself. But she isn't.

She grabs Sean's arm tighter. Dares him to do anything.

"What's happening?" June asks, rushing into the room, and there's something almost scared in her voice.

"It's fine, June," Sean says placatingly, like he's got this all under control, which infuriates Mal more. "She's upset about her daughter and taking it out on the wrong person."

"It's *not* fine," June says.

Guy and Elva have joined the edges of the fray, standing in the cramped front entrance. A crowd has gathered behind them in the open jaw of the doorway, trailing like a tongue onto the concrete porch. Mal hates causing a scene, especially when she catches Papi peeking around the hallway, silently pleading for Mal to keep it down and not accidentally beckon Mami — *don't rouse the sleeping beast.*

Still, Mal tightens her grip on Sean's arm, digging her nails into his skin, but he just stares her down like he's amused by her cattiness, like he's testing to see how far she'll go.

June's huffing, "This is absurd." She's prying Mal off, but Mal — instinctively swatting his wife away — strikes June across the face. Hard.

"You stupid bitch," Sean booms, grabbing Mal's arm like he's going to twist it — or snap it. June holds one hand to her face and the other to her husband like he's a giant toddler she's protecting from a bully even though he's got Mal in a lock-down.

"Wait, wait," Esteban's calling in his political oratorio. "Let's all calm down." His voice carries a sense of authority and reason that normally reassures Mal, but right now it infuriates her. She *needs* her brother on her side, not pandering to these pendejos.

"He *knows* something, Chuy. I know he does. He — " Mal hears herself screaming as if through a tunnel. "Where were you today at twelve thirty?"

Sean releases Mal and it takes every ounce of strength she has not to spit on him.

Abuelo and Esteban are holding Mal as Sean's family flanks him.

"With *me*," June insists.

Of course, June's protecting her husband. Lying for him. That's what women do in this godforsaken Valle. Cover shit up for rich, entitled assholes.

Esteban exhales. "Now, Sean, come on. My niece is missing. Give my sister a break. She's dehydrated, probably low blood sugar. Stay and help, okay? We need all hands on deck."

Griselda steps forward, looking like she's a kid again about to confess something and scared of the punishment. "I should have told you this earlier . . ." She's speaking to her mother. "I took Amaranta to a protest."

"What kind of protest?" A slithering up Mal's spine.

"The kind I usually go to . . . with Harlan . . ." Griselda's voice trails off.

"Oh, Gris . . . you didn't."

Why weren't you watching your sister? It echoes between Mal's family.

"What were you protesting? I didn't hear about any protest," June says, and Mal wonders if she can really be so clueless about what her son's been up to, but then again, it's a hazard of motherhood, not to know what the hell your children are doing.

Harlan looks at the ground where the wet cake has mashed into the carpet like vomit. "Dad." It comes out small and embarrassed.

Sean rolls his eyes but keeps his lips pressed in a thin line.

"We were freeing calves," Griselda says. "Nothing happened. We just . . . let a few calves go." But her expression is wracked with such guilt Mal doesn't believe *nothing* happened.

June interjects, "So you think my husband, what? Kidnapped Amaranta in retaliation for some hijinks with my son? That's outlandish."

Esteban placates, "No, of course not, June. We're all overwhelmed here."

Mal turns to Sean, unable to wrench the record from the turntable despite her daughter's admission. If anything, it convinces Mal even more. "You *know* something. I see it in your eyes. My daughter was *at your ranch* . . . and Renata went to those protests! What did you do to them?"

Sean stares at Mal with something that vacillates between fear and pity.

"Answer me!"

But before Mal can stop the trainwreck she started, Mami's wheelchair is parked in the hallway. "Guy?" Mami's rasping.

Mal had forgotten that Old Man Callahan was even standing in the doorway. He hasn't said one word in his son's defense, which is odd even for these ricos.

"Guy, what are you doing here? You should've called first. My husband's home." Beneath the scrape of Mami's voice there's a hint of coyness.

Old Man Callahan turns as red as his grandson and averts his gaze, gathering Elva and shuffling through the crowd, but Mami's wheelchair glides with an eerie swiftness, and she's yelling after him, "Why'd you leave me and our baby? You promised you'd take care of us." This last part comes out as a screech. A girl, pleading.

Their baby? *Their baby?* It hits Mal like a gale force. She can't chalk this up to one of Mami's demented outbursts. It makes too much sense. The blue eyes. How Papi never treated him the same as the rest of his kids. Because Benny *isn't* his kid? Maybe this is why he's always treated Benny so cold and formal. Why he was all too happy to let Mal raise him as her own son. Mal had always thought it was because his birth heralded Elena's disappearance and Mami's breakdown. But what if it was because he always knew Benny wasn't his son?

She turns sharply toward Papi, whose face has crumpled like his day-old *Valle News*. His shoulders sag and he slumps into the nearest chair, burying his face in his hands.

Mal, in her frenzied pursuit to get Sean to talk, threw her family under the bus — and they didn't learn *anything* that'll help them find Amaranta. She should've taken Sean out in the backyard and had a private conversation. What the hell is wrong with her? Why did she have to act just like her petulant, vindictive mother?

She'll apologize to Papi later. Or maybe she won't.

And what about Benny, pobrecito? Should she tell *him*? Not while she's so damn mad at him about taking Gus to the station, that's for sure.

For now, as penance — before either woman can spew anything else — Mal dashes to Mami's wheelchair and wheels Mami to her bedroom, passing the godforsaken ofrenda for Elena on their way, its candles perpetually alight. She's tempted to blow them out.

She won't add Amaranta to it, dammit. She just won't.

Before Mal heads to the game with Chuy, she locks herself in the bathroom and calls Gus. *Pick up pick up pick up.* He answers on the first ring.

"Did you find her?"

"No." She crawls into the tub, clothes on, and curls into fetal position.

"We'll find her, amor." But his voice betrays his equally broken heart.

"Have you been home yet?"

"No, why, what's up?"

"Don't go home," Mal whispers through her tears. "Or my brother will arrest you."

She explains everything while he listens as he always does.

"If they need to question me, I should go down to the station and answer them. I have nothing to hide. You know that."

Benny won't railroad him. He said so. But Benny's not the sheriff. Benny's not in charge. Benny can't *guarantee* Mal the rest of the
force won't twist Gus's words.

And, worst of all, Benny's a *Callahan*. Half of one, at least.

"Not without a lawyer, *please,* Gus. Just . . . wait, okay? Wait
until we find Amar. We'll sort this all out."

Why is this their life? Why are they so cursed?

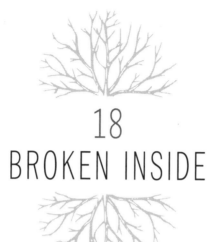

18
BROKEN INSIDE

al huddles against Chuy on the edge of the dead zone. The
stadium pulsates. She can't believe they haven't canceled
the game — her whole world has stopped. How is the rest
of the world still running? The chaos at Mal's house might've
deterred non-football fans, but the rivalry against the Spartans
from El Centro has still drawn a massive crowd.

As the cheerleaders high-kick and chant and the goalpost clock
ticks down the seconds, Mal imagines Elena, vibrant and energetic,
jumping and cartwheeling with her royal blue and gold poms, her
flyaway skirt twirling around her like a whirlwind. But the image
shatters when La Siguanaba's hooves stomp her sister's head like a
cantaloupe.

Mal scans the crowd for her girl. Some teens run away. Not
Amaranta. Not even after what Iggy said about Amar finding *proof*

Gus murdered Elena. And frankly, that was impossible. There was no proof because he didn't — *couldn't* — do that.

Sean, maybe. And *his* wife, June, might cover it up. But not Mal and Gus.

So what *had* Amaranta found? What would make her *think* she'd found proof?

The line at the snack bar winds across the opposite end of the field, running parallel to the end zone. Nachos, popcorn, hot dogs. It all curdles Mal's stomach.

Amid the crowd, a figure near the entrance of the concession stand holds a sign. It's not fangirling over a football player but instead features a young woman's picture and the plea, HAVE YOU SEEN RENATA RUIZ?

Squinting, Mal recognizes the woman as Renata's mother, Carmen.

Should they call her onto the field with them? Are the girls' disappearances connected? Would highlighting the search for Renata distract from or add to the urgency of the search for Amaranta? Mal feels like an asshole even debating this.

"Don't be too hard on yourself," Esteban says, and Mal realizes he's been speaking this whole time. "We never know what anyone's truly up to. Even family."

"Yeah, like Mami." She nudges her brother. "Why don't you seem shocked about Benny? Did you know he was a Callahan? Did Papi know? Is that what your beef's been about?"

Esteban's face hardens. "I had my suspicions. Benny's blue eyes...they don't run in our family. Green maybe, but not blue. And he's been so opposed to me accepting any help from the Callahans. It's like self-loathing, like he's trying to reject a part of himself."

Mal takes a breath, trying to process this. "So you think he knows?"

"I don't know if he knows for sure, but I've always suspected there was something deeper behind his anger. It's like he's trying to fight his own blood."

"Speaking of fighting our own blood, your kids are shit," she mumbles.

He guffaws a hard, appreciative laugh. "Wow, your filter's vanished. Okay, I wasn't expecting that, but good. I like this real and raw version of you."

"The version where my baby's missing so I don't give a flying fuck about anything?"

His sigh comes out as a deep *whoosh*. "No, of course not. I didn't mean . . ." He sighs again and slings his arm around Mal's shoulders, meaning to comfort her, but his weight's a burden that almost topples her forward. She leans into him, stabilizing herself. They used to wait together like this with the rest of the band in itchy polyester uniforms to march at halftime.

"Let's start over," he says. "My kids are shit. Tell me why."

"They've got some sick altar in their armario with at least a dozen jars of blood, each labeled with a name. Did you know? The blood could be from classmates, friends, or victims."

The corners of his mouth twinge. "Ay, come on." He squeezes Mal tightly in a half-bear hug. "You pulling my leg, sis?"

"I'm dead serious. I saw the jars. And there's a mini fridge with more jars . . ." She turns to look him in the eye. "Listen, last weekend, Amar spent the night with your kids and was acting strange since. I dropped the ball, I admit, but this is some frightening shit, Chuy. Sharon downplayed it, but I'm worried they did something to my girl."

Esteban shakes his head, a mixture of disbelief and concern. "I'm sorry they scared Amar. I'll . . . get to the bottom of this and set them straight, okay? Trust me. But I seriously cannot believe they would've *hurt* their prima. They love Amar. We all do."

Mal glances up at the scoreboard as the halftime whistle blows. Time has run out.

The team retreats from the field while the principal motions for Esteban and Mal to join him at the half-yard line. A microphone's brought center field. The band blares a fanfare.

Esteban guides Mal, keeping pace with the energetic music that feels more like a dirge. Her brother waves and smiles, acknowledging the crowd's cheers. Mal sweeps the stands again but can't see Benny. She does see the *other* Callahans. The sight unsettles her. Their whole family sitting all regal and composed after what just happened. Sean fixes a cold stare on Mal like he can't wait for another chance to fight when his wife can't intervene. The only one showing a smidge of concern is Harlan. He's not sitting with them but canvassing the stands with flyers of Amaranta along with Griselda and Yessi, who are holding up pictures of her girl.

The cuates stand out in their chic goth, a black stain on the bleachers. Esteban must notice them too, because his smile falters as he eyeballs them and mouths, *I need to talk to you.* Yeah, like they'll admit anything to their father.

He begins his speech, but Mal's already dissociating.

She tunes out the sound of the crowd, Esteban's voice, the pernicious braying of the horse-headed woman whom she can feel waiting at her periphery — and listens for Amaranta. *Thump-thump. Thump-thump.*

Esteban hands Mal the mic. Her mouth sandpapers. She's never been adept at public speaking. How can she convey her fear and grief to these people when one of them might be *hiding* her daughter?

She must be speaking because Esteban isn't snatching back the microphone. He's nodding, tears in his eyes.

She mentions Renata's name and points to Carmen, who remains by the concessions, still holding up the sign. "Help us find our girls,"

Mal hears herself imploring. Her plea hangs in the air, and a palpable tautness engulfs the stadium, crackling with an undercurrent of unease. It's as if the crowd hadn't seen Carmen until this moment.

Esteban takes back the mic to wrap up their time on the field with something that must be inspiring because the crowd erupts in cheers, the band strikes up again, and the cheerleaders rush onto the field, but Mal's already striding toward Griselda and Yessi, who've *finally* been joined by Benny. She has to find out what's been going on in the investigation.

Esteban's huffing as he catches up to her. "That was great, sis. It'll help. I know it will. Okay, I'll go have a talk with my little shits then check on you in a bit."

She barely registers his words, her bowels churning as she turns her attention to her younger brother. "Benito, ¿qué pasó?"

He rubs both hands vigorously over his unshaven face. "Well, first of all, Gustavo's nowhere to be found. Have you heard from him?" Mal shakes her head, and he lingers on her response a moment like he's waiting for her to tell him more before he raises his eyebrows and continues, "My lieutenants have been scouring CCTV footage from both the school and Johnny's. And I double-checked the footage from Sharon's. Her and the cuates' stories check out: she was home drinking, and the cuates got home around one forty-five, but Amar wasn't with them. She last appeared on their cameras Saturday night, looking fairly upset. She took off walking down the block by herself."

Mal's insides pickle. "I still can't believe Sharon didn't *call* me . . ." She also can't believe she's judging her ex-sister-in-law for being irresponsible when this feels like it all comes down to Mal's utter negligence, but she keeps this part to herself. "Where'd she go?"

"Like I said, she was on foot. We could ask Sharon again but . . ."

"Yeah, she's a drunken dead end. What about Oscar?"

"Nothing fishy on Sharon's security cams. He talks to Sharon, grabs a drink, and tends to his bike." Benny brightens. "Oh, I did obtain Amar's phone records. She received a two-minute call from an unlisted number at precisely twelve thirty-eight today, shortly after the dismissal bell. It could be a burner phone, one of those prepaids anyone could purchase from a store like Walmart. The number has no other inbound or outbound calls except to Amar's phone. We tried calling, but no one answered and voicemail isn't set up."

"Okay . . . so . . . who do you think she was talking to?"

He lets out a low surge of breath and rubs the stubble across his face again. "In any other situation, I'd say a drug deal or . . . you know, a john."

"Amaranta? Drugs or sex work?" What Benny is proposing is light-years away from her daughter. But then, midscoff, a sickening thought strikes her. "Could it be Oscar?"

"Maybe, but if he ever had that burner phone, he hid or tossed it. I don't think so, though. The school footage shows her walking off campus with him . . . carrying a box of pamphlets. He was off camera for two minutes and thirty-four seconds. Then he's back on campus cleaning and taking down the booth and chairs. Looks like she kept walking toward Johnny's."

"Except, he could've *done something* to her in those two minutes and thirty-four seconds, Benito. Aren't there cameras in the school parking lot? Did you check his car?"

She can't stand the thought of her daughter scrunched in his trunk, gasping for breath, pounding from inside, calling for help as the air dwindles.

"He took one of Sharon's vehicles. And yes, we've checked it. No signs of Amar or a struggle."

"So, did she get to Johnny's? What did the rest of the cameras show?"

"Johnny's cameras are grainy and don't show her going inside. No one fitting her description went inside."

She leans closer. "What about the outside ones?"

He hesitates, choosing his words. "One...might've caught a glimpse of a girl from far down the street." He clears his throat, a hard, loud implosion. "She got into a beige or dirty white truck, a Ford or Chevy. The cameras are more of a deterrent for vandalism or theft than for capturing details. The picture's fuzzy, but we're trying to clear it up."

"You think it's Amaranta?" Mal can't believe he's being so obtuse.

"It's hard to tell right now, but maybe."

She scoffs. "Someone gave her a ride...to Gus's? That's what you guys think?"

He shrugs. "I mean, we're looking into it. Gonna clean up the resolution and see if we can get a license plate. And, of course, talk to Gus as soon as we can find him. You're *sure* you don't know where to find him?"

"No, I don't. I'm trying to find my *daughter,* Benito. And Sean Callahan drives a white truck, you know. It's time to look into *him* instead of chasing the same dead end you cops have been insisting on for twenty-five years." She's yelling. People are staring.

Benito winces like she's slapped him.

"Mom," Griselda whines. "Everyone in El Valle drives a white truck."

"True, but that doesn't mean I'm wrong."

Benny shakes his head. "You just hate the Callahans."

She almost retorts, *I don't hate you,* but she's caused enough distress. Now is *not* the time to tell him that he's one of them. The thought of it makes her sick. Why did Mami have to drop that bomb today of all days? But maybe more than anything, why didn't Mal realize before now? Has she been so blind?

While she's lost in her thoughts, Griselda fills Benny in on what happened at the house before the game. He sighs. "Promise me you won't go off on the Callahans again. Their threats are not empty. We don't need a defamation case. Just leave them alone and let me do my job."

"Then *do* your job, Benito. Find my daughter."

He inhales slowly like his patience is wearing thin. "Esteban texted me he's got bloodhounds coming in from San Diego tomorrow. I don't know how he managed that, but it's a good sign. The powers that be are taking this seriously. With Esteban's high-profile campaign, there's no way Amaranta's case will slip through the cracks. That's one hopeful thing, anyway. You go home and take care of yourself. You did great out there. My team and I are doing everything possible to find my niece."

"Don't give me that official bullshit. And you know perfectly well I'm not going home. Not while my daughter is still out here."

He squeezes Griselda's shoulders. "You gonna be alright? Stay with your mom?"

Griselda nods and Benny weaves away through the crowd out the gate.

Yessi squeezes Mal's hand. "I'll keep checking with gente here. Text me." She kisses Mal's cheek. "We'll find her, yunta."

Like she's just seeing her, Mal stares at Yessi, whose face is all scrunched with concern. It's weird, right? How Yessi is acting?

"Why didn't you help your tía search for your prima like this?" Mal nods toward the concession stand where Carmen's still holding up her sign. "Why are you *so worried* about my daughter but don't seem to give a shit that your own cousin's been missing a whole week?"

Now it's Yessi's turn to look like Mal's punched her, and deep inside Mal knows she's acting crazy and irrational and lashing out at those closest to her, but something's broken inside her. A gauge exploded. A giant fucking hole where Amaranta should be.

Griselda puts her arm around Yessi and scoffs loudly. *"Mom,* you don't have to be such a b — " She stops herself before she says *bitch.*

"No, mija," Yessi says. "Let her get it all out. She's in pain." Yessi turns to Mal. "Honestly, yunta, I didn't think nothing of Renata running off since she's always doing shit like this with some guy or another. Your 'jita is a baby."

Mal lets out a shaky breath. "I'm sorry, Yess."

This paranoia isn't like her. It's like she's downed a bunch of Red Bulls and listened to hours of death metal on full blast. She's jittery. On edge. Angry. She wants to punch something.

But it's not her friend's fault. She may be a slut shamer, but who in this town isn't?

"Don't worry about it. I've got you." Yessi still looks hurt, and Mal can't blame her, but she simply nods as her friend disappears into the crowd toward the stands. Her brain feels so fuzzy. She *should* talk to Renata's mom, though. They should be working together.

"Mom," Griselda snaps when Yessi's out of earshot. "That was messed up. Why are you acting like this?"

"I don't know, mija. I don't . . ."

Griselda sighs. "Let's just go home. You're exhausted."

Mal shakes her head *no,* but before she can elaborate, Esteban pops by with his grim cuates in tow. He holds their shoulders like kittens by the scruff. They stop in front of Mal.

"My kids have something to say to you."

In unison, creepy AF, *"We're sorry, Auntie."*

"For?" Esteban prompts.

"Scaring you," Xochitl says, void of emotion. Machinelike.

Xolotl quickly adds after his sister, "We promise we didn't do anything to Amaranta. We don't know where she is. We're just as worried as you."

Yeah right. They're just trying to avoid a grounding. Still, she's gotta give Esteban some parenting cred; this is more than they've said to her all day.

"I'm taking the cuates home for a serious talk about their behavior," he says. "And revoking car privileges. In fact, you two..." He squeezes their shoulders tighter, making them wince. "You're driving home with me. We can leave your car in the parking lot overnight."

They wouldn't dare groan in front of their father, but Mal recognizes the severity of this punishment. Esteban knows how to hit them where it hurts.

"We'll search again first thing in the morning, sis. I'll be home with these two rascals all night, but call or text if you need anything. Oh, hey. Do you need a ride?"

"No, Gris has her car."

"Take care of each other, then."

As he ushers the cuates through the exit in the chain link surrounding the field, his words reverberate through Mal. She knows he's not trying to echo Mami, yet somehow his sentiment parallels what's been running through Mal's psyche since Mami first screamed the phrase at her when she was seventeen: *She should've been watching her sister... taking care of her.*

"Come on, Mom," Griselda says, threading her arm through Mal's. "Let's head home."

"We're not going home."

As the whistle blows, signaling the next half of the game, Mal scans the bleachers while the crowd mills back to their seats. Sure enough, center row, the Callahans (sans Harlan who's still talking to folks in the crowd) sit straight-backed, heads high. Bunch of pendejos. If Benny won't find out what they're hiding, Mal will do it on her own.

"I'm going to Sean Callahan's house to find my daughter."

19
CHASING GHOSTS

Griselda chases after her mother beelining through the parking lot. "Wait, what?"

"Give me your keys."

"What are you talking about? He's not home. He's up in the stands with his family. Didn't you see them?"

"Exactly. We have a narrow window here. The second half's starting, so we have, what, an hour? Where's your car? Click the panic button."

Griselda rolls her eyes. "I know where I'm parked, Mom. God. You're acting *insane*." She grabs her mom's arm and steers her toward the side street and clicks unlock. Her little Honda lights up. "I'll drive. Benny said to take you *home*. You need rest."

Mom snatches the keys and rushes to the driver's side. "I'm going with or without you, mija."

Griselda gawps as her mother buckles up. She can't let her do this. "Why are you so fixated on Harlan's dad? He's the enemy to your *business*. Big bad wolf of the *meat industry*. But, Mom, why would he *kidnap* my little sister? Jeez. Are you listening to yourself? Where would he even keep her?"

"In his house. Which is why we're going to find her."

Even as Griselda protests, a small, hard shiver pebbles her gut.

Maybe Sean *is* fed up with the protesters? It's the idea she floated by Harlan earlier. While he dismissed it because his dad's a professional . . . a community man . . . Griselda's still mortified this all comes down to what *she* did at the protest.

It's just, the worse she feels, the stronger her armor grows. She can't show Mom how terrified she really is. Mom's already losing it. Griselda has to be the strong one.

Maybe more than anything, though, Griselda doesn't *want* Mom to be right. She doesn't *want* to be the reason her sister's gone.

Mom starts the engine. Griselda groans but climbs into the passenger seat. If you'd asked her before Thursday, is Harlan's dad capable of something like this, she would've said adamantly *no*. But after the calf rescue . . . maybe there's the slightest seed of doubt planted. Anyone's capable of anything. Griselda included.

Even so. This is breaking and entering they're talking about.

"Mom," Griselda starts, buckling her seat belt as Mom pulls away from the curb.

"Mija, Harlan's un amorcito. He's grown on me too, okay? You've known him forever. So it's probably hard for you to see how *messed up* his dad is. But believe me, mi amor. Sean Callahan is a *monster*."

The way Mom was grabbing Sean at the house, it's clear some shit had gone down between them. It's just, maybe she's fixating on him because of whatever happened in the past. Maybe she's ignoring the obvious as a result. "Mom?" She probes gently. "Why *don't* you believe Benny that it could be Gus? That Cucuy guy?" Griselda clears her throat. "I saw him today. When I was collecting samples in the sea. He was . . . I don't know . . . watching me."

"What?" Mom's tapping on the steering wheel, clearly agitated.

"Yeah, he creeped me out . . . right before I talked to you at the old house. So like, around the time Amaranta . . ."

"What are you suggesting?" Mom brakes harder than necessary at a stop sign and the car jerks, locking Griselda's seat belt, which scrapes against her neck.

"I'm just concerned we're looking in the wrong direction. Like, I get that you have a past with Sean and all. But maybe that's clouding your judgment?"

"Did Amar mention Gus to you?"

"Why would she?"

Mom's knuckles are turning white against the steering wheel.

"Look. I know Gus too, okay? We have a history. *It's not him.*" She says this last part with parental finality.

"What kind of history?"

"I . . . helped him search for his daughter when Elena went missing. We . . . searched together. We . . . helped each other get through that time."

Ewww. "Helped each other *how?*" A nauseating sensation crawls up Griselda's throat. "Isn't he, like, way older than you? Weren't you a teenager? Wasn't he a *dad?*"

"It wasn't like that."

Griselda stares at her mom shifting all ants-in-her-pants — and a horrifying realization begins to dawn. No. That's too . . . she blocks it from her mind. Abruptly steers the ship back to calmer waters. At least, calmer for Griselda. "I still don't understand why you're so hung up on *Sean,* though."

"Because," Mom snaps, veering them back into the middle of a steep drop-off. "If we don't find something on Sean, Benny will arrest your father." She clamps her hand over her mouth, but it's too late. It's had the intended effect.

Griselda feels like she's going to throw up. She's stunned into several seconds of silence.

The town whirs by like dark, oceanic waves as Griselda tries to process.

The inky blots in her subconscious. That creeper at the edges of her memories.

He's her *dad*? What the actual—?

"Does Benny know? Is *that* why he has nightmares of El Cucuy? Does *Amar* know?"

"I . . . maybe."

"*Mom*. Are you *hiding* him?"

"No." She lets out a sigh of frustration. "You can't understand. He was distraught when Noemi disappeared. He devoted his entire life to finding her. Even after the police stopped, he put his life on hold. He could've started over anywhere. But he kept searching for his daughter. This town may have its rumors, but that's all they are. Rumors."

They cross Main Street and approach Harlan's opulent neighborhood.

Griselda's chest tightens so badly she pulls out her inhaler and takes the requisite two puffs and then another. "They say he *killed* his *daughter . . .* and now . . ."

Mom's face gets all crumbly. "He didn't. *He did not kill her.* Okay? He was home with her when it happened, so people say . . ." She sighs. "Screw what people say. You can be watching closely and still . . ." She makes a little choking sound halfway between a hiccup and a sob. "Noemi was supposed to be in her room. His wife at the time was working the night shift. He was grading papers and fell asleep at some point. Gunshots woke him up. Could've been someone scaring off a predator. Hunters. Or military drills.

"At any rate, he got up for some water.

"Noemi's bedroom light seeped through the door crack, so he assumed she was still in there. The front door was unlocked, but he thought he'd just forgotten to lock it. That was the only thing out of place. He checked the front yard but didn't see anything. So he locked up and went back to bed.

"The next morning, she was gone."

Mom pauses, swallowing hard. Normally Griselda would reach out to comfort her in some way, but this is too messed up. What is her mom even saying right now? It sounds rehearsed. Like, is this what Gus has been feeding her all these years?

Griselda's known Mom needed therapy since she was a kid, but if she'd known her mom had been brainwashed by a suspected serial killer, she might've recommended more stringent treatment.

"If he'd only checked on her . . ." Mom's more whispering this to herself than recounting the tale for Griselda now. "Did she go outside to see what the gunshots were? Was she out there already, and the gunshots were aimed at her? He's been obsessed with figuring it out ever since. We've . . . we've been obsessed."

She looks at Griselda like she's begging her forgiveness.

Griselda won't give it to her.

"His ex-wife took off to San Diego and became a holistic yoga teacher, and everyone else gave up on Noemi eventually, but he stayed and kept searching for answers. That's sheer devotion."

"Or a guilty conscience."

Mom says nothing as they slowly pull up to the Callahan mansion.

"We should park at Tío Esteban's but there's not enough time. Just turn the corner."

She's only doing this so her mom doesn't get herself arrested. Amaranta doesn't need that on top of everything else. She's doing this for Amar, she tells herself. They'll deal with their murderer for a father later. Right now, Griselda's gotta keep her mother from flying off the handle. And besides, Harlan gave Griselda the code for emergencies or whatever, so if worse came to worst, she could claim she had permission to be there.

Mom parks and they get out.

"Try to look natural," Griselda whispers, opening the trunk and pulling out a bunch of reusable grocery bags and two pairs of gloves. "It'll be less conspicuous if you're helping me bring groceries."

"And the gloves?"

"We don't want the Callahans to press charges. You already threatened them. Now we're breaking and entering. They could send us to jail."

"Benny wouldn't let that happen."

"You're acting just as entitled as they are, you know."

"What are you . . ."

"We don't *own* the police just because your brother works there, Mom."

Mom rolls her eyes, stuffs the gloves in her pocket, and grabs two of the bags. They're empty, but she fluffs them out so they appear full. Then they haul ass, bags in tow, up the long driveway. *Act like we belong here,* she reminds herself, standing up straighter.

At the grand mahogany door, its door handle a deep rustic brass, there's a touch keypad. No buttons. It's one of those fancy electronic doors. If you put in the wrong code too many times, it calls the police department and security system office.

"Do you know the code?" Mom asks impatiently.

"Yes. What were you planning to do if I wasn't here?" she hisses. "Smash a window?"

How did Harlan say she should punch in the code? Shit. She wishes she'd paid more attention. The panel is flush and empty until she swipes her sweaty palm across the pressure-activated sensor, and it lights up with numbers. She's never entered the code herself. They better not have changed it. She dons the latex gloves and presses the code — 6 7 7 9 — and with each press of her gloved finger, a soft chime resounds until an audible click unlocks the door.

Mom, who's also slipped on her gloves and balled up the shopping bags, opens the door and rushes inside before Griselda can tell her about the security alarm. If she doesn't enter the next code within forty-five seconds, it'll be a rave up in this bitch.

Griselda chases after her mom, crossing the threshold into the foyer where she reaches for the invisible control panel she hopes is where she thinks it is — flush with the wall above a crystal bowl filled with fake glass candy. She enters Harlan's birthday — 0 8 1 9 0 0.

It's like he wanted her to break in.

The display screen flashes DISARMED, and Griselda releases a long exhale of relief.

Her mom is already searching through the house, opening every door — closets, bathrooms, cupboards, pantry. Griselda rushes to Mom's side, hissing out where everything is like some crazed realtor showing her the house. Mom's making a mess. So much for inconspicuous.

"What are we looking for?"

"Your sister."

"You can't genuinely believe she's —"

Mom's using the camera app on her phone, taking pictures of random things.

"Where's Sean's office?"

Griselda points down the hall past the grandfather clock. "Third door on the right."

Mom rushes down the hall and disappears through the doorway as if sucked through a dark tunnel. Griselda sighs and helplessly follows her.

The office is grand with a large television on the wall, a dark distressed leather couch, and a huge Venetian desk, items neatly stacked and tidy as if it's never been used except for an array of colorful Post-its stuck across the glass and a small tray with a single, half-full shot glass beside the wide-screen desktop computer.

"He's a total control freak," Griselda says. "He'll know someone's been in here."

Mom ignores Griselda and continues snapping photos with her phone.

Griselda checks her own phone: 8:47 p.m. The game will be ending soon. She peers out the window, across the lawn, and over the wall, where she spies Tío Esteban clearly yelling at the cuates in their own house. They don't have their usual smug expressions on their faces anymore.

She didn't realize Sean could see Tío Esteban's house from his office.

She cracks the window to see if she can catch what Tío's yelling about.

"But, Dad . . ." The sound is muffled, but she catches some of the conversation. "It's *fake* blood . . ."

"Mom," Griselda whispers. "Look at your brother. He's so mad."

Mom comes to the window and listens.

"Serves them right," she says. "They scared the shit out of Amaranta."

"What'd they do?"

"I don't know. Just keep helping me look."

Mom's never been the paranoid type, not neurotic or hypervigilant. It's weird to see her acting so much like Abuela on her bad days.

Griselda shuts the window and follows her mom through the rest of the house. There are fewer windows back here. They're in the family room now, close to Harlan's room.

It was bad enough during the day with the Callahans here. At night, it's utterly creepy. All these twisted antlers and bulging animal heads that jut from the wallpaper.

Griselda steadies herself in the dark, pressing her hand to the wall as she walks forward. There's an indentation behind a slat of wallpaper. Tracing it, she uncovers a hidden seam, concealed beneath a deer head. Her hand trembles as she pushes it aside, and it *opens*. No way. There's a goddamn secret passage? She did *not* mean to prove Mom right.

She sighs in surrender. "Mom? There's a room back here."

They enter the cramped space. Despite herself, Griselda's abs constrict. She has *no idea* what they'll find in here. Harlan's never shown her this before.

She takes it all in.

Hunting gear. Wet soil. Gun oil. Across the room, a locked glass safe looms like a watchtower, guarding what it churns within its guts. Mom rushes in.

"This is where he keeps his guns."

But it's not the guns that catch Mal's attention as the hidden mud-room spins and blurs around her. It's *her . . .*

Alongside the animal heads and antlers bolted to the walls, La Siguanaba's disembodied horse head—bloodied at her stump of a neck—drips thick welts of blood down the side paneling. With a low, guttural creaking from somewhere deep in her throat, she turns—and the corners of her mouth spread into a menacing smile.

Mal presses her knuckles hard into her eyes and box-breathes in for five, out for five.

But La Siguanaba does not disappear when Mal stops counting.

She grabs Griselda's hand to try and ground herself in the present moment, but when she clamps her daughter's fingers, she recoils. The hand is not warm and soft. Not her daughter's at all. It's bloated and swollen, rubbery. Mal whips around to Griselda, now floating in the middle of the mudroom as if carried by unseen water. Her skin is a sickly shade of moss. Her crow-black hair wavers, undulating like seagrass.

Mal can't tell if she's screaming. She's locked in place, her heartbeat plugging her ears. She can't hear anything but the roar of water rushing over her. Suddenly, Griselda's spun upright, still hovering in the air. Her eyes blink open. She's distraught. Something's choking her. Those bulbous hands reach for her neck, prying at the unseen force. Her eyes, bloodshot, roll back.

"Mom!"

Mal tugs at her daughter, yanking as hard as she can to snatch her back to the ground, away from La Siguanaba. *You can't have her!*

"Mal!"

The voice isn't coming from above. Not from the mouth of the dead girl choking midair.

Mal's yanking at Griselda when she realizes her daughter, very much alive, is standing beside her, stock-still, watching her mother in horror.

Mal was never grabbing Griselda, was she?

In her hands, ripped from the wall, is one of Sean's rifles.

"What's going on?" Griselda finally whispers, her voice shaky. "Why'd you start screaming? Why'd you grab that gun?"

The chills clamp Mal first in the chest then spread to her entire body.

"Mom, you're really scaring me," Griselda whispers, reaching out like she wants to put a hand on her mom's shoulder but is afraid even to touch her.

"I'm sorry, mijita. I——" She wants to explain about La Siguanaba haunting her. But the way Griselda's staring at her makes her realize there's no way this rational, empirical, college-educated creature will understand. She'll just make Mal feel like a superstitious idiota chasing ghosts. And Mal can't bear that right now. Not when Griselda could be in danger.

That vision was *clearly* her elder daughter.

Mal sets the gun down slowly.

Not only does she need to find Amaranta *now*——she needs to keep Griselda from harm.

"That's a car in the driveway," Griselda hisses, grabbing Mal's arm and tugging her back through the panel and down the hall, into a room with a plaid comforter on the bed.

"Is this Harlan's room?"

"Yes, there's a back door."

"Hang on, let's check the closet, under the bed, and in the bathroom."

"Mom, I told you, I was here earlier." It's like she's playing twisted hide-and-seek.

"I still have to check."

"They're *home*. We'll get arrested."

But Mal's already pulled away from Griselda's grasp and is digging through the closet. Under the bed. She flings open the bathroom door and flaps aside the shower curtain.

Griselda grabs Mal again and yanks her, too hard, through the back door, shutting it softly behind them and whispering, "Run."

"Where?"

"Tío's." She nods toward the back fence.

Mal runs.

"It's too high."

"I'll give you a boost."

"And you?"

"I'm not the one they're upset with." Griselda squats and grabs her mom's foot to launch her over the wall.

Mal grasps the brick and strains to pull herself the rest of the way. "These people are dangerous."

"They're not. I'll meet you at the car."

"Gris!" Mal hisses, but her daughter's already running back to Harlan's room via the Callahan back door, so Mal jumps onto Esteban's lawn and sprints to his back door, thudding on it like a child left out in the dark. The seconds stretch. She's about to knock again when the door swings open. Her brother's eyebrows shoot up like birds startled into flight.

"Mal? What are you doing back here? Come inside."

"They have her," she chuffs as he ushers her into the kitchen and shuts the door.

"Who? Amaranta? Who has her?"

"The Callahans."

"In their house? Did you see her? Is she alright? Let's call Benny."

"No, Gris."

Esteban's eyes flicker with disbelief. He places a gentle hand on her shoulder. "Mal, Gris is fine. She's an adult. She can take care of herself. Are you alright? I know you must be . . . shaken. Maybe we should sit down and talk. Just you and me."

She refuses to sit at the dining room chair he's offered—she's too upset—but she explains everything except La Siguanaba. The break-in, the gun room, the guns.

Esteban seems unimpressed. "When was the last time you ate?"

"Why is everyone so concerned with my eating? I'm fine."

Tears are streaming down her face.

"Sis, you're exhausted. Let me take you home, or better yet, sleep in the guest room."

"I can't sleep. Amaranta . . ."

"Should we call your therapist? Do you have her number on your speed dial? I could call her for you." He extends his hand for her cell phone.

She pulls it out of her pocket, feeling sheepish and ridiculous, but says, "I'll call."

Instead of her therapist, she dials Gus. It's ringing when there's a knock at the front door.

Mal's trembling hand clutches her cell phone as she follows Esteban to the door. With tears still spilling onto her cheeks, he swings the door open, revealing Griselda, dripping with sweat from the humidity, her hair frazzled, her eyes wild.

"Gris! What happened?" Mal's shaking her head, the tears still flowing. She can't stop crying. Gus is asking her over the receiver if she's okay.

"I told Harlan I came to check on him after everything that happened earlier," she explains. "That my mom was just stressed and didn't mean all the things she said and did."

Mal's grip on the phone loosens; it dangles by her side, a voice calling, *Hello?* as her sobs turn into hitched and hiccupping breaths. She leans against the doorframe for support.

Gris grabs the cell phone and says, "Hello?"

The cuates descend the staircase, no longer smug vampires but plain-faced, pajama-clad children. Mal hasn't seen them this unpretentious and down-to-earth since they were little. Esteban's saying something about Mal needing to secure her own mask. Griselda's voice hisses into the phone, snotty and superior, "We've got this under control. We don't need you."

What a way for her to talk to her father. But it's unfair of Mal to expect anything else.

The cuates regard Mal like a curious zoo exhibit. They may be chastened but they're still not well-mannered.

Mal lunges at them.

"Where is she, you little shits? What have you done with my daughter?"

Griselda and Esteban pull her away, whispering to each other about Abuela's Ativan and Mal needing sleep as though she can't hear them. "Abuelo said the Ativan's missing. We need to get some from the farmacia."

The cuates are laughing, and Esteban yells at them, "Upstairs, ya!"

Like a wild thing thrashing against its cage, Mal's whimpering and struggling against her brother and her daughter. "I can't sleep. Not until I know she's home. Where is she? Chuy? Gus? Where's my *baby*?" She's devolved into body-wracking sobs.

Esteban's patting Mal's hair while Griselda looks at her like she's lost her mind and maybe she has. The vision of Griselda drowned . . . that can't be what's happened to Amaranta. It fucking can't be. She refuses it. *Mathematician in the Sky, don't you let her be dead. Don't you let her!* Mal can't breathe. She has to believe there's still time to save her. Forty-eight hours. That's what Benny says. They still have time. She's not getting these visions of the hellish horse-headed woman for nothing, right? There's *got* to be something Mal can do.

Her daughter's body will not be sluiced from the water.

She will not salt the earth with her daughter's bones.

20
RIDE OR DIE

Eventually, Mom stops crying and Griselda drives her home. But once there, Mom plants herself like the screwbean mesquite in the center of the front yard, refusing to move, whimpering, "I'm not going inside until my daughter's inside."

The sticky black tar of night has settled around them, the only relief coming from the dim glow of streetlamps and the porch light Abuelo left on, which lures a swirling mass of night bugs, their bodies flickering like sparks. Empty tables and chairs from the search party scatter across the yard like remnants from an abandoned carnival.

"Come on, Mom. You're no good to Amar like this. Get some rest and we'll start searching again first thing."

But Mom droops, deadweight in Griselda's arms.

Griselda feels like a parent trying to coax her inebriated and petulant teenager into the house when unfamiliar headlights flash and dim as a car she doesn't recognize pulls into the driveway behind her Honda.

Her stomach lurches as Gus steps out. What's *he* doing here? He nods at her and she instinctively steps back. "May I?" He's already reaching for her mom, and something primal in Griselda rises up to fight him, but the way her mom leans into his embrace freezes her in her place. She watches, a mix of horror and disbelief rooting in her gut as El Cucuy holds Mom, stroking her hair and whispering consolations.

She can't believe he's her father. It's trashy and telenovela and awful. They've officially entered *The Twilight Zone*.

When Griselda was a teenager, she was so mad at her mom for taking off to God knows where — presumably a boyfriend no one was allowed to ask questions about. Mom was an open book with a single sealed-tight chapter. She would just *shut down* if you tried to bring it up. Now Griselda knows why. She was hiding this monster.

Griselda tries not to picture El Cucuy hurting her sweet, funny, beautiful little sister. But if her undergrad years have taught her anything, it's how to question *everything*.

She can't let this lie. There's too much at stake. Her hermanita is *missing*, and Benny needs to question this guy. Mom said as much. Even if she can't admit it.

Griselda dials Benny and walks to the edge of the lawn, distancing herself from the creepy tableau of her parents huddled beneath the mesquite tree, rocking back and forth.

When he answers, she breathes out, "El Cucuy's at our house. Come get him."

"He's there now?" Benny sounds like he's shuffling through papers and eating something doughy.

"Yep. It's creeping me out. Pendejo, you have to tell me the truth, okay? Did you know he was my dad?" His explosive throat clearing tells her all she needs to know.

All these years. Everyone's been lying to her.

Benny finally says, "I'll be there as soon as I can," and hangs up.

At the same time, Abuelo Beto has emerged on the front porch and is scowling at El Cucuy, still holding Mom, who's somewhat more pacified but still cooing through her tears that she can't go inside without Amar.

Gus glances at Griselda with a forlorn expression, his eyes asking, *Truce?*

Griselda brushes him off with a scoff and looks away.

Abuelo spins on his heels, disappears behind the door, then returns a moment later, brandishing Abuela Vero's black cane. He holds the cane as high in the air as he can and yells, "Get away from my daughter! El Diablo!" His voice crackles. His face is screwed up with fury.

It would be comical if it weren't so tragic.

El Cucuy raises an arm, as if protecting Mom even though she's not the one in danger. *Why couldn't Abuelo have done this yesterday? Before Amaranta disappeared?* Griselda has half a mind to let Abuelo beat the shit outta this guy anyway but thinks better of it. She runs to him so he doesn't pull a muscle or trip on a clod of grass and accidentally smash his face in or break a hip, the way elders do.

"Come on, 'buelo," Griselda says. "I already called Benny. He'll take care of it."

Abuelo snaps his head toward her and blinks as if he's coming out of a haze. Thick brows furrowed, cane lowering slowly, he looks like he's about to respond when Mom shrieks, her voice sharp and high-pitched, "You did *what?*"

Before Griselda can answer, Mom turns to El Cucuy and hisses,

"I *told* you not to come here. My brother will *arrest* you. ¡Vete, ahora!"

"You need me," he says, squeezing Mom's shoulder. "It'll be alright."

At the very least, all this Cucuy drama seems to have distracted Mom from her grief.

Abuelo shakes his head and exhales a weary sigh, leaning onto Abuela's cane, its rubber tip wedged into a crevice between pavers where the stubbornest weeds poke through, the ones who've resisted the vinegar and digging fork.

Griselda's phone vibrates in her pocket. She fishes it out and a message from Harlan flickers on the screen: Hey, any updates? Sorry about my parents, they can be real jerks. Just wanna remind you, I'm here for you no matter what. Hit me up anytime day or nite, okay? ☺

A gnawing guilt that refuses to be named niggles at her. She tucks the phone away without replying.

In a few short minutes, Benny pulls up, his lieutenant with him. He's got a little jelly on his shirt. Griselda called it; he was eating a donut. Normally, she'd laugh and call him a cliché, but right now, her stomach hurts. She feels responsible for all this.

"Gustavo Castillo," Benny says, his voice all authoratative as his lieutenant holds out the handcuffs, which seem like overkill and somewhat theatrical to Griselda but whatever. "We need you to come in for questioning in the disappearance of your daughter, Amaranta Veracruz."

"Is he under arrest?" Mom asks.

Abuelo emits a snort of skepticism at the same time Mom moves protectively in front of El Cucuy. "It's okay, amor. They can question me. I have nothing to hide." He extends his hands.

But Benny relents. "We don't need handcuffs if you're agreeing to come with us."

"Where are you taking him?" Mom asks.

"We're still waiting on that warrant to search your house," Benny says to Gus. "So we'll just head to the station."

"You don't need a warrant. I can show you around my house."

Lieutenant Hernandez Pierce steps forward, her voice firm yet calm. "Mr. Castillo, we appreciate your cooperation, but you have the right to legal counsel. Do you waive that right?"

Gus shrugs. "Lawyers never did much to help."

"I could call Esteban," Mom offers, but Gus shakes his head.

As Gus ducks into the backseat of Benny's sedan, Mom runs past Abuelo into the house, and Griselda lets out a sigh of relief. She knew it was the right thing to call her bruncle. He's always good in an emergency. But practically before her exhale's complete, Mom's running back out the front door again, keys in hand, and jumping into her Jeep.

"Goddamnit," Griselda groans, then realizes she's said it aloud in front of Abuelo. "Sorry, 'buelo."

"Well, don't just stand there, mija," he replies, pointing the cane toward the Jeep. "Don't let her go alone."

Griselda sprints to the passenger door, waving down Mom, who's already backing out like a bat outta hell. "Wait!"

Mom slams the brake and mouths, *What?* all dramatic, like, *you've done enough damage.*

"I'm coming with you."

Mom doesn't talk to her the whole dark drive over, headlights casting long shadows down the dirt roads. She stays silent even when they pull up to what might've been a seaside cottage a few decades ago but now looks more like a shack.

Does Griselda remember any of this from when she was very

young? Mom's brought her here before, hasn't she? That's why El Cucuy blurs the edges of her memory. Why Benny has nightmares. "Maybe we should've waited until morning," she mutters more to herself than Mom, who doesn't respond anyway. Mom's never been one for the silent treatment. It's disconcerting.

El Cucuy sits in the back of Benny's unmarked police sedan parked just outside. Why did Benny just leave him out here, uncuffed? He could run away. Or did Benny cuff him after all?

He nods at her unusually quiet mom to head inside without him. Griselda follows and is immediately assaulted by the smell of decay. It's not like at the house she grew up in, overrun by squatters. It's not that kind of moldering, not feces or mold. But there's a definite musty stench. The way a convalescent home can smell. Hospital antiseptic mixed with sadness. Griselda wants to wait in the car but feels compelled to babysit her mom. She hates feeling this way.

The interior is a chaotic maze of clutter; thumbtacked maps seeping red with scribbles paper the walls, like in a serial killer's lair. It's like the scene from *Se7en* when the detective and devoted husband, Brad Pitt (Harlan has a guy crush on him too, so they've watched all his movies from *Thelma & Louise* on), enters John Doe's insane notebook-cramped apartment with Morgan Freeman as his police partner. That's how Griselda feels in El Cucuy's house, only, she's terrified to find out what's in the box. There are literally boxes *everywhere*. Files and legal boxes stacked and teetering, newspapers yellowed with age strewn across all the furniture that's likewise buried. The guy's a freaking hoarder. Griselda has to sidestep around the maze.

Benny and his lieutenant are already donning gloves, searching the place.

Griselda shivers so hard her teeth literally clack with an audible chatter that makes her feel like a cartoon character. She's only ever had chills like this once before, the time in tenth grade she had mono (same time as Harlan, go figure — damn him for making her watch so many horrors and thrillers alongside his rom-coms).

El Cucuy was *too calm,* bringing them here, wasn't he? Maybe this is some kind of trap.

She clamps her goose-pimpled arms around her chest, glancing at Mom. The house seems to cast a soporific haze over her, as if she's been dosed with that sleepy-time tea with the little bear on the box. Her eyes flutter and she collapses into the only armchair not buried under layers of clutter, drawing a tatty, plaid throw blanket from its back around her shoulders.

Griselda's read about a predator, the jewel wasp, that hijacks a cockroach, turning it into a pawn and unwitting mealhouse. The wasp stabs her victim in a precise area of the brain and injects it with a neurotoxin that zombifies the poor roach. She takes away its sense of fear and will to escape, then drags her groggy, compliant victim to her burrow, laying eggs inside its body so her young can devour it from the inside out. The jeweled mother keeps the roach alive but docile, ensuring fresh organs as sustenance for her offspring.

Is that Mom and El Cucuy, only he's the wasp? Has he been feasting off Mom?

It's hard to see her badass butcher mom this way. Griselda kinda hopes there's another more plausible explanation as she stands before one of the walls, reluctantly taking a closer look: photos, articles, and notes connect with tangled strings, the clippings all sensational, some from literal tabloids: "Chupacabra Rampage in El Paso Leaves Family Pet Mutilated: A Warning to Us All?" Next to it, an old, faded article from a local Texas newspaper details a young boy's mysterious disappearance, the word "Chupacabra?" scrawled in Mom's tight, anxious handwriting across the top. "La Llorona Spotted Near Rio Grande, Mourning Turns Malevolent," accompanied by a grainy photograph of what appears to be a woman in a high-collared, lace wedding dress at the water's edge.

It's absurd, yet Mom has meticulously annotated the margins, circling dates and names. Another section of the board is dedicated to El Nahual, with several articles from villages in Oaxaca, where livestock were slaughtered under the full moon, the villagers whispering of a shapeshifter seeking vengeance.

A cluster of articles covers sightings of La Siguanaba, replete with sketches of the horse-headed woman Mom's been terrorizing them with since childhood. "Does she go after men? Or girls???" a note questions, the suggestion alone enough to make Griselda's skin crawl. "Has anyone actually seen her by the Salton Sea?" another note asks, underlined several times and strung to pictures of Noemi, Gus's infamous first daughter, then her own Tía Elena.

But what churns Griselda's stomach is a picture of Renata. She's only been gone a week. Mom's been here recently, working on this madness. It all feels like proof that Gus gave Mom a whopping glass of Kool-Aid, which she's downed.

"What the hell is this?" Benny asks, holding up a jar. Griselda's stomach sloshes when she realizes the jar is full of a macabre array of teeth.

"It's the evidence we've collected." Mom's tone is weary as she defends her grim harvest.

Lieutenant Hernandez Pierce, gloves on, lifts a jar and inspects its contents. "No, these are teeth. Mixed with fish bones."

"You've been collecting fish bones?" Benny stares at Mal like he's just seeing her.

"Anything the lake turns up."

They move into El Cucuy's bedroom, which is surprisingly meticulous, with jersey-knit sheets and a floral comforter. It smells of sandalwood, and the bathroom is clean with ordinary accoutrements. All this may possibly gross Griselda out more; this must be his and Mom's "sanctuary."

But across the hallway a door is closed. Benny turns the knob. It's locked.

He calls through the hall, "Hey, Mal. What's in this locked room? You got a key?"

Griselda's chest constricts.

She wants to call out "Amaranta!" and pound on the door, but she can't move or speak. Fear has glued her to the hardwood behind Benny and his lieutenant in the dim hallway. They're gonna find all the missing girls in here, aren't they? On piss-stained mattresses smelling of ammonia and desperation. Or chained to the furniture. Or dead. She pulls her inhaler from her pocket and puffs it twice.

"We don't go in there." Mom's voice is right on Griselda's back.

"Well, we're going in there now," Benny declares, shoving his shoulder hard against the door, but it doesn't budge.

Griselda tries to quiet her mind to listen for any sound from within. Voices or scratching or crying. All she hears are the wasps and the line from *Se7en,* only now it's *What's in the room?*

"Go get Gus," Benny instructs his lieutenant.

When she returns with El Cucuy, he's sweating profusely. He stops beside a visibly shaken Mom, who squeezes his hand.

"That's my daughter's bedroom," he says barely above a whisper.

"Would you please open it?"

Is it Griselda's mind playing tricks on her, or does a light flicker from inside Noemi's bedroom? "Is anyone in there?" she asks.

"Of course not," Mom scolds. But the way Mom's shaking, maybe she's worried too. Or nervous. Or both.

"Gustavo?" Benny snaps. "A key?"

"I lost it ages ago. Somewhere in this mess." He seems apologetic. But he's probably putting on a show.

The buzzing intensifies. *Bzzzzzz.* A wasp's nest. In the walls.

"Fine. Let's just break it down," Benny says. He steps back, readying himself for a much more forceful entry than before. Normally Griselda would warn that he's gonna break his shoulder, but before he can act, a soft, almost imperceptible click halts everyone in their tracks.

"What the fu——" Benny exhales at the same time Mom gasps.

The door, previously locked tight, swings open slowly, creaking on its hinges as if inviting them in. No key, no force.

The wasps' buzzing grows louder, then suddenly ceases, leaving an oppressive silence. The warm scent of sandalwood is replaced with a pungent gas-station bathroom stench. You know the one. Piss all over the floor. Walls. Ceiling. Ammonia. And is that——hay?

Griselda braces herself.

Mal clutches Griselda, pulling her away from the doorway. *You can't have her!*

In the center of the musty, dust-covered teenage girl's bedroom—— a Hello Kitty, pink-bowed mausoleum untouched for twenty-six years——the horse-headed woman flickers into view. Her onyx mane obscures the edges of her face, her blood-red eyes pierce through the dimness. She grabs the girl that Mal now notices has been cowering beside La Siguanaba.

The butt of a rifle slams into the girl's face. Her left cheekbone and jaw. And her teeth.

Her teeth scatter across the thick layer of dirt and dust bunnies soiling the hardwood.

21
WHAT DESTROYS YOU

Mal slams the screen door and sits on the porch, wrapping the blanket tighter around her. She can't get warm enough. The whole world has gone cold and bleak since Amaranta disappeared.

The faintest glow illuminates the Chocolate Mountains beyond the desert, the Salton Sea in the distance shimmering against the inky dusk.

It's been a whole night without her daughter. It's Saturday morning. Mal should be heading to work, and Amaranta and Papi should be coming into the carnicería to pick out this week's meals. Instead, she's sitting here, alone, and they haven't learned a damn thing.

They had nothing on Gus. They never do. Bunch of dumbasses, Mal would usually think. Except this dumbass is her baby brother she loves like a son, who happens to be half a Callahan by blood.

She sighs. She can't fault him for doing his job. But she does. While they're sitting on their thumbs at Gus's place, combing over what she and Gus have already gone through countless times, her baby girl is still out there somewhere—along the shore of the hundred-mile lake or in the desert, or in some sicko's basement.

La Siguanaba takes girls. Mal didn't want to believe it. She should come for terrible men, not innocent daughters. But there it is.

Does she deliver them to men? Or anyone who's called upon her? Is she a summoned demon in that way? Does she do the dirty work of others?

Or is she stealing them for herself? Her own sick pleasure?

Either way, what's clear to Mal is that they should've searched Sean's place harder. He's the one with that secret room. All those guns and trophy heads. She saw a vision of a dead girl in his house too. They need Benny to get a warrant for *Sean*, not the same tired scapegoat this whole fucked-up town's been after for two and a half decades. But Benny's gotta do everything by the book, or the sheriff will have his badge, and, oh, guess what? The Callahans have the sheriff by the balls. Or maybe Benny's working *for* the Callahans after all? Covering for them?

She shakes that thought away. What's wrong with her?

She finds out her mother was having an affair and suddenly she's rewriting history. Benny's *Mal's* son in all the ways that count. She knows the kind of person he is.

He's not really a Callahan. He's not.

And even if he *were* . . . he's more like Harlan than Sean.

Mal's exhausted to her core.

She's been telling Benny as much since he made Gus open Noemi's door, pobrecito. Or rather, since that damn Lieutenant Hernandez Pierce, quiet as a mouse, went around back and broke

Noemi's window, unlatching the door from inside. That's what everyone else had seen, at least. But Mal knows La Siguanaba was there for a reason. She just doesn't know *what*.

Is La Siguanaba messing with her? Testing her? Taunting her? Pretending she has a chance of finding her daughter before she . . .

"Amaranta," Mal whispers into the nothingness. *"Ahhhh . . . Mar . . . Ahhhhhhhnnnnnnn . . . tahhhhhhh!"* Her voice has risen with each sylla-ble, until suddenly she's screaming at the top of her lungs. Her head droops, slack against her neck. She's soaking wet, teeth chattering so hard she'll break them. And her teeth do crack. They shatter into the water at her feet. *Plunk, plunk, plunk,* fall the teeth, white as the seagulls scattering from the toxic sea. White as the bleached fish scales floating to the surface. White against the menstrual blood-water suddenly rising. She clings to the knotted roots forming at the bathtub's bottom, curling her toes into the sandy playa.

Elena simmers into focus, just beyond Mal's reach. A teenage girl stirring a pot. Carne de rez, a thick primal cut, ruddy in the broth. Separating meat from bone. Elena stirs.

Mal watches her sister through the bathroom doorway as the walls tattoo themselves with sprays of blood—*Destroy what destroys you*—through the gangrened hallway, into their old kitchen, decay-ing around her, smattered with rat droppings, until the pot splatters to the ground.

And then something rises from the broth—Amaranta rises, dressed in school clothes, jeans and a tee, with a pair of highlighter-yellow Converse.

Mal clambers out of the tub, naked and shake-legged as a foal, stumbling, fevering toward her daughter. A thick cord connects them. Mal follows it, but Mami blocks her, chewing through the ropy placenta, blood dripping down her chin. Before Mal can push Mami away, Elena grabs Amaranta and squeezes her tightly, and together, the two girls evaporate. Like water in the desert heat. They disappear.

And all that's left is La Siguanaba, picking up the pot, returning it to the stove. Her horse's maw smiling that wide-toothed smile, dripping saliva.

As she screams again, Mal's maw splits open, a pink pitaya bursting from a cactus. She is the horse-headed woman, cantering into the fields. Her mane scraggles down her blood-soaked back. Dogs are barking and there's Benny, gripping an industrial flashlight steady. *"What have they found?"* Mal's screaming. Benny turns, his bright blue eyes burning through his chupacabra face, his black nose scrounged with dirt and mud. *"Benito! Tell me what they've found!"*

Mal's not sure how long she nodded off, but by the time Griselda starts hollering for Mal from inside the house, the sun's a ball of pink fire above the mountain peaks.

"Mom!"

Mal scrambles up, heart palpitating.

Griselda's clutching her phone, no, Mal's phone, waving it in the air. "You got a notification! Find My Phone! Mom!"

"What? What happened?"

"It found her!"

22
A LAMB, BLEATING

SOMETIME AFTER NOON ON FRIDAY

A whooshing in Amaranta's brain. Sopping. Freezing. Brain freeze.

An ice storm in the desert? Shhhhhhh. Hushing. Or is that her, breathing hard?

Short-circuit.

An ice storm in her brain. Thick, jagged pieces of hail. Iggy's fond of saying, *When hell freezes over.*

Can you move, mijita? Try. For Mami.

Her limbs won't obey.

I can't.

Come on, try.

Her body is heavy. The pungency of petrol. And something sickly sweet.
The slushee. She's covered in red.

Cherry-red ice. Her clothes are soaked and sticking to her skin, both with sugar and wetness and sweat. Has she peed herself? She's shaking uncontrollably. Her whole body juddering.

She can't keep her eyes open. Everything's sideways. She's sideways. It's dark in here. Or is it dark outside? She can't tell.

She has to get out of here.

She tries to stand, but her legs wobble like a foal's.

Maaaaaa. She tries to call for her mother but nothing comes out of her mouth. She tries again. Spittle drools down her chin.

What was in that slushee?

Maaa. She's a lamb, bleating. Only, she can't tell if she's making any noise or not.

How far away from town is she? Or is she still *in* town? She can't see anything through the slits in her eyes. It's all blurry. Like her eyes are covered with gauze. Are her eyes covered?

She can't move.

She's read about being trapped in your body—locked in. Is that what she feels now?

Get up, Amar! Come on, mijita. Mami's here, let's go, I've got you. Ma, reaching out her hand, looking Amaranta straight in the eyes, assuring her.

She gathers all her strength and heaves herself against a wall, using its unfinished texture like flypaper against her unsteady palms, pulling herself to kneeling, then precarious standing.

She takes a step, then another, still unsure where she is or where she's going. *Maaaaaa?* She tries again. *Greeee?*

Is sound coming from her?

Or is that the scraping of leaves and branches against—what? Glass? A roof?

Pins and needles jab her feet and legs. It's like she sat cross-legged too long. She has to drag her legs to step. She feels against the rough drywall. A garage?

She blinks several times, trying to focus. It's like she's got chlorine in her eyes. Everything's hazy.

Maaaaaa. Mama. Ma. *Come get me. Come pick me up. I'm sorry I didn't tell you sooner—*

One dead foot hits something hard, a rock, no, a concrete step, but it's too late; she's keeling forward, too drowsy and confused and unbalanced. She would brace for impact if she could.

The pain shock-waves through her. It starts at her face and chin, then reverberates through her neck and down her spine. She's a broken faucet. She's spurting warm water. A bathtub. She's drowning.

Arrorró mi niña . . . hush-a-bye . . .

Her cheek pressed to the cold, hard concrete, half her body sprawled jagged on the painful step, she blinks again. All she can see on the ground beside her is a small white pearl. Shining in a crimson pool.

Her tooth.

She would put her hand to the burbling fountain of her mouth if she could. She closes her eyes. The woman with the long oil spill of hair at the edge of the water turns her head. *Follow me,* she neighs.

23
LAST FREE PLACE IN AMERICA

The man with snakes coiling around his neck has no front teeth and no daughter of Mal's, he insists, no girl or woman in this RV for years — and not cuz he's got no game. He's a straight shooter, him and his snakes.

Mal's skin prickles as he spits out *straight shooter*. She doesn't believe one goddamned word from this snake catcher's mouth, his sibilants broad and sloppy.

"Put that thing away," Benny orders but does nothing to stop the slithering. "Let's go through this again. Your full name's Francis Miller, but people call you Bull."

"Like a bull snake, docile unless provoked. I don't bite, but I can sure as shit choke the life outta you if you bring me to it." He holds the snake to his face — tender as a beloved family pet or an injured bird — and kisses it.

Mal recoils. It's not his eccentricities she has an issue with. But this guy could have her daughter stashed somewhere in this snake-skinned hellhole. "Why'd my daughter's phone ping from your RV?"

"We're getting to that, Mal, hang on," Benny says in a tone Mal takes as condescending. He turns back to Bull. "You've lived in this spot for the past ten years, give or take a few months, so you're well-known around these parts."

These parts is Slab City — a desert outpost dubbed the future of homelessness by big-city newspapers. Others call it the last free place in America, built upon the remnants of a decommissioned Marine base. It's where Skid Row meets Burning Man, home to the Slabbers, not a baseball team but drifters, addicts, oddballs, army vets, bohemians, and outcasts. It's where dogs Papi calls rez dogs roam around the plywood and RVs.

Just weeks ago, Mal, Papi, Amaranta, and Esteban, ever the optimist, had visited the camp for his campaign — while Slabbers lack traditional amenities and addresses, Esteban's adamant about their voting rights. The people here don't have addresses, technically. There's no post office. But even unhoused residents have the right to vote, Esteban explained fervently, Mal and Amaranta by his side, clipboards in hand, signing folks up. Like Claudette, who lost her home in Long Beach due to medical bankruptcy. *People can adapt to anything,* she said. No trash collector. No flushable toilets. When there's no other choice, humans learn to endure.

We'll give you a reason to endure, Esteban assured. *I promise you that, Claudette.*

"Yep, been boondocked here near on a decade," Bull slobbers. "Won this beauty in a bet. She's a classic. A 1980s vintage Winnebago."

"Yeah, she's a beaut," Benny placates. "So you haven't seen a teenage girl around here? No one hitchhiking or asking for directions or a place to stay?"

"Nope. Just me and my snakes," Bull says, his tongue flapping against his gums, in the excess space between his lips. The wheeze in his voice isn't from cigarettes; his camper doesn't smell like smoke. It's from the toxic dust storms. "The sun out here, it does things to people," Bull says with a flicker of a smirk. "Makes 'em see things."

"What's so funny?" Mal cuts. They don't have time for this. Where's her daughter?

"Did I tell you this guy's a mixture of hemotoxins and neurotoxins?" He kisses the snake again. "I wouldn't wish this venom on my worst enemy." He's been reciting a dozen junk facts about rattlers since they arrived. He's shaking and wriggling his fingers in the air like he's playing an invisible instrument. All those snakebites have caused neuropathy.

"Why would her phone lead us to your RV if she's not here?" Benny presses, holding up Mal's phone. On the Find My app, a blue circle hovers over this plot of land with a small thumbnail image of Amaranta smiling up at them.

Bull shrugs. "Not every bite injects. It's a lottery. One in three lucky bastards won't get no venom at all."

Backup's coming. Benny's finally getting something right now that he's shifted focus off Gus, who's back in action, searching the desert outside with Griselda and Lieutenant Hernandez Pierce. For now, Mal and Benny just need to keep this snake creep talking. Did he set his sights on Amaranta when they were campaigning the other week? Did he follow her to school then drag her back here?

"Come on, you don't remember us from when we were here a few weeks ago?" Mal prods. "My brother, dad, and daughter were with me. You must've seen us."

"Nah, never seen you before today."

Mal can't take her eyes off the diamond scales coiling around his neck and shoulders, ridges so thick and woolly, the reptilian body appears furlike.

"As I was sayin', after gettin' bit and goin' to the hospital more times than I have fingers, I learned to catch 'em. So when I see rattlers around here, in someone's yard, where kids are playin', I take 'em to the desert a mile or two out."

Mal almost asks if he takes the snakes or kids to the desert, but he points to a map, soiled and crumpled, hanging on the wall beside a naked woman with—you got it—a snake coiled around her nether region. It's marked with yellow stars.

"What do the stars mean?" Benny asks.

He traces one and says, "Where I've had . . . encounters."

Benny squints at the map. It's the surrounding Sonoran. The stars circle the Salton Sea. "Encounters? With who? Or what?"

Bull chuckles but it quickly escalates into a coughing fit and Mal covers her face with her shirt to avoid his spittle flying at her. "A bit of both, I reckon. Animals, people, some old remnants of the past."

"You'd better not mean *bodies*," Mal snaps.

Bull shakes his head. "No, I don't mean *bodies*."

You never know. Since cemeteries in the Slabs are as much of a problem as self-dug porta-potties, a few years back, a flood carried dead bodies across the washes. The corpses floated through the desert like rafts ablaze on their way to Valhalla. The phone calls, too, flooded the lines.

Mal wishes they could crack a window. Bull's RV is too hot. And cluttered. Bottles of all sorts, a free two-year-old Mexican restaurant calendar taped to the wall, and various bits of food, tools, and curiosities litter the space. Everywhere, crisp shed snake skins. And, of course, Bull with a rattler draped around his neck and shoulders like a noose. Like the disgruntled man who called deputies from the nearby hot springs to report that his brother-in-law had allegedly threatened him and other family members with a rattlesnake, coaxing the snake to bite them.

The last dispatch Benny shared wasn't funny at all. She and Sal stopped laughing and sobered up. Like too many calls, it went unresolved.

A female subject called 911 from the Slab City skate park and advised dispatchers she'd been drugged and kidnapped before disconnecting. Mal can hear the dead hum of a phone line reverberating through her skull. Could Amaranta be at any of those spots on Bull's dirty map? Could those stars be not snakes but *girls*? Renata went missing out here too.

Bull's snake facts might be diverting them from something obvious. She retrieves her phone and dials Amaranta. Mal's mothergut clenches. It rings from somewhere inside the RV.

She springs up, and the rattlesnake bows, constricting its body into a tight line. "What have you done to my *daughter,* you sick shit?"

Three weeks ago, Mal was the sister of the senator-to-be. Professional, proud. Now she wishes she had her scimitar. If this guy's done *anything* to her baby girl, she will gut him and slice the meat from his bones.

Bull backs up a few steps, his hands out like *stay calm,* which infuriates Mal more. "Hey, hey, I don't have your daughter." His tongue is too thick. It comes out garbled. The snake around his neck stays taut—like a dog's tail pointing to danger.

Amaranta's phone stops ringing and goes to voicemail. Her voice makes Mal's eyes sting with tears. *"If I don't know you, I doubt I want to. If I do, I'm probly already with you."*

"Sir, return the snake to its tank," Benny says, grasping Mal by the arm to hold her back.

"Amaranta?" Mal pushes past Benny and Bull anyway and flings open the bathroom door, revealing a cesspit. She gags at what's splattered all over the shower/toilet combo and shuts the door but not quick enough. It's not blood but shit. Literally everywhere. "Amaranta!"

Bull coaxes the snake from around his shoulder into a tank inside a grungy, broken-down fridge. The rusted door reads LIVE SNAKE! BEWARE in shaky script.

Mal draws back the accordion door to the bedroom where a thin, stained mattress props atop a shelf, uncovered pillows and a threadbare blanket wadded at the head. The fug of stale sweat and body odor and God knows what makes her eyes water. She covers her face with her shirt again and tries lifting the bed to ensure it's not a secret compartment. Despite her efforts, the bed won't move. She yanks out the drawers, their hinges protesting, and kneels to search beneath. "Amaranta? Are you down there, baby?"

Coiled snakeskins and tumbleweed-like dust and debris.

In the kitchen, Benny's saying, "Look, Bull. We need the facts. Why is this phone in your home?" He holds Mal's phone up again and points to Amaranta's picture in Find My Phone. "This phone is associated with a missing child. Where did you get it?"

"Well, shit, why didn't you ask that before?" His lisp creates a foam of spit around his mouth. "I was out lookin' for rattlers and bombs yesterday when I came across this in a knapsack and brought it home to charge cuz it was dead. Out here, one man's trash is another man's gain."

"What kind of knapsack? Where?"

"I don't know. A kid's backpack."

Mal's breath hitches. She reaches for something to brace herself, grasping the sticky residue of the trailer wall. "Show us exactly where you found my daughter's backpack."

He pulls the map off the wall and points to a yellow star a mile outside Slab City, back the way they came between Niland and Salvation Mountain.

"Did you see anyone out there with the backpack? Did you see or talk to this girl?" Benny pulls out a clearer picture of Amaranta, which Bull squints at then shakes his head.

"Nah, I never seen her before."

"Like hell you haven't," Mal spits. "She was *just here* a few weeks ago. We were here with my brother."

"Who's your brother?"

"Esteban Veracruz. He's running for office. Don't tell me you didn't notice us."

"I try and avoid stiffs in suits." His hand holding the picture of Amaranta trembles like he's shaking a Polaroid.

"You have any warrants against you?" Benny asks.

"It's nothin'. A while back, I got into an altercation with a guy over me supposably trespassin' in his yard on the mainland. I was catchin' a snake, but he called the damn cops. I was just trynna keep it from hurtin' kids. I didn't mean no harm."

"A minute ago, you mentioned looking for bombs? Did you plant bombs?"

He wheezes a chuckle. "God no! I'm keepin' folks safe. Why would — ?"

"Okay, so why are there bombs out there?"

"The Marine base. Government fuckers leave 'em lyin' around. I deactivate 'em, but if I don't know how, I call the fire department."

"Was there a bomb near the backpack? Did you see any debris?"

Bile burns Mal's throat. Benny's asking if he saw pieces of her daughter blown to bits.

"No, no, nothin' like that. Just the backpack."

"You see anyone else out there? Near the backpack? A newcomer? Tourist? Townie?"

"Nope. Just the backpack in the dirt all by its lonesome."

"You have it here with you? And I'll need that phone."

Bull heads to the cockpit, Mal close on his heels, her breath so ragged from anxiety she may need to ask Griselda for a puff of her inhaler.

Bull rummages through a pile of shit in the cockpit before retrieving the backpack and a cell phone from a charging port and handing them over to Mal, but Benny plucks Amaranta's phone away before Mal can examine it. Her breaths come in short puffs as she opens the backpack instead. Her baby girl had it with her yesterday morning when Mal dropped her off at school. Despite the tang in the trailer, this backpack still smells like Amaranta. Inside, art supplies and a sketchbook Mal flips through. There's a sketch of Iggy with hearts all around it. Mal's been so caught up in her own drama . . . her daughter's relationship should've been obvious.

Meanwhile, Benny scrolls through Amaranta's call history and messages. "I don't see anything suspicious other than the two-minute call to that burner phone I told you about."

"Call it, see if anyone answers."

A few seconds later, "It's disconnected."

"She didn't pack any clothes or overnight things. And this was all she had with her when I dropped her off at school." The tears are rolling down Mal's cheeks. "I don't think she ran away, Benny. She was just going to school . . ."

If Bull's telling the truth and he found her backpack in the middle of the desert, what does that mean? Did she throw it out purposely? From a trucker's window? Someone else she was hitching a ride with? Or is she here in Slab City, and she just dropped it accidentally?

The other possibility is glaring her in the face, but she can't bring herself to envision it. She refuses to acknowledge it. She's trembling all over and squeezes the backpack to her chest.

"Mal," Benny whispers. He's standing beside her. How long has he been calling her?

"Huh?"

"I hate to say it, but we should get the team set up where he found her backpack. Get some dogs out there."

"Cadaver dogs?" Mal swallows back sour gastric acid.

La Siguanaba, blood-soaked and bedraggled, tugs at Amaranta. Mal chokes, a thick root gnarling guts to throat.

Benny grips Mal's shoulders, but she feels nothing. "Not just cadaver. Not yet. I'm still hopeful we'll find her alive. You hear me? This is only a precaution. Don't give up hope. We need your tenacity. Come on, boss up, Mal."

She nods, tears hot and sticky against her cheeks, pooling among yesterday's makeup and the crust in her eyelids. She forces herself to feel the weight of Benny's hands upon her and urges her lungs to expand as she gathers breath. One, two, three, four, five. Shaky and painful but she manages to hold the snake-funk air in the box of her rib cage before stretching her mouth into a wide O and releasing.

Bull watches her with interest, and a swishy sensation overtakes her. She whispers to Benny, "What if he *is* lying, and this is a ruse to get us out of the camper?"

"My team'll be here any minute. We'll scrub this place and the surrounding perimeter. Half of us will stay and the other half will search the desert. She could have a tent or someone else with an RV, another Slabber, maybe. Someone she met when she was here before?" He clears his throat with a violent inward implosion. "We won't take this guy's word on anything."

Bull makes a hurt face and puts his hand on his chest.

Mal stifles back the image of Amaranta stuffed into a shit-stained holding tank or storage container beneath the trailer.

"Let's go, Bull, you're up," Benny says, clapping his hands. "Take us out to where you found my niece's backpack."

"Your niece, huh?" Bull grabs a baseball cap, tucks his unkempt hair beneath the brim, and is heading toward the side door when a cactus-sharp cry slices through the fug. It's Griselda's voice, coming from outside.

A daughter's scream can signal countless things. Delight from rainwater puddles after a monsoon cools the blistering heat. Terror from a cockroach fizzling on the bathroom wall. But this is unlike any sound Mal's heard her daughter make yet.

Benny rushes out of the Winnebago with Mal. They scan the yard, Bull a step behind, carrying a large contraption that resembles a dentist's plaque scraper, only broom-sized.

Mesquite and headless palms clump around the dirt and weed-covered lot where Griselda isn't. Neighboring Slabbers have come outside to peek. They leave well enough alone, but they also protect each other, or so they told Mal when she was here with Esteban, Papi, and Amaranta.

Does that mean they protect each other from justice too?

"Gris!" Mal calls, praying to the Mathematician in the Sky that she's *not* screaming because she's found her sister sawed into pieces in the Winnebago's holding tank.

She dashes around the trailer, stopping short at the horrifying scene before her.

Gus holds his rifle aimed at their fallen daughter.

24
DEATH RATTLE

hat the fu——?" Benny's gasping when Mal understands what's happening.

Griselda's curled onto the hard-packed dirt, contorted in anguish. Beside her, mottled brown and tan blurs into diamonds, the taut body coiled into a staff with a pair of fangs curved and sharp as Mal's butcher knives. The rattle sizzles as Griselda clamps her leg where two flame-red puncture marks burn brightly, droplets of blood oozing from the slits.

Mal's first reaction is to sprint to Griselda's side, but she knows better than to cross the snake's path. On hunts, Papi called this sound the death rattle and warned Mal to steer clear.

Gus's finger is on the trigger, but Bull interjects—"No need for that." He locks eyes with the snake, extending his snake hook and muttering, "Up to your mischief, huh, Lucifer?" With a flick of his wrist, he secures Lucifer, immobilizing its fangs. Lucifer hisses and thrashes, fangs striking the air as Bull lifts the pole, Lucifer in a taut coil. Only then does Bull turn his attention to Griselda. "Lucky girl. Out of any rattler, it was old Lucifer. Son-of-a-bitch is a dry biter."

"How do you know?" Mal asks, rushing to poor Gris, who's pasty and dripping sweat.

"Lucifer's old as dirt. His fangs are pretty much calcified. But no venom doesn't mean you don't need no doctor. These suckers get infected quicker than you can say *antibiotics.*"

Mother's instinct tells Mal to crouch down and suck the venom from her daughter's wound, but Papi taught her better. She could spread the poison to her mouth or ingest it.

She kneels and strokes her daughter's hair, thinking of her vision in Sean's gun room. Her daughter's corpse thrashing midair, choking. "We need to get her to the hospital . . ."

But her intestines kink at that too. That hanging girl could've been *dying,* not dead yet. She could be *Amaranta*—in the desert right now, needing Mal to find her.

Mal can't make this impossible choice. "We still need to search where Bull found Amaranta's backpack. Our forty-eight-hour window . . ."

Benny says, "Mal, I'll go to the desert and keep you updated. You head to the hospital."

Mal turns toward Griselda. "Does it burn, 'jita?" She presses her hands to her daughter's wound, feeling for warmth or swelling. It's not blistering or discoloring. Bull might know a lot about snakes, but Papi's taught Mal about treating wounds in the field.

Griselda barely swivels her head *no* but winces. "It just hurts. And itches."

"That's a good sign," Bull says. "Like I said, dry bite."

"We still need to get you checked out," Mal says. "You look like a ghost."

"I'll take her to the hospital, Mal," Gus offers, gun finally lowered, his expression somber but earnest.

Benny frowns. "Mal, are you sure that's a good idea?"

"Benito, get off his back. He cooperated with your all-night search. What else do you want? He's a good guy. And her *father*." Mal expects Griselda to protest like her bruncle, the way she's been shooting daggers at Gus all morning, but she doesn't. Maybe she's in shock. "Thank you, Gus. Be careful. And text me what the doctor says."

Gus lifts Griselda as easily as a felled coyote from his yard and carries her toward his truck, Mal watching helplessly after them.

Old-school country western wafts from the radio, somber and soporific as elevator music. Griselda wouldn't have pegged El Cucuy for a Johnny Cash or Tammy Wynette kind of guy.

As the chills overtake her, she huddles against the passenger side door for support, curled as best she can to keep her bitten leg from rubbing against the bucket seat. Why'd she get into a truck with El Cucuy? The wasp's nest buzzes. *Bzzz.* Her thoughts molasses.

She tries swiveling her neck to look at him (Where's he taking her? Back to his den? To make her a zombie cockroach?) but her head won't obey. He's a shadow in her periphery. Black mold that was always growing at the edges of her life, suffocating her, only she had no idea.

The puncture marks on her leg itch like hell. She crosses her arms tightly to keep from scratching. She has questions for Gus that won't form past the cotton in her brain — *where are we going?* — her tongue wools over. She drifts in and out as Tammy croons, "*Stand by your man.*"

Harlan. She should call him. He'd *do something*. Like after the calf rescue. He said he fixed it. But maybe she got attacked by a rattlesnake as karmic payback for taking Amaranta to that shitshow. For nearly killing a guy. Or what if Raul was lying? What if she *did* kill a guy? What if she's being punished? Even if, according to Bull, she's one lucky girl.

Hay bales stacked like bricks shadow cornstalks sagging like defeated saguaros. Her eyelids grow heavy, then droop altogether. Everything blurs. When she reopens her eyes, the truck's crossing the fizzled, rootbeer-colored New River. She closes her eyes. Did she text Harlan to tell him what happened? He should meet her at the hospital. "Ring of Fire," Johnny's deep baritone. But she can't concentrate. Her eyes open. The cemetery, rows of tract houses. She's drooling onto her neck.

Why'd she get into a truck with El Cucuy? Why would Mom do this to her? Why would Benny allow it? She wants to protest but can't. *Bzzz. Where are you taking me?*

El Cucuy puts the back of his hand to her forehead. She's too exhausted and feverish to resist. "You're burning," he says in a voice not unlike Johnny Cash. *I fell into a burning*—"We're almost there. How do you feel?"

She droops. Renata stands by the side of the highway, waiting in the dead of night while Griselda pulls an all-nighter in her San Diego dorm room. A set of hands twine around Renata's throat then toss her limp body into the Salton Sea like a haul of toxic fish. Griselda turns a page in her textbook. The pier rusts. The sea burns. She falls into the flames. They consume her.

* * *

When Mal was a small girl, sometimes a man would walk the beach with what looked like a Weedwacker a school groundskeeper or the maintenance crews at city hall used. Curious, she'd asked her papi what the man was doing, weeding the sand.

"Mijita," Papi chuckled, patting her atop her head. "Es un metal detector."

"What kind of metal's he looking for?"

"The ricos ran off so fast they left their jewels behind."

"He's searching for treasure?"

"Quizás. Está buscando algo precioso." He hoisted her atop his strong, fisherman's shoulders, and she giggled as he carried her inside the beach house. "Stay here with Esteban and watch your hermanita. I need to fetch your mami from that rico, uppity hunting lodge." Mami started working in town when the hurricanes destroyed the resorts on the sea. "If I don't keep a close eye on that woman, she might disappear." He winked.

Mal hadn't thought of that in years. How prescient and chilling his words were.

Later, with Gus—the teeth, the map. Mal has spent her life hunting for girls.

Now she yearns for a different kind of detector. A tool to unearth her most precious possession from the vast expanse of dirt where the search party has resumed in the Sonoran Desert that sprawls for hundreds of miles until it reaches the sea. Her brothers, Yessi, the neighbors, they're all here. Benny's team arrives with German shepherds, the cadaver dogs sniffing out traces of decay, bypassing rodents and the skeletal remains of smaller mammals, while the missing person dogs lead their handlers through dunes and arroyos. *Mathematician in the Sky, let the right dogs find my girl.*

Mal tries not to think of her visions—the dogs sniffing out

Amaranta in the bloodwater broth with Elena and the rest — all the girls hooked together like monkeys in a barrel.

Benny calls her over in the middle of their search. Kneeling down, he brushes the dirt away from a set of tire tracks and points out the grooves etched in the ground. "See these?" He takes a photo with his phone. "All-terrain vehicle. Could be hunters or someone out here for recreation." He scans the area and points to another set. "These are different. We'll get them back to the station, see if we can get a make and model."

A few feet away from the tracks, Mal crouches next to Amaranta's backpack, which they've brought to approximate where Bull found it in situ. A stiff breeze skitters a cluster of pink salt cedar flowers past the backpack. Mal reaches for the petals, uncovering a glint of brass half-buried in the underbrush. Using her T-shirt like a glove, she picks up the spent shell, its weight cold and grim in her hand: a .300 Weatherby Magnum. She holds out the shell casing for Benny. "What if Amaranta was walking around? A stray bullet . . ." The thought roils her intestines so severely she has to box-breathe — *inhala . . . one, two* — several times until her bowels settle. "Could you find out who was registered to hunt out here?"

He takes the casing. "A lot of folks hunt around these parts, Mal," he says, handing it back. "We'll look into it, sure, but it's likely a dead end."

Mal slips the casing into a small evidence bag. Benny's nonchalance stings. He's discarding her fears too easily. Like he discarded Iggy's grandmother's wheeze of a warning. Nelly mentioned bullet shells in the desert and look where they are now. Look what's in her hand. She said La Siguanaba and El Cucuy were out for vengeance. Behind Noemi's door, La Siguanaba and a girl getting hit with a rifle. Is the horse-headed woman *helping* El Cucuy kill the girls? Where's *he*? Why has only La Siguanaba shown herself to

Mal? Could the pair *represent* someone in the real world? Sean and June? Grandma Nelly's words rattle through Mal like tin against metal, ticking like the hands of a clock. They're squandering their forty-eight hours. Maybe Benny *should* be listening to so-called mother's instinct. The police are getting nowhere — again.

"Benito, we're in the *desert* like Nelly said. She specifically said we'd find bullet shells."

He shoots her a pitying look, then pinches the bridge of his nose. "We can't go chasing some whack ghost stories que no tiene ni pies ni cabeza."

The party searches until the night grows frozen and the desert sky becomes a knitted blanket punctuated by stars — a child's flash-light peeking through a quilt after bedtime. They search until Gus sends a text urging Mal to come to the hospital.

As Mal climbs into the Jeep, Benny's radio crackles. "We found something on a security camera near Johnny's." It's that window-breaking Lieutenant Hernandez Pierce back at the sta-tion, her voice distorted by static. "Footage is closer-up than we got before."

Benny casts a glance toward Mal, like he's weighing whether or not she should hear whatever Hernandez Pierce will say, but Mal's in for a penny, in for a pound. "Go on."

"The image still isn't as clear as we'd like, but it's another angle confirming what we saw before. A man in a hoodie interacts with a girl who looks a hell of a lot like Amaranta. She leaves with him . . . voluntarily."

Benny clenches his jaw. "Get me a screenshot of the man ASAP."

"Can't see his face. It's obscured by the hoodie."

"Of course it is," Benny mutters. "Get it anyway."

"Roger that."

Mal says, "You know she didn't go to Gus's. Where else would she have gone? Would she have gotten in a truck with Oscar? If he told her it was about her tía or the cuates? Did you find anything else on him?"

"Not yet, but we'll figure this out." He says it with such conviction she imagines a world where she can believe him.

Then she crumples that world like trash in the hands of a god who doesn't give a fuck about girls in the borderlands. Or their mamis.

25
STEAL THEIR FACES

The house sheds its velvet each night at the edge of the desert lake. Long before Abuela's rage sloughed toward her daughter, a woman turned nightly into a horse, or rather, half of her transformed. Some of El Valle believed her a cuento, a tall tale, told to frighten children. Only, La Siguanaba was no cuento. Her misfortune occurred in the deepest time, long before the days were measured by longing, before they were measured at all.

Abuela's fingers twitch. She's rewoven this story so many times, she knows it better than she knows what she had for breakfast or her grandchildren's pesky names. Her gaze elongates as she relaxes on the patio, surrounded by the potted plants Abuelo planted because they were bright and made his wife smile. The familiar restlessness in Abuela's eyes signals what Ma calls *another episode*. Ma says Abuela went crazy when her other daughter disappeared. Amaranta tells her *crazy* is an ableist slur lobbed at the misunderstood.

"The sun's nice today, isn't it, Abuela?" She adjusts the sun hat on her abuelita's head.

The elder woman hums, her voice like a violin bow skittering across the strings. "Mmm, it's warm . . . like the sun on the shores of the Salton Sea . . . just like where I met her."

"Met who, Abuela?"

Abuela turns, her ojos like two cat's eye marbles. "La Siguanaba, mija. A long time ago, by the sea. She had long, beautiful hair and was washing it in the water. But when she looked at me, her face was like a horse's skull, and her eyes, pools of darkness."

"Ma always tells it differently. The horse-headed woman haunts the sea at night."

Abuela blinks at the sky under her wide brim. "She dared show her face to me in the light of day."

"Maybe because you're so brave."

"You know, 'jita, my family took a different route to El Valle than your abuelo's. My mother, María del Rosario Flores, had been in California since the beginning of time."

"For time begins with story, and story began with the People," Amaranta finishes. She's heard this many times.

"That's right, mija. They were waylaid in the orange and almond groves, traveling up and down California for the orchards before they made their way past Los Angeles, down into the bowels of the state, for the water."

"They came for the sea." Amaranta tells this next part to her abuelita like she's reading from a storybook. The elder woman closes her eyes and listens. "But María del Rosario — sometimes called Mari by her lovers, for she had many suitors, so lovely was this woman who longed for a glitzier life — Mari wanted to be in the movies.

No Mexican and Native women were. Still, Mari longed to be a star. Unfortunately, she died in childbirth before she ever got the chance, but she passed that longing on to her daughter."

"Mmm," Abuela murmurs. "My mother died much too young."

"When Vero Flores was a teenager who wanted nothing more than to escape El Valle, instead, she went to a party where she met a young man with eyes the color of the alfalfa fields."

"Not green, not brown. Alfalfa? Mmm. That's right."

"And although she still clung to her mother's dream that she was destined for more than El Valle could offer, Vero tried to let it go — for Beto. For loving Beto Veracruz."

"A damn shame."

Amaranta giggles. Good thing Abuelo's not out here or he'd be hurt.

"Only, when the Salton Sea called the glamorous Hollywood stars of the day to its beaches and offered Vero a second chance, she found she couldn't let go of her dream. She roamed the shores, luring those with wandering eyes."

Abuela's eyes are laughing now. She sees how Amaranta's shuffled her story with the horse-headed woman's, but she approves. "Ay, mijita. Never follow a beautiful woman by the sea or you'll be lost forever."

"I thought she came for bad men . . . drunks."

"She came for girls too. She was jealous of the girls for being so beautiful when she was cursed to be so ugly. The face of a horse, imagine? She wanted the girls so she could become them, for a while. Lure in men with their borrowed beauty."

"And that's why she took *you*, Abuela? Because you were so beautiful?"

"Sí, chulita. Solía ser la más bella que todas."

Abuela says this without a pinch of irony, perhaps not even

realizing she sounds like the evil queen in the fairy tale, the one who steals her daughter's youth and beauty for herself.

"In the days of my people, we called her Macihuatli in Nahuatl. *Matlatl* means net. *Cihuatl* means woman. And that's what they said she was — a Net-Woman, capturing men."

"Abuela, how did you escape her?"

"Maybe I didn't." Abuela leans back in her wheelchair, crossing her hands behind her head. "La Siguanaba and El Cucuy were gods, mija, married, in love. Until Cucuy betrayed his wife and tried to cover up his misdeeds by murdering his lover. When his wife found out, she turned him into the beast he was . . . El Chupacabra. But he still couldn't help spreading his seed. He had sons. All dogs."

Ma says Abuela's dementia-addled brain mixes all her stories up, but Amaranta loves the remixes she and Abuela make together. "What became of the husband and wife?"

The swirling patterns in Abuela's eyes drift away, like marbles abandoned midgame. "There was a hurricane the night she had a daughter. It destroyed everything."

Amaranta opens her eyes. This place is dark. So dark. And cold. She tries to wrap her arms around herself but can't. She can't feel her limbs. She can only feel the relentless cold.

It stinks of dead fish. The foul stench of a toilet overflowing. Her mouth is seeping. She wants to press her finger to the empty space. She imagines it's tender, fibrous, squishing.

Mama, Malamar, come find me.

Her eyes drift shut again.

26
BLOODLETTING

Benny drops Mal off at the yellow loading and unloading zone of the hospital tarmac, promising to return her Jeep in the morning and update her about the hoodie guy. Mal barely has the energy to pat Benny's arm before stepping out. His team has already combed the hospitals for Jane Does. But Amaranta isn't a nameless girl.

The sharp tang of the hospital antiseptic greets her with bitter citrus, triggering countless nights of rushing Gris to the ER for nebulizer treatments and corticosteroids. Amaranta was spared these traumas. Her childhood was always simpler, more carefree. Until now.

Outside the hospital entrance, nurses on break cluster around, some smoking, beside anxious family members awaiting news. And there she is — La Siguanaba in the shadows. Half-beautiful, half-grotesque, she fixes her bloodshot eyes on Mal.

Mal wants to run at her. *Where's my girl? What have you done to her? Where are you hiding her? Give her back!* But she can't make a scene. Not since witnessing the forty-eight-hour lockdown on Mami when she broke down after losing her daughter. Psychotic, they said. But it wasn't psychosis. It was grief. Mami never fully recovered, and Mal's beginning to understand why. She bats away the flies buzzing around her as a disconcerting idea roots like a pig for fungus in her gut——

Why wasn't the horse-headed woman in the desert? Does she only show up when she's *after* a girl? Hunting her? Has she come to the hospital for Griselda? Like an angel of death?

Or is Mal's mind crafting monsters from despair?

The photo of Elena and her imaginary horse has spent twenty-five years above the perpetual flame of her ofrenda. Has staring at the last painting created by a missing girl bred delusions in Mal?

Mal crosses her arms and strides through the hospital doors, ignoring La Siguanaba for once. They say the sign of the cross can ward her off——some men bite their machetes, but Mal's not that crazy. She checks her phone for the room Gus texted her, beelining past the nurses' station. The nurses are so burned out, charting and chugging back energy drinks, they don't notice her.

In the room, Griselda lies in the hospital bed, looking small and pale as a child. Her dark hair clings to her forehead with sweat, her cheeks flushed red. Her eyes resemble black beads. Gus stands when Mal comes in, but she motions for him to sit back down as she perches on the bed, atop the stiff white sheets covering her daughter. Griselda may be a grown-up, but even grown women still need their moms. "How are you, mijita? What did the doctors say?"

She rolls her eyes. "That Bull guy was only partly right. His stupid snake still had *some* venom so they gave me the antivenin and said it'll be a rough night but I'll recover."

Mal climbs the rest of the way into the bed with her daughter, keeping only her dust-clotted boots hanging off the edge. She squeezes Griselda tightly, swallowing a thick glob of guilt for taking Griselda out to Bull's trailer.

She pulls back the sheet to check Griselda's leg. It's pink but not bright red, inflamed but not bulbously swollen. She holds her free hand an inch away from the wound and works her way up her daughter's body as if performing a limpia. When her kids were little, she would recite, *Sana sana colita de rana, si no sanas hoy, ¡sanarás mañana!*

They stay like this, Mal holding Griselda until her daughter's breathing steadies, and Mal can tell — like when Griselda was a child — she's sound asleep.

Mal's done everything right and everything wrong as a mother. She checked on them. Knew their friends. Kept a watchful eye. She thought she was protecting them, dammit. Mal loved who she loved, but she'd convinced herself she was shielding her daughters from her drama. She was keeping them safe.

Her children have eaten thousands upon thousands of meals, three square a day, except when they're sick or on special occasions when she cut the corners off the squares and the meals have been nothing but sweets. Cake for breakfast. Pancakes for dinner. Even Benny. He would've starved if not for Mal. She kept the electricity and water flowing. They've been loved. Thousands of lullabies, in English and Spanish. Doctor's appointments, lessons, haircuts, staying up late to quiz them for exams. Griselda accepted to grad school. Benny, the youngest detective in the department. And Amaranta. The world's supposed to be her oyster.

Gus wanders out of the room into the hallway. Mal will talk with him later. Right now, Griselda needs her. Still, she can't put Amaranta out of her mind. Is she hurt? Is she safe? Is she cold? Has she had anything to drink or eat? Does she know Mal loves her?

Does she know Mal's searching for her? She hates that she can't reach through the fabric of the Universe like a blanket. Can't pull back the threads and find her little girl.

As Mal holds Griselda's hand while she fevers through the night, the strangest thought floats to the surface of her consciousness: *Siguanaba, if you have my girl, keep her safe.*

Mal would swear she was awake, but Amaranta stands beside the bed, eyes shining.

She came home bursting from science camp last summer because scientists found ripples in space and time, proof that every proton and neutron from those in our little fingers to our hair follicles to every thrum of our heartbeats hums in tune with the rest of the Universe —

"We contain a bit of everything that's ever been or will be. Inside of us. Like, inside our cells. Our atoms. We're the music of the cosmos. There's *proof,* Ma."

"*What* proof?" Mal wants to know.

Amaranta had given her mathematical equations Mal didn't understand. But her daughter's joy was lambent. She flashed from within.

When Mal went into labor with both girls, she told Gus to stay away. Not just to shield him from the pain of reliving it all but also to protect them both from the inevitable whispers. She knew how quickly word would spread, giving people another daughter to use against him, another reason to accuse him of wrongdoing.

She'd knelt on all fours in the throes of labor, braying like a wild horse. Her breasts swinging heavy, belly drooped low, she released primal, guttural sounds as she split open the gates to the otherworld, tearing the veil of creation to pull her girls through —

She'd sweated and toiled and shit, not entirely alone but close.

A nurse held her hand. Not her demented mother. Not her

disappeared sister. Not her vainglorious sister-in-law. Not even Yessi, although her comadre would have if Mal had asked.

Mal could've allowed Gus in. But she chose to birth her daughters alone.

Maybe it was pride. Look what she could do all by herself—push her girls out like the meaty pulp of plums ripping through the purple skin. Like a new Universe bursting from the tight singularity of a black hole. She did it too. She was that stubborn and strong.

But she can't do this by herself. She needs help *losing* her daughter. Her whole bright Universe and all her thwapping music. Her bright connection to the rest of time and space.

She can't be alone through this.

Mal's eyes flutter open to a hospital room drenched in inky light. She blinks. Amaranta fades and there is only Gus, leaning against the doorframe, watching them, his usually muscular body sunken and small. A nurse has refilled the bag of fluids dripping into Griselda's veins. Her heartbeat beeps its sturdy rhythm on the monitor. The pain starts in Mal's chest then radiates to everywhere in her body. Her baby is still missing. Mal fights the image of Amaranta lying blood-scrubbed and vacant-eyed in a ditch beside alfalfa, coyotes sniffing her early rot in the dusky wind. It hurts too much.

The door creaks open, and Esteban and Sharon enter, passing Gus, accompanied by one of the cuates. Xochitl, who looks paler than usual, her bitchy, vibrant energy subdued, clings to her mother's arm for support.

A twinge of guilt overtakes Mal at the memory of screaming in the cuates' faces...was it yesterday? The day before? The forty-eight-hour window squeaks against its pane. A fog has settled over her neurons. Her back aches from curling against the hospital bedrail, wedged into the metal to give Griselda ample room. Mal closes her eyes and breathes.

Is it 6:00 a.m. now? She's losing track of time. She's losing herself. Exhausted doesn't cover it. Spent. A fetid rag. A wave of grief passes over her, threatening to pull her under, but she fights it. She needs to pull herself together. They have six hours before the window slams shut.

It takes Mal a groggy second to realize that only she and Griselda are in the room. Esteban, Sharon, and Xochitl are talking in hushed whispers in the hallway. Gus is gone again.

She gently dislodges her arm from beneath her daughter's head, her joints protesting as she stretches. Pulling herself to her feet, she joins her family in the hallway, easing the door shut behind her.

"Why are you all here so early?" she asks, her voice hoarse. "What happened?"

Their faces are grave as they turn to her. She keens, as if she's missed a step on the stairs. When no one says anything, she spurts, "Did you find her?" The image of Amaranta in a ditch burns her vision.

"It's not about Amaranta. There's been an incident with Xolotl." Esteban's voice is distant, threaded with something glass and shattered.

"Vampire mierda otra vez?" Mal darts Xochitl a look; her niece seems to have shrunk, her haughty grown-up demeanor replaced with a brittle vulnerability, like a child wearing their mother's makeup all smudged across their face.

"We were just trying to scare her . . . we didn't mean . . ."

"You wanted to scare your own cousin? That's sick."

"Enough, sis," Esteban intercedes, his voice echoing in the sterile chill of the hospital. "Xochitl's already beating herself up."

"We . . . cut her during the ritual but never wanted to . . ."

Sharon's hand tightens on Xochitl's arm, a silent plea for restraint. "What the actual——" Mal stops herself. "When?"

"At the sleepover."

"Is that why you're here? To confess?"

"Xolotl's getting stitches. Damn kids. They both cut themselves. Apparently, he cut too deep." Esteban's ragged. He looks more like Papi than ever. Aged and gray and stressed.

Sharon adds, her voice thin and strained. "It was just a game."

Mal can't suppress her vitriol. "It's more than a *game*, come on. My daughter's *missing*. Your son needs stitches. You two need to wake the fuck up."

Behind the cuates' twisted theatrics lies a heartbreaking reality: two kids desperate for the recognition of their parents. Esteban lavishes his attention on the community; Sharon, on the mirror or the bottom of a glass. Mal would feel sorry for them, except they've dragged her daughter into their ill-conceived pseudoritual.

"Do you think Amaranta ran away because you hurt her?" Mal manages. "Is that what you're saying?"

Xochitl draws back like she's floundering for her brother's protective shoulder. "I mean...we sort of threatened to cut her again...at Dad's fundraiser...so...."

"Jesus, Chuy. Are you hearing this?"

"I'm sorry, Mal. I didn't..." Her brother's face scrunches into an expression she recalls from childhood, a little boy who's failed at being a protector.

Gus approaches, holding three Styrofoam cups of coffee, furrowing at the palpable tension. "What'd I miss?"

Before Mal can reply, a soft creak behind them draws everyone's attention. Framed by the hospital door, Griselda clutches her IV pole like a lifeline, her face a pale contrast to the bold graffiti of her hospital gown.

"Mija, are you feeling okay?" Esteban asks his niece, but she only nods. He looks toward Mal, and she can tell he's about to ask what they can do to help, but she's so mad at his kids she can't continue this conversation without blowing up.

She raises her hand to him in a gesture they both know means *Enough,* and he nods, watching her with a pained expression as she hooks her arm through Griselda's and motions for Gus to follow them back into Griselda's room.

"Can we go home?" Griselda's voice is barely above a whisper, her sleepy eyes fixed on Mal, who fixes the hospital gown slipping down her shoulder.

As they turn away, Mal steals a look back at Xochitl between her mother and father. Makeup scrubbed from her face, no fancy clothes and accessories to hide behind, no brother with whom to close ranks like smug-faced soldiers. Without all that, she's small and singular and out of place. Like half of her is missing. But beneath her insecurity, there's something else. Something that reminds Mal of herself when she was that age — fierce, fiery, and utterly terrified.

There's nothing auspicious about getting bitten by a venomous snake and spending the night in the hospital, especially when Griselda's supposed to be out searching for her missing sister, but instead she's made everyone waste a whole night and morning because of her stupidity (again!). Nothing auspicious, except for what she sees after being discharged, while the nurse is rolling her down the hall in a wheelchair (she can hobble with a crutch, but they're legally required to roll her since the injury was to her leg).

Mom's finishing the paperwork with the insurance desk. El Cucuy said he'd wait outside, probably too uncomfortable in the room since Griselda was awake and alert and still creeped out.

Granted, he *did* drive her straight to the hospital and not to some bunker. But that didn't mean she had to embrace him with open arms. Just because he (so far!) checks out as *not a serial killer* doesn't mean she wants to spend holidays with him. He abandoned her for twenty-three years. How do you come back from that?

She hoped Harlan would come visit her in the hospital since he doesn't live far (just on the other side of Cattle Call Arena), but he's been MIA all morning. The doctor insisted they ensure Griselda was out of the woods and responded well to the antivenin (which they make from horse blood).

So as the nurse is wheeling her out, she happens to glance into a room where a big hoopla's being made—family, balloons, flowers, hugs. Someone has come out of a coma.

Griselda's heart thuds.

She recognizes the chubby, goateed man in the bed, the one who woke up.

She texts Harlan again, cupping her hand over her phone in case the nurse is nosy and tries reading it over her shoulder.

Holy shit! The guard from the cattle yard is at the hospital! He's awake! We didn't motherfucking kill him!

27
UNA PLÁTICA

Home from the hospital much later in the day than anticipated, Mal yanks a rotisserie chicken from the fridge, a gelatinous layer of fat cocooning the bird. The once crispy skin now wears a translucent sheen under the fridge's cold light, giving it a rubbery texture. Amaranta would hate this, but she's not here and her family still needs to eat, so Mal needs to hold it together. Yesterday and the day before, she made a rash of bad decisions because she was running on fumes. Amaranta needs more from her mother; she needs Mal to stay in this for the long haul.

Her therapist's words come to her, or was it Chuy who said it? — *Secure your own mask first.* It's true, but she doesn't need platitudes. Motherhood is more complicated than that. Secure her own mask, sure. But she'd still secure her daughters' first each time.

Jellied chicken in one hand, Mal grabs a wilting head of lettuce and positions herself at the cutting board where she peers into the steel blade of the cleaver at the deep etches in her face. She's aged a decade in two days. Mal holds the knife farther back, trying to capture her whole reflection. She hasn't showered in more than forty-eight hours. She's wearing Amaranta's T-shirt with an atom and the words YOU MATTER. Amaranta laughs at that. Mal freezes, knife halting midslice. She listens, but the laughter's in her head, a cruel trick.

The idea of succumbing to her mother's realm of lost women, bereft of a daughter, sickens Mal. She stifles a rising glob of phlegm, swallowing it back down. *A man with a hoodie in a truck. A girl got in voluntarily. Tire tracks. Amaranta's backpack in the desert. Shell casing.* What she's forcing herself not to think, but it's invading her every waking moment anyway: *A body. A body*—inside her rib cage, her own heart is a flat-iron steak, tenderized.

She's determined to start searching again after lunch, but where? They've already torn the town apart and half the desert. If her visions of La Siguanaba started again when Renata disappeared . . . is La Siguanaba leading her toward the girls? Or distracting her?

What if she could induce a vision? Summon La Siguanaba somehow? For guidance?

Does one call a monster the way one calls a god? With some kind of prayer?

Should she close her eyes? She clutches her knife, feeling a bit ridiculous.

O horse-headed woman, show me the way to my daughter.

Just then, Mami wheels herself into the kitchen, and Mal braces for her mother's customary coldness.

Instead Mami reaches out and gently strokes Mal's arm, a touch so unfamiliar and tender that it sends shivers down her spine. When is Mami ever nice, much less maternal? This sudden display of warmth catches Mal off guard. She sets down her knife but then worries this is a trick and she'll need it to fend off a Mami attack.

"I never knew how to relate to you," Mami coos as she pats Mal's hand. Mal waits for Mami's claws to dig in. "You were always your father's daughter. You loved your books, fishing, hunting. You were more his than mine. He even loved you more than me." She talks to her own reflection in a compact mirror.

"He did not, Ma," Mal sighs. She doesn't have time for this. Mami finds ways to turn the conversation back to herself, even now, when Mal's daughter is *missing*. "Chuy learned all that too, and you showered him with affection and devotion. He was a damn prince."

"My Stevie? Oh, my boy was easy. You were tough."

"Okay, I don't have to listen to this right now." She doesn't have the strength to fight her delusional mother.

But Mami says, "I blame myself. That toughness? Makes you a good mom . . . Not like me. I was too soft."

Mal doesn't know whether to snort with laughter at the absurdity of her mother believing herself *soft* — or sob with relief that for once, even if it is the dementia talking, her mother has admitted Mal's a good mom. Since Mami's such a shit mom, it shouldn't matter what she thinks of Mal's mothering skills one way or another. But it still makes a difference to Mal.

"You could relate to your papi," Mami says, and there's the sharp edge to her voice Mal's been awaiting. "I hated that about you."

Mal teeters forward, bumping into the cutting board and grazing her thumb against the blade. The tiniest of cuts, thinner than a papercut. But it stings.

Something clicks into place. Has Mami's misplaced rage been meant for Papi all this time? She hated him so much she cheated on him? But Old Man Callahan left her and their child? Could Mami have been brokenhearted? Mal always thought Mami had the most devoted husband—he's doted on her all Mal's life. But maybe Mami's still a spurned woman. The OG Siguanaba.

"You know, Ma. I wasn't tough. Not like you're saying. But I *had* to be independent to clean up your messes."

"My messes," Mami says, as if she's chewing on the words. "My messes."

"I didn't mean . . ."

Her messes became all of their messes. Like Mal's done to her own daughters. Like she's been doing to everyone she loves lately. Mami may never be able to admit that she was angry at herself but Mal has become mother enough to mother herself. And however Mal parses it, she's been acting like Mami since Amaranta disappeared. She needs to apologize . . . to everyone she's been hurting . . . her daughters . . . Yessi . . .

Mal's not a soft woman, true, but she's not a cruel one either. She doesn't snap at her family and friends who've done nothing but love and support her. As soon as she eats something to keep her blood sugar up, she'll go to the front yard and talk to Yessi, who's still leading the search party even after Mal made a colossal fool of herself on Friday night and accused her friend of—what? Caring too much about a girl who's practically her niece?

"No, no. You're right. I did leave messes. I left Elena a mess . . ." Mami lets out a sigh. "Pobre Elena, just like her mother."

"What do you mean?"

But they're interrupted by Gus, who walks into the kitchen and says, "I just got off the phone with Benny."

"What did he say?" She picks up her knife again, its cold steel a reassurance in her hand.

"They need us all to come in for lie detector tests." He plucks up a piece of the dark thigh meat and slips it into his mouth. "Formality."

"He's *still* on your ass, huh?" she scoffs, sliding the knife through the head. The two halves break apart. "Get out the ranch, will you? And a purple onion."

He opens the fridge and retrieves the requested items. "We all need to go in, not just me."

"Papi," Mal calls toward the living room, slicing the lettuce into strips. "Did Benny ask *you and Mami* to come to the station?"

"Sí, pero I told him how hard it would be to get Mami down there. He says I can go solo when Lupita comes to relieve me."

"When *is* Lupita coming? Have you called her?" She peels the waxy outer layer of the onion, then slices that globe in half, her eyes stinging. She should've bitten into a spoon. The skin around her eyes is already red, raw, and itchy from crying for the past two days.

"She doesn't answer."

"That's fishy, no?"

Gus gets out a big salad bowl, and Mal's struck by his familiarity with her kitchen. She plops the chicken, onion, and lettuce in and shakes it around.

Papi comes in, saying, "Oh there you are, Vero. I'm still looking for your vitamins."

"I made salad," Mal says, reaching for bowls, including one for Griselda, resting in her bedroom, when a set of electronic chimes tingle from her back pocket. It's a ringtone she never uses, a child's xylophone that grates on her nerves. Her pulse trills as she pulls out not her own phone but Amaranta's. "It's not a call," Mal says, her voice trembling as she stares at the screen. "It's a reminder for an appointment. She was supposed to be *tutoring* someone right now. I'm so stupid I didn't think of this before!" She clicks on the alert. "She started tutoring a classmate in physics. Holy shit, what's his name . . ."

"Alberto?" Papi suggests. "Teo? I know there's a 'to' in there somewhere."

"Mateo!" Mal shouts, a sudden rush of clarity hitting her. "I can't believe I didn't tell Benny about him! He's a new friend!" She thrusts the phone toward Gus, showing him the screen. "Look, there's an address! And it's not far from her school!"

Keys in hand, she's already rushing toward the front door, salad abandoned.

"Are you going now? Do you want me to go with you?" Gus asks.

"Papi, are you okay with Mami and Gris without us? Yessi's still outside with the search party if you need her."

"¡Apúrate! Go see what you two can find out!"

Before they set off in Mal's Jeep, Gus runs to his truck parked on her curb and grabs his shotgun.

The boy who answers the door at Mateo's house is round and pimply, his disappointment evident as he takes in Mal's haggard appearance. He was clearly expecting Amaranta. A sharp pang of preemptive grief strikes Mal, a glimpse into a future filled with moments like this—each door opening to reveal yet another person who isn't her daughter.

"Can I help you?" His neck rolls beneath his chin as he speaks. Mal feels an instant connection with this kid, an outsider like her, she can tell. But he's giving her side-eye, reminding her she hasn't showered, changed, or run a brush through her hair in more than two days.

"We're looking for Mateo," she says.

"That's me." He shifts his weight and avoids eye contact. His shirt reminds Mal of the Amaranta-borrowed shirt she's wearing, only his isn't stain-covered and foul-smelling. It depicts Neil deGrasse Tyson throwing shade and his hands in the air with the caption: Y'ALL MOTHERF*CKERS NEED SCIENCE. If this kid's a science geek too, why does he need tutoring?

"My daughter was supposed to tutor you today. Have you seen or heard from her?"

Mateo glances at Gus before locking eyes with Mal. "No, but I was hoping she'd come back."

Mal's chest flutters. Could this kid have given Amaranta a ride somewhere? She pictures him in a hoodie driving a white truck. "Come back from where?"

Gus shifts beside her on the square concrete block that serves as a porch.

Before Mateo can answer, a woman's voice calls from inside the house, "¿Teo? ¿Quién es? ¿Está aquí Amaranta?"

He widens the door, and Mal's gut lurches.

Standing in the small dining room beyond the doorway, holding a bright green paddle of cactus, it's the woman from the football game—last seen holding the sign that read: HAVE YOU SEEN RENATA RUIZ?

"Renata's favorite." She holds up the sticky nopal like an apology. "I cook when I'm upset. Helps me think."

"Carmen?" Mal whispers, grabbing Gus's hand for support.

"Entren, por favor," Carmen says, her voice overbright as she invites them inside. "Disculpe mi hijo, keeping you out on the porch." She ushers a stunned Mal inside and pulls out the dining room chairs, covered in plastic, for her and Gus to sit at the little glass table bedecked in fruit-embroidered doilies. "¿Quieres tomar algo?"

"No, thank you," Gus declines a drink, filling the space of Mal's shocked silence.

"I've been meaning to thank *you*," Carmen says, nodding toward Mal.

"Thank me?" Mal's breath hitches. Amar's been *here*, at Renata's house, more than once.

"Sí, you and your . . ." She nods toward Gus, and Mal realizes she should introduce him but remembers what Benny said in the car outside Sharon's—Carmen still believes Gus had something to do with Renata's disappearance.

Mal clears her throat and simply says, "Husband."

Carmen smiles, apparently oblivious. Gus is just an idea to her like most of the town. El Cucuy couldn't be this kind-eyed man sitting down at her dining room table. "You and your esposo for bringing up Renata's case. You put her in the public eye." She picks at the spines on the cactus pad in her hands. "La policía, este pueblo . . . they've been slower to look for Renata. She's older, not a child like your hija. Everyone calls her a puta just because she dated guys. Last I checked, sleeping around's not a crime, but they act like it is. They don't care about her como el senator's niece."

"Even with my brother running for Senate, no news cameras have shown up, and it's been two days since my daughter disappeared," Mal says.

Carmen scrapes at the nopales with her knife, de-spining the paddle, cutting it into strips. "Pues, mira. That's how it is. At least our girls are en el sistema. Mi hija was born aquí. They have to pretend to care. ¿Mi opinión?" She waves her knife in the air. "Mi hija was too good for this backward pueblo. She only stayed por un tonto."

"Do you know *who* she stayed for, Carmen? Who was she waiting for out there?"

Carmen's head moves like a dandelion swaying in a breeze of denial and motherguilt—Mal should know; it oozes from her too. "Nadie más knows what I'm going through pero tú. Es un club muy terrible, madres de desaparecidas." Her voice has grown thick, like she's swallowed a handful of rocks. "I never felt welcome con las madres del PTA. Pues, nunca tenía tiempo. Trabajé from sunup to sundown most of Renata's childhood. I missed so much of it."

"Not by choice," Mal adds softly, thinking of Carmen plucking radishes like eyeballs from the sweltering fields sunup to sunset every day of Renata's too-short life. "Pero tell me about Raul. Didn't he drop her off out there? Why would he leave her on the highway? Have you talked to him?"

"Raul's harmless. They've been together since they were kids, on and off. Renata siempre ha estado, cómo se dice, *boy crazy*. She's so smart but couldn't focus on her estudies."

Mal doesn't say anything about Yessi's chisme that Renata got arrested for a sexual encounter with one of those boys. Instead, she says, "The last time I saw her at work, she said she wanted to be an environmental justice lawyer."

"Sí, but she wouldn't focus. No como tus hijas. Renata always had her eye on some boy or other. Tus hijas son brillantes. Amaranta was helping Mateo with his physics."

Mal eyes Mateo suspiciously, then points out his T-shirt. "Looks to me like you already grasp physics just fine. Was my daughter really helping you?"

Mateo shifts uncomfortably. "I mean . . . she was cool to hang out with. Even if she did talk about my sister all the time."

A fist curls in Mal's stomach. "Why? Did she even know your sister?"

He shrugs.

"What kinds of things did she say about Renata?"

"I don't know, I mean, she liked that she was brave, wasn't afraid to be herself, even when people talked shit about her." Mateo's voice is low, as if he's sharing a secret.

Carmen interjects, "La gente en este pueblo have nothing better

307

to do than talk smack about mi hija. They didn't know her. They saw what they wanted to see."

"Did Amaranta say anything about feeling unsafe or worried about anything?" Gus asks.

"No," Mateo answers quickly, shaking his head. "Nothing."

Mal stares at him. Despite her empathy for this guy who probably doesn't stand much of a chance in the cruel high school arena, she fights the urge to shake his shoulders and beg him, *What aren't you saying?*

"Then why was Amaranta coming over, if you didn't need help?"

Mateo, red-faced, replies, "She had a major crush on Renata. It was pretty clear she was interested in my sister, not me. But I liked spending time with her anyway."

"You're talking about my girl in the past tense," Mal notes, hackles raised. But she's mad at herself for not seeing it. The way Amaranta was looking at Renata last Saturday, not jealousy or admiration—*affection*. She liked her. She's thinking in the past tense too. All the things she missed. How much more did she overlook?

Tears well in Carmen's eyes, bagged by crescent moons. She swipes at them hastily with the back of her hand, leaving wet streaks on her sun-worn skin.

They say it's usually someone the victim knows. Someone she already trusts. So many missing girls. So many people they trusted. Who was the guy in the hoodie? The lieutenant said a girl got into the truck willingly. It's a hard knot in Mal's stomach. "How old are you, Mateo?"

"Sixteen."

"What kind of car do you drive?"

Carmen slams the knife on the cutting board. "Are you accusing mi hijo of something?"

Mal's not used to being the one without a knife.

Things aren't adding up. Amaranta has a crush on a missing girl then goes missing too. Mateo has a crush on Amaranta and feels spurned by her feelings for his sister. And now the mother is slamming a knife, upset that Mal would accuse her son of . . . what? Doing something awful to both girls?

"Let's just calm down," Gus says. "No one's accusing anyone. We're just trying to find our daughter, and we're hoping you might know something that'll lead us to her."

"I don't drive," Mateo answers sheepishly. "Not yet."

"Know anyone with a white truck?"

The other mother puts down the knife altogether, nopales abandoned, and leans against the counter. "Your daughter's boyfriend. What's his name, Mateo? The one who comes with Raul sometimes to take Renata to those protests?"

"Harlan?" Mateo says.

Mal's skin itches where Sean grabbed her and twisted her arm back. "It's his dad's. I've been trying to get Benny to look into it."

"Benny?" Carmen asks.

"My brother, Detective Benito Veracruz."

Carmen gives Mal a not-so-subtle look like, *Of course your daughter is getting all this attention when one brother is a senator-to-be and the other is a detective.*

Mal dismisses the side-eye. "Unfortunately, even Benny can't cut the red tape in this town that protects the Callahans."

"Oh, we know the Callahans." Carmen says this with such vitriol, she practically spits on the nopales. "Mi hija was last seen right by where her papá dropped dead from heatstroke in the Callahan fields when Renata was a baby." She looks at Mal with tears in her eyes. "I can't bring myself to go out there, and I don't trust la policía," Carmen says. "That Callahan land is cursed. Nothing will grow on it."

"You think she was *on* Callahan land when she disappeared? Not just by the highway?"

"Sí."

"Did you tell the police?"

"They don't listen to me."

Not even Benny? Has Benny been listening to Mal? He arrested Gus. He's having them come to the station for lie detector tests. Even Papi! When they *should* be hauling Sean's ass in! It infuriates Mal.

"Why are you so sure?" Mal asks, but before Carmen can respond, a sharp pain pierces through her temples, and she keels forward, slamming her head against the glass tabletop. Mal's jerked from Carmen's dining room and plunked through the stygian darkness into a scalding bathtub, Mami's hand thrusting her underwater. *"Breathe! Breathe!"*

As Mal's hands wrap around the edges of the porcelain tub, something slides into her mouth—burning, metallic, acrid. A bridle and bit, breaking her teeth. Mami's voice cracks, wild. *"Breathe! Breathe!"* Her voice distorts into a ghostly scream, reverberating through Mal's eardrums. Papi does nothing to stop it. And since he stands there merely looking on as Mami dunks her daughter's head under, Papi might as well be the hand holding her beneath the burning liquid.

Mal blinks the spume from her eyes. Amaranta in her yellow Converse thrashes in the hellish boil. She inhales the water like soap bubbling at her mouth, foam filling her nostrils, burbling her scream, reverberating through Mal's eardrums.

La Siguanaba hovers in the corner, her horse's maw releasing a silent scream as she grasps Elena, who bleeds out on the bathroom tile. Amaranta boils in the pot of steaming sopa, the bloodwater broth—

Mal lifts her head from Carmen's fruited doily and gives a compulsory shake like eking out the water stuck in her ears after a dip in the briny depths, pushing away the clomping sound of hooves reverberating through her chest cavity. The hordes of teethlike shells crunch beneath each *clop, clop, clop* through her nightmarish visions.

Gus's hand is on her back, gently massaging circles, and Carmen's staring at her not with horror or shock or even the concern one might expect for someone who's just appeared to have a seizure. Carmen's gaze conveys recognition. Understanding.

"She came to you, just now, didn't she?" Carmen lowers her voice as if afraid of invoking the spirit, and Mal's chest tumults. She tries to say *yes* but can't form the word aloud so she just nods. "Mi abuela told me cuentos de La Siguanaba cuando era una niña. Pero I never believed. Not until Renata went missing." Carmen's tone, solemn and fervent at once, reminds Mal of telling her own daughters ghost stories they never believed. "But since then, I've felt her presence, lurking, waiting. It's like she's feeding off my grief."

Since Mal first saw the horse-headed woman in the fields between the bonfire and home, the night Elena disappeared, *no one* has affirmed what she saw except Mami, and everyone said Mami was crazy.

"Wait..." Mal trembles at the door Carmen has opened. "Has La Siguanaba been haunting you too? Have you *seen* her?"

Carmen doesn't laugh or scoff. The room goes silent, except for the faint bubbling of something on the stove. "Sí. And smelled..."

"Maple and ammonia... like wet straw?"

"Exactamente así. She's been telling me to search the Callahan land, pero after mi esposo..." Her voice breaks. She takes a deep breath. "I can't bring myself to go there alone. Y la policía won't help. They found nada. End of story."

"Benny doesn't believe me either."

Carmen shakes her head. "They think I'm loca. Maybe I am."

"You're not crazy," Mal says. "Madres de desaparecidas, like you said. Maybe she comes to mothers."

Then why did she come to Mal when Elena disappeared? She was a sister, not a mother.

Except, she *was* a mother to Benny, wasn't she? Mami was useless.

What if La Siguanaba had visited Mami, but Mami ignored her?

What if the horse-headed woman snagged Mal's attention because no one else was listening?

Noemi's mom, Luz, moved to San Diego shortly after her daughter disappeared. What if she left to get away from the haunting?

Gus holds Mal's hand under the glass table but says nothing. He won't gaslight the women the way other men do. He just sits there, staunchly quiet and supportive as Mal takes it all in, the tiny details of the home: the worn-out sofa with a crochet blanket, the faded family photos on the wall, the small television playing a telenovela on low volume. The void left by a missing daughter.

"If La Siguanaba's been trying to get our attention and now she has it, what do we do?"

"No sé," Carmen replies. She's resumed her chopping—the nopales no longer in strips but tiny, slimy chunks.

"Which part of the land do they say nothing grows on? Could you show us on a map?"

Carmen nods, and Mal whips out her phone's map, zooming in near the banks of the Salton Sea.

"That's near where I grew up," Mal says. Carmen's not the only one with trauma on that land. It's where Gus lost Noemi and the Veracruzes lost Elena. And it all belongs to the Callahans in one way or another, except for the small patch that belonged to the government before they gave it to Papi. Plus the ghost town that now only consists of Gus's house and a closed-down dive bar. The rest, the Callahans kept for themselves or leased out to the geothermal companies. And now, with Esteban's backing, they're striking a deal with the lithium companies for cell phone batteries. It's where La Siguanaba first started haunting Mal.

"Here's how mi abuela told the cuento to me," Carmen says. "Back in those days when el mundo was young and wild, La Siguanaba had a daughter."

"She was a *mother?*" Mami never told Mal this part.

"Sí. Pero El Cucuy, a married man, was taken with her daughter's beauty and youth. He couldn't control himself, he said. She was a hunter's trap. Rather than facing the music, confessing his sins, he silenced her." She makes a slicing motion across her neck.

Mateo rolls his eyes and plops onto the couch, grabbing the remote.

His mother ignores him and keeps telling her story. "La Siguanaba, when she found her daughter, estaba furiosa, una tormenta de ira y desolación. She hunted El Cucuy, y lo castigó, turned him into the beast he was inside, una criatura de la noche, doglike y fearsome.

"In return, he cursed her with the head of a horse. La cabeza de una yegua.

"Pero El Cucuy no aprendió. He sired boys who became men who would cover their mistakes with blood. Men who would blame women and girls for their lust.

"La Siguanaba realized her mistake too late. Vio que en su rage, she'd made it worse para las mujeres y las niñas, las inocentes.

"Así que ahora, ella wanders, un espíritu de venganza y protección. Drawn to places where injustices have been done, especially a las niñas y mujeres, las envuelve en sus brazos to shield them. But sometimes, trying to protect them, she carries them away forever."

When Carmen walks them to the door, Mal promises she'll keep the other mother updated. Her story might have given Mal another lead. Somewhere else to look.

Or is Carmen just trying to throw Mal off the scent of her own son?

28
NONE OF OUR BUSINESS

riselda's only been home from the hospital a few hours but the house, sodden with grief, seems to hold its breath. Mom's room where Gris has been recovering smells like arnica and Vicks VapoRub (even though these have nothing to do with healing snakebites, Abuela insists on using them).

Harlan hasn't returned her calls or come to check on her. More importantly, he hasn't inquired about Amaranta or shared any updates about his search. Has he given up on finding her?

She checks her phone, hoping on stupid hope that Amaranta's called or texted. But then she remembers, they found her her-manita's phone with that snake guy out in Slab City.

She wants to scream all her impotent rage into the void but that would scare her abuelitos. Abuela's been wheeling herself in every hour, insisting on applying fresh ointment and checking on her leg dressing. Since Amaranta's disappearance, it's as if Abuela's become a mother again. The one Mom says never existed, lurking in there all along and needing to be shocked back into herself.

She put up a picture of Amaranta with a fresh vela burning on the ofrenda for Tía Elena. Griselda hates it. Not because of Abuela's prayer for both girls. *That's* fine. But because Tía's *not* a girl anymore . . . that ofrenda's been up for too long. Griselda can't stomach a vela staying lit for her hermanita for more than two decades. It's too painful.

Abuelo's been on the phone all morning, calling everyone in town and anyone they've ever met in Yuma, Palm Springs, Riverside, San Bernardino, or San Diego. All the outlying empires. His desperate plea has cycled on repeat into Griselda's recovery room. But no one has seen Amaranta. They'll keep an eye out.

Mom left with Gus, following a new lead on Amaranta. At least Mom *told* them she'd be with her boyfriend this time; she's not skulking around in secret anymore. Their once-complete family puzzle now has a misfit piece. They've lost Amaranta and gained Gus — a sickening exchange.

Abuela wheels into the room again, arnica and poultice aromas clinging to her rebozo. She parks beside the bed, her rheumy, clouded eyes gleaming with mischief as she takes Griselda's clammy hand in her warm, weathered one. She opens her other hand to reveal a small compact mirror; it glints in the scant evening sunlight filtering through the window.

"Hey, Abuela? When's Lupita coming back? Her daughter's not still sick, is she?"

Abuela's lips pucker into a thin line, her demeanor so tart she could put a bowl of pickled jalapeños to shame. "Ayyyy, I fired Lupita last week!"

"You fired her? When? Why? Do Abuelo and Mom know?"

Abuela huffs, her shoulders squaring. "I can do what I want in my own house."

A bubble of laughter rises in Griselda's throat. So testy. "I know you can, Abuela. Of course. But why'd you fire her? Did she do something wrong? Did she hurt you?"

Abuela's grip on Griselda's hand tightens. "I didn't need her anymore, es todo. My daughter takes good care of me. Why should we pay someone else when my daughter can do it?"

Griselda frowns. "Which daughter? Elena?" Is Abuela confusing her for Elena again?

Abuela gives a little shake of her head, her silver hair tufting about her wrinkled face. "No, my older daughter, Mal. She digs the worms out of my wounds."

Griselda lets out a surprised chuckle. "Worms, Abuela?"

"Well, maybe not worms. Mal cleans them out."

With Abuela's free hand, she pulls something out of her pocket—a crinkle of plastic she brings to her mouth. It's one of those marzipan candies she loves, wrapped like a rose.

Griselda looks closer at the compact mirror in Abuela's hands. It's silver and ornate with swirling engravings. She's never seen it before. It looks antique. Like real silver.

Abuela catches Griselda's gaze in her mirror. She winks, takes a pair of tweezers from the pocket of her house dress, and begins plucking at stray chin hairs. "My damn eyebrows moved down to my chin! I look like a goddamn horsewoman! ¡Mira! These jowls." She sighs and puckers her lips like she's sucked on a sourhead. "I could've been a movie star if not for those hurricanes wrecking everything before I was discovered. Or if I'd married a movie star instead of Beto." She blows a raspberry at the mention of her husband's name.

"But, Abuela, where did you get that mirror?"

"Mira, mijita. It's a buried treasure." She turns it this way and that in the light. "Look how it shines."

Abuela is a magpie with a nest of other people's things she's stolen over the years. She collects trinkets and junk she calls treasure. The familia finds their stuff in Abuela's room all the time. But this mirror's unfamiliar among the usual baubles she hoards. "Let me see it a sec?"

Abuela clucks disapprovingly, and, before she can hand it over, Griselda's phone starts ringing. Amaranta? Griselda darts a glance at the screen, her stomach somersaulting, but it's Harlan. Abuela uses the distraction to wheel away. That sneaky magpie.

Griselda answers, "Why're you ghosting me, pendejo? My sister still hasn't come home, and everything is shit. I needed you. I thought..."

"I'm so sorry, I've been out of range. I didn't mean to ghost you..." Harlan's staticky and a little out of breath.

"A snake bit me."

"What? What kind of snake?"

"Rattler."

"Holy shit, Gris! Are you okay? Did you get antivenom?"

"Yeah, a snakebite's the least of my worries." When she says it aloud, the weight of it compresses her chest with the force and vehemence of floodwater—she's a broken dam. Sobbing hurts her whole body. Even her leg. But mostly, her heart. "Where could she be?"

"I wish I knew."

"Did you get my text about the security guard?"

"I told you it would be okay!"

"Hospitalized for three days isn't exactly *okay*."

"You know what I mean." He clears his throat. "Hey, sorry I'm not there. I would've brought you flowers and a teddy bear, you know that."

"Where *are* you?"

"My dad feels bad he stuck his foot in his mouth with this whole thing . . . you know, at your house Friday. He fucked up pretty bad, he actually admits it for once. Acted like a real asshole. We just wanted to help but we ended up looking like the privileged jerks we are."

"Your dad said that?"

"More or less."

"Hmm."

"Anyway, he said we should take a step back, lay low for a while. Stay out of your family's hair."

Griselda snaps, "Or he's just trying to avoid getting accused of kidnapping again."

"Yeah, I guess." Harlan chuckles, but it sounds pained. "So anyway, it's hunting season—"

"Wait, *you* went *hunting?*"

"I didn't want to, believe me. I tried to stay so I could keep helping you with the search." He sounds as annoyed as he used to be in junior high, a chastized boy eager to grow up but under the inescapable thumb of his family's name and reputation. "But my mom twisted my arm . . . like I said, my dad . . . They went on and on about how irresponsible I was, undermining our family's business and do I know how hard my family's worked and how ungrateful I am, blah, blah, blah. They wanted to make it, like, a family trip or whatever. My grandpa came too. It's supposed to teach me a lesson." He sighs deeply, a long staticky pause. "My family's so messed up, Gris. Their money, their legacy . . . it's all they care about. I want out for good, you know? I want to go to San Diego with you."

She lets that set in a moment, unsure of what to say. When it's clear he expects a response, she sighs. "Honestly? I don't even know if I'm going back." Her throat gels as she says it. She hadn't realized its veracity until she said it aloud. Not even school feels important without Amaranta. Is this how Mom felt? Why she dropped out of school and got her GED? Why she never even went to college? Everything else fades away when a sibling does.

Harlan sounds like he's crying when he says, "Keep me posted, okay? About your bite and your sister and everything."

"Sure."

"Hey, Gris?"

"Yeah?"

"I love you."

He waits a few seconds for her to say it back — she can hear his breathing through the static, ragged and erratic as a wounded animal — but when it's clear she's not going to say anything, he disconnects the line.

As Mal and Gus drive home to see if there are any updates on the search party before they head out to the Callahan land, Gus says, "That kid's unrequited crush on Amaranta was unsettling, wasn't it? Carmen might be sending us on a wild goose chase."

Mal offers a soft, rueful chuckle. "We're no strangers to those." She's intended it as less of a jab than a reflection on the common ground they've shared their whole relationship. All those teeth in the sand. They've spent their entire love on a quest for a missing daughter. The painful irony isn't lost on Mal. "I'll ask Benny to check on Mateo."

When they pull up, there's a truck parked in front of the house. It's not white, but beige is close enough. It's bathed in mud, tires caked. Mal tries not to catastrophize, but the moment she steps onto her property, the stench of decay and sodden earth hits her.

It takes a beat to register what's on her porch: two men — one tall, stringy-haired with a hipster beard and handlebar mustache, the other stocky with a buzzcut—have hauled a grotesque bundle onto the paved walkway.

A monstrosity shrouded in a tarp. It sags and bulges, blood oozing from the corners.

Mal takes a step back, stomach coiling, head reeling. It's a carcass.

A massive one. Much too large to be her teenage daughter. A cow elk, from the size and shape, no antlers like the bulls, at least five hundred pounds.

Mal pictures it beneath the tarp, stiff, glassy-eyed, patches of fur matted and missing. They've wrapped it to keep flies from laying eggs in its wounds and orifices. But the inevitable endgame is clear in Mal's mind—the squirming worms tunneling its softening flesh.

These are the hunters from the carnicería.

Dried mud smears across their camo gear like they've sprouted directly from the soil. Hipster Beard wears a second layer of hair, every strand a dustbin of grit and crisp leaves. His khaki camos are splattered with a palette of maroons and browns—blood and offal. Buzzcut, no cleaner, bears the same crust.

"What are you two doing here?" Mal chokes, covering her nose with her T-shirt, not because of the carcass but the sweat-mud-blood combo ripening from the hunters. She's not usually such a lightweight, but this is too much.

"Hey, Mal," Buzzcut grunts, wiping sweat off his forehead with a bandana. "We brought you the elk to process as agreed." He holds out two crisp hundred-dollar bills, clean except where his fingers touch them. The men look too satisfied with themselves.

Gus clears his throat to say something when Mal clearly can't form a response, but Yessi comes to Mal's side in a flash, arms akimbo, and cuts him off. "You two pendejos have some gall. Her daughter's *missing*. Have you been in a hole?"

"In a matter of speaking," Buzzcut chuckles, the teeth around his neck jangling. "Been out camping this whole week. Took us that long to make the damn kill."

Any other time, Mal would tease them for taking so long — these doofuses. But all she can think about is that they've been gone a week. She last saw them the day Renata disappeared.

The wet copper of blood stings her nostrils. She checks the time on her phone. Two hours past noon. Amaranta disappeared at 12:36 p.m. on Friday. It's now Sunday afternoon. They're hours past the forty-eight-hour mark. It'll be dark soon.

Butchering the elk would be easy. She could shove her earphones in, turn up the music, and drown out the world for the hours it took to carve apart this animal.

Yessi narrows her eyes. "You guys just show up here like Mal's your personal butcher. How did you even get this address?"

"Wait, Griselda's missing?" Hipster Beard asks. "Damn, that sucks ass."

When they came to the carnicería looking for Mal, they thought she was a man. How do they suddenly know her elder daughter's name? Who are these guys?

"You've been camping all week? In the desert?" Mal asks.

Hipster Beard — "Yeah, why?"

Mal's breath hitches. "Have you seen a girl? She was wearing a backpack. Or someone dropping her off?" It's like she's swallowed cactus spines.

The hunters exchange glances. It's Buzzcut who finally speaks. "We didn't see nothing but wildlife. Sorry."

Mal gives them a long, hard look, trying to gauge whether they're hiding anything.

Hipster Beard reiterates, "We promised to bring you the elk

from our hunting trip so you could cut it for us. That's it. We didn't know Griselda was missing."

"Griselda's not missing," a sharp, tense voice calls from behind Mal.

It's Griselda, hobbling out of bed again.

Mal wants to cuss the hunters out herself. Her daughter is supposed to be resting.

"You know these jokers, mija?" Yessi asks.

"Hey, Marcus. Cole," Griselda says, leaning against Mal and the doorway for support. "Yeah, they go to protests with us sometimes." She turns her attention to the men. "What's up with the dead animal on our doorstep?"

Buzzcut says, "Harlan said Mal's the best butcher in town."

Griselda covers her chest with her arms. Buzzcut and Hipster Beard . . . Marcus and Cole . . . have been staring at her tits through her sheer T-shirt since she came to the door braless. Jackasses.

Yessi huffs loudly, rolling her eyes. "Well, clearly she can't carve that elk up now. Get it out of here."

"We can't unshoot the damn thing. The meat won't keep," Buzzcut grumbles.

Griselda, deadpan, says, "You'll have to butcher it yourselves or take it to Beef Tooth. They've got a full setup there. They can handle it."

Hipster Beard scowls. "Beef Tooth? Come on. We're not taking this to the Callahans. We've had enough trouble with them already."

"Where've you been hunting, huh?" Griselda challenges.

Buzzcut mumbles, "Screw the Callahans. We'll poach on their land if we want."

They're naive like Harlan, thinking they can have their cake and eat it too. Get what they need from the Callahans while so-called sticking it to them. Eventually, you have to decide which side you're on.

"I don't care where you take it," Yessi says, "but you have to get it off this porch."

"We don't have time for distractions, guys; my little sister's been missing a couple of days," Griselda adds.

"Oh shit, we didn't hear about a kid —"

Mal cuts Buzzcut off, "Both my daughter and Renata are missing." She watches them carefully to assess their reaction. They've been gone a week. Do they really know *nothing*?

"What the hell? Renata's missing too?" Hipster Beard scoffs. "We just saw her a few days ago with . . ." He looks supremely embarrassed and uncomfortable, and Mal could swear Buzzcut is eyeing him like, *Dude, shut the hell up.*

"What guy?" Mal demands. "Where was this? When?"

"We were heading out to the desert and saw her near the Salton Sea with some guy. You know how she is."

"Come on," Griselda says, rolling her eyes. "Don't be like that. Did you see the guy or not?"

"Hey, it's none of our business," Buzzcut says, holding up his hands all *don't shoot the messenger.*

"If you know who she was with, you need to tell the police."

"Come to think of it," Hipster Beard says, lifting a corner of the tarp and dragging it back toward his truck. "We didn't see nothing."

29
HELLHOUND

Griselda feels useless, sitting around the house with a swollen leg when she should be out looking for her sister. Instead, Mom took *Gus* out searching. El Cucuy. The world feels upside down. Amaranta's missing. Harlan's hunting with his family. El Cucuy is her father. And Griselda can do nothing but nurse her damn snakebite.

She called Benny as soon as Marcus and Cole left, warning him they were acting suspicious as hell and he should question them ASAP. Now she texts: Any word?

Looking into them, he texts back a minute later.

I didn't tell you on the phone cuz mom was standing right next to me, but I think they were scared to talk in front of Gus.

We went thru all that the other nite. Moving on.

She sighs. Tries calling Harlan again. It goes to voicemail.

There's got to be something else she can *do*. Maybe she should call the news stations in San Diego and see if she can convince them to come down here and cover this? Spread the word?

Abuela's slumped in her wheelchair beside the French doors to the patio. She's staring out into the garden but turns when Griselda flops onto the flowered couch to pull up the YellowPages app on her phone. "Elena?"

"No, 'buela." She's tired of playing the dead girl. "It's me, Gris."

Abuela nods. "I saw her with him."

"With who?"

"She thought I didn't know, but I knew. A mother knows."

Abuela holds up the mirror again. Griselda had forgotten. She reaches out for it now.

Abuela clutches it but Griselda pulls it from her grasp. "Sheesh, 'buela."

Her stomach drops as soon as she looks closely. Engraved on the mirror are initials. Curlicued calligraphy. G.C. + E.V. Beneath the elegant inscription, a smudge. Brick-brown. Rust. No. Not rust. Blood.

A knot twists in Griselda's chest. The initials, the dried blood.

Gus Castillo and Elena Veracruz. Holy shit. The thought of Mom's boyfriend with her disappeared tía makes the bile snake up Griselda's throat. That same boyfriend who was just in their house. Her own father. She's shaking violently. What did he *do* to Tía Elena?

What did he do to her *hermanita*?

Griselda thinks back. Didn't she see Amaranta holding this mirror the night she came home? Didn't her hermanita tuck it under the mattress?

"Where'd you find this, Abuela?" She's trying to keep her voice calm so she doesn't upset Abuela and send her into hysterics, but it's hard.

"I told you, mija. Buried," Abuela sighs, exasperated. "Why don't you listen?"

"Buried *where*?"

"Under the mattress."

Griselda's chest *thwacks,* a battering ram pounding inside her.

Did Amaranta know about Gus and Tía Elena? Is that why Gus . . .

She can't breathe. Where's her damn inhaler? "Did Benny see this?" She searches in the drawers of the coffee table to see if there's a spare inhaler in there.

"Why would Benny need to know about my treasures? It's pretty, isn't it?"

"*Abuela.* Did Gus see this mirror? When did you find it? Did you show anyone?"

Abuela cuts her off, snatching the mirror back and wheeling away from the glass doors toward the television, clicking it on and muttering, "It's none of your concern, mija."

The mud pots burble and hiss, their sporadic eruptions splattering muddy water across the windshield like hot, steaming raindrops. The Jeep shudders across the washboard road as Mal and Gus navigate their way toward the Callahan land.

Gus maneuvers over ruts and potholes as Mal scans the geothermal field that fuels these acidic pools, spurred by the San Andreas Fault running beneath. Some look like puddles of urine while others appear as human-sized monsters made of mud, rising into cones from the fetid ichor. What other monster lurks out here? The horse-headed woman is nowhere in sight. Are they on the wrong track again?

Carmen said La Siguanaba takes the girls by accident. It feels more like she's been *targeting* the girls in Mal's life. She haunts mothers. What about fathers? "Has La Siguanaba ever appeared to *you?*"

Gus slows the Jeep around a spurting mud pot. "Nah. I still don't get it. If she goes after men, if she's a woman scorned, what could she want with kids? Guess that's the thing about ghost stories. They don't make sense."

Like the stories about Gus.

"I've just . . . felt like I've been losing it more than usual. You know how she came to me the night of the bonfire when Elena vanished? It started again Saturday night . . . *out here.*"

He makes a quiet grunt of acknowledgment, like he's considering.

The earth belches, splashing droplets of acid rain across the windshield. Gus turns on the wipers. After a few moments of silence punctuated by the *swish, swish* of the acid smearing across the glass, he says, "Did you know lightning and thunder are the same phenomenon?"

"What's that got to do with a monster following me around?"

"What if she's not going after the girls at all but showing you where they are?"

The hairs on the back of Mal's neck prickle. If that were true, what has La Siguanaba been showing her? The girls pulled from the ground like roots, all tangled together. The girls choked or drowning or hit in the face with the butt of a rifle. The girls in bathtubs or sopa pots, boiling. These mud pots could've swallowed Amaranta and the other girls. They could've been dumped in these boiling pits. Boiled away. All that would be left is salt and bones.

The horrifying truth hits Mal full force and she lets out a choked sob. She's known all along and hasn't wanted to admit it—

Mal and Gus haven't been searching for missing *girls,* laughing and bright-eyed. They've been searching for *bodies.*

Deep down, she must've known that. She *did* know that. But she couldn't focus on it. Until now. She has to prepare herself for the worst. She might find her daughter's *body* out here.

The image of Mal and her girls laughing and dancing in their shared bedroom shimmers. Mal should've been more of a mom and less of a sister, but she couldn't have loved them more if she'd split herself in two and given them each a piece. That's what she did. It's not just Amaranta she's looking for. It's half of herself.

They near a patch of land distinguished by its surrounding fence, taller than Gus, with barbed wire strung atop and a thick chain and padlock the size of Mal's fist. Affixed signs read: NO TRESPASSING. PRIVATE PROPERTY. POACHERS WILL BE SHOT ON SIGHT.

Mal hops out, mud squishing beneath her boots as she strides toward the thick steel disc of padlock. "What are they hiding back there?"

Gus pulls out his shotgun from the back of the Jeep. He slides back the pump handle, opening the chamber with a crisp, mechanical *ch-chuk*. "We'll have to shoot it off."

Mal watches as he aims the shotgun at the padlock. The first shot rings out, and shrapnel flies, but the padlock holds. Gus tries again, but the same thing happens—shrapnel everywhere, no breakthrough.

"It's not working," Mal shouts over the ringing in her ears. "We'll have to ram it with the Jeep."

Gus nods, handing her the shotgun. "Get in the passenger seat."

Mal grips the shotgun as Gus reverses to get some distance. Then he floors it. The Jeep barrels forward, crashing into the gate with a resounding *clang* before it buckles and gives way. Mud spews as they roar through the weed-rampant fields. Beads of sweat pour down Mal's face and neck. She's ready to aim at anyone who fucks with them. Even the horse-headed woman.

That's when they hear it. The growling of another vehicle's engine not far in the distance like thunder leading them toward lightning. It's heading for the sea.

Mal unbuckles, pushes back the soft canvas of the Jeep to reveal the star-nettled sky, and perches herself gingerly atop the bucket seat, shotgun cocked and poised against her shoulder.

Griselda, shaking, takes two puffs of her inhaler, then dials Benny's number. She texts Mom while the phone rings. Are you okay? The message shows as delivered, not read.

Of course, it's El Cucuy! God, Griselda was so stupid to listen to her mom.

Benny answers, "Gris? What's up? I told you I haven't talked to Marcus and Cole yet."

"Benny, you need to come over. Now." Her breath is ragged. She gulps in air. "Abuela found something under Amar's mattress. It looks like something Gus gave Tía Elena . . . I don't know how Amar got it. But, Benny," she pauses, her breath hitching. "It's *proof* that *Gus*—"

He cuts her off, "Come *on,* Griselda. What're you doing?"

"Benito, listen. I'm not being paranoid. I'm serious this time. *Gus* killed Tía Elena. And Amaranta found out. I think that's why he . . ."

"What *proof*?"

"A mirror with their initials. And blood. It's probably Tía's." Tears are streaming down her face. She can't believe she let her guard down. Let Gus drive her to the hospital and stay the night in her room. Let him in their house. He *is* the monster she thought he was. What did he do to her hermanita? She'll kill him. "Mom's out at the Salton Sea with him right *now.*"

He makes his weird signature half-sigh, half-grunt sound then says, "Fine. I'll be right there. Don't show it to anyone else."

After she gets off the phone with Benny, she dials Tío Esteban to tell him what's going on. They'll need backup. Abuelo hobbles into the living room, hunched but alert as she explains over the phone what's going on.

As soon as she hangs up, Abuelo declares, "I'd better go out there too."

"No, Abuelo. It's dangerous. And you're . . ." Griselda hesitates, her throat tightening.

"A viejo, I know. But that's mi hija out there. And mi nieta. I have to go help them. That's what a father is for." His face ashes over as he grabs his coat and car keys.

Yessi appears in the doorway. "Abuelo, wait!" She glances back toward the TV where Abuela Vero is engrossed in her telenovela. "You can't go out there."

Abuelo's face is set. "¡Necesito hacerlo! Yessi, take care of my girls, eh?"

Tío Esteban was so concerned about Griselda taking Abuelo to the Salton Sea the morning before the fundraiser. Just a few days ago—feels like forever. Now she's sending him out there, alone, into the precarious night, unarmed, possibly after a kidnapper and murderer.

She texts Benny and Tío Esteban what Abuelo's doing, her fingers trembling.

"Gris, no te preocupes. He'll be okay," Yessi says, but she sounds nervous too.

Griselda tries her mom to let her know Abuelo is coming, but her text bounces back. A cold dread settles in her stomach. "I can't reach Mom. Her phone must be out of range."

* * *

Gus catapults the Jeep across fallow fields, surging toward another vehicle. Mal braces herself, eyes fixed ahead. She's a hellhound unleashed, barreling toward the brine-swept beach of her youth. If she believed in God, she'd say it was a miracle. If she believed in fate, she'd call it that. Amaranta might call it entangled particles — what one does, so does the other.

A white truck comes into view, its form fractured by the Jeep's headlights cutting through the dust. The truck fishtails, turning too sharp on the soft washboard.

"What the hell are they chasing?" Mal's voice is a sharp, frantic shriek.

Gus pushes the Jeep faster. "Can't see."

They've passed the so-called cursed land, heading straight for the sea.

Mal wraps her muscles to her bones, steeling herself. As they close in, the truck skids, revealing a girl sprinting through the fields. Her long dark hair flies behind her like crows flapping in the wind. Canary-yellow Converse pound the dirt, now uneven with crops.

She runs toward the sea like a sprinter toward the finish line.

30
CLAWFOOT

ONE HOUR EARLIER

Amaranta kicks the empty box of Johnny's fries with cheese and taquitos away from her in the bathtub she's been using as a makeshift bed in her grimy prison. She can't believe she actually ate in this filthy-ass tub, but hunger has a way of erasing pride and sanitation. He left her the food along with a jug of fresh water. The dried cheese and avocado crusted to the carton look like maggots.

At least the toilet flushes and there's running water to wash her hands and splash on her face and under her pits. It's so hot in here. She was freezing at first—like she'd stripped naked and locked herself in one of the meat freezers at the carnicería. But ever since the fuzziness wore off, she's been burning up.

While she was passed out—first from the roofied red slushee

he gave her and then because, like a dumbass, she'd knocked herself out on a concrete step in his garage — he must've changed the lock on the bathroom so it locks from the outside.

Since she came to and couldn't get the bars off the windows or pick the lock with her fingers, she's been entertaining herself by reading the ring of graffiti around the bathtub. *End of the line. Destroy what destroys you.* She was chained to the tub's clawfoot but managed to wriggle out of that a long time ago. Nothing under the sink could be a tool. She tried blunt force, knocking the door down with her body weight, starting at one end of the small bathroom and then launching herself at the door as hard as she could, but after a dozen futile attempts, she was pretty sure she'd dislocated a shoulder.

Plus, her head was killing her the first day. She thought it would split apart.

And the hole in her gum where her tooth dislodged. At least she didn't choke on it.

The water and food are gone. She doesn't know if he's coming back or not.

She kept hoping Ma or Griselda would find her, but they haven't come, and Amaranta won't die in this godforsaken hole that smells of piss. The drip, drip, drip of the leaky faucet reminds her of hooves, clomping.

She lifts the toilet tank lid. It's heavy. Especially since her shoulder throbs from playing human battering ram against the door. The constant *plink-plink* of that leaky faucet nags her to hurry up. At least this plan doesn't involve knocking herself out. Again.

With a deep breath that hurts more than she expects, she lines up the lid with the lock. Time to see if all those movies with cool breakouts were a bunch of lies.

She jams the lid against the lock and wiggles it. At first, nothing happens. *Shit.*

She repositions and tries again, considering how she might use the ball and chain bobbing in the toilet tank if this doesn't work. She bangs the porcelain down as hard as she can and, to her surprise, the doorknob cracks! It's decapitated, hanging like a head from a broken neck. She wriggles her finger inside the mechanism to pop the lock and voilà!

It really doesn't seem like that should have worked. Amaranta doesn't believe in luck or superstition but something otherworldly might finally be on her side.

Thank you, Mathematician in the Sky! Thank you, thank you!

The door creaks open and she rushes out, worrying she should've saved her weird prayer of gratitude for when she actually escapes alive. It's still up for debate. The rest of the house is as squalid as the bathroom, if not immensely more so. He's not still here, is he? She pads slowly on the tiptoes of her Converse just in case, still clutching the toilet lid to use as a battle shield.

When it's clear no one's watching her but rodents and roaches, she drops the tank lid with a *clang* and sprints for the front door into the night. She's run through El Valle's fields countless times but never the ones out by Ma's old house and, besides, everything's different in the dark. She squints into the night but she's still all buzzy and lightheaded from her fall to the concrete plus not eating enough over the past few days.

Which way to the road? Which way to Gus's house?

If only he hadn't taken her phone. Not that she could've charged it anyway.

She darts through the rutted rows of vegetables, mud clinging to her Converse. At a chain-link fence crowned with barbed wire, she stops. NO TRESPASSING. PRIVATE PROPERTY. POACHERS WILL BE SHOT ON SIGHT. Private property means someone lives here, right? She scans her surroundings, squinting into the loamy darkness where mud pots steam like soup on a stove. Beyond that, the geo-thermal plant glowing like Oz.

A rustling in the underbrush snags her attention, and she glances down at the dirt where she finds a hole large enough for a coyote to squirm through, maybe even a pack of coyotes.

She can fit. She drops first onto her hands and knees, then her belly, and crawls, the chain link scratching at her back. On the other side, she wipes her muddy hands on her clothes.

A dim light in the distance sends her heart muscle thwacking against her rib cage. She charges in that direction until she comes to a small outbuilding resembling a wooden cabin. A flickering glow emanates from the two front windows. Maybe there's a farmer out here she can borrow a phone from. She knocks but no one answers, so she pulls the door open with a loud squeal. "Hello?"

She expects a rustic scene—a table with bowls of porridge and a flickering candle, maybe?—but quickly realizes she was mistaken about the purpose of this hut.

Terribly mistaken.

A dark, sticky coating of . . . is that blood soaking the wooden planks of the floor? She picks up her feet and sure enough, the soles of her Converse are stained red with it already.

A clump of dread lodges in her throat.

Butcher knives and hooks hang from the ceiling, swaying as if someone just bumped into them. She half expects to see Ma with her bloodstained apron pop around the corner. The air reeks. Putrid with a steamy, hot shit that'll clog Amaranta's nose forever. She pulls her shirt over her face but the thin fabric doesn't help. The stench chokes her.

The flicker of light isn't a candle but a single fluorescent bulb throwing everything into a weird, shadowy relief. There, smack in the middle of the room, a beheaded deer splays on the butcher table.

Its bodiless head with eyes wide open looks . . . sad. Like it's asking Amaranta to *do* something, but what can she do? Someone's already done the worst. Below, a large galvanized-steel tub collects offal and blood. The hot shit makes her gag.

And then, in the corner, a pile of coyotes just tossed together like stuffed animals in the donate pile. They could be sleeping, all tangled up. But they're not. It's a real-life pet cemetery. It's like a monster's lair and these are the remnants of its meals. She swipes angrily at her tears. Dizziness grips her. She tries to force her legs to turn and sprint back outside when she sees, in the crack of a wooden floor plank beside the offal tub, a string of colorful beads she recognizes.

They dangled from the ears of the most beautiful girl she's ever seen up close. A girl who flashed her a bright smile behind the counter of Ma's shop.

Another whiff of the sour tang hits her nostrils, walloping her hard in the gut. What the horrifying hell happened to Renata in this cabin? The tears are falling freely down her face now as she bends down, pinching the beads from between the floorboards. Behind her, the door hinges squeals. Someone else is here.

She spins around, but before she can say anything, Harlan, wide-eyed, shouts, "Amar! You're okay! Your sister's gonna be so relieved!"

Amaranta clutches the beads in her palm. "You?" She's so upset — not because she ever liked or trusted Harlan (she always kinda thought he was an insincere douche) — but because of how it'll shatter her sister. Griselda trusted him completely. "What did you *do* to Renata?"

Harlan shakes his head, his whole face flushing so red it's almost purple. "No, you don't understand. It wasn't like that. I didn't . . ."

"I *know* these are her earrings."

But then his dad and grandpa flank him in the doorway. And Amaranta can read in their eyes what they're thinking. She's in the way. She knows too much. She has to go.

She squeezes the beads tighter, backing toward the splayed and dripping deer on the table, the pile of coyote carcasses, searching her periphery for another exit.

Sean holds up a gun, but Harlan shoves into his dad and hollers, "Back door! Amar, run!"

She doesn't hesitate. She lunges around the butcher table, almost slipping on the blood-splattered floor as Harlan grabs his dad and grandpa, holding them while she fumbles the door open and flees again into the star-drenched night.

Behind her, she can hear Sean barking, "What are you *doing,* you idiot? She'll ruin everything for you!"

"They all do," his grandpa bemoans, his voice such an ugly growl she can't believe it took her so long to piece it together. What a monster he is.

A minute later, a truck engine roars to life.

She races toward the flickering lights shining at the geothermal plant.

Would they believe who was chasing her? The men who own this land, the building, practically everything in this town?

The mud pots hiss and burble like a bruja's cauldron, the ground softening then sinking altogether. She stumbles. A scalding hiss of liquid spurts at her leg like one of those venomous dinosaurs in *Jurassic Park.* The pain is sharp, like a jaw clamped down on her scorched calf. She screeches, but the truck is coming. She has to get up and keep running.

She puts pressure on it and fumbles. It hurts so dang bad.

She's going to die out here, isn't she? They're going to kill her like the other girls?

Just then, a woman appears beside her, midnight-black hair covering her face.

"Renata?" Amaranta whispers.

But when the woman looks up, she's not a woman at all but a horse. Her gaping nostrils flare, her fiery eyes like jeweled marbles. And like that, Amaranta recognizes her. She was there in the tub, when Amaranta was passed out. She kept her company while she slept.

"La Siguanaba?"

The horse-headed woman grabs Amaranta's hand, pulls her up, and tugs her past the mud pots, zipping through the fiery chasms, navigating deftly until they're back in the vegetable fields, tromping across cabbage heads and toward the sea.

31
MALLOW MAR

S he's not a hallucination, right? Gus sees her too? Mal chambers a round and takes aim, steadying the shotgun despite the rumbling of the Jeep. She fires. Once. Twice. *Click, click, boom. Click, click, boom.* The recoil kicks her shoulder as the truck's driver's-side tires burst like balloons caught in a ceiling fan. Its tail swerves, shattered tires flapping against the ground and spewing shredded rubber. Sparks fly from the rim, scraping the sandy shoreline as the truck teeters precariously.

"Gus! It'll hit her!" Mal screams as she clutches the shotgun and crouches low, quickly buckling her safety belt and clasping the door handle. Gus punches the accelerator and hurtles them toward the truck skidding along the beach, churning up dirt and debris.

"Hold on!" Gus yells back. He jerks the wheel and positions the Jeep to intercept the spun-out truck. The world tilts, ground and sky jumbling as metal screeches and the two vehicles collide. The Jeep shudders from the impact to its back bumper, and they're tossed around in their seats, but Gus's gamble paid off. The truck stills.

If birds scatter into the dark night, they bleed into the blackness.

Mal unclicks her buckle and tumbles out of the Jeep with the shotgun. Amaranta is still out there. They need to detain the other driver — Sean? — so he can't hurt her girl. But she can't bear not holding Amaranta a second longer.

She throws Gus the shotgun, calling "Don't let him go."

Lightheaded and whiplashed, she sprints toward the water. The beach house isn't far, Mal realizes, gaining her bearings as she runs.

The girl in the water is half-drowned and gasping, bedraggled. Her dark hair, soaked and matted to her face, gives her a ghostly appearance. For a split second, Mal's terrified she followed a ghost down here — that she's caught La Siguanaba, who only looks human until she lifts her terrible maw. For a split second, she is Renata. Elena. Noemi. She is all the missing girls blurred together.

Then she calls out, shaky, unmistakable, "Ma?" She pulls back her hair and there she is. Her eyes lock on to her mother. She stumbles forward, knees buckling the second she's in her mother's arms.

"Amaranta!" Mal's clinging to her daughter, their tears mingling with the salt of the sea drenching them both. Mal breathes in the top of her daughter's head as if she's just slid from her, screaming. "Did anyone hurt you? Did they touch you . . . did they . . ."

"No, not like that. Ma — "

"¡Ay, Dios mío! What happened to your legs? They're scalded!"

"I fell into one of the mud pots," Amaranta sputters, voice thin as a fledging's chirrup.

Then Mal sees the gaping chasm between Amaranta's teeth. She gasps and cups her daughter's face. Dried blood crusts her mouth and chin down to her neck where bright, red stains bloom across the collar of her T-shirt. Amid the sour stench of blood and lake and sulfur — an unmistakable cherry-sweet, sugary smell on Amaranta's clothes. "Who *did* this to you?"

"Ma, listen —"

The thunderous clap of a shotgun cuts her off.

Mal quickly pulls Amaranta close and then pushes her behind herself for protection. She should've kept the shotgun.

From the shadows, a figure is racing toward them, gun in hand.

Amaranta tenses. Just as the figure becomes discernible, her daughter calls out, clear and devastating: "Mom! Harlan killed Renata!"

Mal looks to him, in disbelief and shock. She shakes her head.

But he's crying. And not denying Amaranta's words.

Mal thinks back to what Yessi said. Or was it Benny? Raul was bartending at the lodge. Harlan was supposed to be Raul's alibi, which should've worked both ways. If Harlan had ever been a suspect. Mal doesn't understand. "Weren't you at the lodge all night Saturday?" She exhales, still hoping maybe her daughter got it wrong. "Raul *saw* you there."

"I'm so sorry, Ms. V. I never meant . . . it was . . . I came to the lodge later . . . my dad and grandpa . . ." He's hyperventilating.

Mal almost has the urge to comfort him but checks herself hard. She'd put her faith in this *one* Callahan being a good guy. There was hope for the Callahan men because of Harlan. Are all the Callahans just disgusting and irredeemable? Griselda will be crushed. What does this mean for Benny? Mal is crushed.

"Why?" she cries when his voice cracks like a whip through the air at the same time —

"Stay back!" It takes Mal a second to realize he's not commanding her and Amaranta but the two other figures emerging from the truck: Sean and Old Man Callahan. All three are clad in hunting gear. Harlan points the gun at his family even as he trembles. "I mean it, Dad. Grandpa. Leave Griselda's family *alone*."

Sean and Old Man Callahan freeze, the former's hand still on the shotgun, the latter's face a portrait of bewilderment and rage.

When Harlan moves in front of Mal and Amaranta to protect them from his family, she sees what he had been blocking before.

Ahead, headlights slash through the night, glaring a lurid light on Gus's torn body lying beside the wreckage. Blood oozes from his left side. Mal stops herself from running to him. Her cry is guttural, shredding through the horrible tableau.

Like a hunter swaggering over a downed prize, Sean towers over Gus, mouth twisted. Despite his son's protests, Sean keeps his shotgun trained on Mal and Amaranta.

"You shouldn't have come out here," he jeers, as if they're poachers on his land like the signpost warned: POACHERS WILL BE SHOT ON SIGHT.

"What the fuck did you do, Sean?" Mal screams, the raw, visceral shock reverberating.

One hand holds Amaranta. With the other, she digs her nails into her palms to keep from running to Gus and stanching the wound, which seeps like a squash flower oozing on the comal of dirt. Sean's gun won't allow it.

These long and painful years, Gus has been maligned as El Cucuy. He's borne the brunt of the town's scorn and cruelty. A grieving father turned into a beast. When it's been the princes of El Valle all along. The wolves among them.

"You sick fuck. Why?" she cries again, a lament breaking inside her.

"Anything to protect my son," Sean says. "You can understand that. It's not personal."

"Dad, Grandpa, we don't have to do this!"

Mal grasps her daughter's hand tighter, and Amaranta squeezes back. She scans the ground for Gus's shotgun. If she keeps the Callahans arguing, she can figure out how to gain control of this situation, at least long enough for Amaranta to escape. Could she call Benny or Esteban from her cell in her back pocket? Or have Amaranta do it unnoticed?

"Harlan, how'd they rope you into this, honey? You couldn't have meant to . . ." *Kill her.* It hits Mal. Renata's dead. Her poor mother.

Harlan, gun aimed at his father and grandfather yet glancing back over his shoulder, admits, "I didn't mean for any of it to happen. Renata came on to me! She threatened to ruin everything with Gris. I just wanted her to stop talking. I didn't mean . . ."

Mal fumbles with her phone. The screen unlocks by facial recognition, so she can't unlock it unless she holds it up to her face. Could Amaranta peer down into the screen from behind her without being seen? They look so much alike they can often fool tech.

"You were dating her?" Mal nudges. "Renata?"

Harlan gasps. "It's like Grandpa says. We're cursed."

"Move out the way, boy," Old Man Callahan barks, raising his rifle.

"Stop, stop, you don't have to kill them," Harlan cries, sounding like a little boy. It's horrifying. The gun wavers in his grasp. "Just . . . stop," he pleads, his voice barely above a whisper. "I . . . it wasn't supposed to . . ." he stammers. "Renata wanted me to run off with her. To choose her. But how could I choose her over Gris? Renata was just filling time. I know that makes me an asshole, but Gris is the love of my fucking life."

It makes you a murderer, Mal thinks but doesn't say.

Old Man Callahan's mouth twists into a snarl, but he remains motionless, caught in the tension of the standoff. "These people keep ruining our lives. I should've gotten rid of the whole family that night."

What night? Mal's about to ask but Harlan cuts her off.

"It's not like that, Grandpa. If you do this, Gris will never forgive me."

"She'll never forgive you anyway, son," Sean persuades with a cold edge. "Now, stop messing around and step aside."

But the headlights of an approaching vehicle flash, wavering everyone's attention. The car speeds toward them, screeching to a halt a few feet from Sean and Old Man Callahan.

Benny bursts out, gun aimed, face twisted in rage. "Drop the weapons!" he shouts.

"Benito," Mal shouts back. "They kidnapped Amaranta! And killed Renata!"

"We didn't kidnap her, Ms. V," Harlan insists, seeming genuinely surprised. Or is that an act? She can't tell anymore. "I wouldn't hurt Gris's sister. I told you."

Mal turns to Amaranta. She should tell her daughter to run, but in her confusion, she stammers, "You didn't get in a white truck with them?"

Amaranta's response is quiet but clear: "No."

"Then with who?" Mal demands, her voice breaking.

"Your brother."

"Benny?" Mal gasps, staring at her brother, his gun trained on Sean.

Amaranta's voice is barely above a whisper, but it's enough, "No, Ma."

"What do you mean?" Mal sputters, trying to process what her daughter's just said.

Amaranta looks at the ground. "Your other brother."

No. Mal slams it shut. Just no. She's shaking not only her head but her entire body in negation, seeing herself and her brother as kids, sitting cross-legged on her bed eating candy while everyone else slept. Her refuge in the nightmare that their house became —

"Chuy!" she giggles, taking a piece of candy he's snuck her and stuffing it into her mouth. *"Where did you get this?"*

"I always provide for my familia!" He laughs back. *"Mallow Mar!"*

In unison, *"A marshmallow! And a s'more!"*

"No . . ."

"Ma, he . . ." Amaranta's trembling, her voice stuttering. "Tío Esteban took me . . . I think to his house first and then to your old house. It was . . ." Tears are running down her cheeks. "Awful."

"No," Mal finally moans aloud, her guts churning. "No."

Just then, another vehicle arrives, ferrying Papi and Esteban.

32
OUT IN THE OPEN

Amaranta blanches at what she finds in Old Man Callahan's office — not just her sister's bare ass on his overwrought mahogany desk or Harlan pumping furiously like an edgy and agitated primate.

How many times had Amaranta stopped to blow a kiss to her tía Elena's ofrenda in the tiny foyer of their home? How many times had she seen the picture hanging there? The abuelos cherished it, a testament to Tía's last known accomplishment. The image was seared into Amaranta's memory by the hundreds of candles that've burned over the years in her honor.

Elena, holding her painting of a bay horse in a verdant field.

It had looked so free, so regal. Burnt-sienna coat with a long, jet-black mane, galloping through that green expanse like it could ride into forever.

No wonder Tía Elena had won a blue ribbon for it.

Amaranta always thought the painting must be displayed at the school or the fair, maybe even in a museum. Or, like Tía herself, the painting had simply vanished.

But no.

Here it is. That same painting, hanging on the wall behind Old Man Callahan's desk.

Understanding prickles like cactus spines in her gut. Like seeing a ghost.

Like Tía's beckoning to Amaranta from the horse itself—

Find me, mijita. Come find me.

Amaranta stumbles out of the office, dumbfounded.

The blood-smudged compact mirror.

It's Tía Elena's blood. It has to be.

G.C. + E.V.

She thought it was Ma's boyfriend. That would've made the most sense. El Cucuy. But he doesn't have Tía's painting hanging above his ornate desk, does he?

So it's not Gus Castillo, but . . . Guy Callahan.

Gross.

Old Man Callahan.

And E.V.

Elena Veracruz. Tía Elena.

But Old Man Callahan's wife's name is Elva, isn't it?

And Ma's always going on about them. The land barons. Robber barons. How Elva kept her family name since her family was one of the original so-called founders of the town.

What did Ma say her last name was?

Vaughn.

E.V.

So . . . this mirror belonged to Old Man Callahan and his wife. They'd monogrammed everything around this stupid mansion.

A rush of excitement pulses through Amaranta, threaded quickly by fear.

She knows what happened to her aunt. At least, she thinks she's solved the mystery. She imagines how Ma will feel, and Abuela, if they finally know the truth. And Renata—could this help with her case too?

She needs to run it by Tío Benny, who's not at the party. He hasn't been answering her texts lately either. Can she ask someone to drive her to his house or the station? Iggy would do it.

But she needs to be careful. Tía Sharon said she was in danger without that mirror. Amaranta guesses she needs it for evidence. Or blackmailing. She's still not sure how Tía Sharon factors into it, but Benny can help her work it out. He's the detective.

Before she can leap to her feet, a pair of footsteps approach. These aren't the beastly unistep of the cuates but shiny leather shoes. Expensive. Fancy.

She raises her gaze to his impeccable suit and tie.

"Mija, why are you sitting on the ground all by yourself? You should come enjoy my party! There's a band."

"I know, Tío. It's just . . ."

"That coyote scared you?"

She sighs. Since Tío Benny's not here, she might as well try out her theory on Tío Esteban.

She spills her guts in a hushed whisper in case the walls have ears, telling him everything, from what happened at his ex-wife's house (not even omitting what his bloodsucker kids did) to the inscription on the mirror and how she mistakenly believed it was her ma's secret boyfriend to how she now believes it must've belonged to Guy and Elva. And now, the painting in the office. It's such a relief getting it all out in the open.

He frowns like he's deep in contemplation. Not angry or surprised so much as intensely focused. "Do you have the mirror?" he asks. "So we can show Benny and have his forensics department test it."

She nods. "Under my mattress, at home."

"Okay, good. Tell you what, mija. Meet me after school tomorrow. You have an early release day, right?"

She nods again. "I'm supposed to have Johnny's with Iggy, but . . . this is important."

"It is," he agrees, his voice soft and sagacious. "Meet me outside Johnny's, and we'll retrieve the evidence and take it to your tío Benny. Don't take it to school, huh? Just in case."

"Do you think Old Man . . . er . . . Mr. Callahan and his wife could've actually killed Tía? Why?"

He sighs deeply. "It sounds unthinkable, but I guess anything is possible. Let's see what Benny makes of the evidence, okay? Don't worry about it tonight. I'll see you tomorrow."

33
ROOT ROT

Mal forces herself to focus on the deadlock she's caught in: Gus bleeding out on the salt-scattered earth; the hum of Esteban's car, as he and Papi stand behind their car doors, static at the sight of all the Callahan men and Benny, guns drawn. Mal, glass-eyed, cement-hearted, and ready to rush them all with the force of a mare defending her foal from a pack of predators.

"Chuy's working with him," she screams at Papi. The words burn her throat. Then another horrifying possibility dawns. "Or are you all working together?"

Except Papi hates the Callahans. Even if Esteban has some kind of financial or political arrangement with them, if Esteban got himself into some seedy campaign support deal, what the hell would that have to do with Papi?

Esteban says nothing, like he's been stunned speechless. His mouth gapes.

Papi, too, seems shell-shocked, frozen like he was the weeks and months following Elena's disappearance, when he was a ghost of himself.

Sean's gun is still aimed at Mal and Amaranta. But Benny's got a gun on Sean. The stalemate buys her the seconds she needs to scramble through the haze toward her next move. She's poised to signal Amaranta to run behind the truck or Benny's patrol car. Gus's shotgun lies on the ground beside him. She could reach it if she pushes Amaranta toward the truck and lunges forward. Only, the Callahans are such sickos, fucking serial killers, she can't risk making a move that'll get Amaranta shot. Like Gus. Her heart clenches.

Benny's voice crackles into his walkie-talkie, requesting backup and medics.

Sean spits a glob of mucus that lands beside Gus. "You know this won't stick. This is my family's land."

Benny inches closer. "People aren't game. You shot a man."

Sean's face hardens. "Stay back, I'm serious. I'll shoot your sister and your niece in the fucking head." His smirk is gone.

"No!" Harlan and Esteban shout together. Fat tears jet down Esteban's cheeks, and not the fake kind Mal can tell are for show. At least, she always thought she could tell. She has no idea who he is or what he's capable of.

A smile slashes across Sean's face. "I'm not the only one keeping secrets, Senator."

"Whatever this is, Sean, leave them out of it. If you need a target, turn around and face me. Let them go."

"Leave them out of this?" Sean chuckles, irony dripping as he says, almost giddy with self-satisfaction, "You brought them into this!"

Esteban looks like Sean's just punched him. He's shaking his head.

"She knows you're no hero. They all know you kidnapped your own niece. Who'd have guessed you're such a dog, Senator Steve?"

Esteban looks gutted. "Mal, it's not how it looks . . ."

"Come on, cut the act," Sean retorts, his cruel enjoyment taking on a sharper edge. "I watched you from my balcony through your garage windows, tying up your own unconscious niece. You heaved her body out of your ex-wife's truck and flopped her onto your garage floor like a bag of fertilizer. It was quite the spectacle."

"That white truck was registered to your ex-wife," Benny says, recognition dawning. "We had just confirmed it, Mal. I was going to tell you, but I swear I had no idea it was Steve."

"Mal . . . I . . . they're twisting it," Esteban sputters. "I didn't . . ."

"You can't talk your way out of this one. I followed you out here," Sean chortles. "You stashed her in that dilapidated shack you grew up in, what, three days ago?"

Esteban's crying now. "I brought her food and water, Mal. I didn't mean to . . . I swear it, I had no idea Sean was out here. No idea he would . . ."

"Ma, Tío called me from a phone I didn't recognize. And then, yeah, it was a white truck. And then he kept me locked up. It was just . . . scary."

Mal turns away from Amaranta and throws up on the dirt.

The burner phone. Not a john or drug deal. Amaranta's own uncle.

Mal and Chuy had already checked the beach house. She wouldn't think to check twice.

She couldn't have imagined this from Chuy in her wildest nightmares. No wonder La Siguanaba had to intervene.

"But *why*?"

"I took her to my place, but then I panicked and moved her to the beach house . . . hoping I could figure out how to . . . do damage control."

"Damage control! You are the damage! You stole my daughter!"

Sean's guffawing like a deranged orangutan, obviously enjoying this. The winds pick up suddenly, hurling sand and salt into the air.

Mal doesn't hesitate. With a swift motion, she shoves Amaranta behind the truck and dives for Gus's shotgun. As she snatches it, slick with his blood, she uses her momentum to kick out, sweeping Sean's feet from beneath him.

Sean hits the ground with a thud but quickly regains his bearings and scrambles for his own fallen gun. Amaranta's wide eyes peer from behind the truck's door, slightly ajar. Her daughter is momentarily safe. Mal won't risk firing the shotgun with so many people she loves close by — even if she has no idea who she can trust.

She clips the safety, flips the shotgun, and, before Sean can grab his own weapon, she slams the butt into the back of his head with a hard thud. She then kicks his gun out of his reach.

Harlan trains his gun on his grandfather, while Benny targets Sean on the ground.

"My grandpa says you women are a trap. But what I did was *fucking awful*. I'm so sorry . . . I . . ."

"Shut up, son!" Sean yells.

But Harlan doesn't shut up. He's howling with anguish through his tears. "You've always said La Siguanaba can imitate the appearance of a man's girlfriend or wife to catch him cheating. To *make* him cheat. She can drive him crazy. All the men in my family are cursed because of what *you* did." He points to his grandpa, who's gone ghostly white. His shotgun is faltering toward the ground. "I didn't even know. Until I did the same thing to Renata as he did to Noemi." He turns toward Mal, spitting as he talks, pointing the gun for emphasis. "When I went to them for help, Grandpa told me what he did. Fucked her. Murdered her to keep her quiet. And when I couldn't . . . chop . . . Ren up . . ." He's choking on his own mucus. "My dad did it."

He's gagging so bad Mal thinks he's going to vomit, but he pulls himself together. "They think La Siguanaba's after us, but I know the truth. *We're* the monsters."

"Just drop the gun, Harlan," Benny says. "We will work this out."

Harlan's whole body is quaking. "I choked her." He seems to be choking on something too. "She just wouldn't shut up." He looks at them, his eyes wild as a caught animal, spittle foaming at his mouth. "I won't be like my dad and grandpa. I won't be cursed. We deserve what we get."

Benny, slow, calm, says, "Harlan, you all have the right to remain silent, all that you say can and will be used against you in a court of law. Put the rifles down."

"Tell Gris I'm so sorry. I love her. I never meant for any of this."

Dirty tears streaming down his face, Harlan fires three shots in quick succession.

His grandpa. His dad. Then he turns the gun on himself.

34
EL BORRACHO

Those three shots still reverberating, Mal's shaking so bad she can't think straight but she flings herself toward Gus on the ground, the sob she's been holding in howling out of her as she presses her palms to the dark bloom of his wound. "Hang on," she's whispering, rocking against him. Another frantic glance to the truck confirms Amaranta is still safe, her small hand pressed against the window, watching every move.

Esteban rushes toward Mal, reaching out to help, but she swats him away.

"Get away from us," she wails. "You did this!" Her body's shuddering now, shaking uncontrollably.

"Mal, no, wait. He twisted it. I wasn't . . . I didn't . . ."

"Look at her teeth, Chuy! You knocked out her front tooth!" Mal's screaming so loudly her throat burns. "Who are you?"

"No, she fell. I—"

"Where'd she fall, Chuy?"

He hangs his head.

"Why'd she fall?"

Tears are streaking down his cheeks. He scratches his face vigorously. He always scratches his face when he's nervous. She looks toward her papi, pleading, as if he could do or say something to make this better. But he, too, says nothing, just clutches the car door, still immobile, as if he's turned to wax. It reminds her of how — when gardening returned him to the land of the living — he pointed out the swollen shapes of fungi, bulging and bulbous, hiding beneath the damp leaves. *"If you overwater a plant, mija, it can get root rot. See, all troche y moche."* That's their family, festering in stagnant water all these years. Rotted.

Sirens blush their red and blue in the distance.

"Chuy! Why'd you do this?"

"My campaign. She . . . if she told anyone . . . it would ruin us."

"Told anyone what, goddamnit?!"

"It was the night of the bonfire . . ." Esteban starts. As he explains, it's as if Mal's back there again, next to a fire raging in a rusted barrel between stacks of sweet-smelling hay bales. Silver kegs surrounded by teenagers filling plastic Dixie cups or squirting the beer straight into their mouths. It's as if Mal hadn't walked the back roads home, La Siguanaba following her all the while, but stayed a few minutes longer and watched Elena take off in a truck. Watched Esteban and Sharon, who'd been making out, notice Elena leaving.

Esteban groaned and rolled his eyes, complaining, "My mom told me to watch my sisters, and my stupid sister Elena just got in a truck with some old guy. I can't let that slide. Come on."

They followed the truck through the winding roads and mud pots surrounding their old neighborhood. To where they are now.

To the Callahan land. It wasn't fenced then. And they didn't own as much as they do now. But still, the same.

"So what she's with an older guy?" Sharon was saying, exasperated. "They're just fooling around, like we should be. Let them be."

He pulled up in the distance, cut his lights, killed the engine.

It would be embarrassing to interrupt them now. He recognized the telltale signs of windows fogging. Truck swaying. Dammit. He felt like a perv watching.

His dick throbbed in his pants.

Sharon was slobbering all over his neck, and he gave in. Elena was a big girl; she could take care of herself.

Sharon climbed atop him, her ass squashed against the steering wheel, and they were going at it when a commotion snagged at his attention. He nudged Sharon to the side to view the truck ahead of them.

Someone was pounding on the driver's-side window of the truck, screaming and slurring. Demanding they get out and face him.

Old Man Callahan stepped out of the truck, his voice patronizing, jeering even.

The two men were yelling at each other, and the slurring one threw a wild punch.

Old Man Callahan punched back.

That's when Esteban realized it was his own papi staggering to a standing position, hobbling to the truck bed, where something caught his attention.

Esteban pushed Sharon back to the passenger side, his hand poised on the door handle, unsure if he should intervene. He zipped his fly.

He could've honked, scaring them, but that wouldn't have helped Elena.

Speaking of the devil, his sister stumbled out of the truck, semi-dressed, hair tousled. She spoke in a pacifying tone to Papi, who didn't seem to listen and instead grabbed something from the back of the truck.

A rifle. He was half-crazed, and Esteban, through the fog steaming his own windshield, finally understood what he was seeing.

He lurched for the door handle and tugged it open, pitching himself out of his car. The night seemed to still, the distant chirping of crickets a haunting soundtrack.

"No, wait!" Sharon's voice, as if through a tunnel, barely registered in Esteban's ears.

Papi was El Borracho, wild with rage.

"First my wife! Now my daughter!" He held the gun, thrusting it out like a sword, punctuating his every accusation. "¡Chingada madre! ¡Con mi hija! ¡Eres un monstruo!" The word *monster* came out as a growl.

He cocked the rifle, aimed dead straight at the center of Old Man Callahan's chest.

Esteban was running, but not fast enough.

"Papi! No!"

El Borracho's eyes, bloodshot and wild, fixed on Callahan, his hand tremoring as he gripped the rifle. The world narrowed to the gleaming barrel of that weapon, cold and unyielding.

And there she went, a blur of disheveled hair and clothes, dashing in front of Old Man Callahan as she cried out, "Guy!"

It came as if in slow motion: the raising of the rifle, Elena's outstretched arms, and Papi's ojos widening as he pulled the trigger, felling his own beloved daughter like a misguided doe.

A deafening bang shattered the silence. Too late, El Borracho saw what he'd done.

Elena's figure crumpled, her descent to the ground like a tragically choreographed dance. Esteban's scream came out raw and guttural. Sharon stood in the shadows, shaking. She puked into the crops.

The aftermath was silence, save for the pained sobs of a broken father.

"*You* killed Elena?" Mal whispers, searching Papi's face for the veracity of Esteban's story. Papi, El Borracho.

He's hunched and drawn into himself, like he's retreated to a cave, a hermit crab, jabbed and darted back into his shell. He says nothing, and Mal knows it's true.

The police and ambulance are close, the sirens yowling, louder and louder.

"I'm so sorry, sis," her brother's voice breaks, tears thickening his words. "I never meant to hurt Amaranta. I panicked. I was trying to figure out what to do. How to fix this. I had no idea about Sean." He looks directly at Mal. "I took Amaranta to protect our father's secret. This was never part of my plan."

He gestures toward the bodies of the Callahan men strewn about them. And Gus's body beneath Mal. She cups her hands to his side, slick as oil with blood.

"Your plan," Mal scoffs. "To kidnap my daughter."

Esteban winces. "I was always going to bring her home. I was always going to tell you. I just needed . . . time. Amar found out about Old Man Callahan, and I knew that if we went to the police," he nods toward Benny, "the Callahans would accuse us. It was only a matter of time before Papi's involvement came to light . . . they'd twist it and make it like he meant to kill Elena. Like Sharon and I . . . when it wasn't like that. We were trying to save her. I was trying to buy time to figure out how to make this all right."

She glances through the wreckage toward Amaranta, who's still peeking through, her eyes trained on Mal. "You could never make this right," she says. "Why was she so delirious that she fell down and knocked her fucking tooth out, Chuy? What did you do to her?"

"Nothing, I swear. I just . . . gave her some of Mami's Ativan."

The cherry-sweet scent on Amaranta's clothes — slushee, laced with Ativan. Mal closes her eyes and takes a deep breath. She can't believe this is her brother. She can't believe her big brother entangled them in this nightmare . . . with Papi's help.

"Did you know?" she asks Papi. Not that it matters. Not that she'd believe him. They've been lying to her for twenty-five years. "Did you know Esteban kidnapped my daughter?"

He shakes his head. "Mija . . ."

She presses her head against Gus's chest, his breathing so shallow and raspy, he's almost gone. They've taken too much from her. "You could never make this right," she repeats, so nauseous even after vomiting, the thick sludge still rising up her throat. "And her backpack? How did it end up in the desert for Bull to find? Huh, Chuy? Did you plan that too?"

"I dumped it in the desert . . . but I had no idea the Callahans would be out here. That they'd find her." His voice is laden with despair. They could go in circles like this forever, but they don't have forever. She puts her hand up to stop him. He wipes his tears as he stands and returns to their father, then puts a hand on his shoulder and turns back to Mal and Benny. "Let me take the fall. Papi wasn't thinking clearly. He was defending his daughter. It was so long ago. Please leave him out of it. Mami needs him."

Papi's voice is thick. "Mijo, no. This was all my doing, and it's time I— " He's so hunched over, it's a wonder he's still standing. His chest has gone concave, like his heart has been ripped out, his rib cage crushed. "I'm so ashamed of myself."

Mal lays her head on Gus, listening for a heartbeat like a child pressing her ear against a seashell to listen for water. He smells of vanilla, bourbon, and earth in that order.

As the squad cars and ambulance encircle them, Mal asks, "What did you do with Elena's body?"

Esteban nods toward the metal rainwater catch basin across the field. It reminds Mal of a beehive. A sopa pot. The pot the girls were boiling in — and when La Siguanaba lifted them up, they came out all entangled, all jumbled together. *If you find your daughter, you find all the girls,* she was telling Mal.

"They're in the water tank?"

Behind her brother and father, the horse-headed woman brays in the distance before her black hair swallows her face and she disappears.

35
AMARANTA SÁNDWICH

The Veracruz sisters huddle on Amaranta's side of the bed, tucked under the sheets that smell vaguely of Abuela and her poultices — arnica and menthol. Right now, it's the most comforting smell in the world.

Her big sister tousles her hair, damp from the five shampoos Amaranta just gave it in what felt like the most luxurious shower she's ever taken. After enduring three days in that moldy, rat-infested, haunted house where Ma grew up, followed by running for her life and slipping into literal lava pools — honestly, she should wash her hair five more times. She thought she'd never feel clean or safe ever again.

And maybe she won't.

But perhaps this is as close as it gets.

She allows herself to be snuggled as Griselda whispers, as if reading her mind, "Let's never do that again."

Griselda offers her pinky finger for Amaranta to swear on, while Ma emits a loud, snarly snore from the other side of the bed, where she's been curled in the sleep of the dead since they returned home from the hospital.

Amaranta suppresses the urge to pat Ma's head and whisper, *pobrecita,* even though Amaranta's the one who just spent the weekend in hell. Ma had her own hellish ordeal too.

Each sister extends her injured leg — Griselda's snakebite parallel to Amaranta's mud-pot burns. Battle scars. A battle they've won. But it wasn't without casualties.

Renata's smile burns Amaranta's eyelids every time she closes her eyes. She can't help conflating her beautiful face with the beheaded deer's. She hopes there's an afterlife for girls who were wronged. A place where they get to do all the things they should've done in this life.

And poor Gris. They thought Ma was dating a monster, but it turns out Gris was. She fell for a Callahan just like Abuela and Tía. Maybe their family's curse was falling for terrible men.

At least Amaranta won't follow in those footsteps.

She wouldn't call Abuelo and Tío *terrible men* — but they did some terrible things, that's for sure. "I was so wrong about everything," Amaranta whispers, refraining from touching Ma for fear of waking her. "So wrong about Ma."

"Me too," Griselda admits. "I blamed her."

"I'm sorry about Harlan," Amaranta says for the umpteenth time.

Griselda scrunches her face like Amaranta has just punched her. She needs to stop bringing it up, but it's hard. It was such a shock.

"I should've seen the signs," Griselda says after a few moments.

"We're both gonna need therapy now, huh? Like Ma?" Amaranta yawns, and Griselda's eyes widen as she stares into her sister's open mouth. Amaranta clamps her mouth shut. "I look like a jack-o'-lantern . . ."

Griselda's expression softens into what might be akin to pity if it were coming from anyone else, but from her it's more like awe. Like she's impressed with Amaranta. "You're beautiful," she says. "Anyway, Mom'll get you an implant. It'll be good as new."

It doesn't feel like things will *ever* be good as new, though.

They sit in quiet contemplation, their shoulders touching, before Amaranta says, "Do you think I'm crazy for not wanting to press charges against Tío? Ma said I should." She sighs deeply and fiddles with a fraying edge of the bedsheet. "But she says it's my decision. I think it's hard for her . . . he's her brother."

Griselda closes her eyes and takes a deep breath. After another silence, she says, "I don't know." The way she clutches her stomach, Amaranta feels bad. Griselda's recovering from loss right now too. Even if Harlan was a shit person who killed Renata, he was Griselda's best friend since elementary school.

"Would you ever have married Harlan, if . . . ?"

She shakes her head. "No. Deep down, I knew something was wrong. I just . . . I let our history cloud my judgment."

Amaranta squeezes her sister's hand. "I'm sorry," she says, resting her head on Griselda's shoulder.

"Thanks," she says, letting her hand be squeezed. "But Tío. I mean . . . that's hard. He drugged you, hermanita. That's pretty sick."

Amaranta nods. "Yeah. You wanna know the crazy thing? I almost took Abuela's Ativan before all this. Never again."

"Ay, Amar. None of this is your fault. You know that, right? Mom's asking too much of you . . . telling you it's your decision."

"I believe in restorative justice."

"I know you do, chica. I love that about you."

"And I wonder if Tío can . . . I don't know . . . restore this."

"That's a big task. I guess it depends on whether we believe he's up to it or not."

Amaranta nods again, and a few minutes pass in silence before she asks, her voice so soft she wonders if her sister will hear, "Do you forgive Abuelo? And Tío?"

"No way." It's an immediate and firm response. A door slamming shut.

Ma snores again. The rasping of a broken engine.

"Me neither," Amaranta says, but it hurts.

"You don't have to, chica."

"What will the judge decide?"

"That depends . . . on what we tell them."

Amaranta picks at the quilt tucked over the sheet. She stares at Ma's socked feet. They're twitching, like she's running from something. Or after something.

"Ma was such a badass," Amaranta says, and to her surprise, the slightest of smiles creeps across her face. "Out at the Salton Sea. You should've seen her."

"Yeah, even if she can't always see past our family, we have a good mom. I need to apologize to her . . . when she wakes up. I was kind of a bitch about Gus . . ."

The final snore comes out like a hog eager for slop. A loud snorting pop.

"I heard that," Ma says, turning over, pillow-creases lining her face, her hair disheveled, eyes veined with scarlet streaks and swollen as blisters. "You can't take it back."

She pulls her girls toward her, creating an Amaranta sándwich, her ma and big sister, the pieces of bread flanking her.

EPILOGUE

What does it mean to stand in the shadow of a family tree, its branches broken by betrayal? Mal would ask herself this long into the night for the rest of her nights. No hay paz cuando una familia has split itself into pieces, even for one another.

When they dredged the water tank on the Callahan land, they found the missing girls.

Bone shards and teeth filtered through the rainwater, irrigating the fields with the girls' remains. Every time it flooded, the lightest and least dense of the bones floated out to the salty sea —

Such was the case with the jawbone Griselda found with Papi.

Forensics, after twenty-six years, finally confirmed what Gus and Mal knew all along.

That jawbone belonged to Noemi.

At some point the Callahans had poured chemicals into the water to try and break down the girls' bodies — which killed all the crops in the immediate vicinity, and, like all wastewater that flows to the sea, contributed to the toxicity of the Salton Sea. The Callahan land was cursed, like Carmen said.

But when Mal found her daughter, she found the other girls. And they finally laid the bones to rest. The jar of teeth — they buried.

Old Man Callahan had bought Sharon's silence; it cost a law degree from Stanford. He didn't know she'd found and kept as insurance Elena's silver compact mirror, smudged with her blood, on the ground beside Old Man Callahan's white pickup while she watched in stoic horror as the three men threw her into the water.

Perhaps it was a coincidence that two sets of fathers and sons threw those girls into the water tanks.

Or perhaps there was something larger at play.

Mal likes Amaranta's version, that there's a great Mathematician in the Sky, watching over them.

Papi would tell her the word for the land is the same for the body in their ancestral language — if he were still alive today.

And maybe that's how it is. Some design beneath the fabric, holding them all together.

Love shouldn't excuse toxicity. But nothing is black or white. Certainly not love.

Was it enough they never spoke to Esteban again? To any of them?

Papi took care of Mami until she died, just a few months after Mal found Amaranta.

Papi followed Mami into the afterlife not long after that. A broken heart, everyone said. And it was probably true. But not only for the reason they thought.

When Mal asked Benny what he knew of his parentage, he shrugged and said Mami had let the truth slip when he was a kid. He'd known all that time. But it hadn't changed anything.

After all the trials and legal red tape, he eventually inherited the Callahan land — and gave it all to Mal.

She kept Beef Tooth for herself. Made it grass-fed. Organic. Cruelty-free. Farm-to-table. Opened another one in Northern California, where she moved to a house beside the ocean.

She parceled some of the land to Carmen.

The rest, she gave to her daughters.

She encouraged Amaranta to testify against her uncle because Mal couldn't live with the idea that her feelings for her brother might influence her daughter to make a choice that compromised her autonomy. Still, Amaranta decided on her own, and Mal agreed that Esteban would do more good as a senator than in prison. He proved that a hundred times over, with every initiative he championed in favor of the people, his community, and his family. Even so, Mal made damn sure he never saw them again—not her or her girls.

He'd created his own prison anyway, in that fancy house on the rich side of town with his drunk wife he'd take back no matter how many vatos she screwed and those leeching monstrosities of kids they'd created. Part of Mal wanted to help the cuates. But they mostly sorted themselves out over time, after college and therapy.

When she moved her girls away, Mal told them, you can love a place without staying.

And of course she also meant, you can love the people without staying. You can love yourself more.

Boundaries, her therapist tried drilling into her.

Love, she would reply. You'll choose a familiar hell over a strange heaven until you reset your heart.

She would always love Chuy. She would always be his Mallow Mar. Deep in her corazón. Even if she never saw him again.

"What are you thinking about?" Gus asks, and she can feel his heartbeat steady against his rib cage as her head rises and falls against his chest. The view from their window is ocean as far as the eye can see. All that salt water. She takes a deep breath.

"Same as usual," she replies, tracing her fingers along the thick rope of skin piled across his gunshot scar.

"The girls will be home soon," he says, reaching for his cane. "We should make ourselves presentable."

Outside the window, a deer peeks from behind a great pine before its whole head and body become visible.

At one point, Mal would've thought of how Papi had taught her to shoot the deer, to respect its life enough to take it. To strip the flesh from its bones and prepare it for consumption. But the deer stares in a way that asks Mal to see her, not through a hunter's lens nor a butcher's. Just a mother's. Just to look. Just to see.

Just to appreciate her for what she is.

Mal spent a lifetime respecting the bodies she dressed and prepared for others to eat. She spent a lifetime nourishing others with her art.

Sometimes, it's enough just to enjoy it for yourself. Not to need anything from anyone. Not to need the animal through the window to feed you or serve your desire for beauty.

And for a moment, the deer flashes into the horse-headed woman who protected her daughter when she could not, staring back at Mal through the reflection, before the deer returns, the tail flickers, and she scampers back into the woods.

ACKNOWLEDGMENTS

My familia and closest support system, my everything: Lina, my writing partner; my badass, horse-jumping, arrow-slinging daughter! I love you! Lucy to my Ethel, or vice versa! My funny, wonderful, sarcastic Jer Bear. The love of all my lifetimes, Andy Roo. Thank you for writing this beautiful life with me.

Mom and Dad, thank you for loving us and keeping a roof over our heads. Thank you for sharing your stories with me and making us laugh! Grandma Marge and my wondrous bros and in-laws — David and Karissa and baby C, and Paul and Mark! My better-than-best Lisa O'Malley Sidhu, for the best carne asada and cheesy potatoes in El Valle! My bruja sister, Avra Elliott, you know. My desert ocean heart with yours.

Bebe and Midnight, boxer and chihuahua girls curled beside me every word I write. Never critical. Always pure and kind. You beautiful souls.

My publishing team! Rebecca Friedman, badass agent and loving sister in my corner, helping me fight for my worth! Helen O'Hare, who uplifted me from the darkness and kept me believing in my voice — thank you for seeing me and Mal! You are the absolute best. Liv Ryan, thank you for standing in the gaps, listening to me, and offering sound guidance and wisdom. All the folks at Mulholland and Little, Brown, I'm deeply grateful and over the moon!

My badass coven of witchy women writers: Kathy Paul, especially for drawing the Veracruz and Callahan family trees to guide the earlier days of *Salt Bones*. Erika T. Wurth, true sister, thank you for scraping me off the floor with a phone call when you shared your beloved badass agent! Sarina Dahlan, your friendship and laughter through the darkest ditches have meant the world to me. Marisa P. Clark, for all the reasons but especially for bringing me back to New Mexico by opening doors with your belief in me. Alicia Elkort, for praying rain and loving me through it all. Dee Lalley, cactus flower crystal ball heart. Sherine Gilmour, all kindness, all realness. Zoila Galeano, for reminding me how far my stories can go. Jennifer Krohn, for our coffee and book chats all these years in New Mexico.

Goddess beta readers and cheerleaders: Rebecca and Juliet Kinkaid-Black, who've offered heaps of support and neighborly kindness at every turn. I love you both and stay so grateful for you! Rosalinda Marquez, you badass hermana, thank you for always being the first in line to support all my creative projects. Y'all sisters: Siân Killingsworth, Leslie Rzenik, Lauren Brazeal Garza, Melanie Márquez Adams, Melissa Morgan, Kat Jastrow Davis, Evelyn Puga, Nicole Stefanko Fuentes, Melissa Balmer. Any other beloved I've missed with my chronic illness brain fog, I love you.

I won't give up, loves. I'll stay fighting for marginalized voices, all of us dreaming in the borderlands. Thank you for staying weird and wondrous with me.

ABOUT THE AUTHOR

Jennifer Givhan is a Mexican American and Indigenous poet and novelist from the Southwestern desert and the recipient of poetry fellowships from the National Endowment for the Arts and PEN/Rosenthal Emerging Voices. She holds a master's degree from California State University Fullerton and a master's in fine arts from Warren Wilson College. She is the author of five full-length poetry collections and the novels *River Woman, River Demon; Jubilee;* and *Trinity Sight*.

Givhan's poetry, fiction, and creative nonfiction have appeared in the *New Republic, The Nation, Poetry, TriQuarterly, Boston Review, The Rumpus, Salon, Ploughshares,* and many other publications. She has received the Southwest Book Award, *New Ohio Review*'s Poetry Prize, *Phoebe Journal*'s Greg Grummer Poetry Prize, the *Pinch Journal* Poetry Prize, and *Cutthroat*'s Joy Harjo Poetry Prize. Givhan has taught at the University of Washington Bothell's MFA program as well as Western New Mexico University and has guest lectured at universities across the country. She was the 2023 visiting professor of creative writing at the University of New Mexico.